The Independent Bookworm

About the Book

Sir Querlak isn't your normal nobleman, but he's dedicated and determined, not only to survive but to bring a golden age to his foef, no matter how many obstacles his swamp ridden foef is throwing at him. How can a young knight find justice and peace while surrounded by ruin and fighting to survive?

In 2002 ADR, the Empire of Argens is still reeling from the usurpation of its centuries-old throne by a ferocious dwarven warrior named Yula and his sorcerous human allies. Not only did they defeat the flower of elvish knighthood, but they exposed the former dynasty as demons in disguise.

When Qerlak lays aside the adventuring life to purchase a knighthood, none of his fellow nobles believe he will succeed. A castle close to ruin, lands nearly abandoned and the surrounding swamps swarming with aggressive Reptile Men, human-sized bugs and other dangerous creatures. Now a greedy neighbor plots an invasion from the eastern hills. By the code of the nobility he wants to join, Qerlak is doomed.

Sir Qerlak can neither ride a horse nor use a lance, and has little more than his courage and love for his people with which to defend this mysterious, exotic foef. Outnumbered, outmaneuvered and out of time, he must face monsters and foes while piecing together forgotten ancient customs and recent chance-met allies. This quest will stretch his strength and subject them all to … *The Test of Fire*.

About the Author

Will Hahn has been in love with heroic tales since age four, when his father read him the Lays of Ancient Rome and the Tales of King Arthur. He taught Ancient-Medieval History for years, but the line between this world and others has always been thin. The far reaches of fantasy, like the distant past, still bring him face to face with people like us, who have choices to make.

Will has written about the Lands of Hope since his college days (which by now are also part of ancient history). He chronicled the adventures of Solmn Judgement dilligently in two tomes of over 1000 pages each (it's now being published as an eBook series and in print) and his Shards of Light series, a sword and sorcery story. He also chronicled stand alone stories like "The Plane of Dreams" or "Three Minutes to Midnight." More of Will's tales of Hope are available at several online retailers.

Find out more on his website: www.WilliamLHahn.com

THE TEST OF FIRE

Tales of the Tributarians III

William L. Hahn

The Plane of Dreams
published by the Independent Bookworm, USA und D
this book is also available as eBook at various retailers

printed On-Demand Publishing LLC, 100 Enterprise Way, Suite A200,
Scotts Valley, CA 95066, USA, www.kdp.com

ISBN-13 978-3-95681-130-2

Find more information on the publisher's website:
http://www.IndependentBookworm.de

I wish to dedicate The Test of Fire to the efforts of those heroes who helped me to see it so clearly. This band includes Kevin Weist and Katherine Weist-Bowers, who were there with me from the beginning and whose exploits need no introduction in either world.

Most especially I wish to thank some of The Lands' newest heroes, Madison McKee Weist, Fraser Weist, and Sarah Frantz, who convinced me that it's never too late (though it's always getting later), and for reminding me that there are times when the last need to be first, because we're all equals in the end.

I'd also like to express my thanks to my untiring beta-readers. Thank you for the time you've put into my story.
Ar Aralte!

A Note to Explain for the First-Time Reader

Sometimes you have to tell a story backwards.

This tale should come after two others, only one of which I have written yet. It is a "demi-sequel" to *The Plane of Dreams*, following some of the characters into later adventures. Each novel can stand on its own, though I certainly hope there is pleasure to be had by reading them in order. Before these stories comes the first tale and I promise to chronicle it someday. The beginning will have to come later.

The Plane of Dreams: a brief introduction

A large band of adventurers returns from the Shimmering Mindsea with piles of treasure. Many things happen, but for our purposes chiefly two.

First, one member of the group, the Elven Pious Warrior Qerlak Barleybane, sees an opportunity to gain a noble seat in an unusual way. By using some of his fortune and borrowing the rest, he purchases the right to claim Mon-Crulbagh, an abandoned foef in the southernmost edge of the Argensian Empire, swearing an oath to the Greatknight of Beryl to take possession.

Second, one of the group's mages, the human Galethiel, has become increasingly interested in the reality of dreaming, and is studying the matter intently. Qerlak offers his companion a place in his castle to pursue her researches. Both believe they are retiring.

But the rest of the adventuring band (known as the Tributarians) falls afoul of a being known as Nightmare, who threatens to take over all of reality if not stopped, and Querlak and Galethiel are dragged into an adventure stranger than any they've ever faced before.

Along the way, three new heroes meet and have an important part to play in resisting the conspiracy by Nightmare's waking-world allies; they later decide to go adventuring together.

TABLE OF CONTENTS

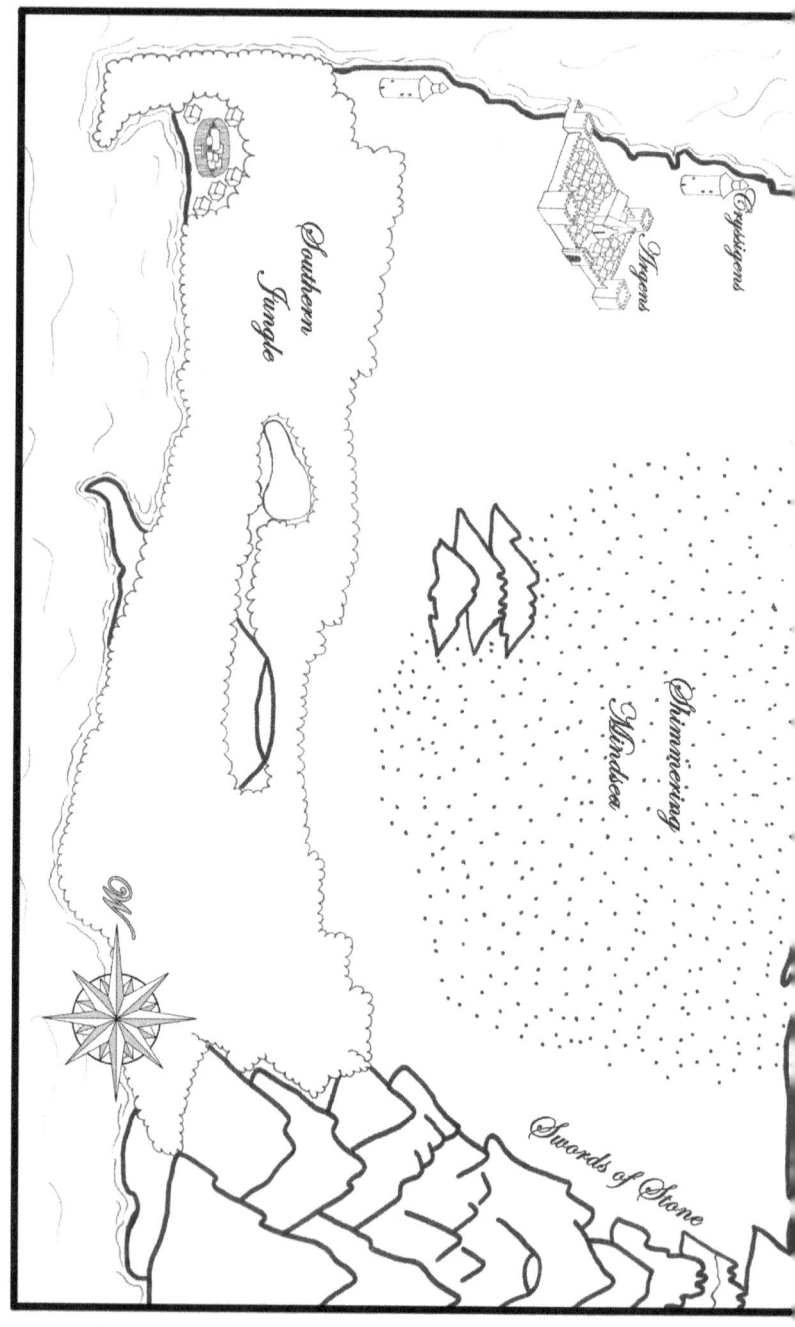

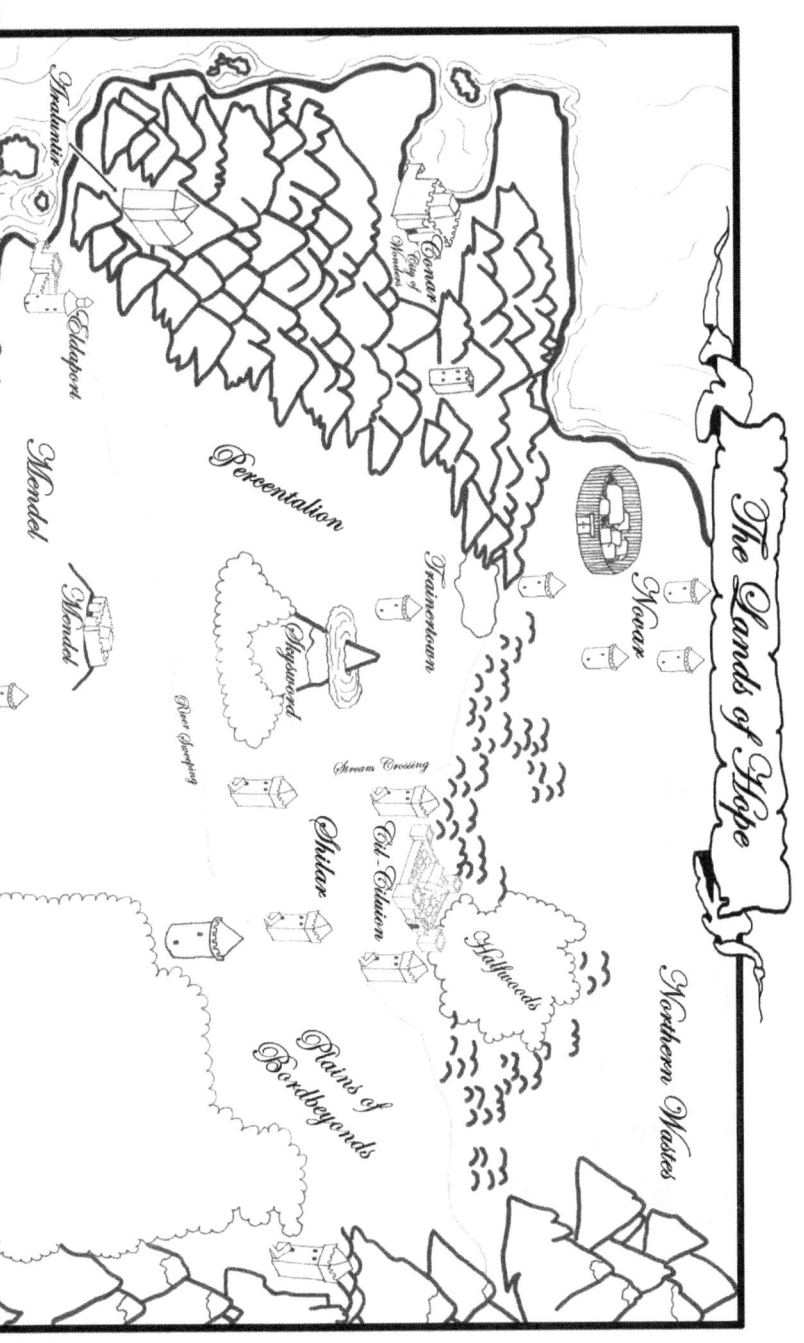

The Lands of Hope

Cast of Characters

From Mon-Crulbagh

Qerlak Barleybane
: Elven Pious Warrior of Argens Hopeforger, formerly of the Tributarian adventuring band and current lord of Mon-Crulbagh

Galethiel the Dreamseer
: Human Wizard and companion of Qerlak, who has unlocked the secret of the reality behind dreams

Sir Seldom Chased
: Human Warrior and chance-met ally of Qerlak, living at Mon-Crulbagh. He is proudly illiterate

Elias Fennet
: Elven castellan to Sir Qerlak

Dekentar Spezh
: Elven guard captain of Castle Crulbagh

Shah-topp Ondaii
: Human engineer from the distant Sunslit Isles

Skeggs
: Elven cook for Castle Crulbagh

Drace
: Elven doctor hired to serve Sir Qerlak

Cecil Disarmle
: Elven squire sworn to Sir Qerlak's service

Severyn Illfellow
: Elven peasant, sentenced to servitude at Castle Crulbagh for previous fraud.

Garr
: Elven youth, Galethiel's acolyte.

From Pritaelseran

Cran-Kalrith Pritaelseran
: Elven lord of a large highlands knighthood, set to absorb his poorer neighbor

Eli'se	Pritaelseran's wife and mother of Hitaelseran
Hitaelseran	Elven youngest son of Cran-Kalrith, sent to raid Mon-Crulbagh.
Zantire Pritaelseran	Elder brother of Cran-Kalrith, accomplished wizard
Dommes	Head butler to Pritaelseran
Guernsten	retainer in service to Pritaelseran
Insis	acolyte of Zantire

From Elsewhere

Torquem'l Beryllian	Greatknight of Beryl and overlord of Qerlak, a Stargazer beset with political troubles in the aftermath of the civil war
Sir Tancrad Coss	Beryllian's vassal and close friend.
Bleys Eversong	Elven Bard attached to Beryl's court
Mo'lem and Larel Barleybane	Qerlak's older brothers, sons of a Greatknight in a neighboring Barony
Bellatara	Halfling Woodsman in a new group of adventurers, originally from the far northern kingdoms
Quarion	Elven Stealthic in a new group of adventurers, having left his family in Wanlock
Ellesmera Altieri	Elven Martial Wizard in a new group of adventurers, having left her mother W'starrah, famous Stargazer Preacher of Cryssigens.

PART 1

Chapter I. Scratch

Castle Pritaelseran: Great Chamber

Hitaelseran looked up at the colossal bronze hawk hanging from the ceiling of the castle's central hall and felt the same as he always did. Its full-sized talons, supposedly stretching for live fish of the pool set into the flagging below, seemed to hunger instead to sink into his own shoulder. Its eyes, artfully sculpted to look down on its natural prey, yet appeared to follow him as he entered down the steps, crossed the room and took his seat at the right end of his father's board. No matter two of the three seats above him would be empty- the fourth son of the empire's greatest knight knew his place.

He was the earliest to attend the summons, as again was only proper. The servants had already been here, refreshing the lights, stirring the pool, and meticulously sweeping every nook of the vast chamber in preparation for what would likely be less than a half-hour's meeting. These jobs done, only the butler Dommes remained behind: his face was flat as he stood against the wall directly behind the great seat, and his eyes were so unfocused as to seem blind. Hitaelseran knew the old elf had marked his entrance, and the time; if he were now to climb upon the table and drop his drawers to urinate, the butler of seven decades' service would get someone to clean it within a minute, and make no reference to the event for seven decades more. Dommes, too, knew his place.

But when his father entered the room, Hitaelseran knew, even as he rose to bow to him, that something was amiss.

Where was Canril? The eldest two brothers were tourneying in Colign, he knew, but the third belonged here at the briefing his father had announced for dawn. The agenda was not impossible to guess. Canril would be assigned the border-raid on Mon-Crulbagh and the youngest son would get the scut-job of surveying the peasants in quiet Lann, showing the flag and enforcing the family rule in an area where no trouble had been seen in eleven decades. But for a son of Cran-Kal'rith Pritaelseran to be late—as the knight took leave of his wife at the entrance, Hitaelseran desperately scrabbled in his mind, and could not recall another time he had met with the man alone.

The magnificent stature and handsome face of his father had the effect it always did. A vigorous forty years in appearance, the lord of Pritaelseran was more than two centuries old and would always strike the very image of elven nobility. His auburn hair carefully arranged to expose his ears and emphasize his lordly visage, the hawk-like nose and high cheekbones; all these led one irresistibly to the golden orbs which held you like a dragon's stare, unless you looked eternally to the ground. His raiment was no doubt perfect, but Hitaelseran would never claim to have seen it: even for him, an Elf and a noble's son, this man's son, it was either eyes or floor.

With an effort, Hitaelseran chose neither, and looked instead to his mother as she turned to leave. In any other household, Eli'se would have been famed for beauty as well as nobility, her outward age celebrated as proof of her wisdom. Only in the perfect knighthood could it be accounted a shame that her hair was white and her face lightly seamed with wrinkles. In Pritaelseran, the peasants looked both ways over their tavern-cups, and whispered it was tragic for such a knight to live shackled to a woman who seemed his own mother. She must have missed her Moment, they'd nod knowingly to their audience; either cowardice or ignorance, and nothing for shame to choose between those. Hitaelseran looked on her and saw a constant mask of formality over sadness. Her husband escorted her with precisely the dignity and deference, indeed, that a man would show to his own mother. She walked down the hall and out of sight with a straight back but an aimless pace, as if already wondering what to do with the rest of this day. In a deep rustle of velvet, she was gone, and the son and his father were alone.

The knight approached the main chair and sat, the signal for his subordinate to do the same. When he spoke, Pritaelseran used no preamble and wasted no time on sentiment.

"The third son has been injured in a fall" he remarked, using the language of a chronicler as usual. "It devolves, therefore, to the fourth son to take his place in the matter of border reclamation."

Hitaelseran's mind whirled with questions, none of which he could ask. Injured how? People fall from horses while hunting, and this was most likely for his chase-mad brother; but his father's mien could not quite hide a flicker of anger as he spoke, and it seemed possible that the fall might have followed corporal punishment of some kind, to which none of the four sons were immune despite their manhood. Whatever the case, the Mon-Crulbagh raid was now coming to him, a chance at glory and advancement, for the low-man on the ladder.

"I shall pay respects in the chapel, for my brother's quick recovery and a good outcome," he ventured, hoping the varied interpretations of his statement would meet with his father's approval.

After a moment in which he stared piercingly at his son down the empty table, the knight nodded once. "You leave at noon, to be in the midst of the adjudication—" by which he meant invading Mon-Crulbagh— "before the third morning. The peasants are billeted and the wagon-train with my retainers is in readiness."

"Then I take my leave of you," said Hitaelseran, rising and bowing before turning at once to go. The idea of a handshake with his commander, much less a hug with his father, never occurred to him. He had his opportunity, and his orders, and that was all. This was no time for self-reflection. If he had taken a moment to note a shade of sadness weighing on his spirits, Hitaelseran would have scoffed and dismissed it, putting it down to his own youth and inexperience. Another year or two in this family, and such a conclusion would no doubt be completely true.

As he reached the top of the steps leading out, his father spoke again: when Hitaelseran turned back to face him, the bronze hawk obstructed his view of the knight's head, so it seemed that the family symbol itself was speaking.

"I trust you will do well with this opportunity. It does not come to you lightly."

Hitaelseran faced the hawk's gaze and tried to keep his voice level at the implied insult. "Perhaps it will prove to be my Moment."

"Perhaps. The rabble to our west shows no signs of true nobility, and it is better this adventurer is put in his place now rather than next season. But war is chance: you may die and yet remain a member of this house."

He could think of no answer to the hawk on this, so Hitaelseran turned smartly on his heel to complete his exit.

⊕ ⊕ ⊕

Garden Court

Eli'se emerged from the curtained alcove onto a balcony overlooking the inner gardens. As she soaked in the bright sunlight with a raised face and eyes closed, a low bell tolled softly once, alerting a trio of unseen servants below, who dropped their rose-spades and ran to a nearby treadmill likewise invisible to public view. As they took turns jogging vigorously on its course, fountains came to life in seven places around the garden, punctuating its star-flower design with the constellation Sword in Crown. Eli'se took in this wondrous view and pondered its meaning awhile in light of her recent fears, then reached back to a statue by the door, carved in the form of Purik Pritaelseran. She tapped its belt buckle once while speaking a few words in the common tongue to activate the embedded proxy. Eli'se overheard the conversation between her husband and her youngest son with increasing trepidation. When she no longer heard the sound of her son's retreating footsteps, she tapped the statue again to end the magic: if her husband talked to himself, she could not bear to hear what he might say.

At a slight gesture from her hand, the bell promptly tolled again, and the servants ceased their running, allowing the fountains to die down and total silence to hold sway. The effect was so smooth it felt to her as if she had cast a spell. Eli'se looked wonderingly at her hand, reminded how efficiently everyone did their jobs here. In more than fifty years since coming south as a bride, she had become fully accustomed to the competence and servility of the staff who worked it. In her first year, convinced her husband must have been a disciplinarian of some kind, she pressed the butler Dommes about it mercilessly. Oath after vow of denial he gave her, and finally whispered "They remember Drayson, milady". Beyond that, not one word would he speak.

Eli'se reached a decision, and turned to leave the balcony, heading for the chapel. Her son, she knew, could not delay

19

his departure for goodbyes to any woman- she would need to meet him by chance. She smiled, as she walked, to think how Zantire, her husband's brother, would ruffle at the very idea of an accident in human affairs. And perhaps he was right, she mused- or rather, like her "magic" with the fountains, it was a matter of perception.

Wizard's Laboratory

Zantire Pritaelseran shut off his scrying spell through the hawk in the great chamber with an angry finger snap. He paced like a caged cat between several podiums and books on tables, consulting his notes and occasionally marking the margins of a page while constantly muttering, as if to himself.

"Reckless, too reckless. Cran sees his retainers as nothing more than spare parts, thinks he can send one in place of another without upsetting the delicate *balance*. But the stars rankle at this—my forecast was quite specific, Canril was to have led the expedition, *then* the signs were auspicious. But now..."

The wizard stopped a moment and rubbed his bald head, as if cudgeling his mind for a forgotten fact. His aquiline features strongly resembled his younger brother's, showing nobility tinged with mental effort, the look of a hardened warrior told to find another gate to storm the castle.

"Where have I left the charts!" he suddenly exclaimed, a touch loud and direct for someone speaking to himself. Indeed, he spoke as if expecting an answer. After a moment of silence, he seemed to get one, and moved to a particular pile of thick vellum sheets.

"There. There, as I recalled, just so. The sign of Balance in the sky presages success indeed, but only for a leader born under its sign. This one, now, the youngest... he has—where is it, blast you—he has the auspices of the Ferret, a summer sign, fire not air, no it's all wrong I tell you! Now, if we contrast the Ferret with Balance... here it is, the birth-chart. Hem, quick mind, that's just what you'd expect from his sign. Unusual loyalty line though, in that horoscope. Not strong—well no, strong but erratic, not sure. This one, he thinks too much!"

Zantire was sitting now, taking in a sliver of light from the morning sky through the arrow-slit in his tower. He rubbed his mouth thoughtfully and nearly let the star-charts drop from his other hand. "He'd have been a fine leader... but now, it seems he is thrown into another's place. I see failure. Yes. Perhaps just as well. I don't like the way that whelp looked at me—at the hawk—as if he knew something..."

The wizard stood with sudden decision, returning some of his charts while keeping others neatly scrolled under his arm as he moved toward the stairs. "I must consult the detailed horoscope. Below. Come along then," seemingly still addressing himself. The mage stopped only to close the door on a small shelf set into the wall, and to flip a lever next to it. As the cogs released, they let the chamber within descend to the lower levels; the wizard moved to the stairs and down, to the ground level and deeper.

The servants of Pritaelseran, most of them, had been on a long flight of stairs leading to the dungeon level of the castle, in one place or another. There were cells to clean when the lord had prisoners, and various things in storage (thankfully near the steps). The butler would never comment, to confirm or deny, whenever someone in the back-kitchen where the staff gathered of a late night, said that Dommes had several times been down to the second level. Everyone knew where that sole stair-entrance was, the one coming down from the wizard's tower and leading into a separate section of the dungeon; but of those who may have been down them, no one would say a word.

And it was only whispered, a rumor beyond a dream, yet never doubted among the staff that the castle actually had four levels beneath its walls.

Chapel of Argens

li'se turned from speaking with the chapel curate as her son entered the main chamber. She saw him stop and look to the eyes of the statue behind her, while he took in the unusual light of the vast room. Hitaelseran was dressed for war, though he could not expect to see action for another two days. With his chain mail under the hawk-gilt surcoat, sword at his belt and winged helm under his arm, he stood straight as a rod and handsome as the day. Eli'se had just time to wonder why he did not remind her more of his father. Then he bowed very properly—become a man before her eyes, she thought—and advanced down the center aisle to her.

The curate bowed to them and withdrew without a word. Eli'se could give the young knight her full attention, as he arrived at the end of the aisle, knelt to the statue of Argens, and then rose to kiss her hand in turn. He had become the perfect knight, she thought—just as his brothers before him. Yet Eli'se felt a chill brush her heart with that thought. Knights, to her experience, made terrible sons.

"I thank Argens first and foremost, mother, for my good fortune to see you before I left. Things have developed rather quickly this morning."

Eli'se smiled, knowing he would take her reaction as a compliment rather than a response to a joke he couldn't know he had made. "I shall thank him too, then, before I complain that he has taken my youngest from me so soon."

"It is but a week's expedition, most likely, and I shall be back before the month is out." Hitaelseran's guileless brow furrowed slightly and she saw the hesitation in him, which curiously gave her a glimmer of hope as he continued. "And we mustn't call the First of the First to task for our affairs, milady."

Now she could laugh and know it would be taken correctly. "Yes indeed, my son, I am properly chastised for my impiety. Will you pray with me now?"

Hitaelseran nodded gratefully at this, and smoothly shifted his helm under his opposite arm to offer his mother the near-hand as she knelt by the front rail before the statue. Then he joined her, soundless and smooth despite his metal gear; the chapel was completely silent for a while, and what each may have said in prayer is not known to anyone.

Yet only halfway through the time he spent kneeling, Hitaelseran's prayers ended. As he waited out of courtesy for his mother, he fell to merely thinking. What always struck him most about the chapel to Argens in the castle court was the extraordinary amount of light within. Not a single candle was lit, though several were there for show completely new and untrimmed. The windows were rather high and set with thick colorful glass, in scenes showing the Great Deeds of the First Flame in such wonderfully intricate detail that they were hard to see at this distance. But from seemingly every corner, light reflected from clever vents and angled shafts, striking polished metal points and mirrors precisely set to spread it around, each one hidden either as part of a statuary scene or in the geometric design of the walls, or even (so they said) embedded as gem-chips smaller than the eye could see within the statue itself. The result was a thickly-walled and private chamber with an eternal hush, yet as brightly lit inside as a cloudy day without.

The statue itself was more than eight feet tall and raised on a four-foot pedestal, towering over all mortals who came to offer devotion. Argens in his prime, armed for war and eyes fixed on a distant horizon, facing east as was proper; under one foot a Demon writhed in defeat, and the bend in its spine indicating total submission, while heretical nowadays, was completely proper for the era when it had been carved. Rather than defend the style or even consider a replacement, Pritaelseran had steadfastly

23

refused to notice the unorthodox curvature, which let a wealth of assumptions go unanswered. Hitaelseran knew that, in silences like that the wellspring of elven noble power bubbled up, and he respected it duly without much enthusiasm.

Yet he almost felt he would prefer candles.

His mother sighed and he rose to assist her up, seeing in her eyes the worry he disdained, the fear he thought more proper for himself, and perhaps even love, which affected him more than the others together.

"You must not fret, mother."

"Or else, my face may wrinkle?" She returned in a merry jest that made her only son gasp with shock.

"Avert!" He cried as if at a curse. "Mother, you are without doubt the loveliest woman in the Barony of Dargor."

"And you, Hitaelseran, born my son, are now a knight full-grown and off to war. May Argens watch over you and bring you home safe."

"I shall be well," he said with a hand on her face, then adding, "and I hope also to make my father proud."

Eli'se held that hand against her face and sighed again. "So, the old war with Mon-Crulbagh begins anew. Good people turned from their homes, our peasants forced to march instead of harvest, lands taken and lost, ransoms exchanged. And deaths. No doubt there will be deaths, as always."

Hitaelseran stiffened at these words; Eli'se could see in his face the response his father had taught him to such womanly concerns. But the youngest son hesitated, and his reply rang a somewhat different note in her ear.

"Those best suited for rule must do so. All the people benefit from a stro—from a just lord. I go seeking not to kill, but to bring the noblest ruler to a people long awaiting him."

The knight kissed his mother, and she released his hand keeping a bright smile on her face until Hitaelseran exited the chapel. Finally alone, she sank into a pew and covered that timeless lovely face with both hands.

Chapter II. Spark

City of Beryl

The first moment Quarion laid eyes on the blue-robed wizard, the base of his spine tingled with a sense of peril. Nothing about her signaled immediate danger. Respect, perhaps, as the tavern crowd to both sides gave way and a few folks stood when she passed. But this mage was clearly of the noble class and would merit such respect whatever her interests. Not very tall, not very beautiful, bearing no staff and her face stamped only with a sense of composed concentration, she moved without hurry directly at the table where the young Stealthic sat with his two companions.

And Quarion knew, even as he rose to greet her, she would wish to hire them. He felt again that charge between his legs and grinned, for danger is what always drove him.

"Milady," he said, gesturing her to the right-hand chair, "You were seeking us?" This drew the attention of Ellesmera and Bellatara to his left. The mage returned his gaze and Quarion ventured another guess, because risks pleased him. "Some matter not suited for a written message or a servant, perhaps?"

After a moment, the lady smiled briefly and nodded, which made the young Stealthic flush with pride. Hold on, he told himself, keep your composure. "I am Quarion," he said with a bow as their guest sat. "May I introduce my companions, the martialist Ellesmera and our Woodsman Bellatara."

"It is true," the lady said to him, "I am in need of discrete persons, such as you and your, your," her voice caught itself at the edge of impolitude.

"We're adventurers," Bellatara said, and the startled mage looked down to her as if a child had spoken out of turn. Quarion grinned; few people could avoid that mistake, until they met the Halfling's steady gaze, and saw the javelins bundled against the corner behind her. The mage grimaced slightly as if she needed to apologize although she had not used the word.

"Yes, as you say," the mage replied, looking then a moment to Ellesmera as if hoping another Elf could supply some balm to this gaffe. But the slim young woman looked back as if no one had yet spoken, so the visitor cleared her throat to continue.

"I need persons able to overcome certain mundane obstacles, and do a good deed without leaving any, ahm, trace of their passing." The mage glanced around the table to let this point sink in. "As you may perhaps know, the high mage P'sodoynam who once served our Greatknight Beryllian died in the civil war last year. Milord has not yet seen fit to announce a replacement for my good friend and colleague, and there are rumors… well, perhaps best to pass over the specifics, but suffice it that he is said to want a person of unimpeachable character to serve his court. This time."

A waiter stopped at their table, behind the mage as if assuming she was the host instead of a guest. With a circling finger, the woman indicated that he should bring a round, which he hustled to do as the tale continued. And Quarion felt another strong tingle of the unknown, but he bit his lip as the mage resumed.

"My colleague passed away leaving only distant family, and his estate is currently entangled with the executors. Ridiculous, really, but the grounds are actually under guard."

The waiter returned with three ales and a crystal goblet of something so richly red as to seem black, setting the last before the mage. A thought nudged at Quarion's mind, but he set it aside to listen more closely.

"To the matter. Some years ago I loaned P'sodoynam a tome of mine, rather valuable, and he neglected to return it before he died." She shrugged elegantly and smiled again. "It's of no importance, except that I need it for my researches rather urgently and this silly audit of his estate—"

"You need us to break into his home and get it for you?" Bellatara was so typically blunt.

The mage sipped and rested her goblet without hurry before answering. "I wish you to break nothing at all, mistress. Having visited my colleague at his home several times I can assure you the guards are easily evaded. By those with sufficient skill."

Quarion's mind whirled with possibilities as the mage unfurled a small parchment on the table to reveal a sketch map of three manor floors, drawn by a neat hand.

"My friend's library is here," she said, pointing to a rear room on the second floor. "I have determined that guards stand outside the front gate, at the main door, and just outside this room. Five in all, but they do not pace, and the watch is kept all night by the same persons." She paused and took in the eyes of the other two Elves at the table, letting a raised eyebrow speak.

"So what?" Bellatara asked bluntly. "Why does that matter?"

"She means," Ellesmera quietly replied, "that they will very likely be asleep in the latter half of the night."

The mage coughed politely, seeming embarrassed, "If not sooner. Thus if you enter the servants' door here, ascend the stairs and then take yourself through the two bedrooms here and here, the passage leads around—"

"Thank you," Quarion said, "we can handle the access. What about the book you need?" As she looked back at him, sipped her wine, and adjusted her robe, he struggled to maintain a mask of calm. Every one of the mage's actions had so far pointed to danger, and he had to bite his tongue or else giggle.

"The book," she replied, "is nearly too thick to grip in one hand. The cover is a deep, dark brown leather and one of the, ahm, symbols on the front is shaped like this." Looking both ways, she leaned over the sketch and quickly scrawled a figure where one triangle intersected an oval shape, with four dots spaced around its edges. The parchment bore the imprint of her fingernail, and Quarion nodded.

"The tome is quite sturdy," the mage continued, "and heavy, of course, as it seems they all are." Here she gave a short laugh, and when Quarion looked to her again, he saw a zephyr-flash of fear, as if she had given something away. The young Stealthic was in fact sure she had. "Put it in a grain sack and notify the barkeep here. I will meet you to take possession."

Quarion looked on his potential employer a long moment, running through several questions it would be useful to have honest answers to. But his inner sense assured him, those would not be forthcoming. That meant only one person's opinion mattered.

He looked to Ellesmera, and thought about what he owed her.

His martial wizard companion sat with hands folded on the table, ale untouched, her face so calm and eyes half-closed, looking as if partway into a trance already. The mage followed his gaze to look on her as well, and they waited.

Ellesmera drew a breath and held it before speaking. "You must have this book at once?"

"Indeed," the mage replied with relief, "I have asked through all official channels, and the very soonest the estate can be settled will be long after my enchantment is ruined. Months of work just in the casting, you see. I never dreamed, my colleague's death was a surprise and, to be honest I have less than a week. At most. Three years' work, I hope you can understand."

Bellatara finished her tankard and thunked it on the table. "I understand payment."

The mage looked down in startlement, then amusement as she drew forth a pouch that rattled on the table the way only coins could. "Fifty silver pieces for each of you. Here is half in advance, to meet your expenses—" here she raised her arm to make a finger-circle again, "with the rest in exchange for the book itself."

Quarion waited to visually poll his comrades. Ellesmera looked pensive; she had the most respect from others, as the daughter of a preacher, but that was far away from here and this was his kind of job. Bellatara's eyes gleamed at just the first installment of the money. She had been the poorest of them before they met, a former slave in fact who had never touched a coin until last year.

Quarion put his hand on the pouch as if he thought this commission easy money. Which it most certainly was not. Grinning with delight at the thought of this deception, he decided to test the waters just a bit. "And of course, you are paying for discretion as well I trust."

The mage flashed a small smile as the waiter brought new drinks for the three. "It is best you not even know my name. Just in case."

"There will be no case," Quarion assured her, rising to bow as she withdrew. "In three days, at most, you will hear from us."

There was nothing in the pace of the mage's exit to indicate any nervousness. No sign in the way she nodded to the doorkeep betrayed a pact to keep an eye on the group. But Quarion's inner sense screamed that she was, and had. His grin was so wide across his face he could feel it to his ears.

When he looked back to Ellesmera, her gaze on him knocked the smile clean off.

The martial wizard always seemed so composed, still nothing to drink, looking over as he sat again, with that quiet focus that made Quarion feel he wasn't wearing any clothes. This was the crucial moment; if his companion started to suspect, she might refuse the commission, return the coins.

"You know something," Ellesmera mused without moving her eyes from him.

Quarion smiled and shrugged playfully. "How to use a cutlass. Pick a lock if it isn't too—"

"Something about her. About the book. This job."

Quarion felt grateful then, that he hadn't thought about his suspicions enough yet. He responded at once, before his mind could take up the task and ruin things.

"It's off, I know that. I don't know what. But this is her place, her regular visit. Everyone knew her." He stopped and swallowed, trying to find words that wouldn't trigger more alarms. "She needed to find us. Or else, people just like us."

"We have only been here a few days," Ellesmera mused, sitting back a little. Quarion began to feel some hope. If his uncertainty was good enough for her, they would get at least to the house. And then they would have to do the job.

"Easy money!" Bellatara cried, grabbing the pouch and spooning out coins into stacks to count them. Ellesmera, roused from her thoughts, began to reach across to the Halfling, but Quarion intercepted her hand.

"Let her play. Nobody in here will touch us tonight. We're under the protection of a great mage."

Ellesmera looked from his hand on her wrist back to him, and Quarion let go at once.

"A mage whose name we do not know."

Quarion nodded. "In a town where we are strangers."

Ellesmera closed her eyes for a four-count without breathing. Still not looking, she concluded, "There are sides here, in this city."

"Right! And we aren't on either one." Quarion flicked a glance to Bellatara, chuckling and stacking coins in fives. He did the math in seconds with half of them still lying loose on the table. The heritage of a merchant's life, which he'd left behind to follow Astor, the Perilsgroom. His hero was urging him to take this job, because it was dangerous. Seventy-five coins there, and the same to come for hauling one book out quietly.

All told, a quarter of what he and Bellatara owed their friend when she bailed them from prison in Wanlock. A debt Quarion desperately wished to repay. Plus the danger. He must have this job.

Ellesmera opened her eyes and watched the Halfling at play a while. With a glance back at Quarion she reached at last to take a measured sip of ale. "We must be cautious."

And Quarion smiled, while within him the Stealthic spirit roared and capered with the sheer unknown of it all.

⊕ ⊕ ⊕

Foef of Mon-Crulbagh

"Dekentar Spezh!" Elias Fennet cried with urgency. "Dekentar, where is Lord Barleybane?"

The guard captain turned at the castellan's call and gave him a perfunctory salute only after shrugging his shoulders. "Last I saw, over there. Sir." He pointed past the road—really a dirt track—and across a planted field to where a group of peasants worked on yet another dike.

Fennet grimaced at the impending ruin of his boots, but duty was all. If the young knight insisted on turning daylong inspection trips of the nearby holdings into three or four night excursions ranging further afield, then the imperative business of the keep would simply have to catch up with him. He stumbled over the fence line and edged around squares of barley, wheat and corn to approach the rice paddy where the peasants worked to shore up fallen supports near an embankment. Fennet only wished that after such trouble, his news could have been good.

As he picked his way through ever-narrower footpaths and snatched his cape from berry-briars between the plots, Fennet tried to imagine how to cushion the blow.

Foreclosure! He only suspected, when he first hired on with Sir Qerlak last summer, that his new employer was of unorthodox background and habits. Lord Barleybane came from a respected family line, third son of a Greatknight with no chance to inherit. And even at that first meeting, Fennet knew that here was a noble he could admire, who wanted something more than wealth or glory from his newly purchased position. He had frankly confessed, he was taking the keep partly on credit from bankers in Wanlock. Qerlak had brought some treasure with him—an adventuring career! But he spoke of it as if proud—and overall radiated such confidence that Fennet thought at the time he was making the right decision to take up service.

Now he wondered, even as he slipped to his knees in the muddy ground near where the tumult was taking place. Fennet looked to all sides for his lord, but the peasants were bunched up so tightly, and so thoroughly covered with mud and dark water, that he could hardly make out one body from another.

"Heave!" came the shout of the tall one on the drier side. Fennet recognized the hunter Chefron Gillthruster, holding one end of a log larger than his waist as other men lined up into the deepening water and tried to level the trunk into place. Everyone slipped and slid against each other, and more water coming through the dike's gaps only added to the difficulty.

With a hammer-beat of dismay in his chest, Fennet saw Qerlak's armor lying near his feet, piled up and empty.

"Good people, where is—"

His question was drowned in the collapse of the log-line, as the opposite end dropped below the water and men floundered up to the surface in a pond over their heads just a few steps away from the downstream side of the dyke. Everyone cried out in frustration or fear. But Fennet noticed, as Chefron grimly clutched the trunk on the landed side, that the other end did not float away or slip further loose. Something, or someone, was still holding on there under the water.

"Back to it!" Fennet screamed, heart racing and not even noting the icy water as he leaped in, to the ruin of his suit. "Back on the log, your lord is drowning down there!"

Even as he gasped and clawed at the slow-turning bole, Fennet could see the miracle beginning.

It was a stone oak trunk, the kind that sank in water, stretching further than the side of a cottage. Hardly anyone had reached it, no one was seriously pulling it up. Yet the deep end started to rise.

And Fennet remembered how right he had been, to stay on.

First the far end of the log emerged sluicing water, then a pair of gauntleted hands, two strong arms and the head of Qerlak Barleybane, spouting muddy water and almost singing in a bass note of strain and effort. Several peasants, Fennet and some of Spezh's guards all joined in, as the log continued up, rising to the gap in the dike and fully plugging it as the lord of Mon-Crulbagh slammed it in place with a squishy thud. The young knight turned to lean his back on the barrier as everyone cheered and children scrambled down from the top to slather clay into the cracks.

"Fennet!" he cried in breathless good humor, "more bad news no doubt. Give me a moment."

Before the castellan could deny or reprove, Qerlak launched into the stream, dunking himself and rinsing at least some of the grime and muck from his chestnut hair and ruddy face. Fennet and his lord made their way out of the shallows, now draining as the dyke was again doing its job. Two noble outfits ruined, he thought, but then remembered, this was Mon-Crulbagh. Nearly every suit of clothing from lord to laborer had mud on the cuffs and hems: washing delayed but never reversed the process wherein all fabrics eventually turned some shade of grey or brown.

"Thanks for your help, good castellan," Qerlak said, yanking off his tunic to wring it a bit drier. Fennet moved to help unwind it and held it out for him.

"As you guessed, milord, the letter from Wanlock Assurers, the one you told me to look out for, has—"

"They intend to call the debt," Qerlak said as he dumped his boots one by one. From his tone, Fennet would have guessed the young knight had learned dinner would be a bit late.

"Yes, milord, by the start of Gryphon. The entire balance, with interest, unless we can make payment."

"And if we could have made payment, you wouldn't be out here." Qerlak stared down at the ground between his feet, and for a moment, Fennet believed he had at last gotten through.

"Your generosity, milord, becomes you as a nobleman. Paying your tithe to Greatknight Beryllian so promptly last winter, feasting your, em, your companions through the new year. And then the matter of the peasant settlement."

"You know, I think I will do the socks as well." The lord of the foef, who had clearly not been fully attending, dropped to the ground and stripped his feet bare, wringing out yet more slimy water. Fennet, still standing with moist tunic in hand, took a slow breath and recited the Elvish meme of patience before continuing.

"The captive peasants, from your, ahm, adventure, were fortunate to be free of the dragon's durance, if I may say so sir. You gave them land here, another great boon. But a settlement stake? That, milord, is where our calculations have come to ruin. There was not enough even of that vast treasure left to grant such beneficence and still meet these other obligations."

"And a nobleman in debt is a nobleman disgraced. Go on, Fennet, you might as well admit it." Qerlak looked up from the

36

ground with that same confident grin, and despite all evidence Fennet found himself hoping against hope that his lord held one more trick up his sleeve.

Before he could continue, they were approached by a half-dozen of the local peasants, led by a small girl with a bunch of wildflowers.

"Milord," said an older man tugging his cap and bowing, "just a small token of our esteem, sir."

From the ground, Qerlak signaled urgently to Fennet, who quickly dropped the tunic over his wide shoulders and hid the horrid latticework of scars on the knight's torso. The little girl was shyly looking at the ground; they might have spared her the sight, and Fennet realized this was of great importance to his lord.

Getting to his knees, Qerlak reached to take the bouquet and complimented it. "So lovely, young lady! And here in the center a lotus, I see; you must have scampered far to obtain that."

She nodded, "Into the pond shallows behind the cottage. Milord. And the red lilies are from the roadside, those were easy."

Qerlak's broad smile faded just a touch as he noticed the foliage surrounding the bunch. "And this? What are all of these small purple blooms among the green?"

"Why, that's heather!" she cried as if nothing could be more obvious. "Don't you know it?"

"I fear I don't, milady. I was raised north and east of here, and we have no…" Qerlak fell quiet, sniffing the blooms as if to do more than appreciate them. His full smile returned as he stood. "Of course I have seen these blossoms, over all the lonely hillsides of my new home, they are more common here than reeds, or grass, or…"

Again, the knight froze without word or movement, and Fennet exchanged looks of concern with the peasants. When Qerlak suddenly laughed out loud, everyone jumped.

"Flame of the First, that bastard," he breathed, then turned to Fennet a moment before snapping in other directions as well. "Fennet, find my horse, I must get back at once. Cecil! Squire Cecil, where are—there, Cecil I need you to speak to the farmers here. We need heather."

"Heather, milord?"

"Yes, not hops!" Qerlak chortled again and clapped his squire on one shoulder. "These small purple blooms," the knight snapped off one from the bouquet to suit. "Like this, sacks of them. Fennet!"

"Milord, Spezh is bringing your—"

"Fennet, find Ondaii and those enormous tubs, do you remember them?"

"The tubs, milord? Yes, I believe we are using one as a, as—"

"A trough, for the pigs! Yes!" Qerlak crowed, then muttered again to himself. "That clever fox, he never told anyone, not even in the journal." Looking up at Fennet again, he rattled on. "Tell Ondaii, he needs to make some lids for them. I'll show him what I mean."

Qerlak was hauling on his boots barefoot and scooping up his armor to throw over the saddlebow, except for the helm which he donned with a slight squish atop his hair.

"Covers, for the pig troughs?"

"And Skeggs! Get the cook ready to help the peasants at their work. This will require—Argens alive, we will need a celebration!"

Fennet had seldom felt so completely lost. "Celebration? Of what, Sir Barleybane?"

"Oh, it doesn't matter, I only need a fortnight or so to experiment. I know! We'll celebrate one year from the day I took possession here! The first week of Serpent." Qerlak's face was alight and Fennet thought perhaps his lord had spent too long underwater. "Tell Skeggs, I'll need barrels of barley, probably three to start."

"Milord, what could—"

"The debt, Fennet!" The young knight laughed and seemed in a fit of hilarity as he advanced to pin another sprig of heather through Fennet's collar. "We're going to set up a week of celebration. All the people coming in, contests, tourneying; prizes, there must be wonderful gifts for all the winners!"

Fennet's brows were so furled they began to impede his vision. "Milord, we will pay our debt, by *spending* money?"

Qerlak only laughed again as he seized the bridle and lumbered into his seat. Checking the horse's stride as soon as it started, Qerlak dismounted, ran to the peasant group, gave the elder man a coin and kissed the little girl's hand, then mounted again and looked down on Fennet with soaking wet good humor.

"It probably won't work. But remember who you serve, castellan. My family name might prove as good as my right arm in defending this keep." So saying, Qerlak used one finger to tap the family crest on his gauntlet, the symbol of the fist clenching a sheaf of grain above the flame of Argens. Then his horse cantered away with the lord of Mon-Crulbagh slowly tipping left, then right, then left again until he escaped the view of all.

Fennet turned to face a grinning Spezh, who spat and summoned his guard to follow their lord home. Behind him, Fennet saw the delegation of peasants, still standing there probably with homely words unsaid and fervent oaths unrenewed. Such loyalty would have silenced the castellan even if he had a clue what scheme his lord was about.

The elder one finally nodded slowly and said "He slew the dragon, that one. Semegorn the fire-worm, held us up there in the hills. Decades. Him and that huge mortal, they killed the dragon and freed us."

Fennet nodded back, smiled weakly at the little girl and said to her, "Thank you kindly for your gift and your inspiration. Whatever it was."

⊕ ⊕ ⊕

City of Beryl

"This city is so *huge* at night!"

Bellatara's whisper, prompting a snort from Quarion up ahead, made Ellesmera smile as she crossed a narrow street in the pre-midnight gloom. She trailed the eager Stealthic with the Halfling between them, moving neither too quickly nor too directly toward the darkened manse of the wealthier quarter near the castle bailey wall.

"City, what a joke!" Quarion replied as they waited for a lone traveler ahead to pass from sight. "Bellatara, how can you say that? This here, this is a cluster of huts near the castle of a lord. When we met in Wanlock, now *that* was a real city."

"Also huge," Bellatara agreed immediately. "And bigger at night, I tell you."

Ellesmera recalled the glory of Cryssigens in the North Mark, and reflected that size was not the only measure of a place. True, Wanlock probably held twice the population of her birthplace, and five times that of this fortress town, but neither in Wanlock nor here in Beryl could one see the glory of the Colors, the pageantry of so many nobles gathered in one place, vying for position and power. Looking to the Halfling between them, Ellesmera reflected that the same town which made Bellatara so nervous gave her nothing but relief. In Beryl, there was but one lord, the Greatknight himself, and no merchant guild or preacher cabal showed themselves in opposition. Not nearly the same level of wealth here either, of the kind her famous mother gloried in and used to further her own schemes. Such a simple job as this, after the stifling intrigue of her childhood, seemed almost too good to be true.

They strolled in leisurely pace toward the district where the deceased mage's house was tucked between gated gardens and retaining walls on all sides, perhaps twenty structures of some real size and wealth just beyond the inner bailey of the Greatknight's castle above them. They had passed a quartet of guards back near the inn and were unlikely to see any more roaming sentinels in a town this small. Quarion sighted the target manse, hesitated a moment while pretending to get his bearings, then nodded toward a narrow alley between properties used for deliveries.

Ellesmera could sense his nervous energy even in the open, but now the young Stealthic practically bounced down the shaded lane, outpacing them both in the night as if he had started running. Ellesmera took Bellatara's hand and let her own night-sight guide them to the first turn, where thirty steps away Quarion was just lowering his body back down from peeking over the stone wall into the back yard of the manse.

He assessed them as they came up, then nodded approvingly.

"What is it?" Bellatara demanded.

"You both move very quietly. Truly, not bad at all."

Bellatara grinned, as she always did from praise, but Ellesmera reflected that this was an interesting observation. A Stealthic, Martial Wizard and Woodsman, two Elves and a Halfling, perhaps as varied and strange a group as she had seen before. Yet all three of them were of small size, wearing no metal and light on their feet. Perhaps here was one key to their hiring.

Quarion kipped up to the top of the garden wall again, hanging easily for a full minute before lowering back into a crouch and facing the others.

"It's just as I thought. At least eight guards, not five. And two of them are pacing between the service door and the front."

"The mage lied?" Bellatara hissed.

"Or was misinformed," Ellesmera put in, but watching Quarion the while for any clue of another explanation.

He looked back at her, then away with a shrug and a spit.

"I happened to see it this time. But I never liked the idea of using the door anyway. Wait here while I time their passing. We'll go straight in the window."

She watched him lay out a length of thin strong cord before going back to his watching position atop the wall. Nearby, Bellatara removed her backpack and cinched the straps so her javelins wouldn't rattle. Ellesmera looked down on her plain tunic and pantaloons and felt a moment of real hilarity pass through her, that there was seemingly nothing she could do, out of her ascetic life, to prepare for such an adventure.

She tucked in her tunic and tightened the belt a bit as Quarion kipped back down.

Crouching together with them he began to whisper, as if a trio of children were playing a secret game.

"Over the wall, then straight to the back of the house on the right-hand side from us. There's a fireplace in the library, according to the plan. I'll lasso the chimney, climb up, then haul you each in turn."

"Are the windows locked?" Bellatara asked.

"Not even closed, I can see from here. There's no one inside, unless they're lying on the floor, and the guards don't pace out back."

"Sounds rather easy," Ellesmera said, again keeping his face in view to gauge his reaction. Yes, a flash of something like pain; not fear, but then how would a son of Astor show that emotion. Quarion also thought this job was easy, but he worried about the unknown.

Yet that look was somehow familiar too.

"One more thing. There can be no talking once we go over the wall."

"But—"

"Not a word, Bellatara. I'm going to show you several hand-signals now. Memorize them and stay quiet. We're taking no chances."

Quarion gestured with his hands only, fingers, palm and wrist turning and forming several shapes. *Stay down. Hold. Back/ retreat/flee. Yes. No. Danger.*

He tested them both for whispered answers, nodded, then put a finger to his lips. Winked. And leaped from his crouch to the top of the garden wall in a single pantherish bound, balanced there looking around, and dropped silently to the other side. Ellesmera boosted Bellatara up and two arms helped drag her across. Then Ellesmera jumped and grabbed the top of the wall and hauled herself over with, she thought, a modicum of grace.

As they slipped across the backyard, moving from moonlight to the shadow of the manse, Ellesmera relaxed her shoulders and steadied her breathing to slow the pounding of her heart. A simple job yes, and nothing terribly wrong with avoiding needless delay. But the voice nagging her inside would not stop. Why trust the mage's word? No reason, except that for a truly illegal act they should have been offered more money. She watched Quarion uncoil his line, swing the noose easily about his head and then up to catch the brick chimney on the first try, and felt a momentary tightness around her own neck as he tugged it taut and began his climb.

Quarion pulled himself aloft using only his arms, letting his legs dangle free to keep his actions completely silent. Ellesmera felt a wash of respect for his agility and smoothness as he reached the top and held one hand out: *Hold.* He looked within intently for what seemed a half an hour. Then he kipped his legs up and through the open window without so much as touching the sill. A moment later, his head poked back out and he grinned down, pointing to the Halfling and signaling *Yes.*

Ellesmera fitted the rope around her friend's shoulders and watched as Quarion hauled her up. Bellatara tried to use her feet but Quarion stopped hauling and signaled *No* until she let them hang there. The muttered curse sounded like a shout and again Ellesmera resorted to her technique for calm.

Her mind began to clear as night-breeze and moving moonlight faded from the conscious mind. Bellatara's easy laughter on the road south from Wanlock, the smell of wildflowers and heather in places where they camped. Quarion's tricks with small rocks, daggers, coins and tankards, making things disappear and come back with a grin on his face. These were her companions, and Ellesmera realized she had felt more at home with them in a jail cell in Wanlock than in her mother's temple. Even as she relaxed, the rope dropped before her and she gripped it, climbing like Quarion had as the Stealthic and Woodsman pulled to increase her speed. She felt a sensation like flying, moving faster than her arms could propel her. Closer to the job that was still off somehow.

A book of some power and worth.

A patron with no name.

For payment, not honor.

The room was vast, dark and quiet, taking up more than half the floor of the manse. Elvish sight was no longer good without the stars, and Quarion lit a small lantern, shining its spot carefully around the edge of the floors to establish that the two doors were closed. He listened at the left-hand double portal, leading to the hallway, then mimed the act of falling asleep. Still shielding the light from that direction, he opened it to illumine the rest of the room.

More than half the wall-space was consumed with shelves, deeply inset and six ranks high to the ceiling. Dark wood and thick carpet were everywhere, and Ellesmera picked up the faint scent of incense for the first time since she had left her temple home. Catching Quarion's eye she furrowed a brow and rubbed her fingers together to signal wealth.

Yes, with a grin. Then Quarion pointed to the shelves and mimed flipping the pages of a book. They gathered at the center to plan.

"Where sh-" Bellatara started, but Quarion clapped a hand over her mouth which she slapped angrily away.

He made C-shaped frames with his fingers, to indicate a very thick volume, then stooped down to trace the oval-triangle-dots symbol in the thick carpet.

Ellesmera signaled *Yes*, and pointed to herself and the far wall.

Bellatara made another signal with her arm, one Quarion had not shown them but whose meaning was plain, and stomped off to the longest wall, where she scampered up a rolling ladder to start defiantly on the top shelf.

Ellesmera scanned the rows before her, using the thickness to ignore more than half the tomes from the start. For some time, there was no more noise in the enormous room than three books made sliding in and out of place. An almost peaceful job, she thought. Using her trance techniques, she slowed her breathing, felt her focus sharpen, started to sense the truth of things in her memory and in the room.

She realized, with only half a mind on the front covers of each tome, their patron was too trusting about this entire job. What guarantee had they offered, to bring her the book and not steal it away? If it was valuable, the mage must have considered that risk. Yet she hired strangers. If the book meant little, then why pay at all? A ritual to be finished, she had said. Certainly, that was an element of casting enchantments; Ellesmera had learned the Sorceror's Tongue and certain spells from the wealthy patrons and tutors of her mother's entourage. But wasn't it rather foolish to begin the work without the tome in hand? And if the loss of lore would be ruinous, then the book itself must be valuable as well.

Her hand almost passed over a rich brown hardbound tome since it was embossed with the symbol of Argens stepping on a supine demon. Then she reminded herself it was thick enough, so she pulled it out to check the front. To her horror, she saw various images in a rich rainbow on the cover.

An ocean wave with glaring eyes, flame that roared without fuel through a maw, muscular piles of rock and mud that seemed

45

of one being, Argens wrestling with a column of stormcloud. At his feet another demon sprawled with its spine twisted in submission, symbol of the Demonbender sect now strictly outlawed in the Empire by its new ruler. And in the upper right corner, the symbol she had seen drawn twice before.

As she pulled it down into both trembling hands, Ellesmera's trance-mind reeled in all the disparate thoughts, from hours or months ago, to an order:

The mage who hired strangers to enter a house too-well guarded, and retrieve a tome now forbidden to anyone. The look on Quarion's face, one of anguish and desperation, the way he looked at the coin-pile when Bellatara was stacking them. The same face he had made when she paid their bail in Wanlock. The one who could make five coins disappear into Bellatara's sleeve for a trick, but always gave them back. He knew this job was sour. But he felt a debt. To her.

Over nothing! She thought. Ellesmera wondered if despite her dedication, the opulence of her upbringing had blinded her to this. A few hundred silver, to men like Quarion, that was wage-labor of half a year. He took this risk to repay her.

"You don't owe me anything," she said quietly, but her companions were so startled they each dropped their books with a sound like slaps of thunder.

"Cark me!" Bellatara cried out, nearly falling from the ladder.

"Who's in there?" a voice from outside the door.

All three began frantically signaling to each other: *No, Back, Stay Down, No, No, Yes, Back…*

The door banged open and Ellesmera dropped the tome to free her arms. By the lantern light her eyes fell across a passage from the random page it fell open to. Sorceror's Tongue: not long enough time for her to read it consciously, but in her trance state the words flowed in like water, letting her play them back as the fight broke out.

Two guards with sword and shield stumbled through, as the book at her feet emitted a short, deep tone and the windows all slammed shut at once.

... thus the procedure for conversing with an Earth Elemental already summoned or otherwise present...

Quarion had pulled his cutlass and instinctively raised it in harm's reach. This drew a reflexive poke from the nearest guard, which he parried. Ellesmera stepped up next to him with her arms raised but palms open.

"Please, we will cooperate."

... compared with what we have already seen for abjuring minor demons...

A book of lore now forbidden by law, and probably undiscovered until tonight. Ellesmera realized with a sinking feeling, even as she eyed the guard near her, this was the job. The three of them were nothing but pawns, in a scandal wished into the open.

Her guard yelled, "Drop your weapons!" but Ellesmera could not comply. Still in trance state, she tried to hold them out peacefully, but the fellow was fooled in the near-darkness and reacted as if she held a knife. He shouted again, drew back and swung for her torso.

Of course, Ellesmera was much better armed than a dagger would provide.

... the caster merely conjures magical Fire in any form or from any source, while speaking the following phrase thus- 'ignita dicta sud terror'.

Without conscious thought, Ellesmera brought her arm up to block the blade, catching it on the flat with her wrist and knocking it out of his grip. Instinctively he rushed with the shield, and she brought her other hand forward palm-out, stopping him cold as he staggered back a full pace.

Quarion and his man, almost disengaged, returned to full alert on the combat with more passes and parries. Shouting

47

from down the hall meant there was no escape. But there was still time--

Ellesmera's man drew his knife and raised it high overhead preparing to charge in. Suddenly the center of his chest sprouted a quivering pole and with an astonished face he fell to the floor. Back on the ladder, Bellatara was already preparing another javelin to cast, her face flaming with urgency.

The ensuing contact is sure to be perilous, but could tell the caster much…

Four more guards piled into the room.

"Bellatara!" she cried. "Stop, come down."

Quarion looked to Ellesmera with a face of agony. She shook her head at him and signaled *No*, then meekly crossed her wrists above her head and dropped to her knees. Behind her, the book flipped pages as if stirred by a heavy wind.

Quarion dropped his blade and also knelt, speaking for all of them.

"I guess it really was too good to be true."

⊕ ⊕ ⊕

The Border of Pritaelseran

Hitaelseran reined in at the top of the gentle incline that would take his patrol out of his father's lands and down, into Mon-Crulbagh. The stunning sky and light breeze lent him the feeling he could ride all day, and still fight come sunset. His eight retainers rode past him toward the end of the road, bearing chain and shield, lance and sword like himself and marked with the livery of the diving hawk. Nodding to his dekentar to take the lead, the youngest son of the foef turned to review the rest of the party entrusted to his command.

Marching behind the dust of the four wagons loaded with tents and supplies, the twoscore peasant levy led the remounts and also carried spears, mainly for show. Even these commoners were in good order, almost marching in step and looking at ease with this show of force. Most knighthoods fielding ten mounted warriors would have to leave only womenfolk behind to guard the keep. Hitaelseran knew, at need, his father could send him three times this number.

All the signs were auspicious as he looked down the incline at the lower country he had been sent to take. This was Hitaelseran's first view of his father's next conquest. The incline stretching north to south was gradual and wide, ambling into lower land over the course of many furlongs. The road here petered to nothing, and the country was visibly wilder and wetter in the panorama brought to his eye. The young knight could see for leagues to the north and west, here at the bottom edge of the Argensian Empire.

Less than an hour's march to the south the view was blocked by quickly thickening jungle growth. On the Pritaelseran highland behind him, cleared fields and a few scattered cottages dotted the view. Ahead of him westward, palms and vines intruded to a point nearly as far north as his men marched. Perhaps once there had been cleared fields here, long ago. But Mon-Crulbagh was fallen far since before his father's day, ineptly led and ripe for conquest by its worthier neighbor.

Hitaelseran cantered to the top of the line again and spoke to his second.

"How long before we encounter any settlers?"

"We'll be well off the incline before nightfall, milord," Guernsten replied. "When I was—that is, in an earlier campaign, we encamped just where you see that line of trees. That's near the start of the Bograwl; not a river really, just a stream but you know how lords need to put on airs."

"And from there?"

"Weren't no villages for another day, day and a half beyond, back then. If you head west of northwest, you'll be coming between the Bograwl on the south and the Sodsluice to the north, and then you'll start to see a few cabins. Or on a course more northerly you'll see the village they call Sluicehill across the river. Maybe a hundred or so peasants, last I checked."

The horses walked easily downhill as the men spoke, visors up on their helms and reins hanging free. Guernsten reached up to stroke the thick faded scar on his cheek while speaking, tracing it from below the ear to the edge of his mouth. Hitaelseran had heard the tale, a Mon-Crulbagh pike scraping through the visor-hinge and just missing the warrior's brain. Weeks before he could eat solid.

Guernsten was certainly over a century old, the veteran of several campaigns under his father. No doubt he was sent to mind the youngest son, but Hitaelseran couldn't find the will to resent his presence here. Guernsten was sensical and spoke plainly, and the young knight was relieved to have a solid opinion on tap.

"What do you hear of this new lord, Barleybane?"

Guernsten shrugged. "Not a real lord, er, so they say milord," with a sideways glance. "A merchant came through the keep two months back, said as how he's of noble blood alright, but a younger son, won't inherit."

They rode a moment in silence, and by the time the dekentar realized his gaffe Hitaelseran was already grinning at him. Guernsten smiled back, then spit. "But he's no knight, you see. Fellow said, he goes about with a basketful of strange, rootless commoners. You know. Mages, a singer, dwarves and mortals, one of them… fights with their hands."

Hitaelseran had heard nothing of this. "He was an adventurer? Like that group in Wanlock, the Tributarians?"

Guernsten looked on his lord sideways again and quietly said. "One of that same gang. The merchant said."

This revelation lasted the pair through several furlongs of silent marching. Hitaelseran found he could form no clear picture at all of his adversary. The beautiful day changed its attractions to different, but still alluring forms as they came lower and closer to the sharp-edged shade of trees and brush parrying the sunlight.

The smell of deep earth, strange blossoms and wetter terrain came to him; the air seemed thicker, heavier but still pleasant in the warming days of Hawk. Midsummer in a month or so.

"I will challenge him if he comes against us."

"Not very likely, milord."

"He's a craven?"

Guernsten shrugged again. "Tales I hear, he fights on foot."

"Dismounted! It's not possible."

"I only repeat what the merchant says, milord."

Hitaelseran held up one arm as if to say, "fair enough". But he added "Most likely, his companions going afoot made him choose their company. But no true knight would refuse the joust."

"If he accepts, you will best him." Guernsten was looking off as he spoke, giving his speech the air of honest prediction rather than flattery. But as Hitaelseran could think of no proper response, there was again silence for a time, and the dekentar continued to look to the north while they rode.

Finally, he stiffened and reined in, pointing to say "There. The bastards, again, look milord."

The raiding-party was now near the bottom of the incline, though it seemed to Hitaelseran's view that all ways into Mon-Crulbagh got continuously lower as far as the eye could see. Trees on the slope were sparse, and in large stretches, as here, there was no brush or other cover. In the afternoon light he could see for an hour's ride to his right and northward. Perhaps eight furlongs off there stood a massive pile of stones, of the kind used for boundary markers in poorer districts. Yet this was cruder looking, larger, irregular and perhaps disintegrating even from this distance. Beyond it another dozen furlongs off, a second pile, and ever-more distantly he could make out four more.

"The border stones, what of them?"

"Do you see milord? By rights your father's house owns the entire incline. Yet mark you the stones. Four furlongs up the slope they are, and see the tracks behind where they've been dragged!"

Hitaelseran reined in to stare, too long for a noble adult. Something about the stones, and his dekentar's tale, rang wrong to him. But it wouldn't do to show indecision now. He signaled for the column to continue, saying "We'll just have a look at this for ourselves."

He spurred his horse across the incline to approach the first marker. He realized only after a few moments, that Guernsten was back with the column, evidently taking his "we" in the royal sense. Hitaelseran didn't blame him for any unease, but now he was committed. With four dozen pairs of eyes on him, he rode straight up and dismounted before the pile.

It was an impressive thing despite its crudeness. Over nine feet tall, and even at this range Hitaelseran could not decide if it were one stone or a hundred. No sign of mortar, yet no mark of plane or chisel either. There were bumps and roundnesses along it, and a suggestion of some order he could not immediately see. Hitaelseran found himself thinking irrelevantly, of a scarecrow in the fields, or tales he had read of the frozen north, where children made fat men from snow.

A moment after he let go the reins, his horse shied with a snort and stepped back two paces. Hitaelseran cursed in surprise, then stomped around behind the thing, to view the scraped earth on the Mon-Crulbagh side.

The sod was indeed clear of grass or cover, a bit wider than the pile itself. Hitaelseran felt a great surge of anger then, that a crime so ignoble—indeed, so childish! —should be suffered to go unpunished. Stalking around to the front again, he faced the thing as he might confront a living thief, with arms akimbo looking up at it and down the row at the others in line.

Right now, there was admittedly nothing he could do. But everyone was watching. The young knight spat full onto the base of the pile, marking some stone and some grass before turning to get his mount. The horse was still a bit shy and it took him two tries to get back in the saddle, embarrassing him further. But by now the line of marchers had passed along and none were looking back, praise Argens. Still feeling something was off, Hitaelseran spurred back to the men.

In late afternoon, they came in sight of a thin trail of smoke ahead, on the other side of a small stand of evergreens, indicating a settler's cabin.

"A fire, in this warmth?" Hitaelseran asked.

"Most likely smoking meat, milord," came the voice from one of the peasant spears, and the knight nodded to him kindly which reassured the man for speaking out of turn.

"We ride by. No punishment unless insult is offered."

As they rode past the copse the back of the cottage came in view. Riding on he saw a small porch, a smoking shed beyond and a chain hanging down with an empty hook still swinging despite the lack of breeze. The settler came out clutching a hoe, closing the front door behind him in a way that signaled the house was not empty.

It was only at that moment, that Hitaelseran rather senselessly recalled that he thought of the border stone as having a front and back as well, despite the lack of any obvious ornamentation.

He and the farmer exchanged a long glance as the raiding party rode by.

"These lands are Pritaelseran's now," the knight informed him with a curt nod.

To his surprise, the man smirked a moment and said, "Be here at week's end and I'll tithe you."

The youth could think of no fitting response to this insolence, so they rode on. From the wooded lands to the right he heard the brief, cracked sound of a horn, once and a few minutes later, again from further in.

"His son, likely," Guernsten said, "warning the village."

"Good!" Hitaelseran replied. "We shan't have to ride all the way to the foef to settle the matter."

Everyone chuckled at this, and Guernsten nodded too but rubbed his cheek a bit.

"Also, shorter ride back."

Hitaelseran looked at him sharply, but if the man knew he spoke of defeat, he showed no sign.

They progressed west of northwest for the remainder of the day, through land rich with life and scarce of habitation. They passed two further cottages, one empty and the other even less welcoming. Sunset brought an air more humid than the day, muffling the sounds of unfamiliar creatures hovering beyond the firelight, and wafting in biting insects attracted to it. And still more horns sounding well after dark.

He stood with Guernsten looking out from the edge of the fire's glow.

"Day past tomorrow, most likely we'll see them milord."

"That long! The lords of Mon-Crulbagh care so little for their people then?"

"Mustering takes time. Longer with peasants, longer still for marching."

"So the old tales are true? He will bring no horse against us?"

Guernsten rubbed his scar awhile without answering. Hitaelseran shook his head as the elements of insult and nonsense only increased the dancing pressure in his nerves. The knight began to kick the ground as he thought, scuffing the rich turf with his boot and exposing soil much moister than on the highlands.

It was just then that Hitaelseran had a flash memory of his last moment before the border stone, on his horse and using that boot to spur away. The daylight showed him—no, a mirage memory surely—the base of the stone still wet, but nothing on the grass before it.

A night-grazing herd of riding lizards grunted and grazed nearby half the night, spooking the horses and hardly calming the men. Hitaelseran and two retainers finally stampeded them off with torches and everyone laughed. But in his tent the young knight tossed and turned, dreaming only in snatches of facing an enormous warrior without his horse or lance.

Castle Mon-Crulbagh

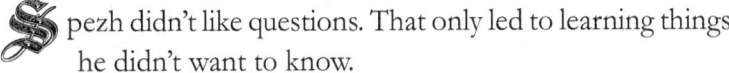pezh didn't like questions. That only led to learning things he didn't want to know.

After arriving back at the castle late the previous night, he heard plenty of questions volleying back and forth. There was banging on occasion, the sound of something dropping to the stone in the main hall, and a curse he could have sworn was his lord's. But Spezh's responsibility was defence of the keep and securing Sir Qerlak's foef. He had checked the guard posts, took a turn around the walls—except for the rearmost western section, which everyone avoided of course—and then went to bed, secure that he was doing his job.

In the morning, he snatched food from the dining board and headed out toward the walls to do it some more. But the world, evidently, had other ideas.

"Dekentar Spezh!" the voice of the castellan was strident as usual, signaling the onset of questions. "Have you seen Sir Qerlak?"

"I have not, sir," Spezh responded with a quick nod and another step toward the courtyard.

"Can you help me find him? It's important."

Spezh turned back with gritted teeth. "Castellan, surely one of the servants—"

"No one has seen him. His bed unslept in, his horse still here. I've searched every room."

A crash from the kitchen behind them indicated that Skeggs the cook was encountering obstacles in his quest for the mid-day meal. A servant bumped through the door in a cloud of steam and smoke, bearing a sharp aroma Spezh could not identify, neither baked nor roasted yet making his entire frame rumble with desire, even with shreds of breakfast still working their way down his throat.

"Milord doesn't care to ride, Fennet, you know that. As for sleep, well…" Spezh let his further thoughts remain unspoken; he himself had slept, and likely Fennet too, but Elves did not need to of course. And the young knight Qerlak was just the sort who might not, an adventurer and active as a bee from a broken hive with one project or another.

"I must report to Sir Qerlak about the task he set me yesterday, on the road, and about, well, certain other matters. Are you saying we are sworn to a lord we cannot locate?"

"Sir Qerlak?" the servant asked, bustling back in with a partner carrying an enormous metal vat between them. "He's in the kitchen."

"He is not!" Spezh shouted involuntarily. Everyone knew the penalty for entering the cook's domain. Even the servants were risking injury to interrupt Skeggs unbidden. But another clanking crash came through the doors, accompanied by a slosh and a vigorous curse that removed all doubt. It was the same voice, the same curse, as the previous night. Spezh gulped and pushed into the kitchen for the first time, followed by Elias Fennet. The morning was not going well.

The first thing he saw was the bloody butchering blade, stuck in the counter before him. Spezh gripped his own ax tightly as he coughed and waved his arm through smoky steam obscuring his view.

But as he took in the scene before him, Spezh felt the morning was about to get better.

There was Skeggs, his hands full of linen as he assisted Sir Qerlak to lift a sheet laden with drek from an enormous vat emitting steamy aroma.

"Fennet, Spezh, you're up, good!" the knight cried as he twisted the folded cloth one way and Skeggs the other to wring out the grainy broth.

Spezh looked at the castellan and chuckled at his bewilderment.

"Look you, they're making ale."

"Ale!" Qerlak cried, as he laid the tangled cloth on the sideboard. "Dekentar, I must ask you to keep a civil tongue in your mouth. Let the good peasants of our foef, who need a drink closer to their daily meal and who lack the benefit from centuries of learning, content themselves with bits of bread tossed in the pot and a few hours of waiting." He stepped up to the two of them and put a strong hand on each shoulder.

"The Barleybanes, gentlemen, make beer."

Before Spezh could properly consider this bit of trivia—drunk was drunk, surely—Fennet asked more questions, damn the man.

"But milord, what would be the purpose here? I mean, if your family, that is, your history is no doubt as proud and noble as I have heard, but—"

Qerlak's laugh was full of such good humor that Spezh smiled along without understanding a whit of the conversation.

"My dear castellan, you let me worry about such fine distinctions. The main thing is, we can do it! I'm sure of it, because this—" he turned away to snatch up a large sack filled with light purple sprigs, "this my friends, is heather."

"So it is milord. And what of it?"

"Can't you tell? Smell this!" the young lord insisted, thrusting a double-handful at each of them.

Spezh shrugged. "Smells like flowers, milord."

"It's hops!" Qerlak shouted, then laughed again. "Never mind, my good guard captain. Suffice to say it will suffice. In my birthplace, we used hops. Riding south to this my new home I kept thinking it was so sad that we had none growing here, despite seeing these covering the downs everywhere! What a fool I was! And that bastard, he never told anyone, I can just bet."

"What bastard, milord?" Fennet asked.

"The lord who brewed here before I came. Not Distallin, most likely, he was hardly around from what I can tell in reading the keep journal. The one before him…"

"Perhaps Maltrak Crulbagh, milord."

"Certainly, or one of the others, it doesn't matter. That's what all these tubs were for, and he never wrote it down." Qerlak's face shone with energy as he moved about, stirring the tub before dashing to the sideboard to resume crushing various piles of grain and carefully mingling them to add to a large crock as he spoke.

"Spezh, do you know the other vat, the one that looks like this one here?"

The guardsman looked down to the tub at his feet, as his heart sank with the expectation of a chore. "This one, milord? Well, truth to tell, there is one…"

"Yes, the pig trough, I know. I need it, can you please clean it out thoroughly and bring it in?"

"There's no room, milord!" Skeggs complained. "Already I cannot walk in here."

"No, not next to it, Skeggs, beneath. It's for steaming the broth." Qerlak stopped grinding and took a quick turn around the inner kitchen area, near the enormous fireplace. "But I don't understand, there should be a pit, in the floor… Skeggs, were you here for the last two lords' reigns?"

The cook straightened up with a hardened face: no Elf liked to give information that could reveal their exact age. "I served Maltrak Crulbagh milord, as well as Distallin and now you."

"But you never heard about this? Blast. Wait, what's here?"

Spezh looked to where his lord had his hands on a section of brick not far down the wall from the fireplace chimney. These questions were only going to lead to trouble, so he took a careful step backwards toward the door. But fate was determined to be unkind.

"Spezh, this thickness in the brick, see the bulge? Is this something to do with the castle defenses?"

With a heavy sigh, Spezh walked past the cook giving his back to the man as he further invaded the sanctum. "No milord, it cannot be- this wall does not butt against the outer keep. I don't-"

"Could it be some kind of secret passage?"

"Sir," Spezh replied with fraying patience. "How should I know? My job is to defend your keep, and I haven't had time nor men to explore every foot that lies inside."

"Nor are you likely to get any," Fennet responded, starting up the old argument between them again. "Our expenses already—"

"Look you," Qerlak broke in, "the bulge runs all the way up to the ceiling."

"Aye sir," Spezh replied, "and all the way to the floor as well."

"To the floor! Of course! Gentlemen, come with me."

"Where to sir?" Fennet asked as the knight brushed past them.

"To the brewery of course!"

Back through the main reception room and into the hallway passing by the empty trophy chamber, Qerlak practically ran for the stairs leading to the mysterious basement level of the keep. Well behind the procession, three servants labored to lug the trough with boiled grain broth in it toward its new home. Spezh called to a guardsman getting breakfast and conveyed the order to clean the pig trough, then grabbed a pair of torches from the brackets and handed one to Fennet as they descended.

Spezh hated coming down here. He'd served around other keeps and even helped storm a small one last year during Yula's revolt, but never had he seen a subterranean level so extensive, connected, and complex as the one running beneath Mon-Crulbagh. Like all children of Hope, he knew that deeper down meant greater evil, and the bogeys of his nightmares shuddered in every shadow cast by the torches as they walked the remarkably clean brick-lined halls.

Qerlak was backtracking to find the room beneath the kitchen, but the lord had never come down here and found it puzzling.

"These hallways don't make sense. Why isn't there one just crossing the way I need to go. What's in here?" He opened one of the many doors leading off each corridor, into another brick-lined, dark room stacked with incomprehensible supplies of the most unguessable miscellany.

"Poles in here. Replacement pikes, I would say. And here? Crocks and pots, ah good, we might be getting close."

"Just some stones in that one sir," Spezh contributed hoping to speed the search, but Qerlak's curiosity was on fire as usual.

"Stones? What sort of—well, Argens' Flame, what an odd thing." He reached to a shelf in this chamber and came back into the hall with what looked to be a crude obelisk around two feet tall, vaguely chisel-shaped, crudely cut and inscribed along its four sides.

"*Per fortior au gens.*" Qerlak slowly read the words in the Ancient tongue.

"There is no punctuation, milord," Fennet put in. "It could be '*Au gens per fortior*'."

"Maybe something like 'from fire through strength', then," Qerlak guessed, "or the other way around 'through strength to flame'. How bizarre- and who needs more than one of these little mottos? There must be dozens of these stone things in here."

Spezh knew it was dangerous to speak but the cellar level made him nervous. "No end to the drek down here, sir. Most of it useless."

From behind he could hear the labored gasps of the servants trying not to spill the vat as they entered the level. His spine began to twitch inside his back and Spezh lurched off down the corridor, just to get this mad adventure over with.

"This way sir. It must be this direction." He charged on with the torch and heard their echoes behind him.

"We came down the steps, turned left- Fennet, did we start out facing the kitchen?"

"Yes, milord. But the turns only take us around the outer sides of the manor house, it seems, nothing through the center of this level."

"I am useless with directions. It was always Meandar who kept track, or one of the wizards, the bard…"

Spezh stopped in front of a double wooden door and waited for the others to catch up.

"What's in here, dekentar?"

"Just some mantlets, sir."

"Mantlets? For defence?"

"I've never been this deep into the cellar," Fennet said, and Spezh could tell the castellan shared his own unease. Qerlak looked at the double doors, nodded, and pushed in.

"See, sir? The mantlets, just five, I stacked them against—"

"The lids!" Qerlak shouted, his voice slapping off the bricks painful to the ears.

"Lids, milord?" Fennet managed. "Like the ones you wished me to have Ondaii make?"

"No need, Fennet, these are the ones. Yes, of course, and look here, the kiln. Marvelous, magnificent, the bastard." Qerlak seized Spezh's torch and danced around the chamber, tapping various shelves, the brick closed-in firepit, and the vat-sized shallow cut near the center of the floor as if meeting old friends. He spun to face the others and Spezh saw again that light, the energy of Hope itself that almost made him a more religious man.

"It's everything we need. Almost. This will save us a week, more, almost two! And here, his grain mixture…" Qerlak seized a rotting burlap bag and ripped the top open, waving his arm at the smell of rotted seeds inside, but then plunging his hand in to closely examine the soggy, moldy product inside as if it were gems.

"Waugh! Hard to be sure, but looks like he was trying to use more wheat than barley. Maybe…"

Dusting his hands on his breeks he spun back. "Now we must get both vats set into the pit here, one with water below. Spezh, can you do that?" Without waiting for a reply, he strode to the spot along the wall where his captain had stacked the metal sheets.

"Let me assist you, sir," Fennet said, but before he could reach him Qerlak had seized one end of the metal sheet and turned back with an edge in one hand as if it weighed no more than a drink platter.

"Spezh, where are the tubes?"

Spezh's heart sunk even lower, into the brick floor. More work no doubt.

"How did you—we took them off sir. I don't know where—"

At that moment the three servants lumbered in, followed by a short slightly built man in bright, spotless robes bearing a light stone on the end of a wand.

"Ah, marvelous, and hello Ondaii, come in. Never mind those lids Fennet asked you for, now we need tubing. Metal tubing, several sizes and probably a dozen paces of it. Over here, men."

The servants lugged the sloshing vat in place and Qerlak, still without assistance, positioned the metal sheet at one end where the flanges on its edges neatly fit around the vat along its long side. He slid the top into place and Spezh cursed to see it neatly covered the entire surface, except for two spots where he had pulled off the tubing.

Ondaii bowed to all within the room, then stepped to the vat and produced his stylus from a sleeve, beginning to measure the diameter of the apertures as well as the distance to various places Qerlak indicated in the still-empty chamber.

Spezh scowled as he scooted from the little man's path. He never liked the strange-speaking foreigner Qerlak hired. And the engineer's politeness only made Spezh like him less. A tiny voice inside warned him that he stood practically alone in his opinion of the annoying peasant, and that usually completed Spezh's bad mood, pointing him in the direction of some prank he could play that would expose the fellow's hypocrisy and supposed genius. So far, matters had not worked out as planned, but next time…

"Yes, we'll need light stones all through these passages. Fuel for this kiln, hardwood if we can get it, swamp brush if not, but no coal, too hot."

As Fennet shrieked about the cost, Spezh wondered if this might at last be his chance to get back to work. But just then the shiny-robed snit turned from his spot on the wall, at a place where a hole in the floor matched one in the ceiling above it.

"Place of smoke, a missing piece here there is."

Qerlak dropped his list of instructions to look over. "Really? That's not good."

"Place of smoke!" Spezh barked, forgetting himself in his bad mood. "Begging milord's pardon, but you fire up that stove there and this entire foef will become a place of smoke. Look at it, nowhere for the fumes to go, they'll blow right through the fuel door here and from then on there'll be no stopping it."

"Built, it is." Ondaii said quietly, in just that word-bent way of his, and now Spezh could feel his own forge heating up.

"Sure, built down here for who knows what devilry! Making ale, not likely. We all know, we've seen, the former lords of this place were insane. Everybody's heard the rumors," he gestured to Fennet who did not respond, and the servants who nodded slightly. "Sacrifices, you ask me. Some kind of demon flame as makes no smoke. By the time you'd lit a wood fire for an hour here, it wouldn't be worth a man's life to try and cross this level to put it out."

"Spezh," Qerlak said firmly, "stop worrying, I recognize brewing when I see it. The flue runs down the back of this kiln and underneath the vats here."

"A chimney in the basement floor!"

"Directly beneath the vats, to heat the water without the smoke you're so afraid of. And over by your feet, it runs up the wall into the ceiling hole above you, and on up through Skeggs' kitchen to run out the same flue as his atop the manor."

"But milord," Fennet asked while Spezh was still gasping for breath at the silliness his lord displayed, "if so, where is the missing piece?"

"I don't know, Fennet, but we need a replacement. Ondaii, with those tubes we'll need something."

Ondaii edged into the place Spezh was standing and began to measure with his stylus up the side of the wall. He could not reach the last two feet and turned to Spezh with a slight nod to ask the favor. Snatching the rod from him, Spezh slapped it against the wall over the little man's head and flipped it as he had been doing until the last rotation took it nearly halfway into the hole.

Taking back the rod, Ondaii bowed his thanks and turned away to speak to Qerlak. "This length of pipe, perhaps will suffice in clay, I can complete in three days. Tubing also."

"A waste of time!" Spezh bellowed. "There's nothing to this hole, it's solid brick just another foot up." So saying he snatched out his ax and thrust it above expecting to hear the solid thunk inside the false opening.

A crunchy sliding noise slightly preceded an avalanche of soot and cinders, and for a long moment Spezh thought this was his end. He was sure he'd swallowed at least a cup of ashes before he could close his mouth. Coughing so hard he nearly fell down, Spezh saw the light of stars as he leaned against the wall and tried to get anything other than dust into his lungs. Dimly he heard voices.

"So, it must need periodic cleaning, that's why the piece could come out."

"Undoubtedly milord."

"Meanwhile, it would now appear my guard captain comes from the southern jungle tribes."

Spezh looked at his arms, armor, boots, even his weapons all coated in ebony soot. He rubbed at his blackened face with hands just as dark and got nowhere. There could not possibly be a good reason for everyone to be chuckling. Just three feet away stood Ondaii, not a speck on his bright robes, looking to him with that fake concern he always affected.

"This is all just a joke to you, isn't it."

"Joke, sir?" Evidently there were still words in the common tongue the fellow did not understand. "Thinking I am how impressive indeed-" and here another infuriating bow— "that you appear with the armor of night. Some warriors, of my home country, arrayed thus, most frightening in battle."

"Marvelous," Spezh answered between coughs. "Drum me up one of those suits when you're done in the brewery here."

"Never mind this, Spezh I hope you're alright, but I did tell you I knew what I was about. Let's head back up and I'll make a list of things you might have seen. Anything we can recover will save us time."

"What time do we need, sir?" Fennet gasped as they were now trotting up the stone steps to the main floor and out the manor hall to the courtyard.

"I must have four weeks. And that's only if I can start two more batches this week. Fennet, when did I take possession here?"

"You arrived in late Serpent, sir."

"No, the date I signed the, ahm, the agreement. You know, the debt."

Spezh was startled to hear of this for the first time, but Sir Qerlak didn't seem to know how to keep a secret from anyone. That tiny voice inside him suggested this left the knight free to speak more often, but Spezh was in no more a mood for self-improvement today than any other.

"Your formal ascension, sir," Fennet always put it so well, "was the seventh of Serpent 2001 ADR. Last year."

"Five more weeks then. We can make it if we—"

Two things interrupted the conversation, nearly at the same time.

From the rearmost western section of the walls, and the tower none of the guards willingly approached, came a muffled report like a dull drum, followed by wooden shutters thrown back on the second floor to emit a puff of white smoke and a flash of long red hair.

"Galethiel! Are you alright?" Qerlak shouted up in real concern.

"We're fine," she tsked down to the courtyard, "my apprentice feels just a little confusion in where to put the reagents."

From within the chamber, an invisible young voice chimed "Sorry, teacher."

Everyone chuckled at this turn, which had happened before, but Spezh shushed everyone and managed to still even his own coughing.

"Quiet! Hear that? A horn."

Even the pigs stopped grunting and after a count of perhaps eight, they all heard it echoing along the road leading to the front gate. And in the further distance, more horns sounding throughout the nearby peasant holdings.

"An invasion, milord. We are not ready for Pritaelseran." Fennet's face was grim. But Qerlak barked a laugh, turning to everyone in order as more folk emerged to the courtyard.

"We're low on men, castellan, but unless I miss my guess, it is they who are not ready for us. Cecil! Squire Cecil, my armor. Ondaii, those tubes and the chimney piece, please. Where is Sir Chased?"

Spezh spoke up. "Last I saw he was heading west to hunt for Reptile Men, sir. Two days back."

"Blast! But that is the deed I asked of him. Dekentar, please send one man on horseback to search for him and pass the news. Fennet, you're in charge here, please see to it the horses are saddled for us."

Qerlak looked up to the tower and the companion with whom he had shared his previous adventures. "Galethiel, you can—"

"Don't say it. I'm coming with you." As the sorceress closed the shutter, the knight of the keep turned back with a fierce grin."

"Spezh, I need every man."

As he saluted, Spezh could see behind Qerlak the statue of a lordly knight wrestling with a Reptile Man, and he knew the struggle ahead would be a joyous one. This job was one he knew, and there would be no questions.

Castle Beryl

Without question, Torquem'l Beryllian preferred his study to the public hall when it was time to think. No cloud of petitioners listening to his every word, no need to make a speech when a good decision would do. Papers on the desk before him instead of councilors whispering reminders in his ear. Even the oak armchair felt more comfortable than his Greatknight's throne of office. On days like today, the lord of five vassal knights didn't want to dwell on his position, as he stood so much closer to losing it this summer.

His door opened to a burst of lilting lyrics and the laughter of his court outside. Blast that bard, too talented and amusing for a lord to get any work done out there. But the portal admitted his closest retainer and fighting comrade, who closed it on the merriment and advanced to the desk.

"The news is bad, milord, there's no ducking that." Sir Tancrad Coss could speak plainly here, instead of settling for a supportive look or nod in the main chamber. Even today, when what he said was obvious, it was better to hear the voice of a friend.

Beryllian gestured to the table. "Which news, Coss, take your pick." He picked up the missives and reports in random order. "The cabal of Demonbenders who escaped from the Barony of Dargor, crossing our border and still missing? Or perhaps the glorious state of our tithing, with my knighthoods dramatically under-reporting in the wake of the war."

He stopped as a knock preceded the representative of the Mages Guild, come no doubt to back up another of his letters, the one demanding a suitable replacement be chosen from among their ranks to replace his last, unfortunate selection. She bowed and returned his gaze without a hint of emotion, adjusting her blue robe before waiting patiently to be called upon. Quiet and unassuming, she might do.

"Loss of labor to that damn migration," he continued, gesturing east toward the distant Far Mark whose promise had lured so many into a mad attempt at recolonizing the uttermost hinterlands of the Empire. "Getting near impossible for the merchants to do any business, entire guilds uprooted and moving east."

"Or a sight near it," Coss agreed, offering support where he could and bringing the mage a drink. "Some remain loyal of course, and we'll straighten out the new census, a smaller tithing. Who could suspect you must face these troubles without the aid of your liege."

"Damn Levigne to the hells he served, that's what I say." Beryllian answered with unfeigned fervor, and the knight and mage in attendance joined him. "May he see no future," the Greatknight uttered one of strongest curses of the Stargazer sect, at which the quiet mage raised her brow. Why had his heart dragged him to revere a minority church, here in the heart of Hopeforger lands?

"Our Baron's chair unoccupied," Coss continued, "imperial troops occupying his capital, and no new pronouncements or judgments from the baronial court in nearly a year. Why Yula keeps him alive and under guard is more than I can guess."

"Surely," the mage spoke quietly, "because Levigne is the highest-ranking mortal known to be complicit in that demonic conspiracy. He is useful as long as he points out others who were aware of Viridian's evil." She paused long enough to sip from her goblet of rich dark wine. "Unlike you, milord, who were merely loyal to an emperor you thought mortal, and thus a guiltless Child of Hope."

Beryllian looked on her a long moment, recognizing her face from earlier embassies. Just three or four days ago, the last one. Persistent and a bit smooth in speech, perhaps she would not do. As he thought about the problem of appointing another mage to his court, the Greatknight realized, he might not have much say in the matter.

"And now," he said slowly, tossing a test before this wizard, "the matter of the break-in, by these three strangers, the stolen book."

"And the murder of one of your retainers, sir, let's not forget." Coss put in.

The wizard paused before answering, yet Beryllian sensed it was not from hesitation.

"Naturally, the theft—well, attempted theft I suppose— exposes a problem for you, milord."

"I know it. My own court mage, having truck with the Demonbenders, and rustic sorcery with the elements, and who knows what else. Blast him as well, we're better off he's dead."

The mage spread her arms. "You could not have known, milord. Indeed, less than two years ago Psoydonam's practices, such as they were, did not break the law. But now, of course, the Guild thinks it wise that your next selection be, shall we say, beyond reproach?"

"A nice, law-abiding Hopeforger no doubt." Beryllian chewed his beard a moment, tapping his finger atop a final letter with tragic news, that he decided not to share. "How about you, milady wizard? Pious, church-going type I suppose?"

She smiled. "My cousin Jameth, lord Beryllian, is the Hopeforger Myster here. I don't think he would forgive my absence."

The gleam in her eyes was momentary, and not wrong, nor even unexpected. But Beryllian grimaced inwardly to see it all the same. Would that lords of the lance could do without wizards completely! But no, they certainly had their uses: most knights like his vassals could not afford one, but a Greatknight was expected to maintain a mage as a sign of status, if nothing else. Still, he thought of church and guild in Beryl both arrayed opposite his current shaky grasp on power, and his instinct was to squirm into some other option.

"Has the Guild examined the accused, in our gaol?" Beryllian could not be sure what drove his sudden question, but the mage's reaction was rewarding.

She coughed in the midst of her wine and needed a few moments to compose herself again. "I? No, I have never seen them there, milord."

Something behind Beryllian's throat began to itch. "Perhaps you could hypnotize the criminals, gain knowledge of exactly what happened."

The mage seemed for the first time a little reluctant, or even afraid.

"That is a serious step, milord; ahm, one which, that impacts your honor if I may say."

"How so?" Coss demanded. "These are commoners, they have no protection against such an interrogation."

"True, sir," the mage replied, recovering her mask. "Yet well we know that those of the noble class despise the power we wizards hold, to search a mind for answers. Besides, what matters it, when your guards are all witnesses to their deeds? Theft and murder, plain as day, or so it seems to me from the reports."

Unusual, Beryllian thought, for a mage to advocate withholding her lore. Yet her tale hung together well. Convict and execute the thief-murderers quickly, bury all embarrassment hanging around the matter. But the itch in Beryllian's gullet made him cough, and the last time he had felt this prompting, his levy was ambushed at the Battle of Tor Perite.

He realized with a chill, this wizard also wanted the accused killed. He suddenly did not.

"I thank you and the Guild for your sage counsel. I shall select a candidate before midsummer." He let that hang in the air a moment before cutting off the mage's imprecation. "If not sooner." Sitting back and attending again to his papers, Beryllian waited until Coss had closed the door behind the mage.

"I don't trust that one," the retainer said and Beryllian laughed in response, clapping him on the shoulder.

"Well done! But then, what mage is worth trusting with your life, eh?" He sighed with pleasure at his shared comradery; here was a man he had entered battle with, practically touching at the knees and each saving the other from the press when dismounted. That element of shared risk cemented their bond, and the Greatknight knew no other way to win or give such faith to any mortal.

Still, the news was bad, beyond question.

"So, milord, what's to be done?"

"About the health of my holdings? Precious little," Beryllian responded. "You're right about the census of course. I won't raise the taxes just to maintain my status, we'll live within our means. What choice do I have, with all our knighthoods sending a fifth less than last year?"

"Actually, not all of them, sir. Remember Barleybane, he sent an extra measure right at year-end."

"Stars of tomorrow, that's right!" In all the poor news of the first three months, Beryllian had forgotten the new year's tithing from his formerly worthless vassal in Mon-Crulbagh.

"Aye milord, that young knight you pledged with last summer, sent in the full tithe plus treasure—actual treasure, gems and old coin—from some windfall he claimed to discover in the hills."

"Is he not content with half the peasants he needs, he wants to conquer even more swamp now!"

"As I hear it, he has received new peasants, some kind of prisoner exchange I cannot tell, but from his western border."

"What? From Colter? I've received no complaints."

"I don't know the tale of it, but the last message from this Barleybane fellow shows he expects to make tithing again, larger than last year."

"Argens' blessing on him then. I remember meeting him Coss, definitely a strange one. Good family, you know the Greatknight's son from Misb, never met the father, but a younger son, that's how it is. Another Hopeforger, of course, I'm getting used to that. He claimed to have been on the Mindsea, came to me from Wanlock with enough money to pay the fee for the entire foef."

"All of it!"

"In cash, I swear to you Coss. Without that, I'd not have made tithing myself. Ever since Distallin, that worthless tourney-boy, we've gotten next to nothing from the swamp. I was expecting to hear every spring we'd lost it to that insufferable bastard Pritaelseran. Still think it's likely. But I needed that money, and the Stargazer sent it to me just in time."

Coss's silence betrayed his embarrassment. Beryllian reflected that only someone this close to his confidence could hear such words at all. A noble close to debt, what an injustice.

"And now," he mused, "our sect has lost perhaps its leading light. You've heard about this?"

He handed Coss his final letter, with the broken seal of the moons and stars signaling an official document of the Argens

Stargazer church. Coss read with painful slowness, but looked up at the climax of its message.

"W'starrah Altieri, dead! Milord, what terrible news, how did it happen?"

"The letter says she died in a great fire," Beryllian said, saving his vassal the time needed to read the rest. "The city was nearly overthrown, less than two months ago, some desert conspiracy and there's mention of a demon, a gryphon, lots more. We get so little news from the North Mark, and now the Hopeforgers will no doubt remain ascendant there as well."

"My condolences, Torq," Coss slipped into familiarity along with a hand on his lord's shoulder. "We all revere Argens in our own way, but you're feeling hemmed in, I can tell."

"I wish the Stargazer would show me the way now," Beryllian murmured fiercely, dropping the letter aslant another on his desk. It was then, in mid-sigh, that his eye caught a word repeated twice in close proximity across the two pages.

"Stars of tomorrow. The missing daughter!"

"Milord? What's wrong?"

Beryllian looked up and realized that even his closest friend could not be brought into this horrible secret. W'starrah Altieri, the light of his church, seeking her runaway child, now dead fighting to preserve peace in her city, for the entire realm. He stared again at the arrest report; before this, only the crime and its implications to embarrass his position had mattered to him. But now the beleaguered lord recognized the only one of the three accused to have a last name.

His itch became nearly unbearable; Beryllian could almost taste the trap ahead. And he knew that he had to do something, whatever it cost him.

"Coss, I need you to depart at once, for Mon-Crulbagh."

"To the swamp, milord?"

"Don't delay, I'll be leaving by early Serpent. An inspection tour, tell Sir Qerlak that."

"At once, milord. I can be there in four days, possibly five. He should expect you within a month. Should I alert the court?"

"By no means! I shall travel with but a modest retinue; if I brought more than ten we'd probably crush the poor fellow's board!"

"No one shall hear from me, sir."

"And Coss. Tell the bailiff to ready the bar-wagon. It comes with us."

"The portable gaol? Do you intend to dispense justice, milord?"

Beryllian looked down at the letters on his desk and quietly replied, "I hope so."

⊕ ⊕ ⊕

Excerpt from the Journal of Mon-Crulbagh

3rd of the 8th, 1947 ADR Talstark Crulbagh

Border war with Pritaelseran; it's almost as regular as rain in the spring, you'll have blood and fire in the fall. He came on across the southern decline, where his roads are better, and headed for the river's ford at Sluicehill. I have considered putting a wayfort there, but manning it is just too hard unless I pull men from the main castle. If the Reptile Men would just stay quiet… my castellan keeps yammering at me about some way to increase the men under arms, but I mistrust the average levy. If that damned fool milord Beryl would leave off the rebellion plots, I could have kept the tithing lower! But I'll never have the knights those cursed uplanders bring, that's certain. Still a few tricks up our sleeves…

I maneuvered to block access to the ford, having pressed the men to arrive at fastest possible speed. Still, with our mounted bow allies not yet up with us, it was a near thing, and if he had the balls to press the attack we'd have been outnumbered almost three to one, and him with more knights. But if we had slowed our speed, he'd have crossed the Sodsluice and maybe taken the village, and I couldn't have that. There's a slight rise southwest of town and a copse of trees nearby—perhaps next time if I get the jump I can march through the village and secure it, and then meet him there. A nice ambush from the glade, if I can draw in those proud metal boys of his.

As it was, we played them off with setting a few fields on fire and marching in the dust to confuse him for our size. By the second day after contact, he was finally onto our tricks and pressed home: cursed flat ground too, perfect for his lancers. My pike stood in and it was a gambler's throw for a quarter-hour, even with me and the personal guard shoring up the center.

But those mounted bow allies came up at last, they honored the alliance and got to his flank. It was bad enough, they can drive a shaft near as well as a foot archer, but their sheer appearance! That shook the drylanders, you could tell: most of his foot ran at the first volley, and those of his retainers who held their piss long enough to turn and charge were met by a heavy squad, which has some scale armor and spears, enough to stand a pass. And of course, you could never match their horsemanship! I laughed through the dust and the wound over my eyes, to see Pritaelseran withdraw in such confusion. We took nine horses and seven suits of armor for ransom- four with men still alive inside. My master-at-arms swears he kept the levy in hand, but I know they're a vengeful bunch when it comes to their lands being threatened by armor-clad nobles. Come to think on it, so am I.

⊕ ⊕ ⊕

Castle Beryl

he dreamt of losing in the arena to a brute with a spiked mace who pounded her mercilessly and hurled insults the while. And when Bellatara awoke in their cell she knew from the instant agony that even the slavers had never beaten her like this.

She gasped just to roll on her side in the bunk, and choked on bile from clenching her teeth to sit up. The stabbing pain in her left side was the sure sign of a broken rib. When she reached her right hand to touch the spot, she realized her two longest fingers were swollen to nothing more than fat sticks. One eye definitely saw better than the other, and the Halfling decided it would be best not to test her feet with the floor so far away from the bunk.

She might never recover, she thought bitterly.

But that was only just. After all, she killed the guard.

Groans from nearby told the Woodsman, despite the darkness, she was still in her favorite company. There was some reflected light from the corridor through the bars, and she let her eyes adjust until she could make out shapes across the way. They would need the time as well; indoors like this only a Dwarf would be able to see.

But there was Ellesmera, must be, sliding to her feet so smoothly and starting those exercises she used, like a dance almost and no sign of the bruises Bellatara saw her get last night. Quarion, a little slower to his feet, stood there and felt himself as she had. The guards had not been kind. It was time to join her comrades. And apologize.

But when she tried to slip to the floor, Bellatara found her feet wouldn't work well. Still asleep, they tingled like a lightning shock and she was on her hands and knees without trying.

"Bellatara!" Ellesmera cried and they both were at her side in a moment.

"I'm fine," the Halfling said to the floor. But when her companions touched her to lift her up, she screamed and felt the parts of her frame that were still wet with blood.

"Sorry! So sorry Tara," Quarion said, "the bastards, beat her like this and no help at all since."

"Why heal the dead." Bellatara ground out as they sat her back against the wall.

"No," Ellesmera said quietly. "We shall not, it cannot be that serious. We will explain."

"She's right, Elle. What could we say? I should have refused; I knew the job was foul when that mage asked us."

"None of us could have foreseen this snare, Quarion. In fact, I don't think we understand it now."

Bellatara watched her friend's composure showing a rare crack as she continued.

"I was wrong to break the silence code. But you don't owe me anything, neither of you do."

Quarion shook his head and pounded the floor in frustration, pulling back with the pain of his own beating. "Three hundred silver pieces, Elle, we can't ignore that. What kind of partnership would this be, what comrade would—"

"I killed him!" Bellatara cried. "Not you. He was going to cut Ellesmera and I killed him."

"Stop." A simple word, not driven by anger or blame, spoken quietly. But Bellatara forgot whatever she was going to shout next; beside her Quarion crouched with an open jaw.

"We are together," Ellesmera said looking to each in turn. "None of us controlled that, but we took the chance, that rainy night in Wanlock. Hungry and nearly arrested, we decided to commit our fortunes, share the risk." She sat back on the floor and smiled. "I cannot explain why I agreed. You?"

They both shook their heads and chuckled.

"But we did," Quarion offered, "and I for one never regretted it. We signed on with that merchant—"

"And then," Bellatara said, "we finally did manage to get arrested."

Quarion swept a hand around the cell. "These are familiar surroundings for us."

"The fight with those bandits!" Bellatara said. "We killed some of them too."

"And the arrest did not last," Ellesmera replied. "We were freed—"

"You freed us," Quarion muttered.

"And we exposed a conspiracy in the marketplace."

"You did that too," Quarion said, "while Tara and I were still in here."

"Well," Bellatara added, "in here, back there."

She enjoyed a laugh with Quarion, though it hurt. Then she saw Ellesmera's fond gaze and quieted down. The Halfling swallowed and reached out for her friend.

"I'm sorry I got us into this, and I agree with Quarion, we're not getting out this time. But I couldn't let him kill you."

Instead of a lecture or a denial, Ellesmera simply returned the Woodsman's gaze, then looked to the Stealthic as they shared a quiet moment.

"But this cannot continue," the Martial Wizard said.

"No worry of that!" Bellatara cried.

"No," she said again simply, and again it carried more weight than it should have. "You fought in defence of a comrade, Bellatara. And Quarion, your suspicions were foremost in my mind when I was thinking about what we had seen. All the fortune, all the risk, each of us shares the same fate. Are we brigands, that we act only for gain? Do we seek glory as the nobles? It must be this way between us, or it will indeed be for nothing. We have no debts, except that we owe each other our lives. The heroes will guide us from this moment forward."

Quarion's scowl melted and he thrust out his hand. "From this moment."

Bellatara reached out with a gasp to take their hands as well. "For another hour or so, I figure."

They were still holding a hand to each other when the guards came. Torchlight was a miniature lightning bolt in those darkened cells, the rattle of the key like the clash of a tourney. Bellatara felt the same sense of danger, as she struggled to her feet moaning and swaying but with both fists clenched, to see the face of their gaolers.

"Here are our honored guests, comfortable and hungry for breakfast I imagine?"

One of them lobbed three trays to the floor, bumping and flipping over to spill their contents on the dirty stone.

"Krem was a friend of ours."

"Owed me money—"

"Be a waste of rope to hang you."

She saw him draw and felt helpless to do anything as the broken rib lanced her just from tensing to punch. But Ellesmera had also arisen, quickly and unnoticed. The blade clearing the scabbard got pushed on its way by her forearm, up and out of grip into the bars. The Martial Wizard had her hands back in her sleeve before the blade hit the floor.

But there were four guards altogether, now all of them drawing.

"Peace, all of you!" came a voice from the back and everyone froze, the guards drawing aside to reveal a tall man in brown robes marked with the sign of Telhol the healer.

"Preacher, you know what these scum did! You most of all."

"Let me pass, please."

"We've got a debt to our friend—"

"And I have my orders, from the Greatknight himself."

That seemed to settle matters, as the guards cursed and slammed their swords home, retreating from the cell. The preacher came to stand in front of Bellatara and looked down on her from what seemed the clouds in this small space.

"And bring more food," he added, getting curses and a slammed door in response.

"Thank you, sir, we—"

"I have orders, madam," he cut off Ellesmera and dropped to one knee before the Halfling. Lightly touching her bloodiest parts, he raised one eyebrow before setting on his palm and murmuring, "*Intakta volar.*"

She felt her wounds close and the pain of her rib faded somewhat, but she was still tender in a dozen places. The preacher withdrew his hand, stood and turned to Quarion next. Checking him in the same way, the preacher instead withdrew a small stoppered bottle, emptied the contents onto his hand and smeared it across the Stealthic's shoulders and back beneath his tunic. Quarion hissed with the pain initially, then shrugged to experiment with the improvement.

Ellesmera bowed to him as he stepped near her. "At all events, holy sir, we thank you sincere—"

"Don't!" he hissed with an effort before deliberately calming himself. In the silence that followed, Bellatara watched his face and wondered how she could be partly healed and still feel worse.

"Kremell, the man you slew, was my nephew."

Ellesmera nodded slowly, and when the preacher moved to examine her, she stepped back and raised a hand to indicate her refusal. He waited only a moment more before stepping to the door as a guard approached with new trays and a feral grin.

"There, I've done what I can. With another few day's rest, they will be fit enough to travel."

"The guard opened the cell and let the Telholian out, setting down the trays ever so carefully into the slop of those previous, and never stopped grinning the while.

"Where are we going?" Quarion asked.

"To the swamp, we've just heard. Never you fear us, scum, we wouldn't touch a hair on your head and have you miss the bar-wagon."

"The swamp?" Bellatara asked. "Where is that?"

"Don't mind where, runt, it's the when of it should concern you. Mon-Crulbagh is the end of the line. Monsters, bogs, diseases. Plenty of ways milord Beryl can dump the bodies of those as whom he'd want never heard from again."

And chuckling theatrically he retreated up the hall.

Ellesmera slowly turned to sit back on her bunk, crossing her legs and resting arms to enter one of her trance states. As she breathed too slowly for any living being, Quarion crossed to the trays and handed one to Bellatara, quietly munching a crust as they watched her. The martialist brought her hands together, rubbing them slowly and hard palm on palm, then with a chanted syllable brought them against her flesh where the bruises and scars were bright. Bellatara felt that perhaps a few minutes passed, or possibly an hour.

"My favorite company," she whispered to Quarion.

He grinned. "For a while longer yet."

Castle Mon-Crulbagh

"Teacher, I can clean this up in just a while longer and then—"

"Not to worry, Garr, you stay here and take your time." Galethiel swung back from the window and tousled her apprentice's sandy hair.

"But I want to help!"

"Absolutely not. There could be fighting, and I must answer to your family for your safety."

"My father will be there. Probably my brother Gerris too." The youth continued arguing even as he grabbed up a cloth to sweep off the remnants of powders that had not exploded.

Galethiel grabbed her riding cape and put a few things into a belt pouch, then paused by the mirror where she adjusted the jewel-feather headband into the masses of her rich red hair.

"Your job, my headstrong apprentice, is to learn to read, to assist me in my research, and to guard this tower when I am sleeping. And now, I add a fourth task, to keep it safe here when I am gone. Can you do that?"

"I will, teacher," he sighed in disappointment. "But what shall I do to be useful?"

"Continue infusing the spell of Light into the next stone."

"But we already have six!"

"And we need scores of them. They are more useful than you know, Garr." Galethiel shivered a moment with recollection. "Lots of dark places in the world."

She turned to descend the stairs and Garr leaped to assist her, reaching for her staff in the corner.

"Here, let me get—"

"Garr!" The wizard shrieked, which froze the boy in place. He snapped his fingers and nodded as he turned to hold the drape aside instead.

"Apologies, teacher, I forgot. Boom."

"Exactly right. Now stay, practice, infuse, and guard."

"I will."

Galethiel took up the Staff of Anun-Re, checked her outfit one last time, then glanced to Garr who was gazing on her in awe. Satisfied she must be making the right appearance, she headed downstairs and out into the courtyard.

Everything there was chaos; soldiers and servants colliding on separate missions, the portcullis slowly rising, horses hastily saddled and to one side a wagon limbered behind a team. Yet when the mage emerged, even the pigs seemed to shy from her path. Everyone was eager to back away from her presence, yet a step behind in doing so which increased their haste. Galethiel didn't know why she had the impact she did, but she knew well enough it was important, for her and her friend.

Qerlak emerged with Cecil in train still trying to pin the livery cape atop his armored shoulders. In one hand he bore a shield with the Lotus of Mon-Crulbagh replacing the grain sheaf in the clench of his family crest. From under his half-raised visor he saluted her first as they converged on the horses held by Fennet.

"You look cleaner than usual," she shot at him.

"You look the same as always," he replied in good humor, but she could sense the tension beneath his tone. "Fennet, I'm

82

relying on you, and practically you alone, to defend this keep while I'm gone. We've not enough men as you well know, but we must pretend we have."

"I understand milord." The castellan hesitated, obviously looking for a word of good cheer to offer.

From horseback, Qerlak leaned down and clapped him on the shoulder. "We'll be fine this time. Keep the gate closed and if it comes to the last resort—let them into the kitchen, and Skeggs will deal with them."

Nothing ever made Fennet laugh, but he turned to Galethiel with a smile and said "Argens' luck to you, milady."

She nodded and mounted up, settling the base of her six-foot staff into the saddle-socket by her foot. Its metal top, with two bands framing a spinning ball of pure hollow gold loomed above her head as she sat. Reining in just back of Qerlak in his splendid enchanted half-plate armor and resting an enormous battle axe across his saddlebow, Galethiel knew the pair of former adventurers were cutting quite the exotic sight to all the staff and retainers. The men cheered as the knight gestured his small caravan forth; first the lord of Mon-Crulbagh, then his human wizard, followed by a soot-drenched Spezh leading three mounted bowmen, and the wagon with Squire Cecil riding beside the drover.

Just outside the walls Qerlak waved to a lone peasant working at clearing brush. The scrawny fellow straightened up and stared, then belatedly tugged his cap and bowed as the other soldiers jeered him.

"We could bring Severyn if you like, milord." Spezh called out. "Maybe your slingers could use him to test their range?"

Qerlak smiled and made no other response as the caravan wound from sight of the castle and its environs. Galethiel spurred to come even with him and they rode awhile in silence.

"Another adventure, perhaps," the knight offered.

"We used to walk everywhere," she fired back.

"Hardly faster this time, we have to match speed with the levy."

"So, this is more of a status symbol?" she grinned over to her companion, but he did not return the gesture and she sensed his worry. "Maybe we should switch horses," she offered, "my seat seems more secure than yours."

Qerlak flicked a moment's glance her way and cleared his throat. "Ahm yes. Your pillion is not exactly suited for lancing. You see the extra stirrup on this side? You could have, um, rode side-saddle if you liked."

Galethiel had never given a second thought to the notion. "You mean like some noble lady?"

"Well, the lord's wife, truth to tell. Fennet found it in the stables and thought it might be more comfortable."

He looked in her eyes a moment, and she could see there the deep waters they both were in. All of it seemed so absurd. Her good friend and adventuring companion had offered her a place in his new keep. She could study there, of course help him when a threat arose as now, and there an end. Galethiel had no appetite to serve as a symbol, of any kind, and she knew that Qerlak understood her. He was the son of the noble class, and an Elf, for Araluntir's sake.

But she didn't need to state the obvious, as up ahead a body of armed peasants came in view, some of their number running up to take their places in a bloc of pikes. Cecil jumped down from the wagon with his own pike in both hands and ran to take his place at their head. The peasants hailed Qerlak as he rode abreast and slammed the butt-ends of their weapons on the ground, more or less together. He saluted them and nodded to Cecil; they joined in behind the riders as all headed off the road and due south now.

Over the lush low country the going was indeed slow, and Galethiel felt her old impatience arising again. Even when adventuring it always seemed to her that things came to a head too slowly. It was a rare sunny morning, thick air and the warmth of summer coming on. They forded the Sodsluice at a point where even the wagon wheels were well above the water-line. Along the way a few more peasants joined the levy, taking their pikes from the wagon and marching in the back of the group; a few youths with slings seemed to materialize as they marched, jogging back and forth on either flank and generally in high spirits. The plodding pace of her horse was well slower than Galethiel could walk, and the mage found her mood growing increasingly twitchy.

Qerlak, to her side, seemed content to await events, and she realized he was not eager for the fray.

The only break in the monotony was a runner from ahead, a peasant boy who seemed exhausted but pointed with his horn-holding hand almost due south.

"Between the rivers, milord. Half a day behind perhaps."

"My thanks young man. Did you see them?"

"My father sent me, sir, when they were passing my house down in the Jungle Close."

"All that way! Ride in the wagon, I'll hear more from you soon."

"Don't you want to know how many there are?" Galethiel asked.

"Of course," Qerlak answered imperturbably, "but the boy's been running for almost a day and a night. When he's caught his breath, his answer about the number will still be the same."

"You're not very curious! And why this direction, how did you know they'd be coming from the south?"

"I've read the journal of the foef. They always come this way, up between the rivers."

"What! Always? How do you know?"

Qerlak looked on her with amusement, tinged with embarrassment. "This is rather hard to explain…"

"To a human?"

"Well, to a commoner, mostly," he replied, and if he gave insult to his friend he did not realize it. "The Argensian nobility, as you may have noticed, are rather proud…"

Galethiel broke his speech with a stream of sustained, near hysterical laughter. Qerlak looked patiently upon her with a raised brow while she gradually recovered her composure. "Yes," she finally managed, "I had noted certain signs of that."

"Well and good! So what you can see now more easily, then, is that such proud persons may never truly be wrong. Traditions form when someone insists they are the best way to do things, I suppose." He coughed and looked away a moment before continuing. "I realize, having been away from my family, that certain customs of ours were never, ah, terribly well explained."

"So what does this have to do with the war?"

"War, this! No, just a raid." Qerlak broke into a smile now. "It's the way it's done, you see. Pritaelseran sends a few men into Mon-Crulbagh come spring, they raid and perhaps burn some things, harass a few peasants. Mon-Crulbagh responds, and as far as I can tell, always wins. That provides the insult bringing the full army over in the fall."

It was Galethiel's turn to stare. "You're not serious. They know they're going to lose?"

"Oh not at all, I'm sure. My peer is likely sending a young leader, not experienced in how this goes. And just a small portion of his total forces." He looked back at his levy and added, "I hope a very small portion."

He tried to lean in for a whisper, but nearly lost balance on horseback and straightened up with a mild curse. "The thing is," he said, "our population is still thin, and we can't afford the traditional retainers we usually would have. The journal talks about 'mounted bow' and even lancers, but it's hard to see how we could afford them, even with more households reporting."

"So, you're bringing everyone."

He nodded. "All I can."

"And if they circle around, attack the keep behind you?"

The knight laughed then, his good humor somewhat restored. "You weren't listening! What they do cannot be wrong."

"So they do it again and again." Galethiel shook her head. "Lucky, if you're right."

"Argens favors the bold." Qerlak's fond smile, her favorite part of his companionship, gladdened the mage, but it faded slowly as they rode even slower.

"At least for a time," he added, "in the fall… we'll have to see. But first, today."

A rider from behind the party rode hard and called out to arrest their progress.

"Milord! Milord, castellan Fennet has sent me to ask about the fire in the cellars. And the grain to be used, and—"

"Of course, right here good fellow, let me repeat it for you as we ride."

There followed a pile of words that sounded vaguely like alchemy, and Galethiel smiled to see her comrade so deeply interested in something close to cooking. She looked back at the rest of the men, and reflected that this pointless poke in a perpetual rivalry could well involve some of them dying.

Qerlak cared about these people, as much as Galethiel desired her researches into sleep and dreaming. She knew those studies had made it possible for the heroes she and Qerlak adventured with to save the entire world from a staggering threat, less than eight months ago. Now, just the two of them, and perhaps suitably, just a small part of their world to defend.

The mage couldn't have honestly said why she was coming along. Was it for the noble goal of keeping this basket of peasants under one lord as opposed to another? Perhaps she simply didn't want to see Qerlak fail, or even unhappy. Then again, maybe she had grown bored of the quiet life this past winter. Whatever the case, she was nearly frantic with the need to get on with it. Everyone else seemed to move so slowly.

The servant took off north, and Qerlak summoned the horn-blowing youth and Spezh forward to make a plan. Galethiel heard snips and pieces as they conversed, and none of the news was good. A dozen lance-bearing knights or more, spearmen with uniforms, several wagons. She didn't know much about how well long spears or sling rocks would do against such an enemy.

Qerlak sent two of Spezh's mounted bowmen ahead to scout out the terrain and locate the raiders. The rest of the party advanced at a faster march pace as the sun set to their right and humidity, as always, grew. Galethiel looked down on the youth who had brought the warning, walking now beside her horse and looking very pleased. It reminded the mage of her acolyte Garr.

"How far to your family's cottage?"

Two steps later, the boy realized the question was addressed to him. Looking up in terror, he nearly fell to the turf and barely kept his feet moving as he gulped repeatedly. "'Tis, it is still several hours south. Milady. Past the glades and near the Bograwl, if it please you."

"We'll camp tonight," Qerlak said, "and get you home tomorrow, before dinner."

The youth nodded and looked down, but managed to glance continually at Galethiel the while. When the levy stopped for the evening, he disappeared to the other side of the fires.

"Everyone is afraid of me," she remarked to Qerlak over a light dinner.

He laughed in his usual good nature. "Well of course, Galethiel! You've spent years traveling with the wrong sort of people, don't you understand that?" He tore another strip of meat from his stick and grimaced as he drank to wash it down. "They call this ale? I'd rather chew the barley grains raw." He looked back to her with a fire-glint in his eyes. "You recall Zoanstahr and Trillien, your fellow mages."

"Of course, we shared everything together."

"Of course," he nodded, "but then Cheriatte the preacher, she had access to miracles. Saling'r, our bard, put an enchantment into his rapier, and for a time I suspected perhaps his lyre…"

"Well, you can summon miracles as well." She replied, not sensing his point.

"Oh, a few, nothing like her. But Engurra, her trance-states, as good as magic, time and again. Even Spitz and Solo, their weapons were heavily enchanted, like my armor."

He waited a moment to let this all settle in while the insects chorused around them.

"Yes. So?"

"Galethiel. My father is a Greatknight of the Barony of Misb. He has a mage, Serruya, a lovely elder Elf, I remember her well. Never used a new spell when one of her best three would do: kind to everyone, we forgot she was a mage half the time."

He smiled a while in recollection, then leaned into the firelight.

"Dear friend, hear me—my father is lord of five knights under him, and not one of them has a mage. Tomorrow morning we will pass to the west of Sluicehill, second largest village in my domain. Eighty-seven persons according to my last census. I guarantee you, there is not a soul in that place capable of summoning light, or detecting magic."

"Very well," she smiled, "but it's only half an answer. They haven't seen a mage, fine, but they have heard of us!"

Qerlak shook his head still grinning. "They've heard of Elven mages, Galethiel. Not a hasty, violent human sorceress with hair of flame and a staff from the ages past. Let us say nothing of how they whisper about their dreams. You are the most famous person south of Beryl, take my word."

Galethiel was stunned to consider Qerlak's point and the rest of the evening passed quietly.

That night, as she was wont, Galethiel entered the Plane of Dreams.

The effort to cross the barrier, formerly enough to awaken and exhaust her, was now a welcome release of somnambulant exercise and a form of reunion. The mesa was still there, which chilled her every time she witnessed its insane height. But the River of Wakening was back in its original course, the halfling-sized trolls whispering into various dream horns were up to nothing especially malicious without the guidance of their former master. Galethiel avoided the plain where the limbs of giants lay strewn.

To one side of the mesa, as usual, was a low-lying place which seemed to mirror the environs of Mon-Crulbagh, its mossy terrain a bit wetter and darker, fewer dream-holes and hardly any of the whispering midgets that dotted other parts of the plane. Galethiel floated without effort above the dream-foef, and right where Qerlak's levy should be a few dream-cones stippled the ground.

She had determined some time ago that to speak or listen at such an aperture was unfair and possibly cruel. But the sorceress could not resist the urge to peek in a few of them as she drifted by. One of the peasant levy lay on the ground lit by embers of a campfire and bore a resemblance to Garr. Through another cone she saw Qerlak himself, and the notion she could perhaps spy on his dreams spurred her with shame, to move on quickly.

Before she knew it Galethiel was above another small cluster of cones some distance away. Her endurance was fraying having spent so long here in conscious dreaming, but as her vision faded the dream-mage saw clearly through one dream-door a handsome youth, surely of the noble class, resting well within a tent embroidered with the sign of a diving hawk.

"Who is that?" She asked her headband, Nomen, and it answered at once as was its special power.

"His name is Hitaelseran."

When Galethiel awoke the morning wore late, and things were finally starting to happen.

Men armed and equipped each other, while Qerlak, looking as if he slept in his armor (if at all) stalked about filled with nervous energy.

"Leave the camp here men! We'll return to it tonight, the wagon too. From here we march to battle!"

This brought a cheer, and Galethiel observed that some part of her self-effacing, polite noble companion was simply born to command others. Not the same way most of these strut-proud Argensians did it, of course. Qerlak was ready to put his body in harm's way to protect his people, rather than using words to achieve the reverse. It affected her too, she admitted as she gestured to him while frantically trying to finish dressing.

"Good morning, Galethiel. No breakfast today?"

"No time," she spat back with a blush. "The enemy, Qerlak, they are led by someone who looks like a knight. His name is Hitaelseran."

"Argens' Balls!" her friend's oath was as loud and sincere as it was rare. He even looked down to the ground a moment. "One of my rival's sons, must be. He has four, I gather." After a moment, he continued quietly, on a most uncharacteristically serious note. "This is bad."

"You mean, you don't want to have to kill him?"

Qerlak looked up then, tried to smile, tried to nod, and turned away without further sign. From that moment on, Galethiel no longer felt hungry, nor that everyone else was moving quickly anymore. It seemed to take forever to get the men together. Finally, Qerlak pointed east-by-south and they set out. He stayed on foot, so she did the same. The youth from Jungle Close led their horses.

At mid-morning they came across a small rise about four furlongs wide and less than thirty feet in elevation. Qerlak stopped briefly, looked about and pointed east to a copse of trees, and then back almost due north.

"There it is, and Sluicehill back over the river that way. Just as the journal said."

While everyone was still puzzling this through, he gestured to Spezh to follow him up the rise. Galethiel followed from steady curiosity, together with growing concern for her friend and impatience nearing the boiling point.

"Spezh, see here we can array the pikemen near the top, the slingers to either side able to fall back when it gets too hot, and the same for your mounted bowmen."

"Milord," Spezh replied still crusted with ashes for some bizarre reason, "we haven't enough levy with us to cover the front."

"No, not now, but later." Qerlak said. "In the fall, when Pritaelseran returns. And if I'm not here."

"But sir—"

"Do you see it, Spezh? Do you understand?"

"Yes, milord."

"Very good, now let's go on, I want to meet them further south if possible."

It only seemed a long time until the scouting horsemen came back in sight, signaling the position of the raiding party advancing north, between copses of lush trees and brush. Qerlak immediately issued orders, and Cecil got his levy in two lines with their pikes lightly grounded and ready to lean forward into the enemy. Spezh and his horsemen advanced along the left flank and began lobbing missiles at the enemy horse, while the young slingers skipped forward to whirl their strips of cloth and loose in no organized way at the spearmen in the center.

Even Galethiel, standing behind and to one side, could see how serious their situation was when the line of chain-mailed horsemen advanced in close order with helms down and lances raised. For the moment they were behind the spearmen, who pressed on with raised shields to take the brunt of the boys' harassment. An arrow in the arm made one of their retainers fall back, and stones crippled two of the spearmen. But the body of men from Pritaelseran pressed on, jeers raining down from those on foot and an eerie silence from the disciplined row of metal men riding behind them.

Qerlak stood before his levy with his ax in hand and shield slung over his back. Galethiel had seen him block a dungeon corridor against fanatical Bedou-uu or undead masses. Qerlak had given solid blows to Kaleg the demon-statue, powerful if impotent against its protection. She knew he would likely never fall in the press, his ax could take down a horse and rider together.

But the others. Galethiel looked at the pike-holders and recognized Garr's father. Nearby Cecil stood at the end of the front row exhorting them to hold steady.

The men would all clash. And some would die, and one side would lose. But it would take forever.

"Cark this," Galethiel muttered, "I'm only human."

She rapped the Staff of Anun-Re twice on the ground, then raised it high overhead, invoking one of the artefact's powers.

Across the cloudless sky boomed a peal of magnificent thunder. The impact on both sides was palpable. The spearmen of Pritaelseran broke and fled, some even dropping their spears on the way. Horses shied and reared as well, making them impossible to control and shattering the line of retainers. Even the Mon-Crulbagh pike staggered and fell back to one side, away from her. Qerlak whipped around and grinned at her as if he'd been given a reprieve; all the men of the foef levy cheered like mad.

From eight furlongs off, the men of Pritaelseran reformed their lines and someone there sounded a horn. Qerlak's men gradually stopped cheering and looked across the lines to where a single mounted horseman, bearing the banner of Pritaelseran on his lance, rode out and dipped the weapon in a signal.

Qerlak sighed deeply and turned to Spezh and Cecil to give some instructions too quietly for Galethiel to hear. She hastened to them as he signaled for his horse.

"What's going on, tell me."

"It's a challenge," Qerlak said curtly, "I'm sorry."

"Sorry about what? Just get out there and take him down, he's not as skilled—"

"Milady," Cecil broke in, "it is a challenge to joust."

The horse arrived and Qerlak made to mount. Galethiel stood in his way.

"You can't! Qerlak," she hissed, "you've never learned to ride."

"Galethiel!" for once her friend spoke with tense urgency, in complete seriousness. "It's ignoble that you are even delaying me. Please. He's a knight, not just some common commander. It's not permitted that I should hesitate. Worse than losing. Do your best, Argens bless you all."

He put one hand on her shoulder and gripped it, then stepped around her as if the farewell were the only purpose of the pause. On his way to mount up he walked slowly, to her mind, just like everyone else. Elves, men, taking their sweet time to die for nothing.

Once again, it wouldn't do. Galethiel stepped quickly past Qerlak's retainers, several yards out into the space between the forces, and planted her staff solidly in the turf. Before any of them could speak, she reached up with one hand and set the orb on top spinning.

"Galethiel!" Qerlak called from directly behind her, still not mounted. Galethiel ignored him as the charge inside the orb built, and the hum of its gathering energy drowned all normal conversation anyway.

She wasn't about to lose her friend. And she was no longer willing to wait.

"Cark this."

⊕ ⊕ ⊕

Foef of Mon-Crulbagh

The thunder blast had caught Hitaelseran by surprise along with the rest of his men. The lord of Mon-Crulbagh, the dastard, had unleashed his flame-tressed human ally before the two sides could properly meet in the press of battle. As he called to his levy and rallied them at what he hoped was a safe range, the young lord knew this called for leadership.

Guernsten, having also brought the retainers to heel, rode up to salute.

"Unfair, milord. Honor has been satisfied, and your father—"

"My father," Hitaelseran snapped back, "will have no cause to complain of the courage of his son. Prepare the men for a second charge, after I pass lances with my foe."

Guernsten began to rejoin, then bit his lip and wheeled away to convey the order. "Again, you bully-boys! Milord will deal with this upstart as he has earned, and then we'll loot the village ahead."

Hitaelseran signaled for the challenge horn, then addressed a quick prayer to Argens for courage and that he might behave honorably. Trotting forward a dozen paces, he dipped his lance with its hawk banner to indicate his call for a duel between equals.

As he waited, the youngest son of Argens' greatest knight reflected on the manifold injustices his father had had to face in this rivalry. Pitted against the lord of a dark wet land, constant rumors of foul magic and monstrous beings with whom he allied against those who should properly rule here. And to make up for his lack of noble character, he employed gangs of peasants to shift the border stones up the hill and steal land from civilized men. Apparently, he employed one of the Nubian savages as guard captain, the man's clothing and armor as black as his skin. Barbarian!

Now faced with honest battle on suitable ground, that adventurer chose to stand afoot, no doubt to lend some backbone to his peasant levy instead of riding as befit a noble lord. Hitaelseran recalled the sight of his own father on horseback, and unconsciously straightened his spine and squared his shoulders in preparation for the joust.

Flame of Argens, even the usurper's squire went unmounted. And no replacement horses! Truly he must be some kind of adventurer, probably an outcast of his family or even a by-blow of his father's house. That would explain much here. Admittedly a large and powerfully built fellow, and that armor looked as fine as anything Hitaelseran had ever seen; the thought that it would belong to him if he won sent a thrill through him.

Hitaelseran's mount pawed the turf with impatience, and for a moment he flashed on the thought of those stones being moved. Certainly, his horse in traces would not be enough to shift it an inch. And the grass, behind the stones, was growing in after just a few feet. Could Mon-Crulbagh be nudging them only once in a while? How would that make sense?

Still the man tarried while speaking to his associates, longer than was seemly to Hitaelseran's taste. Finally he moved to his horse, and yet Hitaelseran could hardly take his eyes from the red-haired mage. She always moved so quickly! How like a human, without hesitation and probably not caring a fig for the consequences. Now she stood forth from the band, and would be directly in her lord's path soon. Already she planted her tall staff, and before he could take it fully in, she had performed some ritual, unlike the first, with no immediate effect.

Hitaelseran tried to put his mind back on the impending joust—with a target so large, no need to be fancy, just place the lance athwart the enemy's center and brace hard—but he was distracted by a growing thrum of energy at the enemy line. To his horror, he could see tiny tendrils of crackling light arcing down from the sky-blue heavens to strike the golden orb atop the mortal's staff. Increasing in size, frequency and sound, they soon looked larger than life, as if a massive storm were raining down atop the open field and centered upon the mage herself.

Now the lord of Mon-Crulbagh was mounted at last, shouting something unintelligible above the din and riding pell-mell toward him. But he bore no lance! He was waving his arms desperately, as if trying to clear a path before his steed, and nearly unseated by its gallop but continuing to—warn him?

Again, the human mage moved too fast. Seizing the staff, she yanked it from the turf, leveled the ball and aimed, just to one side of the charging unarmed madman Hitaelseran saw before him.

Then the world seemed to crack open in a blinding flash of searing heat and jolting pain. Hitaelseran recoiled from furnace air, smelled the burnt flesh of hell, and dimly heard the screams of the damned in some demon's torture chamber. Then a sudden jarring impact made him breathless and there was nothing but sunlight, keen brightness from heaven so sharp and close he could not manage to keep his eyes open. He could not feel any part of his body, though sure he was mortally wounded. Only a kind of strong support behind him and a sense that he was floating, perhaps to his reward.

But the clop of horse's hooves seemed incongruous with his situation. The screams of hell's prisoners faded into something much more mundane, the shouts of men in rapid retreat, and very distantly, cheering. A strong arm snaked behind his shoulders and lifted the young knight away from the support of heaven. Now the sensation of being afloat left him and Hitaelseran slammed back into a body in agony. He realized the heat and burning smell was sourced in himself. He cried out despite all, clawing to raise his visor.

Just above him was the face of a strong, kindly Elf, framed in metal and filled with concern.

"Sir! Sir Hitaelseran, I believe? Are you able to hear me? Please, sir, if you will do me the courtesy of not dying I shall be much indebted to you."

Hitaelseran tried to speak and only coughed, twice, as his throat seemed to need restarting before it could recover the power of speech. At last, he managed, "Sir, milord Barleybane, I presume?" Looking vaguely around to orient himself, he noted that somewhat behind his back, men with the Hawk emblem were in full rout toward the east. Ahead of him threescore men marched up to join their lord, and his heart sank into the turf to know his defeat had happened so suddenly.

"Your prisoner, sir." He tried to draw his sword to reverse grips and hand it over. But his captor forced his arm down resheathing his weapon.

"Keep that, young man, no one has fairly defeated you today."

"Little matter, milord," Hitaelseran replied, "for surely no man can long withstand such sorcery."

In response, his enemy's face screwed up with determination. "No. Not if Argens will help me." Placing his other hand on Hitaelseran's chest, Sir Barleybane incanted a few words in the Ancient tongue. At once, the wounded knight felt something that spoke of walking and rest and courage, spreading through his body as water into sand. Hitaelseran could still clearly feel the places on his hands, face, chest that were burned and scarred, yet he sensed there was more energy in him, more of *him* now to overcome such wounds. With wonder at his core, he sat fully up and stared at his benefactor.

"Remain seated and don't overdo, sir, the effect of the Strengthening is only temporary." So saying, his enemy stood to face his band as they arrived. Staring through their number, he locked eyes with the dread mage as she came up. Hitaelseran felt his skin crawl as it had only on those rare occasions when he met his uncle back home. Her smirk gradually faded to puzzlement under the steady gaze of the lord of Mon-Crulbagh.

The silence was interrupted by a peasant rider on the back of an enormous lizard. As Hitaelseran quelled the impulse to back away from the horror, the servant dismounted and no one else seemed in the least interested.

"Milord! The castellan sends his compliments and wishes to know if the remaining grains must be kept for second use. Also the fuel you requested—"

"Never mind too much about the wood, so long as it isn't coal," the knight responded, and Hitaelseran could not quite credit that this conversation was happening. His defeat and capture, the humiliation of House Pritaelseran directly at his feet, this fellow put below the matter of arranging his kitchen table.

A reckless adventurer, who had saved his life with a miracle.

"And you can give the wort to the pigs, they'll love it. Now then," the broad-shouldered knight called to his men, "I have to get this young fellow home to his family. How much further to your cabin, lad?"

As he lay back and felt the edges of his pain and mortality returning, Hitaelseran belatedly realized he was still not the subject of conversation. His eyes crossed with those of the sorceress, and he quickly looked away lest he somehow offend her again.

"And the son of Pritaelseran, he must be returned to the castle at once. You there," to the lizard-rider, "get back and summon the doctor, we need Drace to come meet us immediately. You men, let's make a cot to carry him back to the wagon."

Hitaelseran watched as the knight mounted clumsily, then pulled the youth with a horn up behind him. He exchanged another long, wordless glance with the woman-wizard, then spurred off south. His men were already out of sight on the way back home. The squire bowed to him and gestured for some peasants to lift their prisoner up and onto a hasty cot formed of a cape tied between two pikes.

The strength of the miracle continued to fade as they walked further north, singing and joking. He was to have ridden this path as a conqueror. Perhaps he would be fortunate. The miracle might drain away completely bringing his death before the pious adventurer returned.

CHAPTER III. KINDLING

Excerpt from the Journal of Mon-Crulbagh

{*In a poorly-kept portion of the journal, undated and with pages torn loose, possibly somewhere after the reign of Bendon Crulbagh, there is a short passage on a page that is torn and full of holes, in ink that has faded with time and a scrawly hand.*}

…-nstant feuds and… dations such that their Greatknights in concert could not… thus the Lord of the Sun sent… who in adjudication set the boundaries along the Sodsluice riv-… didst mark such with Stones of more than three meters in h-… and thus to settle such matters for all time… -ment to ensure that injustice would be faced down where'er it set… peace for a time.

The 10th of the Hawk, 2002 ADR

To One Qerlak Barleybane, Formerly of Misb
and now Self-Styled Lord of Mon-Crulbagh,

Accustomed as I have been in my years of service to the Empire in the manifold ways that the common folk require instruction,

I yet never believed I would have to address such basic teaching to someone that the code of chivalry required me to treat as a peer. I gather the man you claim as your father had older sons, and as such he may have neglected your education, no doubt on the expectation you would never ascend to such a weighty responsibility. And thus, it would appear, the task falls to me.

Let me be clear at the outset, whatever you believe to be your advantage in the matter of the recent dastardly ambush, the final instruction will come to you by season's end. I shall administer that discipline personally and it shall be of a decidedly corporal nature, most pleasant to me and varying on your side mainly as to its length. Pay close heed, that you may be blessed with a brief lesson in noble comportment.

First, you shall administer correction, naturally, to the mystic peasant in your entourage for daring to intervene in a joust legally demanded, as well as for the effrontery in bringing sorcerous harm to one of her betters. The custom calls for one hundred lashes, and the likelihood of the villein's death forms no impediment to the immediate application of punishment. Best if you deal the blows yourself, it may go easier on you when it comes time to reckon your own crimes.

Second, you shall recognize the lawful authority of Pritaelseran over those hectares lying between the rivers Sodsluice and Bograwl, regardless of their current state of development, and turn sovereignty over any such inhabitants as reside there now to my hand. In the disgrace of your interference with the border stones, all such childish pranks shall cease immediately upon receipt of this lawful demand, and proper barrier markers will be erected, at your expense, before the following year.

Third and finally, the fourth son shall be returned by you at once, no further harmed than by the cowardly mystic assault of your witch-thrall, and possessed of his arms and mount as befits his free and undefeated condition. While any penalty should rightfully accrue to you, I cannot expect you to be aware of the noble custom here (nor in any other wise), and in my magnanimity I shall be pleased to remit to you 900 silver pieces. This is in consideration of the upkeep due to a knight, though I greatly doubt your board can possibly provide fare or lodging of that quality. The remainder you may keep, for the nonce, against the instruction which I solemnly promise you, ere summer ends.

In Argens' Name,
Cran-Kalrith Pritaelseran

18th Hawk, 2002

Greetings Cran-Kalrith,

Words cannot describe how happy I am that you should put the best foot forward in sending me your most recent letter. At least, based on your reputation, the contents of your message were the best I expected to see. I am gratified to know my initial thoughts about our neighborly relations were well founded.

As to the suggestions you make in the bulk of your letter, I do heartily thank you for the amusement they brought. The mortal mage in my company, Galethiel, when I had read out your rather pithy notion to her, was rendered quite speechless for some time. With laughter of course; I was surprised at the level of your wit! Previously we had heard nothing of this, I admit. She asked me to say that she looks forward to discussing the full import of your quaint idea of the legal customs personally, as much as I do, and we await with eagerness your convenience to draw closer together for such an intimate conversation, as you appear to promise at the end of your letter.

With regards to your fine son Hitaelseran, allow me to be serious. I assure you, with Argens as my witness, he is well and under no great duress at the moment. He convalesces in my care from his accident and if he suffers any lack from my poor hospitality he is of course too noble to make mention of it. I find in him a blameless example of the best in our noble class. In this wise, you are no doubt correct to imply that his upbringing was proper; indeed I admire the young man very much and am growing loathe to part with his company. I have furnished your son with supplies to write, and earnestly hope he shall tell you in complete confidence about his condition; I shall include any such letter alongside my own.

Your suggested ransom, however politely disguised, would do well were Hitaelseran a merchant or the son of a minor preacher. But be assured, the joke is understood. I shall never reveal to my noble guest that a father set the value of his offspring at silver, when it should by rights have been gold. Whatever you think of my training, I know a hawk's price from that of a hen, and the fee of a knight under such a distinguished banner would doubtless know it too. Let us pass this off as a rare failed jest on your part in an otherwise hilarious letter.

On balance I feel I owe you my greatest debt, both in the matter of the armed embassy you sent to my foef as well as for this amusing letter with which you followed it. Matters delay my attendance upon your lordship for some weeks yet. But rest assured, we shall be prepared to receive you again whenever you choose to visit. You promise your own attendance and I could not be more pleased to hear it. I hope to show you the true taste of Mon-Crulbagh hospitality at that time.

Sincerely, in Argens' Name,
Qerlak Barleybane, Lord of Mon-Crulbagh

The 18th of the Hawk, 2002 ADR

To the Lord Cran-Kalrith Pritaelseran,
from his latest and least son, Greetings,

Sir Barleybane my captor provides me with writing materials and has sworn upon Argens to respect the seal I set upon it. It seemed proper to me, therefore, that I not scruple to use the wax, lest I appear fearful in my current circumstance. I trust his word that this letter reaches you unread.

That I have failed is quite evident, and I offer no excuse. By my inexperience and foolishness, I fell prey to the enemy and am now in his gaol. If you would still place any value on the word of one who has betrayed your trust, believe me now that the blame lies entirely on my shoulders. Neither Guernsten nor any of the retainers or peasant levy failed in obedience or courage, except that which all men might feel on the touch of the unknown. I was fairly captured, if not nobly beaten, and this fact was avowed by Sir Barleybane upon his first words to me.

Neither do I fear ignoble treatment by his hands, though this may be of no importance to you. I am housed in a clean well-lit cell with reasonable comfort, can eat when I wish and allowed the sight of my armor and weapons outside the door, as an assurance, my captor says, that they have not been sold. He expresses the hope they may soon be returned to me, though he offers no further details. I gather from his words that he is in receipt of a letter from you and is composing a response. I am told I may include this letter with his own and thus I have discharged my obligation to you with these few words.

Please inform my mother that I am well, assure her she may not worry for my safety in current circumstances. I have no other words to excuse or explain my inability to live up to the family name, and am content to accept whatever discipline you may see fit to inflict when I am again allowed to return.

In Argens' Name,
Hitaelseran

⊕ ⊕ ⊕

Castle Mon-Crulbagh

 s Fennet trod downstairs to the summons of Lord Barleybane, the accounts-book in his arms felt like it was made of stone. There could be no other purpose for the meeting, and all his warnings, indeed the castellan's direst fears, were coming true. Whatever Sir Qerlak's many fine qualities, which Fennet could gladly list—courage, noble bearing, relentless optimism, and a unique compassion for all those in his care—the fact remained, the knight's son knew absolutely nothing about the value of money.

In the fortnight since the raid, Fennet had made clear to his lord the absolute necessity of reducing expenditures. Yet Qerlak had only laughed and insisted, the Reclamation Festival would go on. Dismiss half the guards, Fennet suggested; Qerlak grinned and threatened to tell Spezh. Make the higher staff go without pay, starting with himself he offered; Sir Barleybane had only turned at once to the paychest and dropped a week's salary into his palms without a word. Increase the tithing for just the remainder of this year, he proposed; on this and only this, Qerlak's smile had faded away, and Fennet knew he must never bring that idea up again.

So today would be the day, Fennet realized sadly, that his lord's fond dream of a celebration yielded to hard reality. The paychest was too empty even to pay the guards another week. Argens save them all if Pritaelseran invaded before the end of summer.

He entered the main hall and saw Qerlak with Ondaii the engineer, Galethiel their human mage, and Seldom Chased, just returned from another of his jaunts through the swampy western lands that Qerlak had assigned him command of. To one side sat the doctor, Drace, with a merchant Fennet had never seen before, quietly waiting their turn as Sir Chased laughed and drank regaling Qerlak with the tale of his adventure.

Why did Fennet's worst news always have to be delivered in public? Qerlak had no sense of lordly decorum, of facts that must be kept from prying ears. In truth, Fennet admitted to himself as he sat to Qerlak's right, he had yet to see a time when his lord had ever been openly embarrassed.

But today, that would change.

"Sir Chased," Qerlak concluded while refilling his goblet, "I thank you again for your extended service to this foef." He turned to wink at Fennet, "Retainers can be hired, but a knight of your caliber is an asset beyond pay. We do, in fact, pay you, do we not Fennet?"

"We do indeed, milord."

"Posh, my friend, 'tis but a means of exercise, these rides," Seldom rejoined while Qerlak filled his goblet as well. The man's ability to absorb strong drink and remain upright was a marvel. "I rather think, as you had hoped, those Reptile Men are well forewarned to stay away from your settled lands awhile."

"A blessing from Argens!" Qerlak cried, "Now the feast can proceed in peace, and you sir, shall by my will stay with us and enjoy it more than any."

"Feasting, say you? And a joust!" As Seldom Chased brightened, Fennet's heart sank even further. How could he disappoint his lord and make him a false-speaker to his friend?

"Oh yes, every kind of food, and of course I hope for some passable beer," Qerlak said, sketching roughly on a map of the area where he envisioned the tables, the booths, and all the rest.

"Milord," Fennet ventured weakly, "do you believe the merchants of Bultarr-r will be filling all these stands?"

Qerlak looked blankly at his castellan a moment. "Oh dear, no, sorry Fennet, I should have told you. I wrote to the lords of Untrebasgh, and Colter and Saec to invite their young men to participate in the combats. And I made sure the messengers dropped off copies with various merchants and guilders as well. No fee for holding a space, as long as they let us know in advance. And they keep whatever they sell, if it's food: just a tithing for anything else."

At this news, Fennet's heart leaped and sank like a dolphin in a storm. "So, they will come, you expect. And their cost to us, I suppose, will be minimal."

"And the crowds, Fennet, think of all the people we will attract to see the swamp-lord and his exotic court. Or that's how we've billed it so far."

All eyes were on him, and Fennet sighed, thinking it was no good to delay further. He flipped open the account-book to the current page.

"It won't do milord. If the vendors who come feed everyone to bursting, there will still be the final feast."

"Skeggs is working on that."

"The need for increased guards, an entire week."

"Cecil will be bringing in the local levy, the pikes will make a good show for us."

"You have made mention of various prizes to be won—"

"Absolutely! This is where the largesse of Mon-Crulbagh will be—"

"Milord!" Interruption was ignoble but Fennet could not hold his temper any longer. "There is nothing, sir. The paychest has not one-fourth the amount we need to maintain the current staff. And you have consistently ignored my suggestions—"

"Ah that!" Qerlak laughed then, and though the situation indicated he could only be driven by meanness or insanity, Fennet found himself smiling helplessly along. It was like a miracle itself: Sir Barleybane laughed as if he had just remembered how, or if someone told the best joke ever spoken. He laughed full and heartily, and with an invitation in it to join him. Fennet knew he would stay, when his lord became broke, when the accursed bankers in Wanlock sent guards to occupy this place and arrest him. He would go to gaol, just to hear the laugh that might come from the cells.

"Fennet, my dear fellow, I have misused you indeed. Please forgive me, there's been so much to do, and I didn't mean—

Argens' Balls, the beer!" Qerlak stood bolt upright and put both arms out in a halting gesture, shouting, "No one leave! I shall return within ten minutes. Stay, stay here!" So saying, he ran for the basement stairs.

Fennet followed despite his orders, and Ondaii padded quietly along behind as Seldom Chased returned to tales of his fight against the Reptile Men with Galethiel. At the edge of the throne room, Fennet saw Drace and the merchant sitting quietly and waiting their turn, one with a face of deep concern, the other with detached bemusement.

As he trailed the knight into the cellar level, Fennet saw him up ahead rubbing the new light-stones to bring up their illumination for a short period. Fennet had been amazed to realize that the wizard and her acolyte were working on just the thing they wanted here. Now, as he followed Qerlak, Fennet had time to think that perhaps he needed to have more faith in his lord's unusual resources.

In the brewing room, the vats were fully laid out and the tubing replaced. Ondaii was there, showing no signs of hurry despite his short stature and the fact that Qerlak had set a hard pace. Qerlak briefly checked the furnace, tapped the tubes and nodded to Ondaii, and then set his hands above the warm finishing vat to invoke with words in the Ancient tongue. Incredible! He was casting a miracle, on the beer.

He straightened up with a deep breath and grinned at Fennet. "An old family secret, Elias. The miracle of Strengthening—"

"The healing you used to save Sir Hitaelseran's life?"

"Hardly that! No, I've seen the followers of Telhol, they follow a much tougher path than I ever could. But Strengthening can lend a bit of something for a short time, to us persons that is. It's helped me in a few pinches, I can tell you. We got our young guest to the doctor in time, and I'm thankful for that. I only knew because I used it on some of my comrades before."

He strolled around the room taking in all the various apparati as Ondaii in the background checked the tightness of rivets and the other fastenings he had devised.

"And now, milord, you will use this miracle on the brew. To save the life of your foef?"

"Oh, nothing so grand!" Qerlak waved off the notion and then grew more serious. "I must say, it feels very good to have this, this part of my old life to bring with me. And it is a bit like what we're trying to do here, Elias. We gather what we've grown, bring it together carefully and with patience."

"And, hem, we apply some heat milord."

"Indeed! Or actually our environment handles all that doesn't it?"

"You are thinking of the invasion now."

"Among other things yes. But we will come through that flame, Fennet, just like this beer. As long as it doesn't get too hot. And then… and then we may really have something here."

He stood awhile in thought, or perhaps prayer Fennet fancied.

"Come, Elias, let's get back up and find you your money."

Fennet's dread returned, but his lord was actually humming a tune as they charged back up the steps. Perhaps this was a question of faith after all.

"Doctor Drace, I apologize for keeping you waiting."

"Not at all, milord, you have many cares I know." The somber man in the black suit rose and bowed properly. "You requested a report on the young knight from Pritaelseran. I have monitored his progress and am pleased to report he is fully recovered."

"No, ahm, no ill effects?"

"None, milord. What a fortunate young man; the last sunny day here in my memory, and yet struck by lightning!"

"It does seem beyond all chance, does it not?" Qerlak's smile was a touch forced as he shook hands with the doctor and let him retire.

Qerlak held up a hand to the merchant who had also risen. "Bear with us, just another few moments, sirrah."

"With respect, great lord, the day draws late."

"And you would have preferred not to spend another night under the stars of Mon-Crulbagh."

"The bugs, rather," the merchant returned with a grin.

"Never fear, my good merchant, you shall have ample reason to be glad of the delay."

So saying, Qerlak returned to the long table and sat. He looked to the others with a straight face, somehow still lit with merriment despite the gloom of the situation. Fennet took up his quill and smoothed down the page showing the desperate state of their cash in one column, the steady march of their incoming expenses in the other. He scanned the figures again, and once again they told of a negative balance within the week.

"Good Sir Chased," Qerlak began, "you mentioned before that I have kept you very busy on the western marches over which I appointed you Captain."

"It has been my pleasure to serve you, milord and good friend," the human knight replied rising to his feet.

"And yet, it strikes me you have had scant opportunity to spend your salary."

"Bah! I am more amused by this so-called work than any entertainment I could devise," the human knight replied, allowing his eyes to drift briefly to Galethiel, and then to one of the serving girls passing through with a giggle. "Or nearly," he amended.

"Then perhaps it is true," Qerlak said, "and I hope you will forgive my curiosity, but perhaps you still have the pay about you somewhere or other."

"Certes, milord. I keep that coin safe in my room."

"All of it?" Fennet cried without restraint. "But, that is, good Sir Chased, that pay, for your past three months and more with us, do you mean to say—"

Seldom Chased shrugged as if nothing could be of less importance. "Perhaps a few spent bits, here and there. Otherwise, in sooth sirrah, I have never troubled to count it out."

Qerlak smiled and took a deep breath. "Do you suppose, Sir Chased, that it would be possible for us to borrow—"

"It is yours, milord, and I give it freely!"

"Nay, not for the Southlands entire, my friend. But If you could allow us to make use of your money until, let us say, the midsummer's tithing? That would result in, what would it be castellan?"

Fennet made furious scratches on his note-paper, and did not take the time he normally did to check the math. "We would be able to pay all the staff in full, milord, another month at least."

Qerlak waited until Fennet's gaze met his, and then dropped cold water on his hopes.

"But there's still the matter of the prizes for our tourney, true?"

"And the added food for the final feast, milord."

Now Qerlak started to smile as if Fennet were playing the game correctly, and the castellan could not help but come along with a small grin of his own as he waited.

"Master merchant, I thank you for your patience and hope to reward it. Please approach the table, my court mage has some business with you."

As the green-robed Elf came up and bowed to Galethiel, she rose as well, like all her other movements quite quickly it seemed to Fennet.

"I have a number of stones I no longer need for my researches," she announced, opening a small box and spilling three dozen gems on the wood. The trader bent down to examine and gently sort them.

"So many, Galethiel," Qerlak murmured, "are you sure?"

She nodded and sat back, thanking Seldom Chased who refilled her goblet.

"Boy, to my room if you would," the knight called. "Under my bed, I believe, it's a pillow-sack, rather heavy, please bring it here."

Fennet could hardly breathe at this turn of events. Was it possible?

"For these," the merchant announced pointing to a pile of three-quarters of the stones, "I can offer you perhaps four hundred silver pieces." Fennet guessed the fellow could sell them for five hundred silver, or better yet, use them singly in barter to even greater advantage; meanwhile carrying the stones would be more convenient than their equivalent in silver.

But Galethiel sat up and the merchant took a step back.

"These here," she said, pointing to the other five, "are worth more than the rest put together."

"Ah yes, I agree, mistress mage. But I have not enough cash for them."

She shook her head and raised a single finger. "These five are onyx, and black agate, obsidian. They must be—never mind, just listen. You will pay me six hundred silver pieces for the rest. For these, I will accept a single silver piece for each of them. In cash, right now."

The merchant could not keep his jaws together, and Fennet's mind whirled with the profit margin he could anticipate. The man fumbled with his pouch and put out a row of five silver coins, one across from each of the darker stones. Galethiel picked up each coin singly, exchanging it for one of the stones, then rattled the coins together like dice before putting them in her robe. "Done, and well done," she said quietly.

"But the rest," the merchant sputtered, "I regret to say, I have not the cash—"

"Nor will you need it, sirrah." Qerlak produced a short list on a parchment. "For I hereby commission you to use that selling price to instead purchase these prizes for our tournament. I believe these could all be found in Beryl: take a look and say you whether you can have them back by the end of this month."

His face alight, the merchant eagerly looked over the list, nodding the while. "A distinguished set of prizes milord. I can indeed have all of these to you within the fortnight. And I shall settle for the remainder—"

"Any remainder which comes to you, good merchant from the intelligence of your dickering you shall keep as a commission." Qerlak put his hand and a mug of ale on the deal, both of which the merchant avidly accepted. "Only see to it that the prizes are of the first quality."

"Worthy of a baron, milord!"

"Worthy of the winners, my good man. Note you, these items are meant to be used."

"As you wish, of course."

The merchant scooped up the gems, bowed his thanks and left with his feet barely touching the stones. Two boys entered, dragging the pillow-sack between them over to the paychest where they dumped the contents with whoops of satisfaction.

"Good Sir Chased, we are quite literally in your debt," Qerlak said, "Fennet here will provide you with a promissory note."

Seldom Chased wrinkled his nose at the castellan. "What, some paper with words on it? Waste not your time, sirrah: my family has been proudly unlettered since its inception." He offered his arm to Galethiel. "Perhaps a turn about the walls, mistress mage?"

Ondaii also bowed and asked permission to retire. "Much work there still is, to be doing of course, if milord kindly will permit me."

Then it was just the two of them alone, in the empty great hall at the enormous table. At last, Fennet had the privacy and discretion he needed. Qerlak sat and looked steadily at him, knowing as he did the game's final moves.

"Thanks to Sir Chased's cash on hand," Fennet began carefully, "we can make our payroll until the festival next month."

Qerlak just listened, so the castellan continued.

"And at month's end, there will be a tithing. First crops in, Argens willing it looks to be a good season, and our rolls of peasants are larger than they were at winter's end."

He scratched a few figures in the margins. "We could repay Sir Chased what we owe. Or we might hire a few more guards, in case…"

"Yes," Qerlak said gently into the empty room. "In case."

Then he turned to look back at Fennet. "But."

Fennet swallowed but could not bring himself to say it.

"But," Qerlak repeated, "the start of next month is also the due date on my note. From the Wanlock Assurers bank."

Fennet nodded. "Fifty thousand silver pieces, milord, as you know."

"Plus interest."

Fennet nodded again, then gasped with recognition. "The interest! Milord, I had forgotten. If we can make a payment of the interest, we can parole the fifty thousand month by month."

Qerlak took his turn to nod. "A mere, what, five hundred silver pieces I believe."

Fennet leaped up. "The paychest, Sir Chased's money." Then he met Qerlak's eyes, and slowly sat again. "But then, we would have no festival."

"And we will have the festival, Fennet. I need you to see that."

"Milord, why?"

"Because Mon-Crulbagh needs it. The peasants here, they have suffered so long, with foul monsters to one side and greedy tyrants like Pritaelseran on the other. And what have they had for protection, these last ten decades, eh? You've read the journal. Clods, and dissolutes, the worst my class could offer, only adding to the wrack and ruin if you ask me. I tell you, Fennet, when the civil war came last year, and all the knights of Argens ran off to fight, it probably came to these people as a relief. A relief!"

He stood up to pace after the echoes of his voice, walking to the raised dais and its wooden throne but too energized to sit, gripping its back then striding in all directions.

"And those poor prisoners, Elias, think of it. That village enslaved to the dragon, we freed those people. Can you imagine what drudgery and terror they endured while this kingdom did nothing to help. There wasn't so much as a record of their capture! And none of them will tell me anything about it. Just kneeling, and thanks and bouquets of flowers, as if they owed us anything. It's an outrage."

"And you, milord Barleybane, you have brought them out of that. These peasants, tradesfolk, the hunters and fishers and children of this foef have hope, because of you."

"Not yet, Elias, not quite yet. They can sense a happier future, but they cannot believe it. And why should they? Two seasons where a lord didn't leave them, or raise their taxes? It's not enough. We must show off Mon-Crulbagh."

Qerlak walked over and sat next to Fennet again.

"I want people from across the region here. Anyone who's thinking about moving east to join the Far Mark, or unhappy with their lives for whatever reason, I want all the malcontents and seekers to hear about what we've done. And come to see for themselves. You know the empty plots, where the best land is. You've had the maps ready for more like the thralls of Semegorn, ready for months now."

"You'll draw more settlers with the festival," Fennet mused. "If it goes well, they'll relocate here."

"And they'll tell their friends before they come."

"And the tithing will grow, we'll be able to meet more of our obligations."

"Yes of course the revenues, I know you must mind that." Qerlak leaned in with a gentle smile. "But Fennet, mind you. They will be happy. Proud. As you said, hope, the real thing."

In the silence, Fennet could only nod his agreement.

"But the interest payment, milord. We won't meet it."

"We will not."

"And Pritaelseran. If you continue to refuse his son's ransom, we'll lose even more in expenses than we already do."

"We will indeed. And that's not all."

"No milord. They will come."

"They will all come."

Fennet waited a long moment. Qerlak, looking directly ahead, started at the silence and met his gaze, then barked an angry laugh.

"What then? Are you waiting for me to pull another trick from the bag, Fennet? I don't have one. Please understand that."

"And yet, milord, the festival will happen."

"It will indeed, my good castellan." Qerlak rose again to pace a few steps away and Fennet spoke to his back.

"And if the bankers come to collect? If Pritaelseran comes for revenge?"

"Then they come! I'll pawn my armor and meet the Hawk-knight dressed in the outfit I wore the day I was born. I'll be gaoled as a debtor, or I'll die in disgrace, or more than likely something even worse will happen."

Qerlak turned back to face him once more. His face seemed to shine with its own light and Fennet felt as he did when Qerlak detected lies on Severyn Illfellow on this very spot.

"But Mon-Crulbagh needs hope, Fennet, far more than it needs me. Whatever I can do, I will. And if I'm taken off, no one will be able to say in truth that I wanted less than their health and safety."

Fennet rose and bowed, saying only, "May Argens grant that you rule a thousand years, milord, if he cares for the people as you do. I'll save every silver bit, I swear."

Qerlak put a hand on his shoulder in thanks. "And if the worst comes," he said, "I swear to you, we won't have to die sober."

Castle Pritaelseran

The post-midnight summons bell roused Dommes with a half-bottle of lotus liqueur already in him. Technically, none of the knight's servants slept any more than their lord, but as he hastened to the throne room the butler straightened his suit and smoothed his hair, slowing the last four steps to reacquire his mask of calm subservience.

What he saw there knocked him all the way to sober.

His lord Cran-Kalrith Pritaelseran stood before the long table, looking as alert and trim as if he'd just eaten well and never drank wine in his life. His left hand gripped and crushed a pair of letters evidently just arrived; his right set down his whipping cane against the table edge where its razor-tines kept it from rolling, but not dripping. And on the floor before his feet lay something more blood than being, its tunic and pantaloons as shredded as the skin beneath and barely breathing through lips too sliced to speak another word of denial.

"The expedition to Mon-Crulbagh failed," the knight announced in clipped tones, something everyone already knew. "The response to my effort at ransom was unsatisfactory, as was Guernsten's explanation for my son's attempt to exonerate him."

He turned back to circle the table and sit the throne. "Clean this up."

"At once, milord," Dommes stooped to embrace the wet quaking figure, focusing past the horror to take comfort that his state of undress was now well disguised in crimson.

"If he cannot walk tomorrow, send him to Zantire."

Dommes swallowed only once before answering. "As you wish, Sir Pritaelseran."

"And bring me the postal rider. I wish to ask whether he stopped along his route, to sleep or for some other unworthy purpose."

"Yes, milord."

Dommes knew his place, and how easily it could be exchanged for that of the man in his arms. He knew also, what treatment awaited the postal rider, having a drink and bite to eat in the refectory right now, joking with the cook and thinking he had decades left to ride this route in peace. Like all of them, Dommes knew what happened to Drayson. He did his best, through years of faithful service, to absolve himself of the need for forgiveness, when he had done nothing to help the last friend he'd ever made.

And tonight, he did not turn aside from doing his duty.

But he did pause, to overhear half a conversation between his lord and the wizard who spoke to men in their minds.

Most of the peasants thought Zantire Pritaelseran a myth, or a nightmare tale told to keep children obedient. The castle staff saw him perhaps once a season, enough to know that real power and command still resided in flesh; they thought he could read their minds at all hours. But Dommes knew enough, from watching his lord and lady, that the communication happened only in a few places, this hallway not among them. The kitchen, he fervently hoped, another exception.

So Dommes listened, and heard enough, before continuing on with his burden in arms. Drips on the floor would have to be cleaned, of course. And a new suit for the morning. But just before that, it was time to save one man from dying, and frighten another into living.

Down the flight of stairs to the kitchen area he kicked open the servant's door and placed the warrior's body on the table very close to the post-rider's meal. The night cook pulled back with a screech, and the courier dropped his tankard to the floor in shock.

"Thalisa, bring the red glass bottle from my locker. Hurry."

Dommes turned to get a bucket of water and a clean rag, but never took his eyes from the post rider the while.

"Stars of Hope! What, what happened?"

Ignoring him, Dommes tore off the remaining shreds of shirt and pants to expose the naked body entire, with its dozens of deep-slicing cuts. It was not intended that a man should survive a razorcane-whipping. Guernsten's breath was ragged, and when the cold cloth hit his flesh anywhere, he groaned like the deep bleat of a terrorized animal. Everything still oozed blood, though it slowed a little with repeated drenching along the arms and legs. By the time Thalisa staggered back in there was as much flesh as blood showing. She shoved one hand deep into her mouth and almost dropped the glass vial with the other.

Uncapping it, Dommes carefully poured out a few drops at a time and focused only on the torso at first, watching as the worst and bloodiest cuts sealed over and allowed the rag to clear the skin. Dommes had held this bottle against the day he displeased his lord, but pushed that thought from his mind now as he shook out a few last drops, and lightly brushed Guernsten's lips with them. Then he threw a tablecloth over his form before the chills set in.

"Tol.. toll trooth," the retainer gasped, and Dommes nodded but shushed him.

"A better outfit, Thalisa, anything from anywhere, go now."

When she left, he looked back to the post rider who had backed up to the side wall in his horror.

"He made a report to milord Pritaelseran which was unsatisfactory."

The rider looked back and forth to the speaker and the retainer, all thoughts of jesting with the cook and perhaps stealing a kiss long forgotten. Which was good, Dommes thought, as he took in the man's gaze again.

"Milord wishes to speak with you as well. To get a report. About the haste you made in carrying his letters."

No one moved and only Guernsten's labored breathing could be heard.

"Another rag and a fresh bucket, Thalisa. I must return to clean, and tell him about you."

"Hopeforger preserve me," the rider gasped. "What shall I say, what shall I do?"

"It is not your word, but mine, that matters here," Dommes told him. "You have already left."

The post rider swallowed and nodded.

"And," Dommes said pointing, "you are taking him with you."

"What? But I cannot, he, regulations, he cannot sit the saddle."

"Then tie him to you! And ride without stopping until you are beyond Lann at least. Milord will send men to follow you."

"But I, he, carrying him will slow me down!"

"Then when I tell milord in the morning that Guernsten seems to have left, to walk the grounds, I will be exposed as a liar. And you and I will suffer together."

He seized the bucket from Thalisa and looked down on Guernsten once more. "I don't know where you can go. Here is some money, may Argens watch over you and bring you to a lord whose faith matches your own."

He straightened up and looked hard at the post rider.

"I shall start in the halls and work toward the throne room. I shall clean thoroughly. You have that long."

⊕ ⊕ ⊕

Great Chamber

Tran-Kalrith Pritaelseran sat with steepled hands in the silence of the darkened throne room and contemplated how long he could take for his revenge. The enemy, apparently quite overconfident despite all indications, foolishly let drop that he was taking good care of Hitaelseran. An enemy worth respecting would have known how to use pain, and perhaps a letter to the boy's mother, as blackmail. No doubt this distaff son saw the coming conflict as some kind of noble match between equals, to be decided on the day of combat with no need to think of the pressures that could be brought to bear ahead of time. Argens Demonbender taught otherwise, and thus the full measure of days would bear a ripe harvest. By holding the boy hostage, this upstart Barleybane gave ample cause for retribution in any degree. The entire foef, now, would be the goal.

He felt the familiar tickle at the edge of his thoughts and looked up to the hawk carving above the fountain.

"What is it brother. You have seen the letters in my mind, I presume? And you have, as always, an opinion to render."

Observations, rather, which you would be well served to consider. Nothing more. Nothing less.

The words whispering in his mind were so very like his own. Cran hated the similarity, the sarcasm and biting wit of his brother's words. Of course, Zantire was far more arrogant and cruel in his actions; a good thing he'd seen reason and stepped aside to let a more rational, patient man rule.

"The issue of Hitaelseran's leadership is closed. No more of your star-charts, thanks; you will kindly focus on what's to be done now."

'Now' is exactly correct, little brother. Send your forces into the low country within the week.

"Nonsense, it takes more than a fortnight to summon the levy. I shall bring the full force of the Hawk down on the swamp-rats this time. The second week of Serpent will be quite sufficient."

Another mistake. In Serpent, the influence of the Chaos cycle will yield too closely to the malice of the Arbalest. Who knows where his bolt may fall this year? But now, in the next two weeks it is still the month of the Hawk, how obvious a hint do you require?

"The stars of heaven need not bless this expedition. Our strength will be quite sufficient to the current goal. Mon-Crulbagh has not a single retainer with a lance; our raid was met by a peasant rabble."

Ah, you were victorious then? I had heard somewhat differently.

"To the hells beneath your laboratory with you! You know what I mean. Hitaelseran was inexperienced, and Barleybane was clever, to use his witch instead of meeting a son of the Hawk in honor. Now with his treachery I am free to seek full retribution."

Word has come to me of this adventuring human, with hair of flame and a temper to match. Some of the peasants even claim to have seen her, in their dreams.

"The quaint superstitions of the lowly! No wonder this Barleybane has been able to cow them so easily. Still, if Guernsten was not lying, she controls the weather.

I will handle her. I know more of the realm of sleep than any Elf alive, much less a hasty young human. Her candle will be snuffed before the battle. Fear not that magery will interfere with your plans, little brother. Only hurry them along, and attack before the end of the month.

"As usual, you have no taste for subtlety. I have dispatched a group under Zanrith to the source of the Sodsluice."

Of course. The borders change with the course of the river, your old land claim. And the Insectirs will rise again to plague him.

"I have sent a man to observe and report on the state of the castle. We will also look into that devilry around the stones, in case this feud comes to the attention of the overlords. And then, of course, the other rumors will have to be addressed."

Mon-Crulbagh's legendary allies, you mean. Which our ancestors have never beaten.

"Nor his remembered, in the past two centuries. They are surely gone by now at any rate. But these matters take patience, more than your stars would allow."

Ignore the signs at your peril, little brother. Time and again I must dig you out from the pits of your own devising. Without my cleverness, you would have lost your seat long ago, instead of expanding your reign to cover the space of three knighthoods.

"You are no more clever than Mon-Crulbagh himself, old one," the knight replied as he took up again the response from his adversary. "Look you in this letter, how casually he refers to being in my debt, as if this were no shame. And to taunt me over the ransom amount! He deserves even less for his ignoble behavior, but for turning down my offer he shall suffer. No, I shall draw him in a while yet, send him another demand, pretend to be angry. Meanwhile, my other schemes will ripen and ensure our victory by the end of Serpent."

Lie to the others, little brother. I can see your fury is no pretense.

Cran-Kalrith bit off his response as he noticed the letter in his fist practically crushed into a ball. He deliberately smoothed it on the table and recited the meme of patience.

"You make sure the witch-woman dies. The rest concerns the lord of the foef, not his wizard."

It shall be done, milord. The voice in his mind conveyed the sense of a wide smile. *Pritaelseran will triumph… despite your distraction.*

With a curse, Pritaelseran shouted the word that cut off the statuette's enchantment and broke contact with his brother's mind. That much, at least, he had insisted on when the enchantment was first laid, an earlier day when his power felt more secure. Recently, Zantire's attitude was becoming too mocking, his plans more secretive. Cran-Kalrith could not decide if his brother's increasing absence from the affairs of rule was good or bad news. But so long as he did his part and removed the element of uncertainty in Barleybane's wizard ally, all would be well.

He looked again on the now-crumpled parchment, and his eye came to rest on one phrase in particular; *"On balance I feel I owe you my greatest debt…"*. What others, he wondered, could there be?

124

He rang the bell for Dommes, and in a minute the butler entered with bucket and rag, bowing to him and regarding the blood on the floor with indifference.

"Dommes, those bankers in Wanlock, when Craltire had his visit there."

"Yes, milord, the gambling, you raised the tithing—"

"The name of the bank, Dommes."

The butler blinked. "Wanlock Assurers, milord."

"Ah yes. I shall inquire with them, where is that post rider?"

"He left sir, evidently at once. Shall I summon a retainer to chase him down?"

Cran-Kalrith waved a hand in dismissal. "I shall have my own man deliver it, no matter. Continue cleaning this, then change your clothes."

"At once, milord."

"And draw from the paychest for a replacement suit, you have earned it."

"Many thanks, milord."

The knight rose to exit the room, stepping around the puddle of cooling blood and fondly imagining the power of debts, and how they could be repaid. Zantire need not know everything.

Wizard's Laboratory

The bald-headed wizard looked through the hawk-mask that formed his proxy link to the throne room, scrying his brother's conversation with the servant. It was important to know everything, for the man who truly ruled this foef. Cran-Kalrith's cutoff word merely broke the mind link, but Zantire could still overhear the knight's questions, and see the fractional hesitation in his servant's reply. Just like his younger sibling, to obsess about debts when all that mattered was crushing the life from your foe.

He lowered the hawk-like viewing mask and looked about his subterranean laboratory, surprisingly well-lit in most places by means of his art. Precisely placed mirrors reflected the two lanterns, and the central pool revealed the light of the stars by means of the man-high mystic lens he had placed atop the tower seven stories above. Light stones were unneeded to see the shelves of books, the nook holding his granary of mystic energy, a few pieces of thick, dark polished furniture, and the shimmer of his Vapor Cloak hanging near the door.

Also standing at attention was Zantire's acolyte, watching his master with that avid gaze he always had when he sensed a scheme hatching. Zantire nodded to his pupil with approval.

"You can tell, Insis, what mission I shall send you on."

"To slay the human witch, master?"

"Indeed. In the heart of her tower while her master sleeps. He will awaken to terror, and know his place, accepting defeat before my brother's battle even begins."

"But her magic, master, mine is not her equal."

"You think so? Does she move so quietly and smoothly as you have trained hard to do?" Zantire put one hand on the man's shoulder, and let it linger there, perhaps longer than usual.

The acolyte grinned, showing teeth nearly black with the lotus-juice he used to propel his visions and advance the lore he sought. "One night soon, the mortal woman will go to sleep and never awaken. If only I can gain access unheard."

"Use this dagger," Zantire said, handing him a gold-hilted blade in a plain leather sheath. "It is drenched in a poison that deprives the voice and breath at once, but kills only with lingering pain. One stab will be enough, though you may of course indulge yourself as you wait."

Insis shivered with delight and belted the blade at once. "But," he insisted, "how to get past the guards, the walls, master? With one or two I can administer the shock-touch and muffle their cries, yet if there are several—"

"None shall see you enter or leave." Zantire said with passion. "For just such a mission have I created the Vapor Cloak, and you, Insis, shall have it."

At this, the assassin's eyes added their own light to that of the chamber, and with shaking hands he turned and reached to the cape hanging on its stand. With a gasp, then a cry, Insis' hand passed through the fabric; sparkles of energy passed up his arm and he staggered back in pain.

"So eager, my apprentice!" Zantire cried with glee at the other's discomfort. "You forget, it was originally attuned to me, much as a staff or other item of power."

"But, master, then how—"

"We shall realign its attunement, together. That is, if you are unafraid to take the risk of death."

Insis held a breath, but his lit eyes seemed to drive him and he nodded fiercely. "I am ready master."

Zantire took up the cloak, which yielded to his hand as if made of finest silk, and laid it upon his main table. Then he attached a set of metal cords to the base of his skull, reaching from the sides of the elevator nook along the wall. Once more he placed a lingering hand on Insis' shoulder, the other on the cloak, and began to incant in the Sorceror's Tongue by which all great spells and enchantments were created. Mystic energy flowed from Zantire's body into both the apparel and the acolyte, and at his nod Insis laid hands upon the Vapor Cloak. At once, the starry sparks of energy coursed up his arm, covering his head and torso as he clenched his teeth against the pain.

Zantire now drew upon his granary as energy flowed from the box in the nook along the cable to the back of his head and on into the spell he maintained. Both men gritted their teeth against the exertion and pain, and one man's nose began to bleed. But the deep groan of wordless agony came from neither the mage nor his follower as the spell reached its peak. The cry ended in a gasp, and the spell energy began to fade.

Insis staggered back from the table, the Vapor Cloak clutched in his hand and wiping his nose with a sleeve before swirling it onto his back. His entire form took on the same shimmer, a misty look that still showed a man, but whose features were difficult to distinguish.

"Go now, rest, and then set out for Mon-Crulbagh. One of my brother's men will spy out the place, he can help you. You cannot fail, apprentice. Slay the witch and break her lord's will with horror."

"I go, master, at once." Insis turned and walked through the chamber door without opening it, while Zantire chuckled long and loud.

Looking back a moment to the pool, the wizard became interested, and a bit distracted by the tiny alterations of meaning he saw there. That he sent his catspaw rather than go himself was a difficult decision, of course. But Zantire realized it would be unsafe to leave the foef in real charge of his indecisive brother, even for a week. Looking at the stars in his pool he still saw death, and the breaking of stones which he took to mean there would be destruction to go with the execution. All well and good.

Another tiny gasp from the granary nook roused him from further observation of these details. Removing the spell-cable, Zantire turned the handle of a glass vial strapped to one side of the box, releasing a syrupy fluid to run into the nook chamber itself.

"Stop complaining," he said to no one in particular, "you know by now your place. Drink there, regain your energy." Here Zantire took up a goblet, and might indeed have been speaking to himself. Then he uttered an arcane phrase in Sorceror's Tongue, of the power and complexity not seen in the current day, ending with one word of the Common speech: "Sleep".

Zantire remained awake, and after a moment, nodded in satisfaction, closed the nook lid, and left the laboratory.

⊕ ⊕ ⊕

Foef of Beryl

The bar-wagon was that perfect mix of boredom and pain, leaving Quarion neither asleep nor awake for what seemed days on end. After departing Beryl, its view of country roads and forest dells fell into sameness for the Stealthic. Sometimes rousing from a half-minute's restless snooze, he snapped up to sight what he was sure he'd seen the last hour, or even the day before. Quarion could swear either the caravan's course was a circle, or else there existed an industrious, malicious tribe of gremlins who constantly ran to carry the entire terrain from behind the procession to the front.

Yet sleep, real sleep, was never possible while the solid-wheeled cart moved. The hard dirt roads gave way only to gravel or paving stones when they passed through a village or over a bridge, and Quarion could never decide whether the ruts of the former or the unevenness of the latter was worse. By the third day his ribs, hips, and skull felt as badly rattled as they had that night when they were caught, and the guards had used the butt-end of their spears on all of them seemingly for an hour. But back then, Quarion had the mercy of passing out. Here, the wagon just kept jarring and tipping and bumping him back to consciousness.

Blissfully, in the evenings they stopped.

The guards let out the trio of prisoners for dinner, to void and to sleep on the grass which seemed like silken pillows; the wagon lacked even hay on the floor. The first night, Quarion went where the guards pointed and didn't mind the grass had an evening dew nor an odor tinged with something like old ale. It was Bellatara who kicked him and jerked her head at the laughing gaolers, before he realized the prank.

But she was always alert to what lay around them in the endless rural stretches of this journey to nowhere. It was of course easier for the Halfling to stand inside the bar-wagon, and Bellatara was constantly noticing new trees in the distance, always first to point out animals to either side.

On the second night out from Beryl, while Quarion and Ellesmera sat near a campfire and slowly munched the same food as ever, it was Bellatara who shushed them with her hands, and seemed to follow the track of a flying thing between the trees. Quarion's Elven sight did not serve him in the copse where they rested, but Bellatara pointed through the ebon air and then winked at her companions.

She stood still as if listening, and Quarion could make out the slightest, highest squeak from somewhere near her. Just as he realized the Woodsman was the source of the sound, the night was torn by a blood-freezing screech; a moment later the guards ducked and cursed as an owl with a wingspan near that of a full-grown man swept close to the fire, looking for the mouse it deserved. Now it was Bellatara's turn to laugh, and the guards eyed her with a suspicion they usually reserved for the preacher's daughter.

For Ellesmera, the gaolers combined spite with fear. Because her hands and feet were weapons, they hobbled her at the wrists and ankles like a picketed horse. Since she seldom spoke and never responded to their jibes, they seemed angrier but hesitated to attempt abuse. Quarion marveled at her restraint and the respect she commanded, and wished he could school his mind to be calm as hers. He tried to simply grin when they leveled another insult, and ignored their loud praise for blankets, ale and other amenities the prisoners lacked. Twice, he had a clear opportunity to acquire a dagger but passed. In the time before the theft was discovered, what could he do alone? And he wasn't leaving without his friends: that much, at least, the three of them had settled.

Sometimes the monotony of the trip was relieved by the sight of peasants and villagers, who invariably came to stare at the prisoners and wonder aloud, as if they were beyond earshot, what they had done. The gaolers were happy to supply them with perfectly accurate accounts, which were met with protestations of horror and reassured with vows of utter honesty. Quarion managed a neat trick by acting the part behind one of them as he spoke, mock-voicing his exact words to the amusement of the audience until the fellow finally noticed. That earned him the butt-end of a spear in the stomach through the bars, which he judged to be utterly worth it.

It also brought the Greatknight himself back from the front of the column, to stare at all parties in turn. Quarion met the gaze of a broad-shouldered Elven noble and saw such a promise of anger and decision that made him long for the ignorant hatred of a yokel-guard. Torquem'l Beryllian regarded Quarion, and his companions, as a problem; that much was certain. And in that lord's eyes Quarion saw a man who could pass judgment without regard for his own pain or another's death.

Why were they still alive?

The knight's eyes passed over him in a moment and spent perhaps twice as long on Bellatara. But when Beryllian came to Ellesmera, who stood last and bowed to him first, Quarion could see the noble's gaze lingered. And he could not be sure—in fact, he could not believe his eyes—but it seemed to him that Beryllian's face flinched with pain, or sadness. He disciplined the guard for loss of control and sharply reined back to the front of the column.

To either side of the Greatknight, two retainers spun their mounts in perfect rhythm, but behind the group Quarion caught sight of the best-dressed dandy he had ever seen. Bright blue outfit with highlights of muted grey, matching boots, gorgeous broad-brimmed hat, a smile that never suffered a fist and hair of spun gold. Immortal Elf with at least a century of songs behind his cobalt eyes, and a bright red painted mandolin slung across his back. He switched his gaze thoughtfully between his

131

patron and the prisoner, then nodded companionably to Quarion before riding ahead.

"Who was that?" Bellatara asked, after swallowing.

"Handsome fellow, isn't he?" Quarion ribbed her before turning to Ellesmera. "I heard the guards talking about him, Bleys Eversong. Been with the court for half a year now, they say." He thought about the distant music he'd heard in the evenings from the front of the caravan.

What did a lord of the Southern Empire need with a bard and a brace of prisoners on the same trip? Quarion could only ask the question, but the tingle of danger that came back to him made him grin.

That night, the bard sauntered to the last campfire, "To sing for the honored guards, and their equally honored guests." Quarion noted that Bleys sang even when he spoke, with words that rose and fell and finished like notes (though he knew nothing of music). He bet no one interrupted this fellow.

Putting one foot up on a rock the minstrel winked at Quarion, who felt a shock all through him while Bleys brought his instrument to the fore, strings held level to the ground as he picked and strummed a famous tune about the great Stealthic Trekelny.

The moon's shifting shadow was his friend,
He climbed the tower walls
All through the temple he did wend,
A' glide past guarded halls...

Quarion smiled up at him, until he noticed the sour faces of the gaolers. Evidently Krem, who they had killed, knew everyone. Bleys was seemingly ignorant of the embarrassment he caused, but held his notes a bit on the phrases that emphasized the great good Trekelny had done, and how he had escaped despite the prospect of certain death. When he finished everyone applauded whatever their personal feelings, just to keep him here on this rare night when the lords did not require him.

Bleys bowed to Quarion who nodded, then turned to Bellatara.

"Now then, what to make of this remarkable person here?"

The Woodsman, also oblivious to any ill-will, hopped up and cried, "Oh do you know this one?" And she started in on the naughty drinking song she sang in Wanlock, to get a meal that night the three of them had met.

Bleys burst into laughter like a silver gong, and he picked up the tune in her key without error, letting her sing the entire thing while perched on another rock. The guards laughed despite themselves, and Quarion thought the Woodsman had never sounded so well.

Bleys took her hand and bowed her to the group before assisting the Halfling down from the rock. Then he turned to look at Ellesmera on the ground and Quarion could sense, this was the entire reason for his visit. Now the bard's face was alight with eagerness; here was a man who shared Quarion's curiosity though probably without a thought of any danger.

"And now, mistress, what sort of tune may I give to honor you this evening?"

Ellesmera smiled briefly up at him and shook her head. "I need no song from you, sir."

"Not food nor drink either, it seems," Bleys returned while studying her closely. "I would invite you to dance but it appears your hands and feet are already engaged."

"You keep a careful step away from her," one of the guards advised, "or she'll snap your neck."

"Did I sing so poorly then!" The laughter at this had an edge of meanness to it, and Bleys never took his eyes from the Martial Wizard the while.

"I was never much for music, I'm afraid," she said quietly. After a long moment, she added, "You sing beautifully, of course. Reminds me…"

"I remind you of someone, mistress? A colleague, perhaps? Maybe I have heard the name."

Ellesmera shrugged. "No one in particular, I suppose. There were many in my mother's house, I mean, when I was younger."

For the first time since he'd known her, Quarion thought his companion looked uncomfortable under the gaze of this handsome, kind-smiling fellow. He knew how to listen, that was certain. Bleys simply crouched to his haunches and cued her.

"In your mother's house? Surely you recall one name, or two?"

Ellesmera looked to one side, then cocked her head deciding to make an effort. "One, a woman, was called Shai, I believe."

"Tambouri Shai!" Bleys' face lit with delight, "Ah, the voice of a songbird, I know of her of course, the toast of Cryssigens. I heard her sing in the temple. Yes, the Crystal City, what a marvelous—hold, you say in your mother's house?"

He looked more carefully at Ellesmera's mien then, and after a moment gently reached to brush her hair to one side before she could bat his arm away. After a moment, Bleys fell back to his butt in the grass, then scrambled lithely to his feet but drawing in his breath the while.

"By the First! Cryssigens, your mother's house, of course, that would explain, you are her daughter."

Ellesmera looked to the bard with a face of rare apprehension. The guards closed up to see what had happened, but Bleys reassured them with a raised hand that he had been offered no violence. Disappointed, the guards stopped, but all the good humor of the evening's entertainment was fully erased.

Bleys bowed to her again, saying only, "I offer you, mistress, my sincere condolences." Then he turned to go, but Quarion dared to step in his way and put a hand on his arm.

"Condolences? What do you mean?"

At close range, Bleys' face showed more signs of the age he probably held, and Quarion had to steady himself not to back away. The eyes, though, showed the Stealthic first puzzlement, then more sadness. Bleys began to speak, thought better of it, then patted Quarion's back and whispered quickly in his ear.

"The Greatknight is a Stargazer. Take comfort in that."

Then the bard moved off before the guards could close in to overhear.

In a poor mood, the gaolers decided that such mysterious misbehavior merited a night in the wagon instead of on the open ground. The trio was escorted back inside and the key rattling in the lock sounded quite final this time.

"I don't understand," Bellatara said with her usual directness. "What does anyone care that her mother is a preacher? She might come, and post bond, or maybe—"

She stopped when the guards all laughed and pointed.

"Argens' Balls, she doesn't even know."

"Doesn't know what?" Quarion challenged, locking eyes with the gaoler, and though he comprised no threat, the Stealthic's surge of emotion for his friend must have come through, for the man took a step back.

"Her mother's dead, haven't you heard?"

"Dead?" The quiet voice came from the corner where Ellesmera sat.

"You're lying." Quarion could hardly speak and needed to grip the bars to stay upright. He knew his friend wanted to remain anonymous, avoid going home, and he understood the feeling. But her mother was famous, beautiful, favored by Argens with miraculous power.

"Dead and burned. Torn apart by Bugs, and ten thousand people saw her ashes fly."

The words were meant to hurt. They did their job.

Chapter IV. Light

Foef of Mon-Crulbagh:
Reclamation Festival 1st Serpent 2002 ADR

Qerlak thought he should have been in serious pain, on the last evening in Hawk, but instead as darkness came on, he felt only elation with a light dusting of terror. Even a human might not have slept the night before the Reclamation Festival.

He climbed to the walls and looked at the fair grounds beyond the moat, where the newly-cleared field was outlined with simple tents to shelter guests without the means to cover themselves. He started to pace the parapet, passing by the gaol-chamber above the gates where Hitaelseran was quartered. Qerlak peeked in and saw him laying back on his bed, perhaps asleep. The answer of what to do with him, he hoped, would be revealed in coming days.

A little further on he was surprised to see a slim, bedraggled form sitting between the crenelments with his legs hanging down outside the walls. His stringy hair, made even straighter by the light rain falling, caused his long nose to seem even more prominent.

"Good evening, Master Illfellow."

Qerlak's greeting made the indentured villein flinch, as if barely deciding that jumping into the moat would not be safer than letting his lord approach. Severyn scrambled back onto the wall and bowed low with cap off. It had been months since Qerlak exposed him as a liar and fixed him to a sentence of indefinite servitude around the castle. The miracle of Detect Lies had worked to impress the peasants on that day of judgment. For its target, it seemed, the fear and awe had never worn away.

"Look you at the wonderful fair grounds we have," Qerlak said, "I know you worked hard to take out that brush, and I thank you for it."

Severyn stammered and looked at his feet. "The wood is only half-chopped, milord. The kiln fires, for your beer."

"Ah, then you do a double-service to this foef," Qerlak said, trying his best to encourage the lad. "I have had no complaints of your work from the dekentar or the castellan."

Severyn shrugged and still looked miserable.

"Tomorrow begins our Reclamation Festival, Master Illfellow. I hope you will have time to enjoy yourself. If, that is, your health holds out." This was a risky joke, for it had been the villein's misuse of pretended illness that had put him in such bad favor with his neighbors and brought him to justice in the knight's court.

But surprisingly, Severyn laughed and nodded. "Skeggs the cook, milord, has put in for my service, at the feast and cleaning up and such."

Qerlak nodded and passed on, leaning in to say, "Try the beer."

When Severyn was behind him, the peasant fled the walls like a man expecting to be attacked. True to say, he had been a rascal for years and done damage to the customs, but Qerlak wondered if perhaps his servitude had lasted long enough.

The knight paced on until coming close to the southwest rear tower and its lone guard. Thinking about Galethiel, he frowned and turned back. Conversation between the two were strained since the raid. Qerlak had never explained—hoped he wouldn't have to—that taking the enemy knight down without a joust was a stain on his honor. She had acted in accordance with their code as adventurers. Would he really want her to hold back next time? Was it cowardice not to speak to her? At a random thought he wondered, if she were taken prisoner or in trouble, might he turn aside from his duties as lord of Mon-Crulbagh to help her. Certainly he would, he realized. So, then.

Qerlak was still on the walls as the skies gradually lightened, and the rain—while not stopping—lessened so much that he could ignore it. This was the first day of Serpent, the start of the summer season so far south in Argens. The Festival. And something was brewing.

He changed into his finest suit, and saw the staff also dressed out in their best. The halls were strewn with fresh rushes, tapestries cleaned for the first time in more than a decade. Even the grounds inside the bailey had been swept and the animals penned up out of sight.

Watching again from atop the walls, Qerlak joined Fennet, Seldom Chased and Squire Cecil as peasants and visitors, primarily from Mon-Crulbagh but also from Untrebasgh and Colter, flowed in steadily through the morning to the fair grounds.

"I hear music," Chased remarked looking about. "And see those bright-colored wagons. A gypsy band?"

Cecil grinned and nodded, "They arrived after sunset, from where I found them in Colign a fortnight ago. I wasn't sure they'd come."

"Well done indeed," Qerlak said clapping his shoulder. They watched the entertainers drawing crowds already; two jugglers, what seemed to be a fortune-teller, and many horsemen.

"Some horse-traders, perhaps," Qerlak wondered aloud.

"And possibly horse-thieves," Fennet muttered in reply, adding "Some of those dancers seem rather attractive."

Suddenly Seldom Chased had vanished from the wall-walk.

Qerlak decided to descend and mingle with the crowds as well. Most folk saw him coming and bowed their greetings, but he overheard plenty of talk, all to his liking. Vendors had goods, the Rom called out games of chance, and more than one stall in three featured food. The crowd continued to grow as the morning passed, and Qerlak overheard many guesses and rumors about what would be seen in the next few days. Most comments concerned the first afternoon's judging, but others expected this or that fellow to do well in the bouts. It was even rumored that the seeress Galethiel would be there.

"And of course," he heard more than once, "Milord Barleybane shall win the joust." Qerlak would have paid to own their confidence in the matter.

At noon, a winded horn prompted those interested in the various first-day contests to funnel into the courtyard of Mon-Crulbagh. Prompted by a strange sensation at seeing so many people making toward his keep, Qerlak returned to the gatehouse and reviewed them.

Many peasants passed by with wondering obeisance and whispered greetings. A few tradesmen from Bultarr-r greeted their lord respectfully, including the most recent, a hawker, introduced by the blacksmith. He brought a hooded merlin to show at the fair, on his wrist. Qerlak complimented the man, and vaguely committed to seeing him hunt with it soon.

Both his manor-owners greeted Qerlak with all the pomp their middling stations could muster and passed more time than he wanted complimenting themselves through him. Prospects of the heightened profits they expected pleased them mightily.

"If there is no further trouble, Argens forbid."

Qerlak settled for a small smile with a steady look, and they took the chance to end the interview.

To his pleasure, several unfamiliar faces passed Qerlak's gaze as well, minor merchants and vendors from neighboring knighthoods; a few gypsies wandered through, including a dark-eyed maid on Seldom's arm escorted like a court lady.

"A simply marvelous day for a fair, milord!" Chased boomed in the full vigor of his best humor.

"And getting better, it seems," Qerlak nodded back to another burst of laughter from his friend.

Among the rest, Qerlak noted a slender elven pioneer with a longbow and one scar traversing the length of his face, faded and almost attractive as he retained full vigor in his spare frame. Several young lads in a roaming band raced through, apparently let loose from mother-strings for the day. Spezh and the guards stopped several strangers bearing arms here and there, evidently come early for the bouting events; they peace-bonded their weapons and were allowed through. Qerlak saw several black Elves, less rare in the southerly baronies, including one in the company of two white Elves, whom Qerlak remembered with a smile as the threesome who turned in Severyn Illfellow. All these and many more made ingress to Mon-Crulbagh.

The afternoon events consisted of an endless series of judgments, for crops, livestock, flowers and other crafts. The two manor owners held pride of place, either pointing the finger themselves or assigning close landholders to serve as proxy in cases where they were competing. Grumbling at that state of affairs was constant, clearly audible and sometimes pithy, but this was the custom.

Sitting his chair atop the reviewing stand, Qerlak found it the furthest thing from boring. He could feel the mood of his people. The peasants took this very seriously, and even more so as it was the first contest they had held in several years. Old claims to fame stood or fell, and new prodigies were found in equal measure. The only item of real note, to Qerlak's eyes, was the unexpected number of clay pots and other crockery; not of the highest quality but certainly ample in quantity.

Before midafternoon, some of the boy-gang ran into the courtyard yelling that a plate-armored knight was coming up the main road, bearing the sign of the jewel-collared boar on his standard.

"The house of Beryllian!" Fennet exclaimed. "What can have gone wrong?"

"Be of good cheer, castellan," Qerlak advised. "Prepare a meal for our guest, then see if you can locate Seldom Chased. He may be, ahm, napping in his room." Qerlak checked his attire, and after a moment's indecision, sent one of the boys to ask Galethiel's presence. His companions watched him go as if to the gallows, and the time stretched on too long as Qerlak wondered why now, of all times, there should come an important message from his overlord.

He stepped up to greet the knight as he dismounted and felt the grip of a fellow warrior. "Welcome to Mon-Crulbagh, Sir Tancrad Coss. Will you do the honor to sit my board and refresh yourself? As you can see, we are celebrating this week."

"Thank you," Coss replied, not committing to any course of action yet as his eyes tried to take in everything. Before he could speak further, Seldom Chased approached, in full attire and wearing the medallion of his office; as always, his entrances created a marvelous, theatrical effect.

"Sir Coss, may I introduce Sir Seldom Chased, a knight of my service, the Captain of the Western Marches of Mon-Crulbagh. Sir Chased, here is Greatknight Beryllian's closest vassal, Sir Tancrad Coss."

The two knights clapped arms in that friendly, competitive way; a mortal Man and immortal Elf, they gazed and grinned for a long moment.

"You asked for me, Qerlak?" Everyone turned to regard the red-haired mage, in turquoise robes, jeweled headband and the Staff of Anun-Re in hand. No one in the courtyard stood within ten steps of her path.

"Sir Coss, may I introduce my good friend and companion of long acquaintance, the mage Galethiel."

Coss bowed stiffly and his eyes told Qerlak much, perhaps that he had overplayed his hand here. Few Elven nobles were comfortable around mages, yet Coss seemed especially alarmed.

"Within, sir, I beg you, and let us hear your news only after a toast. I think you will find the beer interesting. Fennet, it is time; tap the first keg and let us see if my mad scheme has met with any success."

Just moments later, Sir Coss' news was before them.

"Coming here!" Fennet cried, the beer pitcher still in hand, "and arriving in four days or less!" He took a deep breath and tried to compose himself. "How many, er, in your lord's party?"

"I would expect no more than ten," Coss responded. "Including the—the others."

Qerlak was afire with curiosity, but it wouldn't do to show too much interest. "We shall welcome them to our final feast. A fitting ending to the celebrations here."

"Excellent to hear, milord Barleybane. And I'm sure the entertainment will be quite suitable."

"Entertainment." Qerlak stupidly repeated. "Ah. Yes. Of course. Of course we shall have entertainment. No doubt." He exchanged an urgent glance with Fennet, then raised his tankard. "But to your health and that of our overlord, Greatknight Beryllian."

With the rest, Qerlak raised the tankard to his lips. Normally it would have been only polite to offer a choice of wine, but he was too proud, too eager to know how his labors had prospered. The nose told him much, but the final test was always on the tongue and throat.

Qerlak took a long pull, let it slide down the gullet, and rested his cup, thanking Argens with eyes closed as he waited for the others to speak.

"Such a soft taste," Chased remarked, "I vow, 'tis more like honey mead than the bite of beer."

"But the kick is clear!" Coss replied with unwonted enthusiasm. "I can tell," sipping again, "it would not take many of these to put a man on his backside."

"My first effort," Qerlak said with diffidence, "I suspected it would not have the bitterness you come to expect. But on balance, successful I believe."

"Really good," Galethiel said and they smiled to each other more broadly than in the past fortnight.

"Milord," Fennet put in, "the final judging, they are calling for you outside."

The sun headed down, and the ceremonious and mixed honor of selecting the Best Animal in Show from the various fauna winners fell to the lord of the foef.

As Qerlak reached the top of the reviewing stand, he saw an assortment of leashed or caged animals in a rough row before him. Not a single cow or calf, as would befit a wealthier, less disrupted district. But there were several sheep, a goat, three large pigs (or hogs, Qerlak could never tell for certain), some waterfowl in reed cages, and one poor fellow on the far end trying without perfect success to control a young riding lizard.

Fennet stepped in smoothly "If I might offer advice, milord? The sow next to the black sheep is a simply splendid animal. And of course, that would make its owner very proud." He pointed to the older of the two manor owners, standing together with exactly the right body language to suggest a wager.

Qerlak's almost habitual distrust of his castellan's political acumen reared its head. To cover his indecision, he called for Skeggs.

Emerging from his busy kitchen, the castle cook approached and before his lord could even phrase the question, Skeggs' eye lit upon a lovely pea-hen with a well-groomed sheen, one of three presented by a poor widow from the interior. Unlike the other contestants, the woman held the animal in her arms like a cat.

"Argens' Loins," he swore in admiration, "this would be the very touch I need for the final feast!" Skeggs turned to the woman and made her an offer for the bird on the spot.

Qerlak knew opportunity when Argens beat him over the head with it. "I declare this lovely hen the Best in Show," he announced, presenting the astonished woman with a sack of feed large enough to raise half a dozen hens next season. The native peasantry roared its approval, and then the talk of food swept the crowd out to the fairgrounds beyond the castle wall to seek dinner.

Fennet invited Coss to review how his horse had been stabled, and then to visit his room. Galethiel waved in a friendly way and returned to her tower: Cecil and Spezh went with the crowd, and Ondaii had been working on something all day as usual. Qerlak turned to thank Skeggs, and then found himself for a moment completely alone on the judging platform in a nearly empty courtyard. The increased space and quiet brought on a moment of clarity, and the new lord saw several things in quick succession by the westering shadows of the courtyard, that were to stay with him in the days to come.

From the bailey window above the gate-house, the silhouette of Hitaelseran looked out on the crowds below; near the inner keep, the skirl of boys spun wildly in a game of half-tag, half-war; next to a table of local wares judged earlier, a young black human in worn but once colorful clothing examined a piece of crockery as if musing; a stranger in traveling cloak complimented Qerlak on the strength of the keep and asked politely for a tour, which the knight absently refused; and from out on the sward, Seldom Chased roared with laughter as one of the gypsies sang a song with two meanings.

⊕ ⊕ ⊕

s Cecil awakened him, Qerlak immediately realized he needed to ration his drinking better than Seldom's urgings had led him to the previous night. But sampling and celebrating his own brewing had proven an irresistible lure: truly, Sir Chased's ability to drink was beyond belief. The mortal had put down at least five tankards, then bellowed a laugh before walking off without the slightest stagger to bed, his companion the dark-eyed gypsy girl almost draped across one arm. Qerlak's way to bed was unaccompanied; just as well, for his gait wove diagonally across the hall like a leaf in a contrary breeze.

He came downstairs for breakfast, and instead got to chew on a half-dozen complaints regarding the clandestine "roaming" of the gypsy band in and around the foef. Visitors and staff had been waiting his presence to lodge their tales of missing items. Wildly popular for their entertainments, the Rom were decidedly less loved for their alleged sticky fingers. Qerlak decided not to use his power to Detect Lies on just these plaintiffs: in fact, he earnestly wished to avoid making a decision of any kind if he could.

"I advise you to speak with their leader, if they have one, and soon, milord." Fennet put in as he staved off the last of the protesters and shoved a bit of a meal before the knight. Qerlak mused whether it was too early to go back to bed. "One of the night-guards also reported seeing a light, burning in the swamp westward. It was out before Spezh could confirm it."

Qerlak looked up at his castellan while chewing and did not speak for a time. He suddenly felt much less sleepy.

"Probably nothing," Fennet offered.

Qerlak felt an irresistible surge of hilarity at that and spit a bit of food back onto the table. After a few moments of choking and chuckling, he managed to reply, "Probably."

The morning's events comprised some horsemanship displays—the Rom were marvelously skilled—and then the long-awaited pike evolution. Sitting on the reviewing stand, Qerlak felt both excited and helpless, as his peasant-levy led by Cecil took the field. The crowd from Mon-Crulbagh, who knew the four-dozen men in the formation, reacted with affected boredom touched, he thought, with a bit of inner jealousy. The young knight also scanned the visitors; many showed no interest, but some took a more serious view. These villeins bore, not spears or motley implements, but fifteen-foot pikes with spear-heads the length of a broadsword. They moved slowly, but without major error, through the evolutions signaled by Cecil (who was still struggling to hold the full-size weapon steady).

The quarter-turn and half-turns went well, and Qerlak realized his hands were clenching his chair-arms as they approached the finale. Splitting into halves, the pikemen marched to opposite sides of the field, then turned, lowered their weapons and charged each other—interpenetrating neatly between the rows! The crowd sighed and everyone appreciated the maneuver with applause. On an instinct, Qerlak looked up at the donjon window over the gate, where the sun showed Hitaelseran clearly; and clearly, he was impressed.

"Dekentar Spezh," he gestured the guard captain closer and then lowered his voice. "Please invite Sir Hitaelseran to join us this afternoon; with an escort of honor, of course."

"Of course, sir," returned Spezh and stepped off to the walls.

Later, Qerlak saw the prisoner walking around the edge of the courtyard, keeping away from everyone except his guard two steps behind. Seldom Chased also saw him as he emerged from the inner bailey, and with his usual candor he called out a greeting to him, between equals, as if they were long-lost friends. Before Hitaelseran could do more than nod warily, he was getting his arm pumped in comradeship and a slap on the back hard enough to knock the wind from him. Chased leaned

147

in, no doubt to murmur another bawdy jest, and then was off to the outer fair grounds with a roaring laugh, leaving the prisoner behind to gape and recover. Qerlak grinned, thinking things could have gone worse. Welcome to Mon-Crulbagh, my former enemy, he thought. At least, he hoped.

That afternoon brought on the archery contest, and the targets were set up before lunch was done. The best three shooters, or all who hit the bullseye once, advanced to the next greater distance until a winner was found. Several men from Mon-Crulbagh proved to be adequate shots, given time to aim and three arrows per flight; but a fellow from Colter seemed about to take the prize at forty paces when the slender pioneer stood in, having quietly passed until now.

As the crowd cheered in appreciation, Qerlak signaled as always for his castellan.

"I hear his name is Garuth, milord- Garuth Tredwater", Fennet advised. "The staff say he's a long-time swamp hunter who hardly ever comes onto dry land or in public view. But he loves to shoot."

Without warm-up or preamble, like a man used to bowing from childhood, Garuth nocked and placed two of his first three in the bullseye at forty paces: the Colter man hit one, and the others failed to do better than the third stripe. At forty-five paces, Garuth again centered two of three, while his opponent just missed on all of his shots. Ignoring the loud cheers, Garuth motioned a request that the target be moved back. Qerlak nodded, and the show began.

At fifty paces, still without pausing or stopping, Garuth smoothly hit the bullseye once and the second stripe twice. At fifty-five paces, he duplicated the feat. After each flight, the roars of the crowd were deafening. At sixty paces, Garuth suddenly broke rhythm to pause just before releasing: a second later, Qerlak on the reviewing stand felt a slight breeze. Three seconds passed, and then the bowman released and struck the

148

center, following with his accustomed fluidity by another, and then a third on target. Truly, the knight thought, Argens must have guided his arm this day: it was as if no one else were there besides him, just the target and his bow, and the occasional breath of wind.

At sixty-five paces, his second arrow nicked the edge of the target and traveled on, technically a miss. The crowd sighed, and Garuth paused, but then drew his third, closed his eyes, held his breath, and released—another bullseye. Nothing could stop the Mon-Crulbagh crowd after that, as they swept in to raise the embarrassed yeoman on their shoulders, parading him around the fairgrounds before depositing him triumphantly and without ceremony before Qerlak's seat.

"I have never in my life witnessed such marksmanship, Citizen Tredwater," Qerlak said warmly, "though I gather from these others, it is nothing unusual." They cheered their man again as Qerlak turned to take the prize Fennet brought out. As he saw the strong yew bow with inlaid handle-grips of ivory, the knight inwardly blessed his castellan for seeing to a worthy prize. Garuth accepted it without a word, turning to the crowd and holding it aloft for them to see, provoking another roar.

As most of the crowd swirled away to dinner, a second, less formal contest for sling marksmen began. This contest bore no prize other than pride for the winner. But as Qerlak turned to leave, he noticed one of the boys from yesterday's play-pack, fired by Tredwater's example, had picked up an unused sling. Whirling a stone in it, clearly for the first time, he threw wildly and missed the target at ten paces. Nothing daunted, he quickly tried again, and on his third stone he actually struck the inner ring. With a cry of joy, the boy stooped down and began assembling a pile of stones large enough to supply a small war. Qerlak watched him, reflecting that the levy of Mon-Crulbagh featured slingers, cheap and easy by comparison to bowmen.

"These fairs forebode the future" he remarked to Fennet, as he stepped down from the reviewing stand.

"And speaking of foreboding, sir," said the castellan, "where has Sir Seldom been all day?"

It was after dusk when Chased showed himself, looking refreshed as if he had slept the entire time, but with his ebon-eyed escort in evidence to deny it. Qerlak braced him for information, and after only a few jests and a bit of barely-veiled boasting, the knight revealed that the leader of the gypsy troupe was Tel-Woman Messina, the fortune seer.

Strolling for the first time through the center of the gypsy camp, Qerlak was struck by the celebratory mood of the entertainers around him. One man played the squeeze-keys alone by a fire, and his fellows passing by stepped to its rhythm as if the tune gave them the power to walk. The tamboor-dancers shared a small stage crowded with locals, mainly men; they smiled the wider as the few womenfolk frowned. Everyone stopped when the rail-thin shirtless fellow stuffed a rapier completely down his own throat, then pulled it out to slice a tossed orange in three before it hit the ground.

Qerlak easily found the fortune-lady's wagon from the sign of the crystal ball hanging off it, and was ushered inside after only the briefest of delays. The wagon's interior seemed much smaller than it did from the outside, in part because the shelves on every wall were deep and crammed with all manner of nameless serendipity. Despite the cramped quarters, Tel-Woman Messina easily fit, an impossibly-old looking human, withered yet hardened like the walking stick she held for balance. As Qerlak stepped up and in, she rose and bowed to him with deference.

"Greetings, Scion of the Drinking Clan. If you will but be seated, we can begin the reading." She gestured to the tarot-table between them, but Qerlak shook his head.

"No, mother, I am here on business, I am afraid, not pleasure. There have been several complaints—"

"Your future, milord, is my first business," returned the gypsy. "Fate has brought you here."

Qerlak was so struck by the theatrical nature of this reply that he could not immediately think of a response. Apparently like many elderly folk she was going to be stubborn, so he reluctantly decided to aim for the shorter path, and took a seat. He noticed for the first time the scent of spiced incense, and in the silence heard the hiss of a single tambourine, from the dancers next door. He silently muttered a prayer to Argens as the ambience of the low-lit wagon crept over him.

The gypsy woman produced a thick deck of large tarot cards but set them on her side of the table first, instead reaching across to take his palm. She peered down into it at very close range, and the Elven knight prepared inwardly for some quip about his expected long life: but instead Messina suddenly flipped it half-up and scrutinized the edge, below his smallest finger.

"So many crosses," she muttered, as if to herself, and Qerlak responded without thinking.

"My mother used to tell me they were all Signs of Hope." He smiled, but when the gypsy woman looked up sharply and caught his gaze, he felt certain he had offended her.

Yet she only nodded and said "And so they are, milord. So they are."

Messina swung a hooked lamp closer to the table, but then turned it further down and slid the tarot across. When Qerlak nervously and quickly cut the deck once, she offered a thin smile and used a table-knife to push the cards back in his direction without touching them.

"Until you feel comfortable with them, milord."

"Are you sure you have that much time?" Qerlak again spoke instantly, trying for humor. "I am immortal, you know."

Messina held his gaze for several seconds without response. Qerlak had never had his tarot read before—things in his native Inmark were much too quiet and civilized to show any appetite for such low pursuits. This was starting to look like the long way home, after all. But he was already in it, so he shuffled and cut the deck several times, announcing they were ready without feeling he was.

She turned the cards in the pattern known as the Great Wheel, and Qerlak strained to recall what the various positions were supposed to mean. The first one down, he was fairly sure, was supposed to represent him: Qerlak's heart sank when he saw the harlequin with his brightly-colored balls. Covering that card crosswise, Messina laid a face-card, a mounted knight with a large sword; above it, a man with no face and a glowing aura all about him, and below another man with a walking-stave and simple robe. He would not have spoken for any money, but Messina herself broke the silence as she paused mid-way through the wheel.

"So many Trumps," she muttered, "the way, it is difficult to see."

Tempted by this opening, Qerlak could not resist, though he felt he was breaking the rules somehow. "Am I the Clown, then?" he asked, tapping the first card.

Messina looked up quickly, but not angrily, then flickered a smile at the knight. "Milord, the Querent's Card holds not the Clown, but the Juggler of Forces. It indicates that a balance is being maintained. Or must be."

Qerlak nodded, not knowing whether to be abashed or relieved, and Messina looked back to the cards, once again musing as if to herself.

"And Crossing the Querent is the Knight of Staves, meaning likely a single person… probably of noble rank, coming from the realm of Air. Yet the Crown holds the Seer, and the Root has the Pilgrim. So many forces, such great consequence, it extends beyond… a Juggling act indeed." The gypsy licked her lips and drummed her fingers on the deck for several moments. "Ah well, let us see what lies in the past before conclud--"

152

And then she flipped over the fifth card placing it to the left of the first; Qerlak saw it was some scene of the night-time sky, with stars and other bodies, but also the sun.

The gypsy gasped and drew her hand back as if she had petted a snake. "The Cosmos! Itself- the All-That-Is! Too much power, this lies beyond me. I have no strength to understand." Messina looked up to Qerlak with respect bordering on fear. Was she sensing their adventure into the realm of dreams last fall?

She seemed to meditate over the set for what felt like an hour, as Qerlak, completely caught in the spell of the reading, held himself as still as if he were hiding from an enemy. And perhaps he was.

But eventually, Messina rolled out the remaining cards. To the right of the first card, a man working over an anvil with a hot fire in the background; to the far right and further down, at last a simpler card with 5 swords on it, which Qerlak dearly hoped meant something more mundane. Messina looked down on these with outward calm, then tapped the space above the sword-card and indicated to Qerlak that he should place the final tarot there. With a slight fumble, he flipped over a card with two coins on it, and sat back feeling suddenly tired.

The silence was interminable. For a few minutes, Messina did not move at all, but Qerlak could see her eyes darting back and forth across the table like a frog on a hot rock. Presently the gypsy woman closed her eyes and her breathing slowed; yet the Elven knight knew she was far from asleep.

"You have faced danger," Messina announced, and Qerlak began to feel better at such standard fare. But then; "from undying peril in frozen winter lands, to quickly burning death on the glassy face of the desert."

Now *that* was a bit close for comfort! Qerlak tried to breathe normally as the woman continued.

"Your companions pursue scattered dangers beyond this world, yet you remain here, near the site of perils—ah, such trials! The home of dangers *undreamed* of!" Qerlak realized that his forehead was thickly sheathed with sweat, though the wagon was not stuffy.

"You are Crowned by the Seer," the gypsy declared, but still speaking half to herself, "he who knows more than you, and an adversary. By the Root, you draw strength from the Pilgrim. A story begins, and you can be helped by helping a traveler."

She looked from the Cosmos in Qerlak's 'past' to the Forge lying in his 'future', but said nothing for a time. Qerlak, feeling ever more in need of some reassurance, pointed to the penultimate card and asked "What does this one do?"

"That is the Qerent's Despair, what you have most to fear. It is the Five of Blades."

"And it means?"

"Defeat."

Qerlak sat back on that a moment, but something in him took fire and he rankled at the idea that these cards would dictate to him.

"So this," he said, thrusting his hand towards the final card, "must be the Querent's Hope--"

But in his haste he stabbed a bit harder than he wanted, actually touching the card and moving it two inches. With a rush of real fear, Qerlak saw another card beneath the one with two coins- he had accidentally taken two from the top of the deck. Underneath, he caught just a glimpse of a pole of some kind, perhaps the Ace of Staves. But he didn't dare to touch the deck again, and now Messina was staring at the place with fixed intensity.

"I'm sorry, I've ruined it--"

"No, milord, that cannot be. With the tarot, there are no accidents. And nine cards, in a way it is fitting...the Two of Nobles signals clearly a harmonious change. You Hope, lord, to pass the Forge's test, and avoid the threatened defeat, of course. But how? Your cards give us the answer." And here Messina pushed the coin-card further aside, revealing not a staff, but the base of a balance-scale, beneath it, another Trump.

"Justice can harness unprincipled power, and brings to heel even superior force, through a trial." Qerlak sat in wonder at the gypsy-woman's words, and only after a moment realized his jaw was slightly open.

"You have faced danger indeed, milord. Now, you celebrate your triumphs, and you hope for even greater prosperity. But remember, Scion of the Drinking Clan, Argens grants nothing to one who can brave nothing."

She reached over with her claw-like finger and tapped the Barleybane crest on Qerlak's gauntlet, the Argensian flame surmounting a hand crushing grain.

"Argens tests by *fire*! And fire burns until it is put out! Face the triple tests of Fire, lord of the swamp domain; then, you may look to your laurels for a time." With an almost corny pause, Messina stared at her guest before turning the lamp back up.

Qerlak coughed nervously and belatedly reached into his pouch to cross her palm with silver. "I thank you for your wisdom," he managed, "and now, if I might speak with you on the subject of these complaints?"

"My people live to entertain, Lord," Messina croaked matter-of-factly. "Jests can be taken ill, but thievery is another matter. Our law prescribes death for the thief who is caught," she said, laying just the slightest emphasis before continuing, "as it calls down the curse for any who unjustly accuses one of the Brotherhood of the Horse. We do not make this law: it is Fate, which to deny is to invite the curse."

Qerlak felt as if he were fencing with an unfamiliar weapon. "Can you be counted on to reprimand your people?"

"You have but to present the name of any thieves to me, milord, and they will be slain. And they all know this. I will not have my clan trample upon hospitality such as you have shown."

Qerlak, a bit shocked, briefly mulled over whether less drastic alternatives could be impressed upon her, and decided likely not. With a wash of emotions, he left the wagon.

He saw again the gaiety and vigor of the band's entertainments. Nothing had changed: the tamboor-dancers gathered the tossed coins and threw back kisses, the squeeze-keys played even faster than before, and two men lit torches with flames spewing from their mouths. These were mortals, traveling without a lord's protection subject to every kind of accident or risk on the road and the vagary of prejudice whenever they arrived. Their penalty for theft was death. Yet every day they risked dying, to steal another day from the world. The obligation would find no home among these people, and Qerlak knew who would take the blame, in the end, if anything happened. Another ball to juggle.

As he walked clear of the Rom wagons his eye slewed to the western horizon at the flare of a small, distant, yet clearly visible fire in the darkness. As it burned, the knight recalled Messina's words. The triple tests of Fire, she had said. For a few moments he watched, undecided: only Reptile Men could be burning something out there with impunity. Did they mean to attack so many gathered humans, after the lessons he had given them? Unlikely—and yet Reptile Men didn't even like fire, did they? So was it a signal? Perhaps Seldom... but no, he'd disappeared again for the night. Tomorrow, Qerlak thought, tomorrow he would get to it.

Foef of Mon-Crulbagh

The Greatknight's procession rolls past sunset, seemingly forever downhill into a new land. The Halfling in the bar-wagon stands staring east, sensing the large forest in the distance that she can no longer see well. Life of a new order pulses there, and in the gorges to the north with a recently empty riverbed. When they cross the second bridge here, her companions note the lights of the nearby town. But she marks that the water level of this stream is quite high, running above the gentle banks to either side and making the grass look like reeds. Something is wrong to the east, a thing out of the natural order. Once, she catches a scent on the breeze from that quarter, a musk of something never smelt before, acrid and hard and recent. Then it is gone.

Before the light is completely faded from the quartz stone, the mage's acolyte tries again to infuse it with a new spell. He labors in his mistresses' workroom, careful to keep his effort far from the powders, vials, and other gems here as she sleeps. He so wants to impress and surprise her. The great book of spells indicates this is possible, to put the power of Fire into the stone already holding Light. The young man clears his hair, reviews the language in the book's open page once more, takes up the stone and invokes while passing his other hand above it. The energy flows from him, the room brightens slightly with an orange, flame-like glow between his fingers; for an instant he fears he will release the spell now, instead of trapping it within the stone. He focuses, groans with effort, and forces the budding magic down, further down into the gem. Removing his covering hand, the mage's assistant sees the stone, still yellow with Light but now spiced with dancing motes of Fire, and grins at his rare success.

What there is to be gained, by placing a spell such as this within the Light-stone, he cannot guess. The book listed the possibility, and he gauged the work within his reach. Now he feels energized and happy; placing the stone in a safe spot, he throws open the shutters and breathes in the night air while looking east across the grounds. Wait until his sleeping mistress sees the result of his labors. The stars seem to shine down in approval, and by their light the young elf remarks only a few persons still moving about within the castle. One, wearing a traveling cloak, is being escorted out by one of the guards. The young Elf thinks proudly that his job as guardian is already being done.

By the flickering light of the bonfire, the enormous muscled Reptile Man heaves the body of his last opponent into the flames and accepts the grunts and roars of the tribe as the tribute of his victory. There is another body already there, and tomorrow's opponent looks across the fire to him with a toothy grin. All of them look east to the foef where the warm-bloods celebrate in their own way. The idea of visiting their gathering never occurs to his dull brain. His place is here, his victory is here. But a part of the monster's brain wonders, if there might be some other purpose to what they do tonight.

A visitor hanging about the edges of the fair seems to have no special purpose; losing a little money at the shuffle-shell table, sampling a meat stick and certainly not looking for anyone in particular. Gradually, his path brings him closer to the gate of the foef, where guests are leaving as the few castle residents return for the evening. The lord of Mon-Crulbagh does not note this visitor's bow more than those of anyone else as he strides in with furrowed brows and hands behind his back.

Presently one last guest exits just as the portcullis is lowered for the night. This Elf stands at the edge of the moat, twitching at his traveling cloak and looking about with an amateur's skill, the visitor thinks, even as he gives him the secret sign. Noting and returning it, the man at least contains himself well enough to walk a random path over toward the judging platform, vaguely like that of the visitor, that brings them nearer through the departing crowds without haste. They lean together, exchange a few whispered words, then nod as if well-met acquaintances and move off opposite. The visitor climbs the platform, pats the thin silken cloak in his pack and gazes up at the foef to his east

158

now, marking the tower in the back where he will accomplish his mission soon. If all goes well, the witch will awaken only long enough to feel the pain.

$$\oplus \oplus \oplus$$

Foef of Mon-Crulbagh:
Reclamation Festival 3rd Serpent 2002 ADR

ttacked! Qerlak snapped awake to shouts and the impact of bodies driving him deeper into the mattress. Cursing, he struggled unable to see more than muscled forms on top of him: then one assailant kneed him inimitably in the upper thigh- and even as he grunted with the pain, Qerlak wheezed with laughter, to know his elder brothers had arrived.

Swearing with a rage less than half-feigned, he rose up vengefully and threw both down, cursing them for effeminates as he used to do. For their part, the dark pair of bravos draped themselves in the sheets and imitated Nanna, crying for the guard in high shrieks, then fell back weak with hysteria. Seizing the advantage, Qerlak beat them each soundly with the bolster until they swore their fealty forever at the top of their lungs, just before the real guard arrived indeed. The two soldiers surveyed the wrack wordlessly, and then looked to their lord for orders. Qerlak waved them off as he fought to catch his breath.

"What, men, haven't you seen a messy bedroom before?"

The last guard to depart paused only to say "Surely, sir, over in Sir Chased's quarters." Both the soldiers had a good chuckle about that, and Qerlak missed them with the bolster on purpose as they retreated.

He hugged his brothers fiercely, then the punching started up. Both Mo'lem and Larel were taller and rangier than their younger brother, having spent so much time together it hardly mattered which one was speaking.

"When?"

"Late last night. We got up at dawn, and had to beg that castellan—"

"Such a stickler!"

"To give us the chance to arrive, ahm, unannounced."

"Family tradition, we told him."

"True enough!" Qerlak chuckled, adding "I may have to review security procedures, it would appear they're letting just anyone in."

He turned to put on his clothes, but spun back when they both hissed in alarm.

"What is it?"

"Those scars!"

"How did you possibly, I mean what—"

Qerlak looked a moment into their faces, these grown Elves older than he, now shocked back to his juniors by the evidence of his past adventures. Neither one had ever fought in a war— their sire, the Greatknight, forbade them all from participating in the campaign two years ago. Qerlak gazed down at his latticed chest, more than a match for the back, and for the first time felt like the eldest of his father's sons. He shrugged and donned his tunic without further comment; with his old wounds out of sight the brothers recovered some of their usual good humor.

In moments, the two of them fell to the more serious business of praising their brother's foef.

"Argens' home-fire, it's huge!" cried Mo'lem.

"Well, land is cheaper on the fringes than the Inmark," Qerlak demurred.

"Father sends his regrets that he cannot be here," put in Larel, "But we pleaded to go so loudly that—"

"He swore he was glad to be rid of us both!"

Qerlak looked on his brothers with a ferment of happiness and longing. Except for that one brief visit on the way to take up Mon-Crulbagh last fall, he hadn't lived with his family for nearly a decade now. The pleasure he felt at this surprise hummed inside him.

"Good news," he announced, "you're in time for the hunt today."

"Faugh!" said one with a wrinkled nose, and the other, "What carking sport could be had in the swamps of Mon-Crulbagh?"

As he pulled on his hunting togs, Qerlak informed them dryly, "You would be surprised."

Outside the hunting party gathered in the early morning light; nearly all were mounted on riding lizards, including a huge but docile brute for the lord of the foef. Seldom staggered forth in some disarray, bawling for a page to saddle Mystic, and the elder Barleybane brothers saw to their own horses as well.

Cecil and a pair of the mounted horsebowmen prepared to accompany Qerlak personally; the new hawker from Bultarr-r was also present, on foot with a lad who carried an extra falcon. The manor-owning families were represented as well, and Qerlak groaned inwardly to think that even here social purposes would be served, not simply martial prowess. Belatedly he wished he had thought to invite Garuth Tredwater. But the hunter was gone from the festival within an hour of the contest's end, back into the endless marsh.

Yet pushing through the early morning crowd came a strapping peasant elf with a broad smile, two harpoons and a necklace of crocodile teeth.

"Hail, milord!" called Chefron Gillthruster with more enthusiasm than deference, stepping around the question of whether he had actually been invited. "Shall you settle for lesser game, or will we seek an Elder Maw?"

Qerlak smiled and waved for the peasant Elf to accompany the group. "Argens will provide us with suitable sport, citizen," he said, hoping inwardly that it would be so. As the hunt party set out through the castle gate, Qerlak could see the gypsy wagons already in full swing; a game of shells, the cart of spiced meats, a spinning wheel decorated with the trumps from the tarot deck Messina threw the previous evening. Without conscious thought, he motioned them out towards the site of last night's flame.

There was much evidence of fire and track—Reptile Man spoor—at a spot half a league from the edge of the fairgrounds. Most of the hunting party, unaware of any such presence until then, stared and started to mutter uneasily.

"I tire of such simple sport," Qerlak said, in an effort to break the mood. "Let us seek elsewhere." Moving off, he found the party more than willing to follow his lead, and suddenly felt the weight of that trust. If a juggler tossed up stones the size of his head instead of brightly colored leather balls, how long could he sustain the act? Qerlak fell to musing on the possible meaning of many things, even as he tried to keep another, very mundane flavor of balance atop this hillock of plodding flesh between his legs.

The two-day expedition began tolerably well. The beaters flushed a mountain cat early on the first day, but no one could bring it down before it escaped. The hawker demonstrated the usefulness of his raptors several times, unhooding them in turn and pointing toward a partridge, then a mallard and later still a large quail: each time, death flashed off his wrist to climb, stoop and strike, then to be fed and recovered by his boy.

In camp on the first night the atmosphere was spooky yet uneventful; it was clear the brothers were already taken with the challenge of this environment. Qerlak looked at them as they talked of home over roasted fowl and heather brew, and realized that he was already well accustomed to this place. Mon-Crulbagh was not like foef Barleybane at all, and seeing his brothers here reminded Qerlak of that constantly. In one way, their home was the complete version, dressed up and clear and prosperous. But in another view, this swampy, low land was the true foef, for which his childhood seat with all the finery had been a dress rehearsal. Qerlak was making things real here, creating a difference for others; he had reason to be proud. Long after the guests had rolled up, he sat in the shadows of the passing watchman, staring into the embering campfire and wondering about the old gypsy woman's words.

Foef of Mon-Crulbagh: Reclamation Festival 4th Serpent 2002 ADR

arly on the second afternoon of the hunt, the party stumbled across the lair of a Behemoth Turtle. Qerlak heard the shouting from the west and dismounted to wade through thigh-high water toward the fighting.

As large as a hay wagon and able to snap a human chest in its beak, these creatures were much prized for their meat as well as the shell. Even its skin was too hard for the arrows and spears that flew, and aroused to defend its home the monster could charge faster than its foes for a short distance through the muddy terrain. Seldom and Chefron were closest and both quite game for the battle. Chased took its bites on his plate armor without injury, while Chefron stabbed manfully into the crack of its shell. Between them, they essayed its demise after some unseating, splashing and minor bloodshed. It took another three hours to harvest the beast, its former defence serving as a hauling-tray for its meat, hooked behind two lizards. Already close to dinner time, Qerlak decided this was a fitting end to the expedition and signaled for home.

The march back barely began when Chefron called out a warning, seeing ripple-signs on the water indicating a creature of some size. Qerlak, Seldom, and the bowmen were the closest this time and moved in; the young lord spotted a dark shape swimming smoothly and quickly through the shallows, rippling a tentacle, then another and another behind as it lazily fled. With shouts of exhilaration, several in the party lobbed arrows or other projectiles; suddenly, something came to the surface that was large and clearly octopoid.

He could see nothing of bone beneath its skin, yet somehow it stood more than three feet above the water. Mo'lem and Larel swore aloud to see that it bore a crossed belt and brandished a wickedly-curved sword in one fingerless limb. The thing gave little time to mark further details: quickly surveying the group with a large, single eye it evidently made a sentient decision to retreat. In a flash it slipped beneath the water deeply enough to leave no ripple-trace.

The pursuit was half-hearted at best; eventually the return home resumed, spiced with exclamations and questions. Qerlak could see his brothers fully taken with wonder at the strange vitality, the sheer otherness of the Mon-Morteissk.

"You've seen that before?"

"No. Not that."

"What then?"

Qerlak pursed his lip as if to say the full list would take too long. "Reptile Men. Trolls. Gargoyles. A kind of mossy rug that moves slowly and destroys whatever it touches." He gave a tiny smile before adding, "And of course, there was the dragon, Semegorn."

"Liar!"

"There are no more dragons."

Qerlak pointed to the higher hills far north and a bit west in the lowering light of summer behind the group. "Well, there isn't one up there anymore, that's for certain." They clucked in disgust but Qerlak pulled down the mail coif to show the scar from neck to shoulder. "Got me right here."

Their faces as he rode told him a story. Fear, and a bit of jealousy, but not a shred of doubt. Qerlak had always been the truthful one, brothers can't forget.

"It's like the tales we used to tell each other."

"Yes. But those were about Argens. Not our baby brother!"

As the hunting party arrived back at the fairgrounds, all other activity came to a halt and the crowds gathered; everyone congratulated and feted Qerlak for slaying the Behemoth Turtle, as if he had done it all alone. The knight dismounted and cut off a nail from the monster's arm, publicly presenting it to Chefron Gillthruster in praise of his triumph: naturally, the bold Elven peasant was thrilled, and immediately compared it to his necklace at the middle. Another local hero, Qerlak thought. This is what we need, folks in Mon-Crulbagh believing they can do anything.

In all the to-do, Qerlak nearly missed Seldom Chased before he slipped off again.

"Captain, a word," the knight began carefully before walking him to one side from the diffusing crowd. "We have seen some... some campfires at night, recently, off to our west."

"In the swamp, milord? Sooth, this is the first I had known, I thought that fire yesterday an old one. Worry not, this is my march and I shall ride forth at the next sign."

Warning bells of thought hit Qerlak so hard he nearly put his hands to his ears, but instead reached out grabbing his fellow-knight by the arm. "Let us, ahm, let us be sure of ourselves, Sir Chased," he managed, "Let me know before you ride out."

"Aye, milord, certes!"

Qerlak was so relieved that the man did not take it ill, he let him go with good grace. After all, there was no guarantee the fires would burn again, he thought. But the sight of the gypsy spinning-wheel put those ideas steadily down to death.

The evening celebrations were once again more fun than Qerlak could resist. The stories and drinking blended together in a happy haze. Tancrad Coss drank with relish and gawped at the good cheer of the hall, clearly unfamiliar with such informal jollity. Even Galethiel was seen spilling a little wine and laughing out loud at some joke of Spezh's. Qerlak tried to overhear the wit, but his brothers kept jostling him back in his seat for more

165

good-natured barbs about his remarkable companion. Since the first moment, neither one could take their eyes from her.

"Say, little brother, that's a pretty big staff she has over there."

"Can we assume, now, that your, eh, weaponry is up to the same level?"

"Does she own the tower, or the whole place, that's what I'd like to know."

Qerlak grinned tautly as he had when arm-wrestling, a challenge neither of his older siblings had made to him in a decade. "My brothers, one thing, let me tell you," he started, a bit thickly. "Two, actually. Two things, let me tell you. First off, that 'staff' you're both admiring—that staff she's holding? Do you know what happens, if either of you try to lay hands on it?"

He waited patiently, as they both stared at the staff and then back, still grinning but blank. Qerlak leaned in then and said, low and hard, "Boom. And she's just the same herself." That routed the grinning.

"So! Fellows, it's a free empire- here's the second thing—no slavery anymore. You say she's beautiful, and I won't say no. You think she and I share a bed, and I won't say anything. But if you're both so manly, why not walk up and kiss her yourselves?"

One more twin look across the room, and that was the prompt and decisive end of every bit of that. Qerlak wasn't sure any of them could have stood and walked without assistance at that point. His beer was indeed strong.

Suddenly, Qerlak reasoned he must have been asleep because he was laying on his pillow. His body reported no other hint that he'd had any rest at all: indeed, as he tried to focus on what Fennet was saying, he realized it was still the middle of the night.

Something about a fire.

He was forever fumbling at his ties and straps, getting nowhere with dressing for what seemed the longest time. Then he heard a distant bellow, as Chased called for his armor and horse. The thought of his Captain, riding out alone to investigate, put life in his blood and the skill born of desperation into his fingers.

Qerlak was better than half-dressed when he careened out to the battlement level. There it was, clearly burning off to the west, and by its light he thought he even made out tiny forms, bi-pedal and tailed. Mystic's neigh cut through the late-night din, and Qerlak hustled down the steps to intercept Seldom and remind him of his promise.

In the end, Qerlak with Chased, along with Cecil and Fennet agreed to go, and... yes, the knight decided, better to request Galethiel. Cecil ran to ask and carry back her response, and during the long wait, Qerlak was chagrined to see both his brothers up also. They neither needed permission nor asked, mounting up with just swords to come along. It would be quite embarrassing if she refused now.

The time dripped by and he had full leisure to dread the moment. But there she was at last, having taken the time only to dress in full regalia, and as impressive by the torchlight of the courtyard as anyone could hope; Nomen on her brow and the Staff of Anun-Re in her hand. Galethiel knew the value of appearances, Qerlak thought with a small smile, and felt better already.

"You look the same," he said quietly, his first private word since the raid from Pritaelseran.

Galethiel looked at him sharply, then grinned, "You still look terrible."

Up on his riding lizard then (the grooms had named her Bruna, he seemed to recall), and the expedition set off.

They rode out past the empty fairgrounds, the crowds in their own tents or the common ones provided to two sides. Just by random chance, the top tarot on the wheel of fortune was The Juggler. The ride was quiet, for the only ones who knew what to expect had nothing to add as they approached the camp ahead.

167

Qerlak's backside asked him if he hadn't done enough riding in the past few days, and Qerlak didn't have an answer.

By the time he came within hailing distance of the campfire, however, everyone could plainly see that it was empty; tracks of at least a dozen Reptile Men abounded, and the remains of raw meat and tubers were scattered about. On a patch of cleared dirt near the dying fire was scratched a crude stick figure of a man. Even as the party scanned about for signs, Cecil called out and pointed west, where another fire had been kindled about twenty furlongs away.

"A trap," grumbled Seldom Chased. A mystery, Qerlak thought to himself as he remounted and led the party forward.

At the second site, also abandoned, there were no signs of lengthy habitation—just crackling brushwood and claw-footed tracks. On the ground was scrawled what appeared to be a group of stick figures, and then one stick figure apart from them. Within moments, another fire appeared to the west, into the swamp proper by now.

"It's a signal," Galethiel mused, "they want one of us to go alone."

"A trap, as I said!" thundered Chased.

"It must be you they want, milord," said Fennet. "You cannot risk it, of course."

"Of course, I must," Qerlak calmly replied. "On my order, everyone is to advance only three hundred paces further and be ready to charge in, should I shout for you."

Seldom Chased entered into such a long, loud, unbroken and shocking string of curses that he had everyone's slack-jawed attention by the time he drew breath. "I demand, milord, I demand," he concluded, "on the strength of our mutual oath and charge you made to me, as Captain of your Outer Marches, that I be allowed to undertake this adventure!"

"I go alone." Qerlak repeated steadily.

"*WE* go alone!" Chased shouted, unmindful of the nonsensical outburst until Cecil and Fennet began to chuckle. "Milord" he added, somewhat diminished but with his face set in defiance.

And after some further argument and a good deal of neck-rubbing, it was so agreed.

The party rode only a little further, then Qerlak and Seldom dismounted to continue on foot. The steps of the paired paladins were the only sounds to break the midst of the night's darkest hour. Too far behind them, the rest of the party was lost in the ebon as if still at the castle. Ahead, the light of the third campfire framed the thin, slope-necked forms of reptilian figures that ranged agitatedly before it. Gradually, their muttered gutturals became audible.

Stepping fully into the fire-circle with Seldom at his side, Qerlak could see there were easily two dozen, maybe two score reptilian foes. They stood in a ragged half-circle, none on the near side of the flame anymore, a crude palette of coral and war-paint and scale, clutching clubs and shell-shields and lashing their tails in the grip of some powerful emotion. Qerlak employed his father's tactic once more, standing still and saying nothing as he weighed them. While they hissed and muttered and gestured among themselves, the knight realized, even outnumbering him as they did, the emotion they felt must be fear. They were standing up to him for some reason, but clearly would prefer not to.

One huge specimen, perhaps a leader, shambled forth a step and barked in garbled Southern, "You hold feast. You do game. Games for all Mon-Crulbagh. We do games too. We too!" He thumped his still-bleeding chest for emphasis and the others lashed and gibbered in assent.

"What do you want?" Qerlak asked cautiously, aware that at his side Seldom had gently drawn his blade.

"We too want game," gnashed the brute. "You fight, make veektarr soon. We, too, have champion. You fight ours. Make veektarr, winner all Mon-Crulbagh!"

"You expect the winner to fight one of you?" Qerlak asked, and even his blood on the bonfire-side ran cold.

"If no fight, not champion! Murk People live here too! We want games! No weapon, no armor, just fight for make champion." The adversary grinned wickedly then, and the knight figured him for the likely opponent. Qerlak surveyed the powerful tail, the cruel talons, the incisors and rippling back muscles as the leader turned to shout defiance to the tribe and hear their answer.

Seldom leaned in to murmur, "Sooth milord, nature has compensated these beasts well, for their lack of wit, it seems."

Qerlak did not bother to respond, his gaze falling instead to the blazing fire, and his memory of the triple tests. Could he really condemn a subject of his, unwitting, to fight this abomination, he wondered?

The Reptile Men would expect him to decide, not to consult with others or delay—if he did, they would lose some of that fear which was his best weapon. And as the time seemed to slow around him, Qerlak realized a simmering anger was growing inside; he was irked to think of refusing them. Were they not also his subjects, indeed? He had never looked at it that way before...

Raising his gaze, the Elven knight kept his voice calm. "I agree. Will your champion come to the foef, then, after tomorrow's bouting?" Smiling, he watched the big one squirm.

Finally, the Reptile Man grunted, "No—me no trust. You lord, keep word. You come here, alone, after make champion."

"You expect me to be the victor, then?"

The brute's face fell slack as if he'd been hit with a stone. "Yyaass, you veektarr," he croaked, "You lord."

Qerlak nodded once, then turned on his heel and left the encampment, followed after a moment by Seldom Chased, who for once had nothing to say.

"Sir Chased, will you keep this—"

"On my honor as a knight, milord, I shall tell no one, provided you swear in turn that tomorrow night I shall accompany you."

"Done."

The two came upon the waiting party, brushed off every question and returned to the foef. Qerlak finally fell into bed lacking perhaps two hours of dawn, and not knowing what to hope for on the morrow.

$$\oplus \oplus \oplus$$

Foef of Mon-Crulbagh: Reclamation Festival 5th Serpent 2002 ADR

How nice it would be, Qerlak thought, to awaken just once to his own body's rhythm, rather than clamor and cacophony. Outside his rooms and down the hall, the arguing voices included Chased and Fennet, and a woman's as well; his spirits sank as he once again stumbled to dress and dwelt on the possibilities.

Sure enough, this time the gypsy complaint was most serious. Someone had caught Seldom's companion wandering the halls wearing a "bauble" of jewelry from the unused trophy room. She denied all wrongdoing, claiming that it was a gift from her friend: Sir Chased unhesitatingly backed her story. By the time all the facts were stated, over a dozen folks had gathered, still in morning-robes, down in the main hall as the argument drifted into breakfast.

"It was a gift, milords, I swear on my name!"

"And by Argens' manhood, I shall thrash the first tongue to wag otherwise!"

"Yet without question," Fennet put in tersely, "when I last dusted, it was hanging on the wall."

Qerlak could not avoid the problem; clearly a crisis point had been reached. To accuse the girl of theft would condemn her to death, by her own people if not he; to overlook it would invite a rash of such behavior from the gypsies, which the knight knew his own folk would not stand for. And to kill a gypsy unjustly was to invite the curse of the Horse People... accurate judgment before breakfast, reflected Qerlak, was not one of his stronger suits.

"I suggest, milord," put in Fennet quietly while the others buzzed back over the same facts again, "that the matter be put off until tomorrow's final boons and judgments."

"Well put, castellan, let it be so," Qerlak said, and the murmur greeting that decision told him the trial would be well attended.

The group started to break up, when some unseen person muttered "the Test of Truth", and a complete hush fell over the room. Qerlak couldn't stop himself from looking to Seldom, who stared in return, both knights taken aback by the implications of the lord casting Detect Lie on a fellow knight and vassal.

Gathering his wits, Chased said "Aye, I welcome such a test freely." After a moment's silence seemed to refute him, he raised his voice and clenched a fist. "I demand it, indeed! I call for the Test of Truth!"

Qerlak's heart, already low when he left his room, now fell to a spot between his boots; any fool could see the knight was chivalrously insisting on a version of the facts that wasn't remotely true. Qerlak looked to the gypsy girl again, her wide eyes only now showing some inkling of the trouble she had caused; there was not a trace of real guile in her, he sensed, and indeed that necklace did go well with her eyes.

"It is a matter for the morrow. Madam, I'll take charge of that jewelry for now, and I order you to remain only within the castle, and under the watch of Sir Chased."

"That I'll do readily, milord!" she gushed, causing a loud and edgy titter in the gathering. Qerlak took the necklace and was handing it to Fennet when a thought struck him from behind his instincts somewhere.

"Who was it, indeed, that caught the girl, and exactly where?"

The castellan pointed for answer, and the crowd parted to produce the stranger in the traveling cloak, from the first day.

"In truth, milord, it was I," he cooed, already somewhat agitated at his newfound fame. "I was taking the night air and admiring the battlements when this one..."

"The battlements, sirrah, form a part of this keep," the lord of Mon-Crulbagh interrupted with an edge that cut the low babble to silence, "and as such, were refused to you."

The man bowed low and stammered an apology, while Fennet stepped forward with a face of shock. "Milord, did this man—I had no idea, when did this—"

"You are hereupon banished from my fortress on pain of death!" Qerlak punctuated his bellow with an imperious arm and the cloaked stranger practically fell in his haste to stumble out, followed by a guard to be sure he was well on his way.

Qerlak took a deep breath and then another while no one spoke, inwardly amazed at the vigor of this fury. Then he saw Seldom's face, and was minded of the mortal's impending fate; from there the dreadful course of thought moved to the day's bouting, and what came after the victory. Perhaps it was to be expected, that he should feel like the string of a loaded crossbow today. And as the lord of Mon-Crulbagh stood reflecting on these matters the small crowd nearby milled off to finish breakfast, and then turn their attention with all the rest in attendance to the day's combats.

"Dekentar Spezh, has Sir Hitaelseran been allowed out this morning, and given access to his armor and horse for the jousting?"

"Aye, milord. He's first to the field." Spezh replied, adding, "We've, ah, hobbled his mount until it's his turn."

Qerlak nodded but never doubted the lad's honor. Hitaelseran had been given the freedom of the castle twice before and made no trouble about it. In Qerlak's adventuring days he'd spent plenty of time with Galethiel and the others, just waiting in dark stone places. Boredom, that was the true enemy.

Qerlak had no chance to feel bored this day, facing the lists with such dismal prospects.

Prowess by the lance was an unstated given of knightly behavior. The fact that Qerlak had no experience of the weapon or a real fighting-horse, aside from the minimum required at tourneys in his youth, was of no account to the public eye. Even as a child, Qerlak had been a very strong and dexterous fighter, able to handle an unfamiliar weapon capably. But in the tournament, with both horse and lance strangers to his touch, he struggled not to look awful. He thought for a moment of riding on big brawny Bruna for the tourney, but everyone knew that riding lizards made horses nervous, and it would be unchivalrous to take advantage. At least his natural agility, and the deep-cut saddle, should assure that he'd be upright until the moment of first contact.

Qerlak even won his first match, against one of his own mounted retainers, to his great surprise and the crowd's delight; their thunderous cheers brought home to him that this was the largest crowd of the festival. There were easily more than eight hundred people here.

But as Fate would have it, the draw brought him up next against Seldom Chased.

Qerlak leaned down to his squire Cecil and muttered, "Let me have a practice lance, and be clever about it."

"Milord? It will snap on any contact."

"I know. I want to make sure I break at least one with him, and this way I can concentrate on keeping my seat."

Cecil grinned, and pretended to knock over several lances in his hurry, laying the thinner, notched version into his lord's hand.

The tactic worked to perfection: after saluting each other respectfully, Qerlak let Seldom thunder down the lists while he settled for a canter and a low crouch. They met more than two-thirds to Qerlak's side and he leaned into the contact, making sure his shield caught his foe's point while he flailed at the side of Seldom's shield with his own.

It cracked neatly all the same, and Seldom's lance splintered perfectly—like everything else he did—square on the device in the center of Qerlak's shield. The horses galloped on; Qerlak was able to keep his head above his spurs, and the crowd ate it up. Turning his steed without too much effort, Qerlak signaled for a tourney lance this time, satisfied he had kept up appearances.

On the second pass, he went a little faster, and with great effort, managed to place his point on Seldom's heart-shaped shield: but at the last instant, his opponent expertly flicked his blunted point up and caught Qerlak clean across the helm. The results were just what the Captain of the Outer Marches intended, and Qerlak was neatly picked off his perch while the horse charged on, to be deposited unceremoniously in the dust.

The crowd cheered loudly for the skill of the victor, and Qerlak was pleased to hear one just as long (though it sounded very dim, to his ringing ears) when he rose and waved to them. He wasn't sure his head would ever feel right again. On the other hand, had Seldom's lance been sharpened for battle, Qerlak's helmet and all its contents would probably still be sticking to it.

And as the joust progressed, Qerlak saw more proof that he had no cause for shame, as Seldom Chased bested three other contestants in turn, including finally Hitaelseran, who acquitted himself with skill and broke four lances- real ones- before going down in the final match. Seldom took the silver spurs, acknowledging the cheers of the Crulbagh crowd with knightly vigor and grace, shouting out greetings to his lord and Hitaelseran and clapping everyone within reach on the square of the back.

Spezh moved in to help Hitaelseran to his feet. Though the young knight staggered, he made at once to remove his sword-belt and turn it in. Spezh looked to Qerlak who waved off the gesture, and the son of Pritaelseran instead took his seat fully armed and honored to watch the proceedings.

But when Qerlak moved with the crowd to the foot tourney-ring and called for his battle-axe, he felt a plunge of dismay, to note that Chased was moving to enter also, his greatsword at his side.

"Haven't you honor enough, Sir Chased," he asked quietly, drawing him to one side.

"Aye, milord, from you, I have had honor too much; 'tis time to pay you back."

"What? Don't you know what happens to the 'winner' today?"

"Sooth milord, certes I do."

The two men held each other's gaze in deadly earnest, and Qerlak knew it was useless to argue. He briefly weighed the odds of forbidding him to participate. But suddenly it came to him, that here was a situation much like the tourney, and using the horse instead of Bruna. The one truly pious and proper option was simply to let the knight enter, along with the others. And beat them all. Qerlak grinned tightly as he thought of the scaly monster of the night before. Of course, he had said.

The crowd was disappointed, when they saw the two knights among the common folk entering the lists for the foot-tourney with small swords, clubs and staves.

"Carrying over their grudge—no prizes for us--ah, what fairness can you expect from the nobles?"

Qerlak heard the snatches of conversation, saw the worried look on Fennet's face. Maybe he should announce what prize the winner could truly expect. But no.

"Good folk, we seem to have many contestants today," he called to the stands, "and the time draws short. I hereby declare a separate bout for the wearers of metal armor. They shall do battle for... for a purse of silver pieces given by my own hand. The original prize shall remain with the unarmored fighters."

This brought a very satisfactory cheer from the crowd, and as the tourney now split in two, it shortened the length considerably. Even as the ebullient Chefron Gillthruster hit the dust in the semifinals of the lighter bouts—felled by the buffets of a huge black from the southern fringe who eventually won—by that time, it was down to Seldom Chased and Qerlak Barleybane in the armored class. The doughty Spezh could not long stand against the resounding blows of Seldom's padded edge; while Qerlak had put down two dekentars and a Colter man with a kind of concentrated urgency that almost seemed impolite.

The two young knights strode to the square for the final bout; looking back at the stands Qerlak saw Fennet, Cecil, Hitaelseran, his brothers, and Galethiel looking on with interest. Turning to Seldom, he took in the face of the one man here who truly understood the stakes. By Argens, such a handsome mortal. His well-met friend, a shield-brother, yet also his vassal. A blessing from the heroes, that's what he was.

Chased spoke first, extending his hand. "I vow, from this day our comradery shall only grow; and I am your man until the death of us."

"And so swear I," Qerlak responded taking his arm in turn, "to a true knight, the best of my vassals in arms."

Then the heavy whistle of swinging weapons played counterpoint to the muffled clang of wrapped steel on plate. They had bouted before many times and were evenly matched— Seldom's plate armor provided peerless protection from all but the mightiest blows, but Qerlak was a bit quicker, and for strength there was little to choose between them. Qerlak heard his head start to ring again almost immediately, and as the match wore on his arms felt increasingly like stones; the roar of the crowd was feverish, but again distant and its reactions seemed delayed.

The realization crept over Qerlak that he could not win; the thought gave him a burst of will for a desperate chance.

Dodging the next of Seldom's mightiest blows, he stepped aside as Chased tugged the point from the soft dirt, using the interim to reach into his spirit and summon a Strengthening on himself. The wave of resurgent energy was only temporary, he knew, but it could be enough. Swinging into melee again with an edge of speed, Qerlak hammered back with his axe three times in succession, hitting each time and breaking completely past Seldom's parry on the third blow contacting him squarely on the ribs.

There was a black moment, like a blank space over his eyes and ears; suddenly Qerlak recovered his vision and saw that Chased was down, and he was standing over him, leaning on his axe not to join him on the turf. A tide of sound came racing in as if catching up to the miracle, and he heard the cheering, the worried voices of Doctor Drace and Cecil, and the gasp of some large fellow nearby panting raggedly for breath.

And Qerlak knew, deep within, that he was the champion of Mon-Crulbagh. Of course.

That evening all the day's contestants laid up in rest: most of the damage from padded blows returned in an hour or two. Qerlak had fought four bouts in a row, and asked Fennet to bring him a healing potion from the scarce treasure store of the Dream-Quest adventure, which he quaffed hidden in his ale. Still, the lord of Mon-Crulbagh ached in every joint and muscle. He took to his bed nearly as soon as the sun went down; but even a moment of sleep brought visions of Reptile Men in the keep, slaying and eating the staff and their children.

Once he awoke from a fit of rest to see the face of Galethiel, sitting wordlessly at his bedside. Clearly, she suspected something, and had been with the group last night, but she ventured no guess aloud. Impulsively, Qerlak reached for her hand.

"I promise you. I promise, you shall be confirmed in your right to the tower, whatever happens, for as long as you want to stay."

Galethiel reacted in surprise, and for a moment looked searchingly at the lord for a further sign. None was forthcoming, so she nodded once and rose to leave. At the door she looked back, paused, and said only "Good luck".

In three more minutes, Qerlak fell back asleep; but in no time it seemed, he was awakened by Seldom Chased, who barged in demanding again, despite oaths already exchanged, to be allowed to accompany him. A few rough jests, a word of reassurance, and suddenly the knight rose and left without preamble.

Fennet knocked at two hours before midnight, and Qerlak arose to arm and dress. In the corridor, he ran into his brother Mo'lem on his way to the garderobe from the feast still going on in the main hall.

"Why do you not carouse, brother?" he asked, a little fuzzy around the edges but still coherent enough to be concerned.

"It's nothing, a report of another fire on the border, probably just a prank of the savages."

"But you're not wearing your armor."

"See then? That proves it's nothing to fear. I'll see to it—you go back to the feast."

"Are you sure?"

"Sit in the host chair for me, will you? Represent the family until I return. Or it ends."

"I will."

"Thanks", said Qerlak, and then suddenly gripped his brother's arm without speaking further. Qerlak left him puzzled as he exited, and Mo'lem saw his brother looking around as he walked, noticing everything as if he might forget what they looked like.

Qerlak mounted in the courtyard, a riding horse just to get him there, and beside him Seldom was already on Mystic in full battle dress. There was a soft incantation from the corner tower, and Qerlak realized he could see in the mid-evening darkness better even than Elves normally do, as if it were dawn. Galethiel was already withdrawing inside her tower once again, but he waved to her in appreciation, then spurred his mount out through the gate and over the moat. Riding past the gypsy camp, he stared at the closed and darkened door of the tel-woman's wagon.

On the western horizon, a bonfire burned.

There was little ceremony, it appeared, among the Reptile Men. By a fire no larger or better set than those of the previous night, the remains of a dead lizard fighter incinerated in apparent sacrifice; or perhaps it was a crude funeral in imitation of Hope. Qerlak reflected, as he and Seldom dismounted, that little was known of their customs, or their ultimate worth; perhaps that would change now, provided he lived on.

Without speaking, he approached the edge of the bonfire and disarmed, handing his weapons to Chased and limbering up. Looking around by the fire's light, which spoiled his Elven and mage-given sight, he could dimly see the shapes and shadows of scores of the savages: they only hissed and grunted quietly among themselves, but the weight of it was palpable. Qerlak had no idea there were so many—all males? The same brute of the evening before awaited him; the Elven knight noted with satisfaction the scars and blood from his previous bouts, but his heart sank to see how little effect they seemed to have on his massive frame or avid demeanor. He waved Qerlak in with sharpened talons and a permanent reptilian grin, hissing and gargling as his tail lashed with its own life. Stepping lightly, Qerlak ignored the posturing and scanned the ground for catches and divots; on the last few closing steps, he tried to gauge the reach of those arms, resolved to box not grapple with the scaly death-maker.

The circling seemed endless, and then Qerlak threw a jab, which landed clean on his enemy's jaw. He followed with two more, then one, and then two more following that. The knight realized, without his encumbering armor on, there was simply no comparison between him and the Reptile Man for speed. When his foe launched a rare swing at him, it was almost child's play to duck under it, and it would have to be a lucky blow indeed that landed on him from arm's length.

The savage, too, soon realized this, and egged on by the howling mob behind him, he gathered himself to use his best advantage. Head down, he barreled in and reached to grapple Qerlak in hand-to-hand combat. The first time, the Elven noble handled it poorly, reacting as a fighter would in boxing. As the enemy closed, Qerlak tagged him sharply with an excellent shot to the jaw, but then, a man-high column of scaly muscle bore him down, and Qerlak grunted to feel the tail stunning the base of his back, talons ripping the skin off his ribs, and teeth sinking into his right shoulder. Twisting in panic, he managed to break free and stand, as the dirt ground into his wounds and made his nerves scream in raw protest. His foe stood lithely and without effort, moving smoothly to charge in again.

It was time to think about winning this fight, rather than posing for a trophy afterwards. Qerlak gave ground, waiting on the charge until the last moment before stepping to one side and out of reach of both talons. One claw scraped on the way past, but not enough to get ahold of the Elf. That was the way, he thought.

And round after round, it was much the same. Perhaps Qerlak could land a jab or a kick on the way by, perhaps not. Once he tripped stepping backward over a divot of earth and went stumbling down. His foe was bearing in and got a slanting bite on his thigh as Qerlak rolled away and up, limping.

But the fight wore on, charge after charge, and eventually the time and the bruises took their toll on the Reptile Man's animal vitality. Twice, his enemy stumbled so badly that Qerlak could lay a punch on him with all his strength; once the Elf feinted with his head then skipped opposite, and gained so much time that he could repeat his tactic of the morning, and bring a Strengthening upon himself to restore some energy and temporarily close his wounds. Further from the fire now, Qerlak realized, he could see better than the Reptile Man, thanks to Galethiel's spell. In the fringe of the brush, he risked tripping but so did his foe, and his charges were now comically slow. The man-monster's tactics became ever more brute, his direction and timing easier to guess.

In a short while it was clear; the reptile champion had managed to grapple twice more, briefly, and Qerlak was covered in blood, but the savage had broken bones all over his body and could not bolster himself as could the Lord of Mon-Crulbagh. Yet his beastly mind could not accept, or even recognize, the prospect of defeat. The savage bore in once more, and Qerlak simply thrust out a right jab with open palm, thumping him squarely in the chest and knocking him back a step.

"Yield, monster!" he called, holding his arms ready but stepping back. The Reptile Man looked down to where his chest had been hit, as if Qerlak had done a sleight of hand to touch him there in mortal combat: looking back up, he shook his head hard as if to clear it. A thick flap of his own skin slapped down from his cheek over his mouth and with a snarl he bit it off and gulped it down. Then he came stomping back towards the knight, as if starting the fight from the first round but in slow motion. Again, Qerlak thumped him with both hands, shoving the taller brute back four full steps and nearly tripping over his own tail, hanging limp now below him like a tangled sword-belt.

"Yield, moron!" shouted Seldom Chased, worked up to a fever pitch by the horrid struggle he had witnessed. The crowd behind the fire hissed like an angry wave breaking on the shore.

The savage, as if he could no longer hear, straightened up, spit out a gob of blood and roared in anger before charging in once more. Qerlak felt an echo of that beastly rancor and shouted in return as he charged in at full force, driven by all the energy of his hatred and horror.

The two thundered together like rams in heat, and by the bonfire's light Seldom and the savages saw a ghastly caricature of the pose graven in the courtyard of the castle. The Reptile Man's left talons sunk into Qerlak's hip like nails; but his right arm broke under the impact of Qerlak's grip, and the elf again rushed him back to the edge of the fire. With his eyes sparking to match the blaze before him, Qerlak kept up his shout, exerted all his strength and hoisted his foe completely overhead, snapping his spine in the lift. For an instant his silhouette was still against the light, and all sound beyond the fire dropped away in awe; then heaving high, Qerlak cast his foe into the bier and smashed his now-dead body against that of his charred predecessor. A cannonade of sparks, a muttered curse from Seldom and Qerlak's shredded breath were the only sounds.

Qerlak faced the assemblage of his enemies, his blood-streaked face matching their war-paint, and he bellowed again, half-lost in the rush of mortal combat, turning his head in an arc left and right to take in the entire assemblage with the sound. Almost as one, the mass of scaly flesh shivered and drew back, like an enormous dragon recoiling from his challenge.

After a few moments, Qerlak recovered enough breath to bark out, "Who... is champion? Who!" he thumped a bleeding hand onto his torn chest heedless of the pain and shouted, "Champion!... Say it! Champion!"

The mass of flesh squirmed a moment more, and then seemed to spit out a part of itself—a thin and scrawny specimen, perhaps only half-grown and cowering. Bending low to the ground and lashing his tail like a fan, he grimaced and finally croaked, "Veekk-tarr!!"

At once, the others picked up the call, and soon the glen almost shook with the paean, while the masses of Reptile Men slowly retreated. "Vick-tarr! Crulbagh-veek-tarr!" Even when the last of them had passed beyond his vision, Qerlak could still hear, dimmer and dimmer, the echo of his subjects. "Vick-tarr... veek-tarrrr..."

Seldom was there, tearing his tunic to bandage up his lord as best he might, and helping Qerlak back to his horse. The poor mount shied, at first, from the stench of so much Reptile Man upon him, but between them they got Qerlak up in the saddle, and from there his horse knew enough to follow Mystic even with slack reins. As they rode back to the castle in the deepest ebon of the star-lit night, Qerlak left his mind to its own devices. While he felt like a separate being swimming far away on oceans of his own imagining, his neck and face craned back to look at the dying cinders of the funeral pyre, to which his hands contributed and where he easily could be resting now, if he'd had the sense to give up.

A test of fire.

And two to go.

$\oplus \oplus \oplus$

Foef of Mon-Crulbagh: Reclamation Festival 6th Serpent 2002 ADR

It was the first time Elias Fennet had ever disobeyed a direct command from his lord.

He was fretting on the battlements trying for quiet, when Qerlak returned to the foef with Seldom Chased. As Fennet ran for the stairs, he passed the gaol tower and glanced within to see that Hitaelseran, the prisoner, was awake and looking down as well.

"Please," the young knight called out, and Fennet put his head back to the bars. "Convey to milord Barleybane my best wishes."

"I shall, Sir."

Fennet saw the horses ambling back to the stables on their own and caught sight of the two knights in the hallway, headed toward the lord's quarters. Qerlak was getting weaker and slower by the minute, now leaning on his captain's arm as he scraped along the walls and into his chamber. As the castellan came upon them, Chased had just managed to strip Qerlak's tunic off. It had so many blood-stained rips on it, they might have been better served just cutting it away—but as it was, the action of pulling it over the head caused entwined shreds of rib-flesh to pull away with the fabric, and Qerlak could not suppress a groan of fresh agony. Fennet nearly fell to the floor from the shock, and before he could speak the lord forestalled him.

"It's not as bad as it looks, Fennet. Just, just help me to bed and I'll be fine in the morning."

Fennet did not even dignify the statement with a response, much less a plea; he simply turned on his heel and retreated to the hall, calling low for Cecil next door. He dragged the poor lad into the chamber; ignoring the knight's protests he instructed the squire sternly.

"Get him fully undressed and draw a bath, warm water not hot. Help him into it- I'm bringing Drace."

"Fennet, you cannot—" Qerlak started, but his castellan was already gone again.

Cecil froze until Seldom pulled him towards the horror that was his lord's midsection.

Working together, following Fennet's example of ignoring their lord's weak complaints or gasping curses, they picked out the worst of the caked dirt almost tacked into his wounds, along with more than a few scales, a claw-nail and embedded insects pressed into him by the force of the combat. Qerlak was nearly insensible with faintness and loss of blood when they paired on his sides and eased him into the tub-basin. There, the waters leeched still more of the dirt, slime and lichen free, along with a renewed red tide from his body.

Cecil saw Seldom taking note of how much blood their lord had lost; the first time he had ever seen worry cross his confident mien put a chill into the young squire's bones.

"Sir Chased, what could have done this?"

"A fight, my boy—the Reptile Men, it was…"

"Did he fight a dozen by himself? Did you find him out there?"

"The details don't concern you, squire," Chased hissed a bit harder than usual; Cecil knew that keeping secrets was not a natural habit for knights. "It was, he was without his armor, that's why—and let it be a lesson to you—"

Fennet arrived with Drace, the doctor tired but clearly awake, as a man who has heard something frightening. When the healer's face fixed on Qerlak in the tub, he could see enough, even through the murky red syrup that had once been bathwater. Fennet worried that this would be the incident to break their doctor's will. The castellan still knew little of what had happened the previous year, on the Dream-Quest. Drace never spoke of that and refused to leave the castle, yet now he seemed to recognize something in the situation and responded.

"No time to lose, get him back on the bed and let's have a look at him."

Once they laid him out, Drace looked his lord over closely, holding his head within inches of the major scars and wounds: the earth-burns, spark-marks and minor scrapes he completely ignored. His inspection completed, the doctor said only, "By the Hopelords, such ruin," and that only once.

Turning to his long black satchel, Drace selected three rolled cloths and unraveled them right over Qerlak's legs. They seemed organized in some way, but none of the others could make any sense of it. Choosing his tools and ingredients with care, Drace applied something moss-like to the worst of the open wounds, and within moments the others could see the brownish stuff turning dark red as it seemed to draw the fluid out. After daubing some long rib-tears with a yellowish paste, he stitched up the skin there with a needle and a thin cord. Partway through this, he looked up to check a gash on the forehead and noticed with a start that Qerlak's eyes were open.

Qerlak regarded his doctor quietly, calmly, and finally said, "I'm sorry to have awakened you doctor."

Drace lost a bit of his composure at this, and snapped, "You'd have been dead before dawn if you hadn't... milord." He clearly wanted, yet did not want, to hear the details: shaking his head, he returned to his labors. "There's a broken rib here--we'll set that," he remarked, touching the area gently to trace the bruise, and ignoring the smirk of pain that crossed the knight's features. "A few of these gashes are very serious, but I think the drinkmoss will save us from a disease, given milord's ox-like constitution. As it is, maybe a week of bedrest and he can—"

"I shall sit for the trials and boons tomorrow after breakfast, as planned." Qerlak interrupted, as if arguing it would rain when his doctor said it wouldn't. Drace turned to stare, and his mouth hung open just a bit.

"Milord, you are mad."

"Better than likely. Fennet, you and Cecil guide me down there early, so no one sees me moving. I'll get up and down as little as possible, walk slowly, and... pretend to be drunk."

"While you settle the peasant cases!" Fennet cried. "But there's nothing for it—we must try and make a show."

"I'll be fine," Qerlak assured them, and before anyone could offer the slightest argument, he was back asleep, and stayed that way even as Drace continued to minister.

"Cecil," Fennet announced, "you stay with him for the first two hours after the doctor is done. My thanks, Doctor Drace, I do not doubt you have saved the life of Sir Barleybane. Squire Disarmle and I shall keep watch until it's time to get him up. Sir Chased, get to bed, you look a mess yourself. You have not been injured, I trust?"

Seldom rose and looked back at the castellan. Cecil could see his emotion but not name it before the knight spoke.

"Here lies the lord of Mon-Crulbagh with wounds 'pon all his body," said Seldom Chased. "And certes, the Captain of those same Outer Marches where he received his injury wears not a scratch."

"I've done all I can, for now," Drace said, rising at last and rinsing his hands at the side-basin. He rolled up his effects, clucking his tongue at how little medicine he had left, and looking finally at Qerlak as he snored. "This knight is a hero, no doubt—but mad as a loon."

"Thanks for your help doctor," said Cecil, sitting by the bedside, "I'm sure he'll be fine in the morning."

The doctor gave a learned laugh at that, leaving the squire and castellan alone with their lord.

Castle Mon-Crulbagh

Qerlak was not all better by the morning. His body told him, in a loud voice, he would not be all better for the better part of three days in most of his better parts. Not for victory nor love could he reach for anything above his head, and Qerlak felt sure he would carry a wide scar on his upper back, to remind him how to meet a Reptile Man charge, for the rest of his life.

But Fennet worked his usual wonders, this time with a second bath, a change of bandages and a fine long court-robe from the previous lord's closet. Qerlak was seated in the main chair eating breakfast when the servants came in to arrange the benches in the light of dawn, and he cut a very lordly appearance indeed, as long as he did not move too quickly. Severyn Illfellow brought him his porridge and noticed that Qerlak was already having beer.

By the eighth bell the hall was growing quite lively, and the decorations of boughs and flowers that lined the walls caught the light. Nearly a hundred invited guests crowded the board, to eat and talk and laugh, and get a good seat for the peasant cases due to come forward. In the midst of it all, Qerlak sat as solemn as a coroner. All about him, from his seat in the great chair at one end of the main hall, the folks of his foef and their guests enjoyed his hospitality and toasted the good fortune of another year, one they thought the best in living memory. Tull was there with his family, and a few others formerly of Semegorn's Thrall; he saw Alik Malik and that new blacksmith from Bultarr-r (the woman, Felicia? Or Faye, perhaps). Cecil attended to his every need, and carried Qerlak's message up to the donjon, inviting Hitaelseran down to sit at board as the guest of Mon-Crulbagh. He came at once, with his guard keeping a polite distance, and bowed his thanks before taking a seat just two to the left of the center chair.

"I am pleased to see you well this day, milord."

"You honor me, young man."

Seldom was there a short while after, looking a little worse for the wear—Qerlak smiled, knowing everyone else would assume his fatigue was sourced with his lovely gypsy companion. Sir Chased advanced to the center at once and greeted Qerlak with outward boister, as usual. When the knight motioned for him to sit a while, Seldom called for ale and they sat a time in silence.

"Why do you suppose, was it the small one, who shouted first for your victory?" he asked, as if in no particular hurry to solve the mystery.

Qerlak rubbed his chin and thought, nodding to recall the moment of the night before. "They are a savage race, living by strength. It must have been a shame of some kind, to have to say it. So they forced the weakest, or youngest, to do it first."

Seldom nodded at this, and their quiet in the midst of the celebration resumed. Fennet signaled that the peasant cases were set to be brought before him, and Seldom rose to withdraw.

"Stay if you would, Sir Chased. These subjects have labored long and hard, and their troubles are our own."

"Well I know this, milord, and I am proud to protect them, as are you," returned his Captain, and he caught Qerlak's eye with a look that told volumes. "But today, as you recall, I am to be one of those cases. 'Tis not meet I should sit up here until after judgment is rendered."

"I had not forgotten, my friend." Qerlak admitted, "If you would prefer to go first?"

"Nay, milord, these peasants should not be made to wait. They are the strength of this foef; let us have the weak go last." And Seldom smiled bravely, whereon Qerlak tapped him once on the shoulder and let him go. But as soon as his companion stepped from the podium, Qerlak could feel his dark mood returning.

The day of boons was usually the least celebratory of a festival, filled with mundane disputes and settled for the most part by customs. Qerlak both loved and dreaded to hear such cases in his first sitting last fall, but now he feared most that they would end.

Precedents had been set then, new ones today. The peasants coming to ask about a boundary stone sliding into the river, or the true father of a black goat kid, were in deadly earnest. Customs differed with the newcomers, Tull's people freed from Semegorn, and in places these new neighbors caused discord with Mon-Crulbagh natives.

Qerlak listened, praying for wisdom as others stated their case. He knew for a fact he could not be deciding correctly in all matters, yet the onlookers always nodded with satisfaction and murmured loudly of his wisdom. Fawning to the new lord? Possibly from some, but once or twice even the loser of the decision tugged a cap and bowed. Fennet took notes on all of it, and later they would study to see what policies to announce, or any changes to implement.

But Qerlak hated deciding anything alone. When adventuring with the Tributarians, there had always been argument— sometimes too much! But usually agreement followed, and the way became clear. The knight's instincts told him that those who know better, do better.

190

At the luncheon, he leaned close to his young prisoner. "What think you, Sir Hitaelseran? Is there one kind of justice only? Or do we decide for the peasants differently than we do among ourselves?"

His enemy's son looked back to him with a furrowed brow. "Do you ask my opinion on your decisions this day, milord?"

"Nothing so delicate! But can we say there is anything the same when the dispute lies between those of the common class, as opposed to an accusation against a noble?"

Hitaelseran looked thoughtful then, eating awhile in silence before answering. "There are, I think milord, certain… general boundaries that must be observed in all cases."

"Such as?"

"Fairness; not to take a silver coin from one man and three from another if their lands produce the same crop. Honor, also, to grant to each person the dignity that he or she is indeed honorable, unless the facts should indicate otherwise."

"Well spoken, young knight," said Seldom Chased from down the board.

"And third I would list honesty, that one keeps a word once given." Hitaelseran stood with his goblet then. "As you have done with me, milord, and for which I am in your debt."

"I assure you, young man, you owe me nothing. Were it not for the, ahm, less than perfect relationship between myself and your father, I would have long ago granted you the freedom you deserve. As things stand, I earnestly hope you will imagine yourself my guest. Except for the part where you would be free to leave."

The laughter at this was unfeigned, and Hitaelseran joined in. He looked up again at Qerlak and asked, "Has there been further word, milord, from my father?"

Qerlak's first answer caught in his throat, as he imagined how it would be to feel so abandoned. There was no rhyme or reason

191

in Pritaelseran's first, ridiculous offer, nor in his failure to raise the ransom to a proper level. But he needed to say something.

"You might say he owes me a letter. I would imagine, what with the rains..."

"The weather, no doubt milord." Hitaelseran's easy acceptance of this excuse carried an air of sadness, even embarrassment, which rankled Qerlak to see. Surely this young man deserved better than to think his father had discounted him. The third son of Greatknight Barleybane had never been made to feel less than his brothers. But clearly, this fourth son, such a rarity among Elves of any class, had been treated as an afterthought. All the rumors Qerlak had heard of the cruelty, arrogance and presumption of his rival were only second-hand words to him. But in the admirable comportment of this youth he saw the unworth of Lord Pritaelseran in sharp relief.

What was he even about with his prisoner, Qerlak wondered. Did keeping him hostage delay Pritaelseran's invasion? But why no offer of ransom, nor any other demand? And if the proper offer did come, it could hardly be more welcome with the state of the keep's finances.

But Qerlak knew for certain, he would refuse it. He simply didn't know why.

"I'm sure," he said for the public to hear, "that you will see your family very soon."

Hitaelseran nodded, and replied, "And we too shall meet again, milord, upon the field of battle where I shall endeavor to acquit myself to some remark."

On this the room fell quite still. Qerlak raised his tankard to answer, saying, "Of that, sir, I have no doubt. I shall strive only to match you on that day." And with this his sadness returned.

"Justice, Lord of Mon-Crulbagh!" The cry of this new voice brought a sigh from the common crowd just filing back in for the afternoon session. A thin black Man in tattered, once-colorful garb took his place before Qerlak's judgment seat and swept into a low bow.

"Justice, against whom, citizen?"

"Against your predecessor if you will, milord." The room gasped as one at this.

"Denied!" Fennet cried out from behind Qerlak's seat. "This foef recognizes no debt from Distallin Crulbagh. His conduct—"

"Peace, castellan, we will hear this plea." Qerlak nodded that the man should continue.

"I am Macellyn Asseigh, your lordship, once pleased to lead a regular caravan of trade from Wanlock through Beryl and Colter, here to Mon-Crulbagh, the southernmost tip of civilization. Generally my trade ran to household objects, utensils and perhaps crockery, nothing of tremendous importance."

"Go on, sir. Come to the matter of the injustice."

"With pleasure, milord. During the troubles, close on two summers ago, dangers rose high for men such as myself. Yet I was content to take those risks, and with the luck of Astor won through to this keep with a load of expensive crystal goblets. These were expressly ordered by the Lord, upon his word as a knight agreeing to pay my price. But when I arrived, he was all aflame for war and denied ever having made such an order to me."

"The ill fortune of your trade, sirrah," Fennet quipped, and Qerlak could see he was as alert as a fox for trouble.

"Agreed, with all my heart, sir." Asseigh drew breath and turned to face the room. "Yet when milord Crulbagh in addition to his perfidy in the matter of trade, also suborned my guards and drafted them into his war-levy—"

Here he had to stop a moment, as the peasantry rose to their feet shouting in anger. Qerlak could tell, it was not a denial of the man's tale, nor were the people angry with him in any way. But somehow this action of his predecessor was an insult.

"Without guards, milord, my caravan fell easy prey to a pack of the roving Reptile Men not two days' journey north of here. My shipment was transformed to a thin layer of glass dust under their tender care, as milord may have reason to know."

Qerlak barked a laugh that stopped all proceedings, and tried to hold his face steady against the lancing pain it brought him while all eyes turned in his direction.

"We have some slight acquaintance of their ways, indeed."

"Nevertheless," Fennet put in, "we cannot be held responsible for your losses, sir."

"Justice, milord Crulbagh," Asseigh replied, ignoring the castellan. "Justice, for a master of this foef who in times of trouble would not *muster* the courage to behave with honor."

His emphasis was subtle, but strangely effective, and Qerlak could make out repeated references to "the muster" as the peasants whispered among themselves and looked on with angry faces. Qerlak glanced around the head table and got no sign that anyone comprehended this reaction. He was on his own for this case.

"What would you have of me, Macellyn Asseigh?"

"Justice," the merchant said smiling, "to our mutual gain."

"Ah then, my castellan will no doubt be glad to hear this."

"I propose, milord, that you grant to me a franchise, with the exclusive right to deal on behalf of Mon-Crulbagh in a commodity I shall name. All the buying, any right to sell, shall be vested in me for a period of, shall we say, thirty years?"

"Shall we say, rather, three." Fennet shot back.

Qerlak raised one hand for peace. "What commodity, sirrah?"

"Clay, milord."

"What? Clay!" Fennet demanded.

"And what, master merchant, will you do with my clay? Assuming I grant you permission to take it."

Asseigh's eyes sparkled with a vision of other places and persons, and his grin seemed to be his mouth's natural position.

"On my first trip, milord, I would burden a wagon with raw clay so that my poor mules would rue the day they were born. And when I reached the towns of Colter, I would sell it in great grey blocks to craftsmen whom I know, and make a pittance on the sale, really. I might return to you with some of these holes stitched, and perhaps socks that boast more cloth than air."

Everyone chuckled at this, which gave him the power to sweep on.

"And in my return, milord, I would bring with me one of those craftsmen." Silence to hear more. "I would draw him with the promise of a free home in your village, and the welcome of a friendly lord, more interested in his people's welfare than in lining his own pockets. With a charter from my hand and signed by you, giving that man the license to practice his craft free of taxes for five years."

"One!" Fennet yelled, but no one so much as glanced his way as Asseigh continued.

"On my next trip north, milord I would carry with me only some clay, and alongside it examples of the native wares, which I have seen at this very festival—"

"I remember you," Qerlak broke in, "the man inspecting our tables on the first day."

The merchant bowed and continued. "Inspired to compete with my imported craftsman, I would bear a load both lighter— to the relief of my mules—and more valuable, to the pleasure of us both. On this load I shall indeed pay you the fair tithing, milord, and when I return I shall be wearing new clothes for the first time since our Emperor took the throne."

"And on your third trip?"

"More craftsmen coming south, milord, and more finished pottery going north." Asseigh paused for effect, and then added, "in three wagons this time."

The crowd applauded and he bowed to everyone in turn, last and deepest of all to Qerlak.

"Milord," Fennet stepped in to speak low, "you must not be taken in by the man's eloquence. It is true, the records indicate a trade in clay goods, but his terms—"

"His terms, good castellan, I leave completely in your hands to negotiate." Qerlak rose carefully from his seat, stepped down and extended his hand to Macellyn Asseigh. "In earnest, sir, of my good faith that we shall indeed do business and someday soon."

"Word of your good faith, milord Barleybane, has already spread beyond the boundaries of your foef. It drew me here, at first, I admit to beg, but now with much grander plans in mind."

Bowing once more, Macellyn Asseigh withdrew from the court with the grace of a Baron; back at the dais, Elias Fennet watched him leave as if he could see him wherever he went for the rest of his life.

The afternoon cases were a blur, seemingly quite easy for Qerlak to decide and thus providing no distraction from his impending doom. The large mortal black, winner of the peasant-bouting, asked a boon of land and was welcomed heartily, along with several from other places. This season, no one asked for relief from tithing as crops were coming in well. As the hour for cases to be presented drew near closing, the session took on the character of a rolling celebration, with early feasting brought around by Skeggs and his staff, together with enough beer and ale that folks lost count. The talk was heady and spiced with laughter: Qerlak at last forgot himself and was chatting eagerly with Hitaelseran about the jousting; from the corner of his eye, he caught sight of the small wizened gypsy leader standing up from her bench near the back.

"Lord of the Fire-Water Clan," she intoned solemnly, "we have tarried the day and lost the light. We await your judgment." A hush fell over the hall bringing back all the sense of dread he had felt since the morning. Qerlak resumed his seat, sighed and nodded, gesturing the principals forward to rehearse their stories.

196

To his right, Galethiel leaned in with an urgent word.

"Qerlak, I know you think the code is law. But cark that—Seldom Chased is your companion. You owe him."

Qerlak nodded. Galethiel's attitude toward noble practice was something he had already learned, to his pain. But she did not realize the full consequences here. If it came about that the gypsy girl took the necklace, even if he excused his friend, her own people would put her to death.

The gypsy girl had the most to say, rattling on about how chivalrous and kind Sir Chased had been to her, praising the castle and showing her all the rooms.

"The trophy room, milord, how vast and spooky! And then... I saw the necklace mounted on the wall, beneath the enormous sword."

"I see. And did you take it down, mistress?"

"No milord, I swear, I merely said how beautiful it was."

"And I told her," Chased averred, "she would look a Marchess with it on. I insisted she try it."

"Well enough," Qerlak said, "But how did you come to be outside with it?"

"As to that, milord—" the girl's voice caught and the tears began, real fear and not unwarranted.

Chased intervened, "She wondered how it might look under the light of the stars, and I escorted her to the walls to see."

Qerlak turned then to the witness, the one in the traveling cloak who had spurred his anger in the morning. "And that is where you saw them, sirrah?"

He nodded and bowed. "I thought it best you should know, milord Barleybane. How could such a ragged peasant possibly own—"

"Shut your mouth, snake!" Seldom Chased reached for the intruder through the arms of the man's guards. "It is just as she claims, a gift, and I'll put my blade through the heart of the next man who denies it."

The stranger smirked from behind the safety his guards provided, and flicked a glance at Qerlak, then to one side where Hitaelseran stood.

"Strange," Spezh offered, "that's the second time this fellow's been up there on the walls. Back on the first day I rousted him, no idea you had refused him permission Sir Barleybane. I just told him off when he got too close to the gaol."

Now Qerlak looked on the witness with renewed urgency, and his instincts seemed correct. "A spy, very likely." He turned to face his noble prisoner. "Sir Hitaelseran, did you speak to this person?"

"I do not know him, milord, nor do I know all in my father's employ. We did not speak." He let the words hang in the air a moment, then blushed and added, "Last night, past midnight, I was asleep."

Titters and whispers from the crowd at this admission only made him straighten his back and throw up his chin. "If you require the Test of Truth, Lord Barleybane, as I understand you have the miraculous power to assay, I willingly submit."

"We have no need to test your honesty, young sir."

"And I too!" shouted Chased. "I will not cower before the truth of Argens to let an Elf best me." His eyes wild with passion, he said again "I demand the test."

Qerlak looked at his friend a long moment, then turned to resume the lord's seat with feet that felt like stones. His eyes crossed with Galethiel's, sparking with urgency, and then with Fennet's, helpless with anguish. Seated once more, there was nothing to do but pronounce a decision, to either shame his vassal or condemn a young woman to death.

He saw Hitaelseran looking to him earnestly, and his instinct nudged him once more. Seek advice.

"Young Hitaelseran, how would you advise here? We spoke before of justice for common and noble folk alike. Here be one of each. What say you?"

The prisoner stiffened again in surprise, then stepped slowly down to face the three at closer range. Qerlak saw, as he turned back to face him, the Elven knight was moving his lips, either in prayer or the meme of patience. In an instant, his face cleared.

"The charge, I believe, is theft. The item this necklace. Which like all things within this keep belong to you, milord. To dispose of as you please."

"Well said, young man. But one thing further. As the lord and master of this foef, I am not free of obligation. In fact, I owe my—" Qerlak's breath fled his lungs a moment as the revelation flooded in. He stood and came down to place a hand on Hitaelseran's shoulder, then faced Seldom Chased.

"I owe you, Seldom Chased. By Argens, I had forgotten, but I owe you!"

"Milord?"

"A debt, my good Captain and vassal, it cannot be you fail to recall?"

"The coins!"

"Indeed, many of them, Sir Chased. And in token of my esteem for your service, as well as in immediate repayment thereof, I am pleased to make restitution in the object of this necklace, if that should prove pleasing to you."

"Aye, and that rightly milord!" Chased snatched the necklace from the tray where it sat and put it on the astonished gypsy girl, who practically fell into his arms at her shift in fortune.

"And our thanks also to—" Qerlak saw Hitaelseran's face turn from delight to agony, as from behind him the intruder broke past the guards and drove his dagger straight into his back.

"Traitor!" he snapped, "You are a disgrace to the line of your fa—"

Qerlak caught the falling body of his prisoner even as his eyes saw a blurring flash of metal and he felt the patter of something warm and thick across his face. With a single lightning sweep of

199

his greatsword, Seldom Chased decapitated the assassin, whose head and body hit the floor in rapid succession.

"On pain of death," the knight hissed, as the courtroom dissolved in horror and screams.

Qerlak settled painfully to the floor with Hitaelseran lying across his arms like a sack, both men gasping and the prisoner starting to heave for breath. Yanking out the blade, Qerlak saw the green-yellow tinge.

"Doctor Drace! Get the doctor!" Fennet screamed, and Seldom Chased with Spezh roared to clear the room of all visitors.

"It burns, it burns milord!" Hitaelseran hissed, "It burns like a flame, like fire!"

Drace arrived and inspected the wound, then the blade, while Qerlak and Fennet held a tablecloth against the flow of blood. The doctor's bandages and salves stopped the bleeding almost at once, yet the wounded knight seemed to sink deeper toward the final sleep.

"A poison I have not seen before," Drace admitted tightly.

Qerlak again cast the miracle of Strengthening on his enemy, willingly pushing his personal energy into Hitaelseran, and renewing it until he saw stars inside the chamber. But Galethiel's hand on his shoulder presaged an influx of new power, renewing him that he might sustain the miracle. With each casting, Hitaelseran's eyes fluttered back open and his breathing eased; yet the toxin ran on, sapping the strength as the drought land drinks rain.

An hour passed, and another, as Qerlak's closest vassals huddled nearby and whispered or prayed.

Cecil stepped in to report. "We searched the corpse. He had a sketch of the keep itself, and his coin pouch has the sign of the stooping hawk."

The corpse-parts lay in a pool of blood, long since stilled. Severyn Illfellow, bringing more cloths and water, stood back and surveyed the mess. "Don't anyone say it. Another job for me, I know."

The humor was short-lived, but the deadly toxin in Hitaelseran's body seemed immortal. Qerlak finally felt even Galethiel's strength wane, as she leaned more heavily on him sitting there before his dais with the young knight in his arms. Seldom Chased, beside himself with frustration, began to sing his Battle Prayer, part of the love-song of the Dagnaluviran from ancient days and a hymn for knights across the kingdoms. As the verses rolled out from his fine baritone voice, Qerlak dared to hope. The poison was surely of the rarest, most expensive kind, enough to kill four men. But not in this house, not without the leave of Lord Barleybane.

"Ah, there," the doctor announced, as Hitaelseran's face broke into a sweat. "The fever from the poison is breaking. He should survive now."

Struck almost bodily with joy and relief, Qerlak looked again on the young knight across his lap.

"You hear, young man? You have once again obliged me to you by not dying."

"I hear, milord. Yet it is I who owe you." The knight's voice was barely a whisper, but he raised one fist, half-drew his sword, and quietly took the oath of fealty undying, the words that bind an Elven noble to service forever.

Even as Qerlak gave the proper response, Hitaelseran began to sink back toward sleep.

"That's well and good, sleep, my newfound vassal," Qerlak said, "You'll need your rest, on the day your father comes to get you back with threescore knights behind him."

"Aye, milord, there shall be a testing then." Hitaelseran muttered, and snored almost before the words left his mouth.

Qerlak thought that truer words had not yet been spoken in this keep, than by this young man who began the day as his enemy. A testing; Qerlak looked up into the eyes of the fiery

Dream-Seer and blood-spattered Captain who would face it with him.

A test indeed.

A test of fire.

PART 2

CHAPTER V. CRACKLE

Foef of Mon-Crulbagh

The saboteurs working to dam the spot where the Sodsluice River splits from the Fengurr channel are in a precarious position. The Tenser Chasm, in broad daylight, is visible from the town of Bultarr-r, and rather than be spotted by farmers or riders on the distant road they must work at night. More, the head of the channel lies at the top of the gorge, so the crew belays themselves with ropes under the knight's direction and guard. They work to position broken trunks or smaller rocks, blocking the falls where this stream heads southwest into the foef of Mon-Crulbagh. Already their efforts have stemmed the flow to a trickle, exposing more rock-faces and even some small caves to view, formerly drenched and filled with water, now drained and open. But not entirely empty, for from these holes comes a buzzing sound and the emergence of creatures that set the Elves' senses aflame, routing the workers until the knight whips them back into place to finish the job.

Their efforts do not go entirely unnoticed however, as from the forest across the gorge a pair of heads take in the efforts of the saboteurs, noting their results both intended and accidental. The mounted man's thick brows furl in anger, his hands clench a strong yew bow but he takes no action. His partner is also upset at what she sees, clucking at the loss of river water for their people and hissing in hatred to see the flying or crawling things beginning to issue from the caves. For now, the horrid Bugs are drawn to the lights of Bultarr-r, but both these scouts know the consequences will eventually fall closer to home. With a soft clatter of hooves, they withdraw to the heart of the Tenser Deeping, so their people may take council and decide. Without the ancient alliance, all courses are unsure. But as they ride over ground both rocky and wooded, their horsemanship is indeed matchless.

The 7th of the Serpent, 2002 ADR

To the Lord Cran-Kalrith Pritaelseran, Greetings,

I trouble your eye with this brief missive to inform, you are relieved (to whatever extent you might have felt the burden) of any need to ransom my body from your enemy the Lord of Mon-Crulbagh. I have recently been freed, having survived the attack of your spy and saved by the hand of Sir Barleybane himself. As a result of these events, I saw no choice but to repay his miraculous effort by swearing fealty to Sir Barleybane, and in light of that I do not expect to return to Pritaelseran again.

I no longer have a hold on you by service and would not invoke an obligation by accident of birth. Yet I ask as one knighted man to another that you do me the kindness to inform my mother your gracious wife that I continue to be well and happy in my new life. I shall not cause you any further disquiet by attempting to write to her directly and I think on balance this should comprise the final communication between us.

Your upbringing has taught me the meaning of honor and the value of the given word. Please trust I have learned these lessons well, and should we meet again I shall act in accordance with the vows I have sworn to my lord Mon-Crulbagh.

In Argens' Name,
Hitaelseran

Insis is finding it harder to wait. The fair has broken up, stripping away the cover of the crowds; he must take to sheltering in the brush against the rain and infernal insects of this marshy wasteland. His contact, after promising him a final meeting, has not shown up at the agreed place two nights in a row. Now Insis watches while a procession of the Greatknight Beryl arrives, as rumored among the fair crowds. He smiles; feasting tonight, and some banal entertainment no doubt, and probably drinking to excess.

No more waiting. Even without the map and other cautions, Insis is quite confident that his lore, surprise and the Vapor Cloak will easily see him through. He hungers to punish his master's rival, to terrify the sorceress even as he abuses and kills her. He will leave the enemy knight alive of course, to tremble with just how easily his betters have struck the best weapon from his hand. And upon returning to his mage-master Zantire, Insis will surely win many rewards, perhaps a workshop of his own and even a granary such as his master created. Insis whets the dagger, then re-sheathes it to anoint the blade again with its poison, while he waits for one more sundown. If his contact fails or has fled, it will not matter. He will seek the rear tower, and none can stop him.

The daring young peasant lad hunting through the forests of western Lann is too young, by Pritaelseran law, to hold a bow. But father has the chills and his mother cannot do it and still tend him. Hunger is also a law, one lord Pritaelseran has not written. The boy's first find was taken from him by an angry

207

hill cat, stealing his kill and breaking the arrow he'd spent so long to make. Only four left after that.

The wind and distance ruins his second shot, nearer to nightfall, when the youth drifted into the more open country west of the forest, even on the slope leading down into Mon-Crulbagh. The roe deer it startled ran on, but the boy is able to mark the location of his errant arrow, for it stuck in the earth right at the bottom of one of those piles of border stone, halfway up the rise and standing clear of any other brush or bracken. Time presses: the youth marks the spot and pursues the deer, vowing to return for his arrow.

Five long hours later his effort is rewarded with a clean shot and a quick death, though the deer in its death-leap falls awkwardly and breaks another arrow. Poor luck following good, but the youth feels accomplishment for his family will eat tomorrow. He dresses the kill and then turns back, not east-by-south to his cabin, but just a touch west of south, to retrieve his lost bolt.

He finds the spot, but hesitates to approach for the border stones are said to be haunted and poor luck to touch. Still, it would take him hours to make a new arrow, so he sucks in his breath and comes on through the night across the open hillside to where it looms a darker shadow in the darkness. Then the youth curses his luck, for now some vandal has taken it. Where he had remembered it stuck in the ground just on the uphill side of the stones, he sees nothing there now. Searching around he spots the dart, broken into bits and half-buried a pace behind the pile. The youth retrieves the metal head, then shakes his fist in defiance of his lord's enemies down in the swampy land. That they have nothing better to do but cause such pain is proof, to his young mind, that his people live on the right side of this feud. But he cannot abide here long, as the mere presence of the stone spooks him: it has no eyes, yet he feels he is being watched. And his family will need this food.

⊕ ⊕ ⊕

Excerpt from the Journal of Mon-Crulbagh

As if things were not bad enough with this accursed drought, we received reports of an attack of Bugs on Bultarr-r the previous evening. Right in the middle of a feast, no less, when I was trying to look well in the eyes of milord Beryl, and in pops this lackwit townsboy, screaming "Bugs! Bugs in Bultarr-r!" at the top of his lungs. Milady wife fainted dead away- I nearly dropped my wine-cup myself. We had heard rumors of a nest somewhere in the Telser Deeping east of the town, but there had been no reports in my rule, nor my father's nor his. I had hoped the evil hive had died out. I must away with my levy to address this- the pike should spit those foul chitterers, if they can hold their nerve when they see them.

12th of the 5th, 1844 Ramask Crulbagh

Not again, not for a bag of rubies with Pritaelseran's head at the bottom!

I marched double-time on Bultarr-r, with the whole pike levy, just to show them I cared for their welfare. My Castellan mumbled something about a "muster", but I couldn't make heads or tails of what he meant- I must examine him when he's calmed down.

But sure enough, the tales are true- the horny devils can tell when large groups approach, and we never caught sight of them on the first day in town. But there was plenty left to see- wrecked fences, doors bashed in like paper, great bulges in the iron gate where they had forced their way in. And as for the people, I don't know whether my men were more revolted by the ones dead, or those still alive, but in pieces. We helped burn the dead, shored up the gate, and that night I held council with the locals. I decided to take one young lad with us as a guide, and set out with just four retainers and myself, to hunt them more quietly.

Praise the Forger, that wizard had my man take a Fire Scroll- and he with the sense to read it. We found the Bugs alright; alien men with two extra arms, low tusky mounts like horned beetles the size of an ox; and everywhere, those waving, flailing antennae. I still shiver when I write of it. We hacked and slew them like men, and they seemed to come on with no more thought of turning than a wave headed to shore. Still, it would have gone hard without that scroll: I wouldn't have thought anything could make that summer hotter than it was. We took a few heads back to town to prove we'd done it, and the healer says he can do nothing for my man's arm. He'll pension out, and train the new militia, he says- but no more Bugs, and I don't blame him.

Castle Mon-Crulbagh

"**Q**erlak, they're coming!" Galethiel let her frustration show as she followed her friend into the main hall where the others awaited around the conference table. Everyone looked up, more at her than the lord of Mon-Crulbagh, and she felt once again her discomfort with fame.

"Milord, they are coming indeed, and far too soon," the castellan Elias Fennet held Galethiel's chair as the two former adventurers sat, and finally took his own.

The Elven knight smiled at them both and said only, "What's to be done?"

"Prepare!" the two shouted at once, then gawked as everyone else laughed.

"We are in complete agreement, em, milady," Fennet continued. "We must be ready before they arrive, tonight and—"

"What?" Galethiel cut in, "I mean, I know they could be here soon, but I thought we had a few days!"

"The messengers have been coming in steadily, they are well past Bultarr-r by now and here by mid-afternoon at the latest. We must be sure we have enough—"

"Wait, tonight? And coming from the north road, Qerlak I thought you said they always came from the south."

Qerlak's brows nearly touched each other, and even as he drew breath to reply, Galethiel sailed on.

"At any rate, there's no time to sit here planning. Get the peasants in and properly armed."

"They are here," Skeggs the cook answered. "Uniforms, proper implements, I'm just starting the roasted meats now."

"Who cares what we eat!" Galethiel screamed. "No offence, but we need to man the walls, or whatever it is you do to defend the keep. The carking gate is still open! Qerlak, what's the matter with you?"

"My dear sorceress," he replied with a small smile, "why for all of Hope would I want to bar my keep against Torquem'l Beryllian?"

"Beryllian? What are you talking about, I thought Pritaelseran—"

She stopped as the chuckles around the table grew to full-on laughter. Even Fennet, after understanding the confusion, grinned and bowed to her.

"Milady, 'tis not our neighbor enemy who comes tonight, but the Greatknight and his entourage. We prepare for the final feast."

Galethiel looked around at all these bizarre folk, who seemed to think eating and drinking was an emergency. "A feast? Are you serious? You called me out here to discuss, what, whether to serve the greens before the bread?"

"No, Galethiel," Qerlak started gently, "I need you—"

"I don't cook!" she heard herself shouting, even as everyone else kept up the laughter.

"Nor would I order you to enter the kitchen," Qerlak said rising to put a hand on her shoulder. He waited until the chuckles died down a bit. "I would not put you at risk of Skeggs' wrath for all the world." He waited until her grin answered his and they both sat again. "But, my good friend, I do need you to understand the situation here. When my overlord arrives—"

"Oh stop worrying, Qerlak, I won't burn him." Galethiel was still grinning as she spoke, but noticed the slight grimace cross her friend's features. This was another of his noble code problems, and she felt her usual impatience boil up at the thought. She took a deep breath and waited.

"I thank you for that promise. As long as you stand by my side, and, well you know, play the part of a court mage, that's all I need. And it will be very important, have no doubt. I could see from Sir Coss that the subject of magery is quite delicate to Beryllian." Galethiel nodded, recalling the nobleman who left late last night to report to his overlord. She had made him nervous. She made everyone nervous.

"Lord Beryl's own mage died in the fighting at Tor Perite," Fennet put in, "and he has not yet replaced him. That smacks of intrigue."

"What's more," Qerlak said, "his retinue includes a bar-wagon, with prisoners inside."

"Prisoners!" Spezh cried, "Milord, how do we know?"

"Runners have been coming to us every day, dekentar," Fennet replied. "There are three persons in the wagon, and the peasants report they are guilty of murder."

Several folks exclaimed around the table, and Galethiel looked at Hitaelseran, along with everyone else, where he sat quietly on the other side of Qerlak from her.

The youth smiled, saying, "Well, a good thing I've moved to new quarters."

"Indeed," Qerlak nodded to him, "and we are very glad of the vacancy, Sir. However, our main business must be with doing proper honor to Lord Beryl."

"Just get him drunk on your beer," Galethiel quipped, "off to bed and he'll be fine. Then we can finally get to planning for this war."

Qerlak did not honor this comment with a response, though Spezh and others laughed. "We shall set out our best board, and do our utmost to pretend that the meal we serve is daily fare, rather than scraping our stock of spice and delicacies to the bare walls."

"The kitchen and staff are ready, milord," Fennet replied. "Whatever may be the case with these prisoners, I'm sure it will be a most entertaining evening."

Qerlak's smile suddenly dropped off his face and he sat back in his chair. "Argens' Loins, the entertainment."

Galethiel looked around at a roomful of men not breathing and again her impatience itched to have done with this noble trivia.

"Oh come now! Qerlak, you'll… you'll sing some songs. And drink. It will be fine."

Qerlak's face as he looked back to her was etched in grim humor. "It will in fact not, my good friend."

"He is bringing a bard." Fennet said mournfully.

"Fine, let him sing," she shot back.

No one spoke, instead looking to the lord of the manor.

"Galethiel, we are the hosts. It is not seemly that we should rely on our guests to shoulder the burden of—"

"Carking nobles!" Galethiel had no stomach for these sensibilities. "Qerlak, you are taking care of these people, and your neighbor is invading to take this foef away. You tell me he has knights, and maybe spearmen, and the Hopelords know what else." She leaned to put a hand on his arm, trying to speak low but too excited to keep her voice down. "On the Mindsea you did not hesitate over trifles when danger threatened. I'm here with you. Stop playing games and let the damn Greatknight be bored with you, just—"

213

"Many apologies," the voice of Ondaii broke in as he arrived dusting his hands with a towel. "My delay is without excuse, but the process could not an interruption stand." The engineer Qerlak had hired when he first took office sat and nodded to his neighbors Skeggs and Spezh.

"Not to worry, Citizen Ondaii," Qerlak rallied, "I doubt you could have had much to say on the current issue, but perhaps soon when we speak of the coming war."

"With pardons," Ondaii replied while sitting, "but did the august sorceress mention games?"

"It's only an expression sir." Galethiel waved her arm in frustration.

"We were just, ahm, casting about for a means of entertainment," Qerlak added. He looked around the table with a questioning face. "I don't suppose anyone here... can juggle?"

Galethiel spoke, just to break the silence. "If you want, I could cast some spells."

Qerlak and Fennet both blanched visibly, and the knight hastened to assure her. "No, Galethiel—normally an excellent suggestion but with this particular guest I fear it might not set relations in the right direction." He grinned at her and winked as if to say, "but it would be fun to see him squirm". She laughed and settled back.

"Perhaps Sir Chased could sing, milord." Cecil suggested.

"You honor me, lad," Chased replied, "but I know somewhat the problem Lord Barleybane faces, and it won't be resolved by an uncouth retainer banging out a drinking song of women and wine."

"It's a question of having a court, you see." Qerlak said with a sad smile. "As part of my enormous staff, you know, a kind of permanent entertainer for those dull days when nothing is happening." He let the notion hang in the air while many chuckled, even Galethiel catching the humor. "Something I have not gotten around to, unaccountably."

"With pardons again," Ondaii said, "but it might perhaps be a game that will do?" When everyone turned to look at the little man, he continued, "Such as Find the Feather?"

"What," Spezh demanded, "in the Hells of Despair is Find the Feather?"

Ondaii looked back at the dekentar, then around the room with surprise. "You know not this one? A simple game, and easy to watch but hard to play." He thought a moment, "It easier would be to demonstrate than to describe. May I, with kind permission milord, withdraw to gather needed things?"

Qerlak nodded while chewing his lip, and as the little fellow left the room, Galethiel had to speak or explode.

"Now, *now* can we talk about the invasion?"

"We can talk about it," Spezh muttered dourly.

"I won't let him besiege this place," Qerlak said decisively. "It's the safer course and we'd likely hold out, but the damage Pritaelseran could do to our fields and peasantry is unacceptable. No offense Sir Hitaelseran, but I must speak candidly of what I believe him capable."

"More than that, milord," Hitaelseran replied, "Of what my father has himself done in the past. You are correct, it is only to be expected of him." He sat back stiffly. "You must forgive me, but speaking so plainly of him who—"

"I quite understand. We shall not tax you unduly for details of intelligence over such a sore subject."

"But sir!" Spezh objected, even over Qerlak's raised hand. "At least find out the number of lances, how many bows, whether he—"

"Enough!" Qerlak's voice cracked with rare anger. "Dekentar Spezh, no man here doubts your courage or intent. But this is a question of honor."

"Do you want to win or don't you!"

"The matter is closed. When we leave to meet the enemy, my trusted vassal Sir Hitaelseran shall be detailed to guard this foef. I will not send his lance against his own blood. And as you all saw last night, I do not long tolerate spies in my presence."

Galethiel clucked audibly. "Fine then, we meet him in the open. What happens then?"

After a long silence, Fennet spoke. "Then milady, in all likelihood we lose the battle."

Qerlak nodded as if discussing his chances with a game of chess. "Our mounted bowmen are very useful, and the peasant levy under Cecil has done splendidly. There are circumstances where each can be quite effective." He mused awhile and drank. "But there are too many knights. His spearmen, even if supported by bows, I would have high hopes of defeating. Yet against all but the most foolish of knights, we are not enough."

Hitaelseran added quietly, "And my father is far from foolish."

Qerlak pounded the table with frustration. "So many hints in the records. There's been no time to explore further, but my predecessors had resources, maybe unused in centuries."

"Indeed milord," Fennet said, "I have seen the mentions of 'mounted bows' and 'heavy squad' which sound much like retainers. Allies of Mon-Crulbagh in older times."

"Perhaps one of your neighbors," Seldom Chased suggested.

Qerlak shook his head. "I see no sign of any agreement with the nearby knighthoods. Tricky thing, trying to ally with a peer when every knight schemes to become a Greatknight."

"And every Greatknight a Baron!" Chased agreed.

Qerlak shook his head. "The hints in the journal, the tone of confidence and satisfaction… I don't think it was a normal alliance."

Silence ran around the table.

"Maybe," Galethiel said, "the Reptile Men?"

Everyone gasped as if she had suggested a blasphemy. Qerlak grinned to her, saying "An interesting thought. But they never ride. And all the references I can see in the keep journal talk of war with the swamp tribes. I'm hoping, after recent events, they will stay away this summer."

"Milord," Fennet asked quietly, "did you see those references to the 'muster'?"

"What's a muster?" Spezh asked.

Qerlak shrugged. "My predecessors said damn little about it, as far as I can tell. It means to gather, and to get ready. But they seemed secretive, almost embarrassed—"

He shook his head. "I doubt we could unravel these mysteries in time. We will meet them with what we have, and Argens will favor the just."

Galethiel was hearing nothing to her satisfaction. "I'll be ready from now on, Qerlak. You make your plans." She rose to leave, taking in the room full of grown fighting men, pulling back in their chairs a bit on reflex. Galethiel realized she liked that. "If they threaten us, I won't hold back."

At that moment Ondaii re-entered, his arms loaded with an assortment of objects completely unrelated to each other, topped by a blindfold. A half-hour later, Mon-Crulbagh had its entertainment.

⊕ ⊕ ⊕

Castle Mon-Crulbagh

Since she had spoken with the bard two nights ago, Ellesmera had not said a word to anyone. Her companions, having learned her mother was dead, couldn't think of anything to say to her. The guards, she knew, tried to speak to her often; but only from a distance and she had long ago learned to block them from her mind. For nearly three solid days and nights, Ellesmera was with the group only in body. Those hours she spent instead in meditation.

The young martialist had learned to attempt the trance state in all conditions and postures. Sitting cross-legged was only a little easier than standing still, she knew. With wrists and ankles hobbled, Ellesmera found herself adopting many half-there positions that others would have felt stressful. From each of them, she was able to reach the trance state and sometimes very deeply. No need to sleep, no desire to eat, she focused on her inner self.

The grief she expected came on, but with more stealth than noise. The thought of her mother stole into every view, every breath, and then each waking moment with a sneaky swiftness that nearly overwhelmed her. Ellesmera examined a hundred facets of those few words, realizing the truth in them. There had been fighting, monstrous threats, and W'starrah Altieri had died in some heroic, ultimately successful fight against them. For all their years together Ellesmera would not have credited her mother with that brand of bravery, for she abhorred fighting itself; but in sacrifice, surely the favored of the Stargazer would have recognized her calling. Ellesmera felt sadness beyond tears as she calmly put away all regrets and second thoughts. She was here now. Her mother was without question in heaven. Further contact between them, though impossible to expect, was not beyond her ability to imagine.

And as the wagon took one last lazy turn from near-south to near-north and approached a distant fortress, Ellesmera prepared to face the world of words again with her senses as finely sharpened as they had ever been in her life. Quarion to one side of her radiated his tension at their unknown doom and his fervent wish that it would bring danger. It was as clear as wearing a sign around his neck: *Young Stealthic, Hopes for Adventure.* On the opposite side, Bellatara clutched the bars as usual and vibrated with interest at the strange wetland vistas, flights of birds, sounds of the hot wet land near the southern jungle. The bar-wagon rattled beneath the gate and the Woodsman sighed with the loss of her view.

Across the way they saw figures emerge from the main hall to greet Lord Beryl and his retainers. Ellesmera beheld the knight of Mon-Crulbagh and sensed a strong aura of honor, humility and goodwill beneath his outward nerves and careful formality. Beside him the colorful mortal mage loomed tall even discounting her piled red hair and impressive headpiece; in her darting eyes Ellesmera sensed she was biting her tongue, watching the young knight for her cues because of her strong loyalty to him. She thought at once of the vows she had taken with her two friends; and she longed for more of this.

The rattle of the wagon door preceded gruff orders to debark. Their guards slouched around as a strapping Elvish warrior in local livery stepped up with two guards of his own.

"These be the Greatknight's prisoners, dekentar, you see you watch them careful."

"We'll handle them fine," their new gaoler quipped, ignoring the other two and standing directly before Ellesmera. "You're the one, needs no weapons." His face sneered but his eyes spoke of doubt.

She spoke at last, gently and slow. "So few, really, need weapons."

The dekentar clearly did not understand, but laughed at the joke anyway. Drawing his dagger, he sliced her bonds at the wrist and ankle, winked at her, then finger-motioned his men to escort them up to their cell above the portcullis. As they climbed the steps, Ellesmera noted the grotesque statue in the courtyard, man and lizard-being locked in a tense, yet ambiguous grip. She looked again to the welcoming host knight and sensed a load of cares on his shoulders, a struggle like the one carved in stone that assailed him each moment as he jested and clapped backs with his fellow nobles. He needed help. He deserved it.

The donjon above the gate was solid stone with thick-set bar windows looking out to the moat and into the bailey. Her friends flopped down with accustomed good humor and were making light jokes as usual. Within, several beds ready for use, but only one with nicer sheets. Ellesmera looked down on the introductions still happening in the courtyard; one Elven warrior in full chain and sword was introduced with added formality, and the Greatknight seemed surprised to make his acquaintance. The youth spoke smoothly, but kept looking up at the battlement level, at this door. He was until recently a prisoner here, Ellesmera could sense it.

And if he were freed by the noble knight who owned this keep, perhaps the same fate awaited them.

Castle Mon-Crulbagh

Quarion looked around the cell with a practiced eye and immediately saw this had to number among the best accommodations the group had shared. Clean and spacious, with windows letting in the fresh air. Along one wall was a cistern of water, evidently catching some of the light rain on the donjon's roof, with a spigot to allow water to fall into a basin below.

Without being asked he pulled a small writing table over to the window looking out, so Bellatara could stand and see. He chuckled to hear her coo with delight at all the green and brown. Quarion was more interested in the door opposite, and what immediate fate might await within the castle.

Just testing the door on reflex as Ellesmera moved away, Quarion was shocked to find that it was unlocked. Before he could get his jaw to work and tell the others, he heard a grunt and a loud "Coming through!" that warned him to step back.

A pile of towels and buckets entered, carried by a thin young Elf with stringy hair and a prominent nose who sauntered past leaving the door open behind him, to approach the basin without

220

need of his vision. He plonked everything down and set out the towels before turning the spigot to let water fall into the basin.

"I'm Severyn," he said while working, "everyone calls me Illfellow. Because, well long story but I'm the one who gets all the scut work here." Taking a small covered metal pot off his waist he set it down, reached through the open lid with tongs and drew out a glowing coal which he dropped into the filling basin causing a cloud of steam. "Lord Barleybane invites you to bathe and then attend him at tonight's feast. Under guard of course." He looked at them all with an air of dawning alarm, as if suddenly realizing he had been sent to the donjon alone to service three known murderers.

Bellatara shouted with joy and somehow managed to strip off all her clothes even as she crossed the room. Clambering over the edge of the basin, at her shoulder-height, she slid into the water with a happy groan even as Severyn hastily turned away from the sight of flesh few Elves had ever known. He handed Quarion a bar of lye soap which he tossed to his bathing friend.

Quarion grinned and extended his arm. "I'm Quarion, and this is Bellatara—yes a Halfling—and Ellesmera. Thank you for this."

Severyn grinned and shrugged. "If you see a mess anywhere, something to do with mud, or blood, or manure, just call for me. I'm going to get the job anyway, might as well get it over with."

Ellesmera was looking on him in that steady way she sometimes did after her trances. "You have been here some time; in this castle I mean."

"Long enough to learn where all the darkest corners are," he replied, then cringed a bit in memory. "Plenty of those. But none worse, you ask me, than the main chamber itself."

"The place where we'll be feasting?" Quarion asked.

"Not early, of course, it will be full of people," Severyn dropped his voice to a whisper and it seemed the rain came down harder as he spoke. "But late at night, when the room is empty. A ghost. I've heard it."

Bellatara clucked from the tub, and Severyn forgot himself turning to look before spinning away with a yelp. "You don't believe me, you just come along after midnight, I'll show you. But I won't stay, and don't blame me."

"Illfellow!"

The moment of silence was broken by the distant roar of the guard captain, making everyone jump.

"Something's spilled. But mark my words." Severyn fled the room with the door still ajar, leaving Quarion to stare at his two smiling companions as he started to feel the welcome rumble of danger in his gut.

Castle of Mon-Crulbagh

Qerlak couldn't feel his pain through the thick blanket of excitement and dread. When he rose too quickly to grip arms with his overlord coming to table, the stitch of his broken rib pulled him back on a string and made it look as if he had lost his balance. But Qerlak pushed through the disability to give the strong clasp expected of him, speaking fair words that he hoped would mask the sweat of exertion on his forehead. Had it been only two nights past that he won the death-bout? Then just one, must be, since foiling the assassin and expending his last shred of willpower to save Hitaelseran. Precious little of that had returned to him by now.

As he sat back and coughed to cover his grunt of discomfort, Qerlak thought that if Argens could see him through those trials, behaving at a feast should not be beyond him. Perhaps it was time to relax, he thought as he reached for his mug; drunkenness, whether real or feigned, could serve to cover many physical shortcomings tonight.

To Qerlak's right sat Galethiel, Fennet, Chased, Hitaelseran and Spezh. On the left first Beryllian of course, with Tancrad Coss, two more retainers and the minstrel in his resplendent outfit. Added tables on the wings formed an enormous "C" shape in the chamber, with Ondaii and Cecil on one end across from the three prisoners led in by two of the guards. Qerlak glanced to his overlord, who was ignoring them, then back to scan the group.

Within moments, his instincts told him these were not common criminals. The Halfling on her own was a strong argument, as their natural charm was well known; he thought of Trillien the magic-jack and wondered where his old companions were, what trouble they had gotten themselves into since last fall. The ache he felt punched past his anxiety and his first tankard of strong beer, a pain he wouldn't have wanted to shield his heart from. He reached to Galethiel and patted her hand.

But the other two, slim and graceful Elves, looked about and saw everything, always mindful of each other. All three in their own way were very alert, they had an air of constant expectation he knew well from his own adventures. Qerlak imagined they were, despite their youth, a band much as the Tributarians had been. He longed to know more about them, but it was both weak and impolite to ask. Why had Torquem'l Beryllian brought them here?

The meal was served, and Qerlak spotted nearly half the staff laying and removing from the wrong side. He looked first to Fennet, whose face leaked agony, holding his well-groomed hair tightly in one hand as he leaned an elbow on the table. Chuckling, Qerlak turned back to face Beryllian, saluting him with his tankard and giving a shrug.

"We're still a bit, em, rough about the edges here milord."

To his great pleasure, Torquem'l Beryllian laughed out loud and toasted him back, waving an arm to indicate that nothing could be of less concern.

"That may be what it takes out here on the frontier, Lord Mon-Crulbagh. At least the food is very good," the Elven lord said, sounding a bit surprised.

"Is there any particular business you wish to conduct here, Lord Beryl?" Qerlak could not keep the edge from his question, and all he could tell of his lord was that tension ruled him in some way.

"You held court here yesterday," Beryllian replied, perhaps an evasion. "Boons and judgments, after the old customs?"

"We did indeed. The final day of a small celebration we held."

Beryllian nodded. "We passed throngs of peasants on the way, a most marvelous fair to judge by their report." He swirled his drink—only wine, how sad—and checked his head before it turned to glance at his three prisoners. "Any interesting results in court?"

"In court, Lord Beryl?" Qerlak drew breath to compose a careful answer. With a quick prayer to Argens for wise words, he managed to say, "We are still coming to know the local customs, of course."

Beryllian looked at him sharply on that, but said nothing. The meat arrived to distract them both, and Qerlak could see across the way the three prisoners ate with gusto as they chatted with a passing Severyn Illfellow filling the goblets. The villein laughed with them, but then became serious and pointed to the raised dais behind Qerlak's seat, where the throne chair was set. He seemed to be insisting something was true in the face of their doubt. But Fennet rose nervously to signal for the evening's entertainment as everyone ate.

Rising and bowing to all, Ondaii strode to the center of the room between the tables and arranged some of the staff evenly spaced in a circle around him. Each servant carried a different odd object: a woman's hat, a knife, one large white plume, a small wooden carving of a bird, and a half-dozen others. Ondaii in the center held up a long strip of thick black cloth.

"With greatest respect and hoping indeed for your slight enjoyment, I honor to present have the game Find the Feather. There it is—" he pointed to the serving girl holding it who waved it around with a smile. "The band of cloth I shall wear, then all shall march in thus a circle for as long as desires my lord. When he calls them to stop, I ask the question 'what lies before me'." Here Ondaii pointed to the servant boy holding a pot, standing at the place directly in front of him in the circle. "When my lord the item there reveals, he then calls 'where is the feather'. And I shall point to it."

Everyone took in this description without a sound, most of them no longer even eating as they tried to take it in. Sir Coss, looking around the circle at all the objects, cried "But it is impossible."

Ondaii smiled and bowed to this without responding.

"Certainly, the blindfold is thin enough—" Beryllian started to explain, but before he could finish Ondaii produced a pair of shears and cut the long band across the middle, advancing to hand one half to the Greatknight as he donned the other over his eyes.

"Can you see, milord?" Coss asked and Beryllian, holding it tight to his forehead a moment, shook his head.

"Nothing, it's black as pitch."

"Then it's impossible!" Coss repeated, and Spezh among others agreed.

Qerlak sat back and tried to look knowing, but his heart sank when he saw all the items begin to march in a circle around his engineer. Everyone murmured in wonder, and it was clear, whatever else, the game was holding their attention.

Galethiel nudged him. "You have to say stop."

"Stop now!" Qerlak cried, and everyone fell silent.

"What is before me?" Ondaii asked.

"It is, eh, it is the shield," Qerlak asked, forgetting the second part.

Beryllian, caught up in the excitement, shouted, "Where is the feather?"

Without hesitation Ondaii pointed with his right arm halfway behind him at the girl who held it up triumphantly.

"It's a trick!" Spezh cried out, angry that the object of his bullying should succeed at anything.

"Some kind of magic perhaps, milord," the bard suggested with a gentle smile.

"No," Galethiel said, "there's only one wizard here."

Qerlak saw the entire left side of his board staring with open mouths, then turned back to wink at his friend. "Let us try it again."

Ondaii just stood with a small smile beneath the blindfold, as the servants began walking in a circle again. This time Qerlak handled all the speaking duties and once again, the instant Ondaii knew that the wooden bird was before him, he pointed just to its left directly at the feather.

"Simply not possible."

"I am seeing it with my own eyes."

Qerlak thought about the day he taught the wizard Zoanstahr to play chess, a game it had taken him months of focus to learn. How quickly the human beat him! In his engineer, Qerlak sensed a similar mind, able to memorize positions and orders well beyond most other persons, at least without aid of their eyes.

"Would anyone else care to attempt this?" he asked with laughing eyes, suspecting full well no one would dare. He was lord of the manor now, and his guests would speak of the strange entertainment to be had in Mon-Crulbagh.

"Make him do it again!" Coss cried, and everyone agreed. As the servants marched Qerlak let the tension hang, while making sure a different object was in front before calling on them to stop.

"Wait! Wait!" Spezh cried, running around the table end to grab Ondaii by the shoulders and spin him in several revolutions before facing him to the right. He stood back grinning and folded his arms.

Ondaii cocked his head a moment, then shrugged and asked, "What is before me?"

"It's the metal pot." Spezh replied.

Ondaii pointed directly behind him as if at Spezh and the soldier cried out in triumph.

"Hah! That fixed him."

Qerlak coughed politely and the blue-garbed minstrel said "Behind you, good sir."

Behind Spezh the serving girl waved the feather at him coyly. The room dissolved in laughter and applause. Ondaii removed the eye-cloth and bowed to Qerlak, Lord Beryl and finally to Spezh who swore under his breath and stormed off.

"The game is best played by all," Ondaii said. "Will anyone attempt to Find the Feather?"

"Not I," declared the minstrel, "my head hurts simply from watching."

"May I attempt it?" a quiet voice from the end of the tables drew everyone's gaze and Qerlak saw the slender female Elven prisoner standing. Tancrad Coss leaped up with an angry face but said nothing.

Next to him, the minstrel smiled and said, "Hear, hear, milord, let us allow this."

Beryllian nodded to Qerlak, who gestured for the young woman to approach Ondaii at the center and take the blindfold. First, the woman faced each servant in turn, her lips slightly moving as she revolved slowly a full round. Then she closed her eyes a moment, nodding a little, and finally tied the blindfold, which Ondaii checked for her. The servants walked, and Qerlak called out the halt and said, "Before you is the fan."

"The fan," the small woman repeated, then seemed to count on her fingers. It took a long moment, but then she pointed just two places to the right and the room gasped. When the Elf

227

removed her blindfold, she looked Qerlak squarely in the eye a moment; he thought at once of Engurra and did not know why.

Several retainers eagerly attempted the game as the lords and others drank and laughed. No one won, and all the losers loudly declared it was still impossible. The ale and wine made their impact, laughter grew while discretion dimmed. Seldom Chased chatted with the giggling serving girl who held the feather; clearly her night was ordained.

Qerlak sampled the more recent brewing, one where he had tried to restore more of the bitter bite to his work, and wasn't sure if he had gone far enough. He was also unsure if his tongue was telling his mind everything it knew, for this was far from his first tankard. He looked at Lord Beryl, who still had not revealed the reason for his visit, acting in some ways as if he were as unsure of his justice as Qerlak was about the beer. Something to do with the three prisoners.

Galethiel leaned in, having followed his gaze. "I don't think those three did anything wrong."

Qerlak nodded slightly. "They have… come a long way." He thought of the Pilgrim tarot card and felt a charge inside him.

Some of the Mon-Crulbagh folk were calling for a song. Since as host he had provided an entertainment, it was fine to allow the guests to take the stage. The minstrel Bleys Eversong seemed to need little encouragement, though Qerlak noted his overlord's sigh as the man stepped up.

"Lords and ladies, citizens all," the bard began, "I'm sure there are many different songs you might like to hear." He smiled at their outcry as if it was to be expected. The servants all called out for 'The Border Stones! Sing of the Border Stones!', and Bleys bowed his assent to a cheer. As he began to sing, Qerlak was stunned to hear the room join in on several lines; he sat back amazed as if at a joke he all alone had not heard before.

When Mon-Crulbagh fought Pritaelseran,
THEY ALWAYS DO, THEY ALWAYS DO!
'Twas before the day of Viridian the Twelfth-
-and maybe the Tenth too.
The Hawk Lord summoned all his van,
THEY ALWAYS DO, THEY ALWAYS DO!
The Swamp Lord challenged him man to man, and the Hawk said yes-
When the rest are run through.
So say no more it's off to war and they fought the decades through.
And that is why the trees are high and the land is low and green,
But the Border Stones of Mon-Crulbagh have never justice seen.
NO THE BORDER STONES OF MON-CRULBAGH
HAVE NEVER JUSTICE SEEN.

Qerlak's body was afire with tingling prescience and he felt as he did in the tarot wagon, when praying in the temple. He could barely breathe, not just at the lyrics but at the way his people reacted. Clearly this was an old song, probably sung from childhood (though likely never as well as by this skilled bard). Everyone in this foef knew their part—excepting their lord. And it wouldn't do to let on that he was ignorant of these customs. Qerlak glanced at his castellan and saw a face white with anxiety, probably just like his own.

The Hawk Lord's knights struck a manly air,
THEY ALWAYS DO, THEY ALWAYS DO!
And laughed at their enemy standing there
Afoot, and lacking in swords too.
"No sticks and stones will break our bones" they thought on their chargers fair,
So the fields are wide and the summer's tide brings a harvest ripe and clean
But the Border Stones of Mon-Crulbagh have never justice seen.
NO THE BORDER STONES OF MON-CRULBAGH
HAVE NEVER JUSTICE SEEN.

Bleys let the last notes of this verse die away, standing still as if the song might be done. But no one moved in all the hall, the servants looking eagerly in like guard dogs on the leash waiting for the signal. And at last the minstrel continued.

The muster of the swamp stood fast,
THEY ALWAYS DO, THEY ALWAYS DO!

To Qerlak's astonishment, the entire hall erupted in full-throated cheers, shaken fists, and many servants pointing to him shouting "Crulbagh! Crulbagh!". Again that word. He gathered his wits enough to toast them all with his tankard, at which the cheering calmed a bit and Bleys, with a bow, began again.

The muster of the swamp stood fast,
THEY ALWAYS DO, THEY ALWAYS DO!
With pike in arm and sling they cast their vote and lo!
Their aim was true
On a marshy mound they stood their ground, till those knights turned tail at last,
And from west to east at last there's peace… until next summer's been!
But the Border Stones of Mon-Crulbagh have never justice seen.
NO THE BORDER STONES OF MON-CRULBAGH
HAVE NEVER JUSTICE SEEN.

Now the cheers were deafening, yet somehow also solemn from all about him. Qerlak looked to the peasants on his staff even as he lurched to his feet, his balance only slightly affected by the pain of his injuries but moreso by the beer. Still he was carried along on a tide of exultation, as if facing danger again in his adventuring days. Something was definitely brewing here. And he would be a part of it whatever came.

"Citizen Eversong," he cried as the applause finally ebbed, "I am most beholden to you for this magnificent, ahm, rendition. I have never heard—that is, never heard the tale told so well as you have this evening. You honor me."

As Bleys bowed, Lord Beryl cut in. "You like him then, Sir Barleybane."

"Like him! I envy you, milord, that your court should have—"

"Oh, you can have him!" Beryllian thundered and rose to his feet even less steadily than his host. "Bleys Eversong, we thank you for the many, many months of service you have rendered to our court, and release you now from our presence with gratitude. Coss, give him a purse."

Yet another cheer rang through the hall and Qerlak felt his instincts kick. Beryllian's eagerness to be rid of this polished, civil fellow was a warning, but he was thrilled at the prospect of attracting such a light to his court, even for a short time.

Bleys' smile never dimmed through this news but as Coss stood to hold out a bag of coins, he seemed to make a decision. Bowing low he said, "Milord Beryl, there is no price I can put on your kind patronage. As to your monetary generosity— forsooth, I must doubt there is much to buy hereabouts." He waited for the chuckling to die down, then continued, "In lieu of this purse, might I ask instead a boon?"

Beryllian knitted his brows in suspicion and said only, "Ask it."

"Will you consent to tell us what these three are doing here?" In the ensuing silence, Bleys dropped a final word, "And what you intend to do with them?"

He strummed a chord as Beryllian glared at him; Qerlak thought the pressure might blow the Greatknight open like one of his tubs in the cellar.

Coss spoke first, shouting, "It is not your place to question how Lord Beryl dispenses justice!"

"Indeed," Bleys replied, "By his word I have no place at all, as of this moment. So I ask again, what justice will you give in Mon-Crulbagh, milord?"

Qerlak looked to Beryllian still seated, and felt the Greatknight was only now deciding what to do.

"Sir Qerlak Barleybane, Lord of Mon-Crulbagh and my good and faithful vassal," he began slowly, "these three persons in my custody are accused of murder, burglary and numerous other crimes." He paused, taking a deep breath and holding it as the world waited. "By your past, ahm experiences, you are better suited than I to assess their worth and lay it against their deeds. I hereby declare them transferred to your custody, to punish, perish or parole as you see fit. They are hereby exiled from the Beryl domain on pain of death."

Qerlak answered from his feet, but felt the words were not his own. "I accept these three on your behalf, milord. It is my intention to test them, by fire, and in the forge of this foef shall the pilgrims you send me turn evil to good, and further the cause of justice as it is done either through them, or upon."

As one, all the guests rose and by unspoken agreement the feast was finished.

"Castellan, find suitable quarters for all our guests including Master Eversong."

"And the prisoners, milord?" Spezh asked.

"To the tower with them, dekentar, as before," Qerlak replied with just a slight wink.

He lingered letting the others egress, and slowly made his way to the throne-chair to sit and wait for Fennet's return. The lights still burned brightly, but the loneliness of the vast space exerted itself and he fancied once or twice he could hear sounds, as if from the floor beneath the dais. The strange events of the last two hours had driven all the drunkenness from him and the pain of his wounds was in strong evidence. One good night's sleep, for the love of the Hopeforger.

Fennet entered and nodded to his lord, as if expecting him to be there. He helped Qerlak to his feet as they made their way slowly to the bed chambers.

"So milord, it's clear this muster, whatever it is, holds a key to our victory."

"Indeed," Qerlak grunted, "and it has to do with the people, the common folk themselves. I've been thinking. These allies, the mounted bow and spear, it's beyond hope, whoever they are, that they would still be with us. If Elves, of any stripe, one of my predecessors would have mentioned them. But to beat Pritaelseran as often as they did, we must have also had the advantage of numbers."

"Numbers of what milord?"

"Of pike. And sling. As the song says."

They struggled up the steps together and Squire Cecil emerged to assist with the final hallway.

"Squire, the lands within a half-day's walk of the foef give us their lord labor by training for the pike, yes?"

The squire nodded and Qerlak looked to Fennet.

"Castellan, how many empty plots in that range? Four, perhaps five?"

"Only three milord. It's the land closest to your protection."

"Right." They arrived at his door and Qerlak turned to wave them off. "I can fall down from here on my own, thanks. What that song said about the border stones I can't imagine. But my esteemed neighbor was upset enough to demand that I fix it, as if I had moved them. By Argens, I've never seen them!

"It hardly matters in the end," Fennet said, "Pritaelseran will certainly invade, probably within the week."

"Yes, as he has before. It means, if we're to win, there must be more of them."

"More pike, milord?"

"Many more. And we got them by knowing what in the hells of Despair the muster was."

"Rest well, milord."

"No worries there," Qerlak replied as he closed the portal. "For once, a quiet night, praise Argens."

⊕ ⊕ ⊕

Castle of Mon-Crulbagh

Bellatara couldn't sleep in her new quarters, and lay listening to the outdoor sounds wafting on the thick breeze up to the donjon cell. After she and Quarion had congratulated Ellesmera on her mental feat in the blindfold game, they all agreed they felt much more hopeful than they had in some time. A few stories of what they each had seen, and gradually the talk died down leaving her alone with the nature all about this remote keep.

The sound of footsteps on the walk outside roused her easily, and Bellatara slid without noise to one side of the door. No key rattling in the lock—no one had even checked that—and she saw Severyn poke his head through, hissing to awaken all three.

"Well? Are you coming?"

Ellesmera swung her legs to sit on the edge of her bed. "Coming, to the main hall?"

"I told you, I would take you that far."

"But, we are prisoners."

Severyn rolled his eyes, then swung the door back and forth on its hinge. "They haven't lost the key, you know. Sir Barleybane is putting on a show until the high lords leave. I brought your things." So saying, he stepped fully into the room, lugging on his other shoulder three long packs that clunked to the floor with the sounds of metal and wood.

"My javelins!" Bellatara cried, and plundered her pack, overjoyed to see most of her things still intact.

Her companions took out their items, looked to each other, and shrugged before equipping. Severyn danced with impatience at the entrance, lighting a lantern off the cell's torch before signaling them to follow.

"It would be very good for us not to be caught," Quarion remarked as they stepped onto the battlements.

"Or not to do something wrong." Ellesmera returned.

Bellatara sighed. "Yes, of course, but anything is better than another night behind bars."

They crossed the open courtyard and entered the main building, empty and silent. Severyn made the only noise, constantly talking as if to fill the lonely space.

"I have cleaned every corner of this castle, and everyone says it's centuries old. Probably the oldest fortress in the Barony." He gulped as they approached the main hall, dropping his voice to a whisper. "The thing is, lots of previous lords, they didn't stay here so much. Those that did, had strange doings with beings in the outer edges. Swampy things, old things, creatures here before Argens himself."

"What kind of things," Quarion challenged with a grin.

"The Reptile Men, have you seen them? And they say across the swamp Sir Barleybane found gargoyles, even killed a dragon. My pap told me, on the east side near the upland-folk, deep in the woods, bugs the size of horses with shells harder than armor. And all kinds of beast-men."

"Quite a daunting array," Ellesmera murmured, clearly not convinced.

They came into the darkened hall and Severyn stopped, gesturing for one of them to take the lantern.

"You don't believe me. I'm used to that. Over there, by the lord's chair, you listen a while and tell me you hear nothing."

"Show us," Bellatara urged him.

"Not for my freedom and a hat full of silver. I'm staying right here."

"Why not leave then, if you're so afraid?"

Severyn looked at her with the real fear she had kidded him about, then gulped and shrugged. "If you three make a mess, I'm the one who'll have to clean it up. Might as well—"

He stopped his speech with a click in his throat, staring across the chamber behind the group. Bellatara looked, and felt a stab of terror to see a misty shape moving slowly and smoothly across the back of the hall.

It glided from their right nearer the trophy room to the left, where the kitchen lay. So far off the light barely touched it; Bellatara found herself arguing with her eyes, wishing that flowing shape did not hold together so well, or move so clearly. It was the very image of a ghost made by children, spreading a white sheet over the head. Without realizing it she had a javelin in hand.

Next to her Severyn began to choke and garble as his body shook from head to toe.

"Gh-g-g-gho—sss-t!"

"Quiet you fool!" Quarion snarled, but Severyn broke away from his restraining hand and dropped the lantern to the floor.

"Ghhoooooossst!" the villein screamed like a scalded cat and fled the room, his voice echoing from the rafters. Quarion snatched up the lantern to keep it lit as the shadows leaped to the ceiling and back like shafts of lightning.

Across the room, the white flowing thing stopped and turned. Bellatara thought she could just make out a face. The lips curled into a snarl that seemed petty for a supernatural creature. Spurred by revulsion, Bellatara suddenly heaved up her weapon, cross-stepped one pace and let fly with murderous intent.

The missile flew truly and passed directly through the thing to stick in the kitchen door behind it. Now the apparition paused, grinning in a way that suggested the pleasures of the living. With just a hint of a chuckle echoing through the chamber, it turned and continued on, to the stone wall beyond the kitchen doors. The form passed through the solid barrier without slowing and was gone.

"What was that?" She asked her companions in a whisper.

"I do not think it was one of the undead." Ellesmera ventured cautiously.

"Should we alert the guards? Or Sir Barleybane?"

"No!" Bellatara hissed. "We're supposed to be in our cell, remember?"

"Then let us return there at once," Ellesmera said, "before Severyn awakens the staff."

"Wait, I have to get my javelin back."

Bellatara trotted across the room to the kitchen door as the others trailed along with the lantern held high. She worked it loose and yanked it free, then froze at the sound of something clacking.

"Did you hear that?" She whispered.

Quarion nodded. "Like chains. Or bones. From the dais."

They all took a few steps closer to the raised platform, stopping when they heard the distant, muffled clank again.

"Severyn was right," Ellesmera said.

"One minute, let me check something." Quarion advanced to the dais and set the lantern on the floor. It was more than a hand's breadth high and made of wood, with floral decorations carved into the sides. Even as the distant clack echoed again, he put his hands on the central flower, a lotus blossom, and felt around.

"What are you doing?" Bellatara whispered.

"This petal, it's not solid. Hold a moment, there's some pattern here."

Quarion focused intently on the wooden floral carving, gently touching the various sections though Bellatara could see nothing move or change.

It seemed to take forever, but suddenly the Stealthic said "Hah. Here we are." He pressed the eight lotus petals in a certain order, the last one giving in a nail's thickness with an audible click. Quarion pressed the center of the flower without result, then feeling around a bit more, grasped the whole decoration and turned it a step or so clockwise.

The entire center section of the dais more than a body-length across slid jerkily back on some mechanism that creaked and protested with echoes through the hall. Before them, a set of wide stone steps led down into the earth.

They stared into the descending darkness until each of them coughed from the dank musty air seeping up into their faces.

"Now we must go back," Ellesmera said urgently.

"No, not now!" Quarion pleaded. "We have a chance to discover something here, make a name, do a deed for our new employer."

"Employer!" Bellatara replied. "He said he was going to put us to the test, or something."

"Listen to me," he said. "You heard the way that mechanism sounded. All those previous lords gone all the time, that's what Severyn said. And Sir Barleybane, he's only been here a year. This secret passage hasn't been opened in, probably in centuries."

"All the more reason," Ellesmera said patiently, "to let him know."

"You have it backwards, my friend. We look first. If there's nothing there we close the door and, I don't know, write him a message about it and leave it unsigned. But if we find anything—then it's a good deed and we can afford to let them find us out."

"That's—" Ellesmera started, but Quarion was already stepping down. He had the only light so Bellatara and Ellesmera both followed.

The stone steps continued down straight and steep, well beyond a normal flight of stairs.

"We must be below the cellar level," Bellatara said with a chill in her spine at her own words.

"And see the stone," Quarion replied. "It's all of a piece, carved from the native rock. This fortress must be sitting on a shelf, you would need years to tunnel in from the outside."

"It smells wet ahead," Bellatara whispered. "I think I hear water, like waves."

The steps finally debouched into a flat open area perhaps three times as wide as the stairs, empty to the edge of the lantern's light. Quarion held his cutlass and Bellatara her javelin as they inched forward into the cold, humid place.

"Meat would never rot down here," Quarion muttered.

"I hope it turns out to be only a salt cellar." Ellesmera replied.

"Bars," Bellatara whispered, as to their left the lantern revealed a familiar sight and ahead of them the stone ended at the edge of ebon water, stretching on out of view. At the water's edge, something curved and covered the size of a wagon canted slightly to one side, evidently floating and tied off to the floor by chains driven into the stone with thick stakes. As they watched frozen in awe, it moved slightly with the waves and clanked gently against its chains.

"Stay together," Ellesmera said quietly, and they walked a step at a time deeper into the room and close to the floating covered object. Bellatara could see glints of its sides against the light.

"It's made of metal!"

"Mostly," Quarion said, "with some wood between the sides. What is it?"

Shining his light around to the right side, he pointed to a work area with old tables and rotted chairs, then back to the left, within the barred cell a single small chest near what looked like a pile of dull white sticks.

"Whatever's in there must be valuable," he said starting to walk over.

"Beware," Ellesmera said coming to his side, "the prisoner."

"What?"

Now Bellatara felt her hackles rise along with the white sticks, as they slowly stood and formed the shape of something with three legs, taller than a man. It advanced to the barred door with more clacking and clicking, seized iron in its bony hands and began to press the bars apart.

"Helmon preserve us!" Bellatara whispered. She hurled a javelin at less than twenty feet away, but the missile flew directly through the thing's chest without harm, clanging on the stone of the cell behind it. The creature's third "leg" now lashed in all directions, clearly a tail. With the bars pushed apart, it stepped through a rain of rust and crushed cement to advance on the living with large jaws snapping and taloned claws reaching out.

Quarion thrust the lantern into Bellatara's hands and stepped up to cover her, ducking one claw and hacking into the bones of its midsection. The lashing tail caught him flush on the side of the head and he went skidding down hard on the stone floor.

Ellesmera moved up to the thing's side, striking once with her open palm and a loud shout. A rib cracked completely off and before the monster could react, she turned to land a kick on the base of its spine, then spun in the reverse direction to hit with an elbow high on its chest. That third blow was intended to catch the neck, Bellatara guessed, but the monstrous skeleton was too tall. Still, more bones cracked, and the thing went down from the hail of blows.

Quarion, staggering to his knees and still holding the cutlass, roared in fear and pain, bringing it down with both hands on that bony neck, severing it completely. At once the skeleton fell into a pile of bones which lay still.

Quarion rolled to his back and gasped with the effort to clear his head. Ellesmera returned to a watchful pose balanced on the balls of her feet, and calmly said, "*That*, was indeed an undead creature."

"You can tell?" Bellatara asked. "Not the one upstairs?"

A smile flicked across one half the martialist's mouth. "It's the first I encountered. My training, following the teaching of Areghel, I understood that we would have a special power to affect the undead. With that 'ghost' upstairs I felt nothing unusual, but here... with this, this thing, I felt almost a hunger. It had to be destroyed."

"Well you can have them all for my money," Quarion quipped. "Let's see what it was put in prison to guard."

The chest was not even locked and within was a rolled oiled parchment in fair condition. They decided not to break the knight's seal covering it, though at first Quarion voted it was better to know. Staying alert for other foes, they explored the work area and found little vials of brightly colored powders as well as small pots and tubes made of glass, perhaps used to prepare them.

"This could be lotus powder," Ellesmera guessed. "The bright colors, and the fact that there is so little here."

"But those are illegal." Bellatara cried. She had seen lotus blossoms on their way here, clearly the tropical weather supported their growth. And the symbol of this knighthood included a lotus.

"Today, yes," Quarion countered as they headed back up the steps, "but back when this place was last—say, what's all the ruckus?"

The sounds of shouting and alarm came down from above, and Bellatara felt her heart drop. Would they be apprehended again and the door this time locked on them forever?

They emerged with dragging feet to the main hall and were astonished to discover that no one was waiting for them. In fact, nobody seemed to have noticed the huge hole in the floor they came out of. A few guards ran through shouting about an attack, and distantly they heard the voice of Sir Barleybane, himself crying out in fear the name of his sorceress.

Castle of Mon-Crulbagh

Garr was proud to keep watch in the wizard's tower. The teacher was only human after all, she needed her sleep. In fact, Galethiel enjoyed 'sleeping on purpose', as she put it, within her circle of stones on the floor next to her bed. The mage's acolyte could hardly believe the tales she told him, of a strange land where dreams were visible. But when she smirked and told him once exactly what he'd dreamed of the previous night, it put all his doubts away.

Garr reasoned that if he stayed awake, she could no longer peek into his young mind's roving thoughts. And some of those thoughts had drifted too close for comfort to the red-haired wizard and the lore she might show him, of a non-magical nature. Garr was sure he would be dismissed the instant those unworthy notions came to light.

He passed the time by recreating his Fire-Light stone enchantment. Garr was becoming more confident with each pass, and his other attempts to assist Galethiel had also improved since that one success. When he showed it to her, she seemed at first pleased but also puzzled. When Garr pointed out the place in the spellbook's early pages where he had found the enchantment, she congratulated him soberly on being able to read the passages. He had forgotten that was something she showed him early on during his stay; Garr took reading for granted now. But after poking through the later pages, Galethiel could only humph and cluck, then chuckle a bit and shake her head.

Garr decided at first not to tell her about making more of them, and that had been a big mistake.

Just last week, during the Festival, he had accidentally knocked one of the four he'd made off the supposedly-safe shelf (was anything, he wondered, truly safe from his presence). The quartz gem hit the floor and shattered releasing a quick burst of light and creating a patch of fire more than two hand-widths across. Garr shouted and screamed in fear, and before Galethiel arrived the burning flame had touched a pouch of lantern oil. The lizard-rendered fat within had gone up in flames instantly and it was all they could do between them to put it out before the entire lab caught on fire.

Garr put his latest stone, the seventh, carefully in place up on a high shelf where a patch of velvet cloth held the others still against jostling. He couldn't help running through the shame of that afternoon, still fresh in the record of his apprenticeship, so to drive out the memory he immediately took another Light stone and began to infuse it as well.

Even as he cast and used his hands to retain the fire energy within the stone, Garr recalled again the fire spreading beneath the far counter, catching on the lizard-oil flask. How fiercely it had burned. The lab still smelled of charred wood and stone despite his constant scrubbing. But a strange thought struck the young peasant Elf and he completed the enchantment without really noticing. After her initial anxiety, Galethiel was not terribly angry with Garr about the accident. She had asked him what happened of course, but when he kept apologizing, she cut him off—so human! —and confirmed that in fact the broken gem, by itself, had sustained flame for at least a few moments.

Garr had never cast twice in the same evening before and the drain on his meager energies made him sit on the window-sill looking into the courtyard. He was young, and unwounded, and did not need to sleep as his human teacher did upstairs. But Garr was tired from casting, and bored, and still a bit ashamed of his last mistake. As he drifted toward a kind of half-doze, he remembered that after the accident, Galethiel had asked to take two of his stones, and later was talking in private with the small man in bright robes, Ondaii the engineer. The sorceress actually seemed pleased with Garr, even asking him to make more of the Fire-Light stones when he had time.

As he floated in such hopeful thoughts about his exotic, tall, beautiful teacher, Garr could not help falling closer to just a short nap. The keep was quiet, after the feast, and all seemed well. Not really sleeping, just thinking in a pleasant way...

He dreamed of the empty courtyard, and then believed he heard someone screaming in fear. About a ghost? The old keep was surely haunted, Garr believed Severyn when he—no wait, there was Severyn himself running out the front door. How silly he looked, and in laughing Garr came back to himself feeling a bit more awake, even as he fancied he heard the echoes of the screamer in dream.

When he saw a misty shape rise through his floor, Garr was sure at first that he had dozed off again. Like a soft, billowy triangle, the apparition grew to full height, and drifted toward the stairs leading up to the teacher's private chambers. Garr was a bit frightened but also excited—after all, was this not only a dream? He followed with footsteps that seemed quite real to him, up the stairs with the same exertion that he usually felt in the day. He never approached the teacher's quarters unless called.

At the top landing, Garr saw his spirit-intruder move directly through the wooden door. More proof of dream, but if so, there could be nothing wrong with following it. Garr threw back the portal and beheld his teacher by moonlight through the open window, lying within the stone circle while the menacing form of the spirit loomed above her. It was in the shape of a cloaked being, Man or Elf, and Garr could see in one hand a dagger dripping with green fluid. As the hand extended beyond the cover of the misty cloak, it seemed to become more real and firm.

Without thinking, Garr cried out and tackled the form, moving without interruption through its body and falling hard on the stone floor beyond Galethiel's sleeping form. Scrapes on his hands and knees convinced him he was awake. He rolled to his back and heard the clatter of the knife as it fell. But the apparition now came for him with murder in its eyes.

"Teacher! Assassin, help!" Garr flailed at the intruder's face with both arms but touched nothing. The attacker reached for his neck and suddenly the hand was hard across his throat, cutting off speech. The attacker barked out a syllable in the Sorceror's Tongue, and from his grip came flashes of burning light that ran from Garr's hair to his heels. The acolyte screamed in pain and dropped back barely able to stay conscious.

"First the pup," came a rippling voice, "now the bitch." The attacker turned on Galethiel, still asleep, and moved to the corner to pick up his dagger. His hand only became tangible when it extended to the ground.

Garr was dazed by the shock of the attack-spell, and stricken too with fear. If the teacher had been awake, he was sure he'd be unable to stir. But seeing her there still asleep despite all the noise, Garr found he was suddenly able to move, to do something desperate.

Reaching to her bed he snatched off a thick blanket, then he lunged to the far wall of the tower room where rested the Staff of Anun-Re. Garr wasn't sure this would work, but he had to try. From his knees, he balled up the blanket inside his palm, seized the wooden staff, and slung it across the room. Knocking aside some of the gems that formed the circle, it came to rest at the mage's side, and her hand clenched around it as if on reflex.

And as the attacker moved in, Galethiel's eyes came open.

She stood with the incredible speed she always showed, and the intruder stopped in indecision. One sweep of her mighty staff passed through his form; she followed up at once with a pointed arm and a flare of pure lightning, which also shot past and hit the wall behind, ripping a hole in the tapestry. Now he grinned with recovered courage, and the hand with the dagger licked out coming close to her arm as she snatched it back. He pressed his attack, forcing Galethiel to block or dodge as she gave ground.

"Poison, teacher!" he gasped, and she nodded curtly.

She struck again with her staff, then tried a new spell of some kind Garr could not recognize. Neither worked. Garr struggled to his feet and grabbed up a stool, thinking at first to defend himself with it. As Galethiel retreated around the bed, the attacker strode easily through it, grinning with malicious glee.

"There is no escape, mortal witch. Tell where the agony should first pierce your body. Perhaps I have an antidote, if you let me into you another—wha—!" He cried out as the stool passed completely through his head and out the window. Momentarily startled, the assassin glared hatred at the acolyte, then turned again to his teacher, who had taken the moment to make a slight gesture with a spoken word of the Sorceror's Tongue.

His next attack scored across Galethiel's upturned arm. But the blade scraped as if from a harder surface, sparking but failing to draw blood. Now it was the teacher's turn to smile. With a snarl, the attacker reached for her with his other hand, crackling with the same energy that Garr felt such agony from. Galethiel gave ground and fired off another bolt but it had no better effect than before. When she was backed against the wall his hand pressed into her ribs and Garr could see she clenched her teeth against the pain.

He had nothing. Garr snatched a lantern from the table, smashed it on the floor where the assassin's feet should have been, and grabbed the sparker from the sill to light the spattered oil. A small bright flame sprung up, and he hoped to distract him for a moment, perhaps taunt him into pursuing.

To his surprise, Garr saw the attacker look down in alarm, cry out and step away from the flaming area. Breaking his contact with Galethiel, they stood separated by a full pace of fiery stone. The assassin could only sweep with his knife, which Galethiel dodged easily, immediately casting a space of mystic fire directly beneath him. Again the intruder cried out and stepped back, and now Garr could see some real doubt on his face.

Galethiel cast the fire spell twice more, starting to hem her opponent in, though beads of sweat showed her exertion more than the heat of her creations. The mystic flame required no fuel to burn for some time, but it had the usual effect on anything it touched. Now the upper room was filling with smoke from the rug, bed, and more. The assassin did not seem badly hurt, but things were no longer going according to his plan. Just as Galethiel cast another patch of flame under him, he glided back and began to sink into the floor again.

"He will get away teacher!" Garr shouted, staggering for the stairs.

"Garr, wait!" Galethiel was making her way around the edge of the chamber to avoid the fire. She stopped another moment to turn the spigot to the roof-cistern all the way open, so that water came spouting down on some of the flames.

Garr knew there was no time, and without thinking he hurled himself down the stairs toward the laboratory where he had first seen the assailant. Weakened from the shocking attack, he stumbled at the landing and crashed into the room hitting his head against a chair. The misty form was there, just starting to sink into this floor, but stopped at his entrance. Turning back, the intruder looked down on Garr with a face of pure hatred and spite, gliding toward him at knee-level as if the stone floor were a shallow pool.

"I'll be back for the bitch, when I choose," he hissed mistily, "but I'll take care of you first."

Garr backed away to the shelves and used them to slide up to a standing position, but it was too late to get away. The assassin reached again with his open hand and Garr felt the coursing agony of his touch as if every nerve was being sliced in half and laid open like a fish in cleaning. Flailing at the attacker's body did no good, and as Garr weakened, he fell back, one arm reaching up to steady himself. His hand hit the top shelf and a small velvet cloth there.

Snatching out one of the stones, Garr brought it down between him and the assassin's leering face, and in panic, convulsively crushed it in his bare hand.

Flashing light and a wash of flame erupted over his arm, scorching his hair, igniting his own clothing. But the attacker also stumbled back in pain and fear, blinded a moment with the unexpected light. Garr sagged against the wall mewling in agony as his arm and torso burned.

But careening around the corner from the upper stairs came Galethiel, her face a mask of anger and purpose. As the intruder staggered back with his hand also burning, he saw the mage and at once began to sink further into the stone. But Galethiel cried out and gestured: suddenly the floor around the attacker burst into leaping fire for a body-length in all directions.

With a cry of utter terror, the assassin flailed to every side. Then a tiny tenor tearing noise at the back of his cape, which seemed suddenly to catch in the stone floor and ripped a seam up to his shoulder.

Garr had never heard a sound so horrendous from a human throat, the noise a man would make if finding his soft stomach and voice-tube filling with gravel. Garr saw the attacker's body suffer a final convulsion, and from the knees up he became fully tangible. His voice choked to nothing, and Garr saw grains of something granite-like leaking from his eyes, nose, and mouth. The figure stood stiffly in place, his every joint and cavity filled with stone. Even his skin was ashen toned.

With a snap of her fingers, Galethiel dismissed the flames, which this time had not set anything else on fire. She staggered into the room leaning hard on the Staff of Anun-Re and said "Illusions are tricky things. He believed he was burning to death, so…"

Her crooked grin went slack, and Garr felt a fresh wave of agony as he caught her falling body. They hit the stone together, and he savored its coolness against his burnt flesh as a black curtain covered his eyes.

Castle of Mon-Crulbagh

Hitaelseran was on the battlements well past midnight, marveling at the rustic nature of his new home, when he heard the shouting. He ran for the stairs down to the courtyard, noting from the corner of his eye that the gaol cell door was open. The portcullis was closed but the front hall doors yawned wide. Others were running to the wizard's tower, but the young knight moved instead to seek the main chamber; either he had an instinct of something overlooked, or his natural aversion to the sanctum of his own uncle, back home, drove him away.

Passing a few roused servants and the doctor in his bedclothes running out, Hitaelseran came into the main hall and by the light of a single lantern observed the three prisoners, standing next to a hole in the floor where the throne chair once sat. They were buzzing among themselves but as he advanced gripping the hilt of his sword they swung around, and mutually held their arms to each side. The male had a sheaf of parchments in one hand.

"What are you doing here?"

"A secret chamber, sir, we found it."

"And this," the youth said handing it over. Hitaelseran viewed the ancient seal and thrust it flat into his tunic.

"What do you know about this attack?"

"Nothing, sir," the Halfling piped up, "except we saw a, a shape that could walk through walls. We thought it might be a, that we were imagining it."

"But then we heard more sounds from below."

"One of the undead, sir, a skeleton—"

"Hold a moment," the youth cried, growing dizzy at so much revelation. "The Lord Crulbagh must hear of all this. It is for him to believe it or not. But for now, close this portal, and—"

"Hitaelseran!" It was the voice of the guard dekentar Spezh, at the far hall entrance. "Sir Hitaelseran!"

"I am here."

"A man, at the gate, sir, badly wounded. Asking for you."

"Stay here, all of you." Hitaelseran forgot himself a moment, not realizing until halfway to the portcullis that he had no rank to issue orders in this place. At the gate, he beheld a horse in the moonlight, a slumped form clinging to its neck.

"Guernsten! What happened?"

"Milord. Beg your protection, sir. Had nowhere else—"

"Guardsman, open this gate."

"I need orders from milord Barleybane for that."

"I tell you this man is my, my retainer. You can see he's badly hurt. On my authority, I order you to open this gate!"

Spezh's face quirked with anger, then he shrugged, saying, "On your head then." He nodded to his men, and a few moments later, the soldier's body slid off the horse's side and into Hitaelseran's arms. Driven by horror and outrage, he easily bore the bigger man back to the main chamber, trailing a procession of servants with Lord Barleybane at its head, who was also carrying the slender form of his mage. The squire Cecil hauled her acolyte over his shoulder like an oversize sleeping baby.

More lights revealed the main chamber; the raised dais at the back, now covered again, served as a makeshift hospital. Servants brought blankets, pillows, water and bandages; Doctor Drace ministered to each as the lord of Crulbagh sank unsteadily with a small gasp, to sit near Galethiel.

"Yes, milord," Drace muttered with an acid tone, "you perhaps recall your broken rib now. Sit there, sir, I find three patients at a time quite enough."

Qerlak ignored the scolding and laid one hand on Galethiel's forehead while murmuring words in the Ancient tongue. Hitaelseran knew it was the miracle of Strengthening and felt an echo of the rush he had just the previous night, when it was used so many times on him to stave off the effects of poison.

"You stay still," Qerlak advised her, smiling though looking haggard from his exertions. Here was an Elf, he reflected, who needed sleep and was not getting it.

"By Telhol's Light!" Drace exclaimed at seeing Guernsten's slicing wounds. "What manner of animal caused this torture?"

"A hawk, doctor, unless I miss my guess," Hitaelseran said through clenched teeth. "This is my man, Lord Barleybane, just come to the castle as you see him. He was, he advised me on the raid in which I became your guest."

"Then I thank you sir for that," Qerlak replied to Guernsten as he crawled to where the man lay, "though matters may have turned out other than you purposed." Despite the doctor's slaps, he reached in and laid his hand on the wounded soldier, invoked again, then quietly sank back on the wood. The miracle brought deeper breathing and energy to the wounded man.

"Guernsten, what happened?"

"Your father, sir. He received your letter, you said, not my fault." Guernsten's lip-slices broke open as he spoke, and there were dull red stripes under his tunic. "He was... displeased, sir."

Hitaelseran looked into his new lord's eyes and saw there the sympathy he would have hoped for from his sire. A fire began burning in his gut, though he knew not yet what it consumed. Controlling his temper, he turned to look at the sorceress and her attendant. "What happened here?"

"An assassin, I surmise," Qerlak replied, sitting up. His face was etched in worry as he looked to Galethiel. "His body, it's still in the tower... stuck in the stone." His face writhed momentarily, "Part of it, rather."

"Sent," Guernsten whispered, "by your uncle, milord. I heard, in the chamber, I heard enough."

Galethiel stirred, and Hitaelseran sensed she had been awake but conserving her energies. "We managed to kill the bastard. Garr helped, saved my life."

"Milord," Hitaelseran said, "it may have been my uncle's closest follower, one named Insis. I can recognize his face, if it is still intact."

"You would oblige me, sir, if you would look at your leisure." Qerlak smiled. "He won't be going anywhere, that is, until we chisel him loose."

"If it is Insis, milord, you may rest assured that his master will accompany my father on the expected invasion."

Silence at this, and he could tell his new overlord was hesitant to plumb for information. But the fire within burned higher, and Hitaelseran volunteered it.

"Zantire Pritaelseran is well known as a learned mage, milord. Older than my father, he abdicated knightly rule for his studies. Though many whisper he runs the foef still."

Galethiel sat up slowly with Qerlak's hand on her back.

"How skilled is he?" she asked.

Hitaelseran swallowed once at the thought of his uncle's piercing eyes.

"I have heard it said, though I know not what it means, that he has mastered a Mage Command."

"What is that?" Qerlak asked and Galethiel shook her head.

"An ancient spell, closely guarded and only available to those with the deepest affinity and talent. The wizard shouts a single word, one for taking action, and everyone within earshot before him must do as commanded."

"A word for action? You mean like 'eat'?"

Galethiel smiled. "You would think of that one. Try 'walk', I have seen that used on signs in a city. And Astromozepal, Qerlak, remember him! He had the power for 'crawl', and it nearly finished us. One story I heard, about the mage of some Baron or other, who knew 'flee'; his lord never lost a battle. But then the wizard died, and no one knew his secret."

"Could you cast one?" Qerlak asked.

She shrugged and laughed. "In this empire? A human? I'd have to burn the Mages Guild to the ground to get my hands on the lore." Then she calmed and looked him straight in the eye. "Could I? I don't know."

Hitaelseran said, "I do not know which one my uncle has learned."

Qerlak nodded. "But he will likely be there, I agree. And your father of course."

He didn't continue, but Hitaelseran knew what he wanted.

So, evidently, did Guernsten, who hauled himself up on an elbow even as the doctor continued to salve and bandage his naked torso.

"You want a full tally of the Hawk's force."

"Never mind, sirrah, you just rest—"

"Cark it!" Guernsten cried, "I'm no nobleman bound to service. Not anymore. See, Sir Barleybane, see what he did to me. May Argens crush him underfoot for all those he oppresses with his taxes, and the men who will die to help expand his realm."

"Twoscore knights he's gathering in chain and lance, full armed. Each has one retainer in leather, also mounted with sword and shield. He has called for his foot levy, not much training but well clad in leather and spear. Like the ones you saw us lead to you."

"How many?"

Guernsten considered with a wrinkled brow. "Still gathering when I left. But I mark at least a hundred, milord."

These quiet words were like the blows of a hammer in that vast hall.

Hitaelseran spoke to add, "My father and any sons he brings will have plate mail of course, extra mounts and a squire apiece."

"Bowmen?" Qerlak asked, and Hitaelseran turned to Guernsten with the question. He shook his head in doubt.

"Not many, milord. Those as cannot afford the armor, is all."

In the silence after that, Hitaelseran looked through the open front hall doors and thought he could make out the sky lightening ever so slightly with the touch of predawn.

"We need more men to fight." Qerlak put the matter simply.

"Here, sir, are three to begin with," Hitaelseran said, gesturing them over. "They have made quite a discovery and will tell you all about it." He withdrew the sealed parchment and handed it over, then turned to Guernsten. "If I might have your permission, I'd like to see this man quartered in my chambers for rest."

"With all my heart, sir, and my thanks."

Hitaelseran carried his man up the stairs and laid him on his own bed, already passed out with his exertions and the lapse of Qerlak's miracle. His bandages made him look little less frightening than his scars had done. Hitaelseran gazed down on him and felt that inner fire banking ever hotter. Failure and shame were two different things; only one must be borne without response. Once sure Guernsten was asleep, he headed back to the main chamber filled with resolve.

Castle of Mon-Crulbagh

Galethiel stood back as the young Stealthic made the secret door open again for Qerlak's inspection. There were only the five of them left in the chamber: Cecil and Fennet had helped get Garr back to bed in the tower. The lad was burned across one arm and had little hair left, but the doctor had said he would recover well with rest.

"Incredible!" Qerlak exclaimed aloud as it opened, "And under my feet this entire time." He took the lantern and led the three former prisoners downstairs as they chattered about their find. The voices faded from hearing and she was alone in the dark.

Galethiel thought about the adventure in Jengesalamur, deep underground and filled with perils. The mystic black scrying ball that gave her the first real dream of her life. The initial step of her journey to becoming the Dream-Seer: they told her she was asleep for nearly an entire day. Some had argued for leaving her there, but Qerlak had insisted on keeping watch. His was the first face she saw upon awakening with a new sense of purpose. Galethiel knew the fierce bond they had would stand; she had met nobles before but never one so noble.

She was just about to head into the cellars when their returning footsteps echoed up. This time, hers was the first face Qerlak saw and they grinned at each other.

"We'll have to look this over soon." He said, too amazed to recall how dead-tired he was. "For the moment, no one is allowed down there without me. Best if we keep the knowledge as close to the vest as possible. Quickly now, let us close this panel."

"Allow us, milord," the Elven female said. The three young guests closed the door again by pushing from behind the dais and it creaked closed with loud protestations.

"We'll need to get that oiled, I suppose. Ah, Fennet, welcome back, do we have some of that oil left, rendered from lizard fat?"

Fennet and Cecil, followed by Seldom Chased and Spezh filed in, as beyond the windows the dawn was breaking.

"Oil? Precious little, milord. Ondaii has requisitioned nearly every drop for that experiment you asked him about."

Galethiel grinned at Qerlak's puzzlement. "I asked him to try something, a new weapon to help in the battle. It's almost finished, he says."

"You? Asked Ondaii? To do something using all the lizard oil in my keep?" Qerlak spoke in that mock-serious tone he sometimes used when trying to act the strict arrogant nobleman.

"And the new Fire-Light stones," Galethiel added just to tweak him further, and everyone laughed. "Patience, it will be ready soon."

"Secrets all around," the knight intoned mysteriously, taking out the parchment and waggling it at his friend. A bluff- Galethiel could see the seal was still unbroken.

"Cecil, please assign our new guests to chambers within the foef proper. No more guards for them, that is, after Lord Beryl leaves this morning."

"At once, Sir Qerlak."

"Fennet, we'll need a good meal to send our noble guests on their way."

"Indeed milord, I can smell Skeggs hard at work already. Something for the early risers is ready now."

"Very well indeed. Let us see what my predecessor thought so well worth keeping away from prying eyes."

As the servants set out tea and bread with jam at the main table, Qerlak cleared a space on the far end and slipped his hand beneath the wax-sealed fold, pushing the oversize paper down before him so that it overlapped the width of the table. He read intently for several moments and Galethiel sipped waiting with her usual impatience to be doing something.

She watched Qerlak's face, seeing his initial concern and interest give way to flashes of shock, astonishment and something akin to fear. He let the parchments rest on the table.

"Fennet," he said quietly, "I've found the extra men we need. Have a look."

Galethiel stood to read over one shoulder as Fennet took the other side. Galethiel's eye utterly failed to take it in, distracted by the penmanship, the officious language and the bold letters near the top:

We, the lords and laborers of Mon-Crulbagh, *do hereby establish this* Compact of the Muster, *in the year 1591 ADR...*

"Flame of the First," Fennet whispered. "Milord, this cannot, it could never—"

"We know it happened, good castellan. And it answers many things. The added levy, the key to defeating Pritaelseran, Heroes of Hope, it even explains those odd-shaped stones in the cellar."

"Those were for practice?"

"Of course! My more immediate predecessors didn't know what they were for, without this document. So they stuffed them in the cellar, doing no one any good. They probably kept all the steel pike-heads here in ancient times, and swapped them only for the duration."

"I don't understand," Galethiel said, "added levy, what is this muster?"

"Milord," Fennet said with urgency, "you must not take this risk. It would mean surrendering control of the foef."

"Would it, my good castellan? Would it really?"

Galethiel saw in Qerlak's eyes that same light and energy that always meant he would do something heroic soon. Never particularly religious, she had always felt only the Elves had time to waste on devotions to any hero. But she never doubted her companion's fervor, and she had experienced the results.

"You see, Fennet," he continued with his eyes aflame and grinning at Galethiel, "it's very much like our adventuring career. We were all equals there, you must have guessed, there's no way I'm lord over my sorceress here. She does as she wishes, and well, there are sometimes mistakes." He became completely serious a moment, and she put her hand on his.

"The noble code," she said, "in my book, isn't worth a bucket of spit. But I'm here for you Qerlak."

"And I have always known that, Galethiel. Grateful for it, immensely grateful." He drew a deep breath and looked across the room at the others eating and chatting. "The point here, though; we always discussed what to do next. If our doughty dwarf led us in combat, well and good, we all knew our parts. But we decided as a group, whether to go and seek the fight. A good leader would never lead his people anywhere only for his own selfish interest. And when it's the foef's welfare at stake, we cannot afford error."

He put a hand on Fennet's shoulder. "We know Pritaelseran is a threat. Of course I wish to rule these people. I confess to you what you already know, that I live for it. But I also believe with all my heart that the people of Mon-Crulbagh are better off, or they will be if I—"

"Milord," Fennet was so moved he interrupted, something Galethiel knew the Elves normally despised, "you are without question the most noble knight of the Argensian Baronies. But all the more reason to keep your authority."

"We cannot afford such trappings here, Fennet. The muster means the people gain the power to vote for war before putting their bodies into harm's way." He looked to Galethiel again, "We vote on it, just as we always used to. If I cannot convince them, well, I don't deserve the lordship, I suppose. But this is one custom I will not break."

"Will they understand this process, milord? You will ride to each village and steading and ask for their vote, equipping all who agree with pike and armor? Will they be ready?"

"They'll need training of course. But for now, even a show of force will work wonders. And don't bet there aren't some who remember this custom, Fennet. You heard the cheering during that song."

Galethiel saw Qerlak rise with a smile, folding the paper and moving back to the center of the table to join the others. Fennet pulled at his face, and she still wasn't sure what was happening here. But now her chief concern was her friend's energy; happy though he appeared on his lips, Qerlak's hand trailed on the table for support and he sat his chair rather heavily after another sleepless night with wounds.

Others were gathering in the main hall now, and Qerlak roused himself to greet them.

"Master Eversong, an early good morning to you sir!"

"Apologies, milord, I heard a ruckus a short while ago and wondered if I were missing some celebration?"

"Of a sort, sir, of a sort. Please sit and refresh yourself, and my thanks again for that most marvelous song, whose meaning continues to unfold before me."

Bleys grinned a bit sheepishly. "I confess, milord Barleybane, there is a version I must sing when in Pritaelseran, which ends quite differently!"

Everyone shared a laugh at that.

"A man must earn a living milord! But in my judgment, the one I sang was the original. The rhyme scheme works better, for one thing."

"What think you, good Eversong, of the chorus? About these border stones, which have never justice seen? Nor myself, for that matter."

The minstrel was digging into the bread and jam and shrugged eloquently. "I hardly know, Sir Barleybane, except that there are said to be monoliths, or stone piles of some kind, to mark your territory's borders with the Hawk Knight. And I gather… there has been constant fighting. So, a lack of justice in that, I would guess."

"Indeed, it is possible. Ah, Sir Seldom, my excellent Captain, and here again comes Sir Hitaelseran, excellent! Good knights, we have much to plan for and I don't doubt too little time to do so. Sir Chased, I will leave Sir Hitaelseran to read you this compact; you may each be required to spread this news once we—"

"Bugs!" Everyone turned to look at the youth who burst into the hall, exhausted yet still terrified. "Bugs, milord, bugs in Bultarr-r!"

"By Argens' Flame," Qerlak cried, "must everything in history repeat itself?"

"Flying things, milord, we saw them in the skies east of town two days ago. The size of a dog with long beaks like swords before them. And more, milord, great low-built monsters in the far fields, tearing and uprooting crops and some of the outlying houses. My family, they lived in one… I don't know where they are now, sir. The people in town, they gave me a horse and told me to come here…"

Before anyone could say more, the sound of a horn from the castle walls echoed through the hall. Galethiel felt a charge run through her, and looked to her friend, whose face was cracked with dismay.

"No time," he muttered, "there's not enough time."

"It's the invasion signal, milord," Fennet said. "The guards are hearing it from the south, most likely. Pritaelseran is coming."

Everyone buzzed and started shouting, and Galethiel sat frozen with unaccustomed fear. This was like those times when exploring the deep under-city, and attacks came from all directions at once in the narrow tunnels.

Qerlak suddenly stood and pounded both fists on the table for attention.

"Everyone, grab food and get to your chambers. Prepare to leave at once; bring whatever you need to enter the fight of your lives."

"But where, sir?"

"Which will we—"

"I will tell you upon your return! Now go!" Qerlak's voice split with anger and the edge of something else, best not named.

Galethiel ran to her chambers, donned her gear and took up the staff. Looking in on Garr she saw him sleeping peacefully and Doctor Drace dozing on a chair in the next room. Passing the laboratory on her way down the stairs, she stopped and viewed again the grotesque shape of her assassin, frozen in half-stone from the thighs up near the middle of the floor. At the last moment, she noticed the small array of Fire-Light stones on the shelf and took all but one with her.

She was the first to approach the main hall again, and saw to her horror Qerlak alone, sitting with his head in his hands looking down at the floor between his feet. In all her days she had never seen her friend and noble Pious Warrior in such a posture of defeat. She almost tiptoed across the chamber to put a hand on his shoulder, causing him to look up. Tears streaked his face, and exhaustion imbued it.

"Galethiel," he whispered, "I cannot do this. There's not enough time."

She couldn't keep her shock from showing. Galethiel realized, even as she drew a breath to reply, that she had always assumed Qerlak's leadership. He thought he had already failed.

"Qerlak. Do you remember, in Jengesalamur, at the three-way tunnel nobody could decide which one was best, or how to proceed?"

"Remember! Could I forget; we argued there for, what was it, two solid hours?"

"No, *they* argued, Qerlak. What did you do?"

"I… did nothing."

Galethiel swatted his wrist then, playfully but sharp enough to sting.

"You said your piece, and then you volunteered to stand guard by the left-hand passage."

He shrugged while mock-hugging his arm as if truly injured there.

"It was nothing, I tell you."

"Oh, really. And when Solo and Zoanstahr and Saling'r were all done, the swearing and cursing and foot-stomping over, what did we do?"

"We went down one of the—"

Qerlak managed to duck her arm this time as she went to box his ears.

"We went down the *left-hand* passage! And in the chamber, with the black crystal ball, I fell asleep and they argued about leaving me there. About leaving me behind, Qerlak."

"Not permanently, just to look a little ahead."

"Right, and what did you do?"

"I stayed behind. To keep watch, that's all."

"You guarded me, sleeping there. You stopped them from waking me, and you refused to leave me behind. And they all stayed, in the end."

She let the import of this sink in.

"You always decide, Qerlak. You decide what you are going to do, and you leave others free to follow. I am free, and I follow you. And I always will." She pinched his wrist then. "Until you turn into a noble, code-following carking twit like this Pritaelseran. Then I will pack up and leave without letting you know."

She reached into her pouch and put the Fire-Light stones on the table.

"One of these helped to kill that assassin tonight. I had no idea you could even make them a month ago. When Garr showed me what he had done—little fool, he might have killed himself then! And I couldn't find a clue as to why anyone would want to do this weird thing. I told him to make more, just to keep him busy. Then I thought about what you said, all those knights on the field, and I asked Ondaii to help us."

Qerlak picked up a stone and contemplated the sparks inside it. "Easily broken?"

"You can crush one in your hand, if you want to look like poor Garr."

He laughed and put one in a pocket. Galethiel continued urgently.

"The point, Qerlak. None of us knows what will happen. Other people will do as they wish." She shrugged, "We just do our best."

Qerlak thought about this a moment, then reached to squeeze her arm in gratitude. She turned it into a hug and felt the power of his embrace. They pulled back and he asked her one last question quietly.

"And if I make a mistake?"

"Then it's a carking mistake! Was the left-passage the right one? But we won in the end."

Qerlak laughed in surprise, and nodded as if learning a thing for the first time. The others returned then, clattering with metal and packs and conversation. No one sat.

"We are faced with two challenges," Qerlak announced, "neither of which we can afford to lose. Seldom Chased, you and Elias Fennet will ride to the steadings south and east between here and Sluicehill. Load a wagon with weapons and any armor we may still have on hand, Spezh will show you our stores. Read them the compact, give the adult males the choice to follow and if they agree, hand them a pike. Cecil, rally the nearby levy and march for the Sodsluice without delay."

He paused a moment to scan the group. "I will meet you there."

Turning to the three newcomers, he said only, "You young persons, I have said I would test you, and I meant it. You will accompany me to Bultarr-r along with the mage Galethiel. We will settle this Bug problem in short order, and return in time for the invasion."

A raft of questions and objections followed, but Qerlak threw out his arms commanding silence. And got it.

"There's no time. A large group will spook the Insectirs, and fire, not numbers, is the key to their defeat. Each of you, take one of these stones and put it safely on your person. Don't drop them."

He turned to face the rest. "Dekentar Spezh knows the battle site I wish to use. If I fail of meeting you at Sluicehill, I will make for that spot. We still do not have our mysterious allies, but Argens will provide. We will… we will all do our best."

"Master Eversong, are those your traveling clothes? Or do you plan to stay here?"

The minstrel bowed at the chuckles all around. "I have nothing worse to wear, milord, not expecting that I should have to work for a living. By your grace, I would prefer to rest here for the moment, bid my former patron a fond farewell, and join with your army as it gathers. Mayhap you would permit me to sing of this someday."

"Right gladly. Sir Hitaelseran, I charge you with the defence—"

"No, milord."

The hall rang with his denial, firm and clear. All stood aside so the two knights had a clear view of each other.

"You are eager, no doubt," Qerlak said slowly, "to prove the value of your newly-minted oath, sir. It does you honor, but I will not order you to fight your own family."

"You saw, milord, what my sire did to Guernsten. Because of me! Because of what I wrote. I have no family, milord Barleybane, unless I find it here."

"You may not spill your own father's blood!" Qerlak thundered, like a man unwounded and fully rested. A lord, in fact. All in the room drew back from the wind of authority he drove across them.

Hitaelseran too was affected, yet he stood his ground. "Agreed. I shall not joust the Hawk Knight personally."

"Whether he challenges you or not?"

"Under no terms, even to fleeing his approach." Hitaelseran's mouth turned up in a saucy grin as he raised one finger to bargain. "My brothers, however, should I come upon them."

Qerlak considered, smiled and nodded once.

"Fennet, short straw for you, I must ask once again that you remain behind."

"Milord, our guests, I had forgotten!"

"Ah. Yes." Qerlak replied, showing they had also slipped his mind. "Please apologize to milord Beryl when he comes to breakfast. He may stay as long as he likes—in fact, with the few men I am leaving you, he can take possession if he prefers. I shall attend him in a fortnight and explain all, should I survive."

Ondaii entered looking quite tired and dusty but smiling to say, "The weapon is finished."

"Wonderful, Citizen Ondaii, I am sure. Bring it with Sir Chased if you will, I shall see it in combat. Whatever it is."

Chapter VI. Heat

Castle Pritaelseran

In his many decades of service, Dommes had seen Lord Pritaelseran and his elder brother together in person any number of times. But never before had he witnessed them embracing.

No matter, it did not affect his place. Dommes carried the tray with liqueur to a side-table and silently set it down. There was no sign he overheard anything they said, in fervent lowered tones.

"Your loss is my own, brother," Cran-Kalrith said, "we shall avenge Insis and Hitaelseran in the same blow."

"No degree of pain, no length of days will be enough to repay that witch, however she did it." Zantire was moved to a loss of control, another thing Dommes had never seen. His bald skull was blotched with red, his face etched in fury and his hands clenched his brother's thick tunic deeply enough to leave unsightly wrinkles. "Would she were an Elf, that I might draw out her torture in a measure to fit the loss of my Insis."

"The men are ready and we leave with the dawn. Mon-Crulbagh this time has overstepped his place and I will finally achieve the glory my father and his father before him failed to bring home to Pritaelseran. No Greatknight in Argens will control so much land as the Hawk."

"I will be there with you. The red-haired witch is mine, brother, and then you will make short work of these peasants and their adventuring bandit-lord."

"A toast to celebrate our new venture." The knight gestured with the parchment of a recently-received letter and they both chuckled. "The foef is ours already thanks to my foresight. But today is about revenge."

"Together forever, brother."

Dommes was already at the door when they turned. Service without presence was his place, and well he knew it. As he moved down the central hall to the inner bailey, he reflected on the change in his master. Sir Pritaelseran had always been strict and even cruel, but with the loss of his youngest son, pride had broken forth to trample all other emotions. Dommes smoothed down the press of his new outfit, so beautifully and sturdily made, and realized that the price of four such fine suits could have ransomed the boy. He had been at pains to have it made in green and yellow, the house colors, yet as he emerged to the bright sunshine of the courtyard where the troops were gathered, Dommes glanced down at his clothes and saw only stripes of red where he had cradled an innocent man less than a week ago. The suit, though new, seemed ruined.

Before him the mounted retainers, spearmen and a dozen wagons were arrayed in perfect order. To one side shuffled a group of ragged peasants with bows over their backs, standing to attention but destined to do the hauling, digging, cooking and foraging between now and the battle. Dommes signaled two servants to raise the ensign flag indicating the lord was absent, so that any chivalrous opponent would seek him in the field rather than treacherously attack his fortress. Not that the castle had ever seen such a siege in all its centuries, but protocol was most important.

To Dommes' right, Canril stood a step below the top. The third son's arm was no longer in a sling, but his face streamed with angry tears to be left behind from this second, and last expedition against Mon-Crulbragh. The eldest, Craltire, sat proudly in his plate suit with visor raised while the second son, Zanrith, held the reins of his own charger as well as his father's. As the lord and his brother emerged to the portico, the soldiers all cheered till the courtyard rang with the sound. Dommes noticed the only person not there, and this too was his place. He hastened to find the lady Eli'se with time of the essence. Not the gardens, he guessed, most likely the chapel.

Within its quiet walls, Dommes once again saw something he never had before. The lady in prayer was commonplace, standing quietly with folded hands and lightly-moving lips, or perhaps on her knees at the front rail. But now her body lay stretched prone on the marble floor, one hand reaching to clutch the base of the altar, and her fair form wracked with sobs. Even the curate had fled this wrenching scene.

And Dommes decided, rather than break into her sorrow to comfort or cajole, he would rather face her husband's razor-cane himself.

Back in the courtyard, Dommes realized the absence of the foef's lady had gone unnoticed, as the army was already moving through the gates. Canril stood frozen to the step, clenching fists and striving for the calm achieved by statues decorating the façade behind him. As he crossed the courtyard well beneath the level of the young knight, Dommes thought how easily he might have been Mon-Crulbagh's prisoner, instead of regarding the run of this foef no better than the sentence of a criminal.

Dommes had seen what real punishment looked like. With the wizard's rare absence from the foef, it devolved to him now to undertake a chore that made many verdicts seem light by comparison. He headed into the far tower hall and made for the stairs leading down.

Past the three levels other servants whispered of, beyond the storerooms and deeper than even rumor dared guess, Dommes used the keys only he and Zantire possessed to open the lowest chambers, moving toward his cleaning chores with neither hesitation nor enthusiasm. Outside the laboratory portal, two hundred paces from any other living being, but one, his fingers fumbled on the key and his shaking hands dropped them to the stone. He nearly could not continue, but Dommes knew his place. No one would see or recall his service, and that was only proper. He managed the lock on his second try and slowly entered the eerily-lit sanctum.

Nothing else here required cleaning, as Zantire was obsessive about dust and clutter. His instructions indeed allowed no latitude; Dommes was here only to clean the nook where the granary stood. With a deep sigh and bitten lips, he shuffled closer and closer to the spot and beheld again what was left of Drayson.

Within the cubicle nook set against the wall was a space where a large dog would have to hunch and curl to fit. The wizard's granary within, the ever-renewing source of energy that powered Zantire's enchantments, had very little left of what made a man. No clothing, of course: the immortal Elf-flesh stood out as white as ivory and wrinkled as parchment. No arms, just two inches of bony thigh beneath his vitals. No nose nor hair nor ears, his mouth and one eye stitched shut, alive still via a metal feeding tube poking through one cheek and a shallow tray beneath now loaded with excrement. Dommes looked, and did not throw up, and set about cleaning the tray. The sewage had hardly any smell or form, much like the colorless paste the wizard had loaded atop the nook to trickle down through the cheek-tube. Clearing food scraps from the cutting board was more work. Nothing Dommes had ever done was less pleasant.

He finished, and as always could not resist a moment when he looked into Drayson's one good eye. That tiny point of contact lanced the servant with hot iron and he began to weep, as always. Drayson closed his orb, and Dommes always took that as a sign he was dismissed.

"He is gone," he whispered, "probably at least a week, no more spells, no enchantments. You can rest."

The thing in the nook moved its head side to side an inch: Zantire had inserted pins to prevent too wide a field in which his living battery might injure himself. But that small "no", delivered with a groan of pain, broke something within Dommes.

He gently laid hold of the nook itself and carried it off its elevating platform, bringing it closer to the scrying pool. Setting Drayson down on one edge, he positioned him so he could see the reflected visions of the water. Drayson looked down on the surface a few moments, and the image shifted to show the army of Pritaelseran moving west into Mon-Crulbagh.

Dommes could not say what moved him, to cut the straps holding his friend's torso in place. Nor why he fled the laboratory to the upper levels with such haste. Behind him, he heard one soft, merciful splash and knew his friend had chosen his moment as all Elves should.

In the main chamber, he seized the letter Lord Pritaelseran had just received. He had carried messages to his master uncounted times, but never before had he risked his life to read one. A receipt, from the Wanlock banks, showing a debt not lying against his lord's account, now discharged. Dommes dropped the note as if the edges were sharp.

Dommes looked again on his marvelous new suit, well made for a long journey, and decided his best service would once again be without his presence. All the places outside Pritaelseran he had never been. But today he would see at least one of them, and the further from here the better.

⊕ ⊕ ⊕

Foef of Mon-Crulbagh

What Bellatara hated most was feeling useless. It was fine that most other folks towered over her, were stronger, reached higher. She had lived among Men since she was a little girl, after her parents were slain while traveling through Shilar in the far northern lands. The Halfling woman could just try harder, keep up, and wait for her chance to help her friends. Maybe back in Beryl, in that wizard's library, she tried too hard. But waiting was certainly the toughest part.

Now she clung behind Ellesmera as the cumbersome lizards pounded along the road north from the castle. Her innards bounced to new positions and every fifth galumph of the reptile beneath them nearly threw her off into the ditch. Lord Qerlak was pushing the pace, and having to hug her friend so hard it cut off one ear meant that she couldn't even catch the conversation. Bellatara felt about as worthwhile as one of the packs dangling from the lizard's saddle.

They stopped the first night and made camp. Bellatara foraged for an hour in the lush lowlands and came back with excellent kindling plus some herbs and tubers. To her dismay, just as she approached the branches and logs Quarion had laid, the mage Galethiel ignited them with a casual gesture, while continuing to talk with Sir Barleybane. Ellesmera noticed the disappointment— of course, she noticed everything about people—and gestured her over to help with the cooking.

As they took their seats around the fire to eat, Bellatara alternated between wanting Galethiel not to see her pique, and wondering whether she'd even noticed the slight or would care.

"Now then," Qerlak said between bites and guzzles, "by tomorrow afternoon, hopefully we will be on the other side of the town of Bultarr-r and in deep trouble."

"Hopefully, milord?" Ellesmera asked.

"Yes, I'm trying to be optimistic," he replied with a grin. "I don't have a lot of time and I'm counting on us five to handle this in less than… well, as quickly as we can. And you don't need to use titles with us, Ellesmera. Nor you Quarion and Bellatara. I am Qerlak and this is my companion Galethiel. In public, certainly my people like to hear the more formal address, but we are now a group."

He looked to the mage who neither nodded nor shook her head.

"We—Galethiel and I—were once members of a group. A band of adventurers, known as the Tributarians."

"We've heard of you," Quarion said.

Bellatara chimed in, "Everyone has heard of you."

Qerlak tilted his head and thrust out a lip, as if deciding whether to argue. He shrugged and went on. "I sensed that you three were on the same path to disrepute, and I hope I'm right because I need your help."

Bellatara looked at the muscular, plate-armored lord and the blue-robed mortal mage with her cedarwood staff, while her jaw dropped open. Help, from her? A charge ran down from her nape to her nethers, just to entertain the ridiculous notion that she could be useful to them.

"Have any of you faced Insectirs before?"

Quarion burst into a short laugh, even the mention of the Bugs getting on his Elvish nerves. "I am, well, a city boy, Sir—that is, Qerlak."

Ellesmera kept her composure but shook her head. "I've never seen one in my native city. Though I now understand, there were some."

Galethiel pointed to Quarion and said, "You opened the secret door, yes? A Stealthic?"

Quarion swallowed and nodded and she turned to Qerlak. "Like Meandar, or Trekelny."

"Let us hope," Qerlak replied, "for better luck than the first."

"You've met Trekelny!" Quarion could not contain his astonishment, which only increased when the pair of them laughed.

"Yes, we worked with him for a time, just last year. We shared the risk, the dirty work, the decisions, the fighting, all of it. I think from what I know of you that this is something you've already come to understand."

He paused a moment and they all nodded.

"You share the losses too, and they can truly hurt. The Tributarians, we lost a great deal, over our time together. It's a long story, but tonight we'll be hearing yours." He looked at the three of them a moment. "We need to hear it all. Who will tell it?"

Bellatara, along with Quarion, looked to Ellesmera who sighed and took up the tale. She left nothing out, made no excuses and indulged in no speculation. Bellatara was disappointed at how little time it took.

Galethiel leaned in looking closely at Ellesmera. "She's a Martial Wizard," she murmured.

Qerlak nodded, saying "Like Engurra. Good."

Then they both slewed their gaze around to Bellatara. For the first time in months, she wished she were even smaller and harder to see.

"I'm a Woodsman."

Qerlak slowly smiled to the broadest grin she had ever seen from the Lord of Mon-Crulbagh. "And us headed into the forest and gorge-land. To fight Bugs, that discomfit us Elves. Very well met indeed, Halfling Woodsman."

She volunteered the first watch even though three of the others were Elves. Bellatara loved the sounds of the night, and after the thrill of being wanted by the Lord of Mon-Crulbagh, her feet barely touched the ground as she paced the perimeter.

They reached the town the next morning and Bellatara began to sense she had something in common with the tall fiery sorceress. Qerlak met with the town's leading citizens and tried to calm their fears, trooped around with them to view the damage to this door, that gate—all from the smaller flying things so far—and listened patiently to the tales of the heavy ground-hugging marauders from farmers in the far fields.

Bellatara stood in the second row with Galethiel, and suddenly realized, they had both tapped their feet and clucked with impatience at the same time. Galethiel looked down with incredulity on her child-sized companion and for just an instant the Halfling thought she might get struck. But then the human grinned, and chuckled, and after that the two of them laughed so hard they had to lean on each other. Qerlak's quiet cough brought them back to themselves, and whatever had been decided by all the talking was evidently accomplished. They left their riding lizards in the stable, walked through the eastern gate, and struck out off the road for the forest lying directly east.

Finally, Bellatara thought, something worth happening was happening.

She ran off the trail to check signs of spoor, the thin, deep tracks they made, and how high up the doors and fences of outlying cottages were broken in. The image they gave her of the stride and size of the ground-monsters was scary and thrilling. Those jaws would catch her companions right about the stomach, but that was head-level for her.

Just before the forest the group came upon the riverbed of the stream called the Sodsluice, and everyone could see how far down the level was here.

"What happened?" Qerlak wanted to know.

"Argens knows, there's been enough rain!" Galethiel quipped.

"The other river!" Bellatara cried, "I saw it, the other day, the banks were full to overflowing."

"You mean the Fengurr?" Qerlak looked north in the direction of the other stream. "That bridge is just north of the turn we took for town. I haven't visited this far out."

"The two must come together, up there." Bellatara pointed northeast, beyond the forest's edge to a place where a rocky headland demarked the end of Mon-Crulbagh territory.

"Do you think something has happened to change the river-courses?" Ellesmera asked.

"It makes the most sense," Galethiel said. "But we're here to get these Bugs, right?"

The three newcomers looked to the lord of Mon-Crulbagh, who was in turn looking at the mage with a wry face. "Who's to say the two are not connected? Let's go take a closer look. Lead on, Woodsman."

Again she felt that charge run through her, and the Halfling stepped out along the bank until she found a spot to easily cross.

"Agh, this mud!" Galethiel complained coming up the opposite bank. Everyone turned to her. "Well, just look at these boots now!" She fumed as if daring anyone to laugh. Everyone took her up on that, and she joined in.

"Now which way," Quarion asked, pointing almost north along the border of the forest toward the gorge.

"Into the trees," Bellatara said, starting east toward the first pine boles two hundred paces off.

"What for, it will just take long—"

"Now!" Bellatara yelled back without stopping. "Can't you hear it?"

"Hear what?" Qerlak asked, but after a few moments the other four all started as if poked and began to run. The high pitched drone was getting louder and louder now. The distant flock overhead was not, in fact, feathered.

On their first pass, the creatures had to veer off as the group made it just within the cover of the branches before they could be attacked. Bellatara could see six legs on their one-stripe bodies, the middle two flat and sharpened like knives. But the easiest feature to spot was their beaks, also sharp and the length of short-swords. There were at least a dozen of them, breaking back in all directions and circling around close to the ground at very high speed.

"What do we do?" Ellesmera asked.

"We can never outrun them," Qerlak replied. "Maybe not even mounted. Try to kill a few, see if that scares the rest off."

Bellatara kept a tree trunk to one side of her and just poked with her javelin as the wave of Bugs passed through. They were too fast, darting like flies, she didn't come close. Quarion swung wildly with his cutlass, nicking a mid-section but crying out from the pain of a passing claw that scraped his shoulder. Qerlak stood his ground, taking a direct collision from one of them on his half-plate armor while swinging at another overhead. His speed, even in armor, was remarkable. He cut the Bug neatly in half while the first attacker slammed against his breastplate and fell with a crushed head.

Ellesmera stood forth and dodged without striking.

But the wizard.

Galethiel's face writhed in disgust and she called out a word while pointing with her off-hand. A bolt of lightning struck from the tip of her finger to the nearest tree, incinerating two of the Bugs at once and producing a crack from the bole that nearly felled it. The burnt corpses traveled on and struck branches, exploding into cinders that rained down on everyone.

The surviving Bugs wove between the trees behind the group and did not return.

Qerlak examined Quarion's wound and pronounced it clean.

"Let's stick to the trees and get closer to the gorge, keep those fliers off us."

"Well then," Galethiel said, "which way?"

Qerlak gestured to Bellatara, and she hopped into the lead.

"Works fine," Galethiel quipped, "If there's trouble, I can shoot over her head."

That brand of ribbing the Halfling knew well; besides, most of her spirit was lost in the beauty of this forest. She wended her way past thick copses almost without thought, moving up and down through small gullies and berms, following the obvious trail and trying to remain calm when she saw the subtle signs. Habitation, not random enough for the deer or dogs, the marks and care of beings who knew the woodlands well.

"Where are we headed?" Quarion asked from near the back. "Is this still north, to the gorge?"

Bellatara stopped and signaled for quiet, standing there quite a stretch and trying not to look as if she had noticed anything.

Finally, Qerlak gently called, "Woodsman, something of interest?"

She crooked a finger for him to come up, and while gesturing randomly she turned her face to his and whispered, "I don't know, milord. Would it be of interest to know that we're being watched?"

Qerlak stiffened in alarm, but Ellesmera put in, "I agree. Somewhat behind us and deeper into the forest."

"How long?"

"At least a few minutes. They live here, whoever they are. I might have missed them, but I heard the hoofbeat—"

"They are mounted!" Qerlak could not restrain himself and his cry echoed around the glade. "Oh, Argens' Balls, they're gone now, aren't they?"

Bellatara shrugged. "This is their home, they'll probably be back."

"How could horses fit through these narrow trails?" Galethiel asked.

For answer Bellatara walked ahead a few paces, then knelt beside a faint track in the hard earth, larger and rounder than a deer could make. Quarion and Ellesmera exclaimed in praise, but Qerlak and Galethiel just looked to each other with a grin.

"So incredible, and so pleased with herself."

"Just like Treaman."

Before Bellatara could ask, the wind shifted and everyone caught the acrid scent of something unearthly ahead of them. Moments later, they heard the sound of snapping brush and beheld three shiny hard shapes too large for wolves, too broad for belief, and closing in too fast for comfort.

"Acgh!" Qerlak groaned, coming to the fore, "not these things again. Watch out for the mandibles, everyone, if you don't have metal armor they will snap right through you. And when you strike, strike as hard as you can, their armor is as thick as a turtle shell."

Bellatara threw a javelin and watched it bounce from the lead monster's carapace as if from the side of a stone building. The beetle-things moved faster than a man could trot, low to the ground with mandibles nearly an arm long clacking together, while those horrid antennae waved in all directions. Ellesmera spun away to dodge the initial rush, holding back on her strikes and looking completely unsettled.

Galethiel never hesitated but stepped up and slammed down on one of them with her staff, which flared with power and bored a hole into the shell with a loud cracking noise. But the creature had come in close and clenched its jaws about her waist, producing a scream of panic and fury. Qerlak turned from his opponent to strike instead at hers from the side. His enormous battleaxe chopped straight through its back half, and the creature released its jaws as it threshed away spraying the ground with thick green-brown ichor. Qerlak's opponent bit at him without resistance, but the plate and chain held out. The Pious Warrior was unhurt though he could not turn back to face his foe.

Quarion hacked four times at the last beetle while giving ground, the final strike coming away with a chip in his blade but otherwise hardly more than scratching the shell. Bellatara could see him sweating profusely and reacting more slowly than usual. Like Ellesmera, her companion was affected by these horrid things in ways he could not counter. She rushed in from the rear quarter and poked at it from beneath, trying to find a softer spot. On an impulse, she wedged her javelin beneath its second waist and heaved up in an effort to tip it over. But its six legs were too much, and it spun to face the new annoyance. Quarion's blow missed, and Ellesmera's attempt to kick only bumped it a few inches offline. As the mandibles closed around Bellatara, she tried to leap back but only succeeded in getting a few vital inches higher than standing. The jaws closed around her shoulders, pinning her arms and forcing her to drop the javelin. Bellatara screamed in fear and panic, but the sound was drowned out by the slash of a lightning bolt that struck the creature side-on and severed its head and upper body from the rest of it. Not a drop of fluid bled from either half as the smoking body fell away, leaving Bellatara tight clenched in a near-deadly bite from the now-dead monster.

Qerlak, meanwhile, had managed to turn halfway in the creature's jaws and again brought down his axe to cleave the upper body vertically. As his foe staggered off on four legs to bleed and die, he surveyed the field and then ran to Bellatara leaving his weapon on the ground.

"Hold on! Hold, I know what to do." Qerlak braced himself, bent over, took two deep breaths and then reached through the gaping upper shell of the creature and into the back of the skull. He flailed around desperately inside there, and just as he turned to throw up from the smell and mess, the two jaws sprang apart while Bellatara fell into her friends' arms.

"Are you alright?" Qerlak asked her. "Ellesmera, would you check her for injuries, that thing could have cut you in half." He sat back, holding his side and quietly groaned now that the danger was past.

"Thank you, Galethiel." Bellatara was breathless, and still terrified, and disgusted, and all in all had never felt more alive. From the corner of her eye she thought she saw a handsome, bearded face duck back behind a large oak.

No one else saw him; instead the group sat against trunks or rocks breathing heavily.

"So," Ellesmera finally said, "are we in the deep trouble you were looking for?"

Qerlak laughed. "It's starting to smell like it. Let's move on."

Bellatara took the lead again, as Quarion continued to insist they were not, in fact, on a trail of any kind and Ellesmera giggled.

Around midafternoon the land ahead opened up to a steep drop, the southeastern side of a broad gorge, studded with twisted trees in places springing up between large shelfs of stone that seemed sharpened to an edge. North across the gap the walls rose higher, in a stone cliff with two channels for water to fall. The left-hand channel fell in a full roar, while the nearer right-hand cut was merely a trickle.

"The top looks blocked with things," Galethiel said, shading her eyes. Bellatara strained to see but could make out nothing.

"How did you do that?"

"Does the blockage look serious? Man-made?" Qerlak inquired.

"How can you tell?" Galethiel asked.

Bellatara clucked. "It's easy, if only I could see it."

Galethiel laid a hand on her shoulder and said, "There, look again."

Suddenly the Woodsman had a near-view of the gorge wall, as if she stood less than a hundred feet away. She gasped in surprise, then scanned around eagerly.

"Yes! You can see where logs have been chopped and sawed, and no river channel can move rocks as big as that."

"I will send men out from Bultarr-r to clear the channel," Qerlak said, "I should have been watching for this little trick. The Sodsluice water level has already dropped and now Pritaelseran's men can cross where they wish." He looked around to his party in worry. "We need to finish this quest now. Where do Bugs come from?"

In the silence that followed, Ellesmera kept a face of stone and suggested, "I suppose, when a female Bug and a male Bug come to care for each other…"

Qerlak put one hand to his forehead as everyone laughed. "Quite right, I stand corrected. I've become too used to serious men like Fennet and Cecil." He looked to the little Woodsman. "But do they have a single lair, or something convenient like that?"

Bellatara could only shrug. "I would guess they do. Like the smaller ones, or some of them."

"The question," Ellesmera said, "would be, why are they here now?"

"Right!" Galethiel cried, "the Bugs are here and the water isn't."

"There!" Bellatara said. "Near the base of the waterfall, I see a couple of caves. When the water is running they'd be covered, probably flooded."

"Excellent," Qerlak said nodding decisively. "Down we go then. Time to get there before nightfall, and that's when they like to raid."

"See up there, on the hillside to the east," Ellesmera said pointing. "There's a tall pile of stones. And there, further away north, another."

"The famous Border Stones of Mon-Crulbagh," Qerlak murmured, "which have never justice seen. From the song."

"Did Pritaelseran accuse you of moving those?" Galethiel asked incredulously. "Look at them, taller than you are, it's impossible, and they line the entire border, must be a hundred or more."

Qerlak pulled his chin as he gazed that way. "True, all of it. Yet as I recall, the border between us was always thought to be either the bottom of the rise, down here at the forest's edge, or else the course of the Sodsluice now west of us." He drew a breath and slowly shook his head. "Those stones are closer to the top of the rise than the bottom. I wish I could figure that out. And whether the muster is a good idea," he continued, talking more to himself now, "and where my allies are hiding."

"What's that?" Quarion asked, pointing down toward the center of the gulch. "Bellatara, can you see it?"

"Maybe a body, some other things like a pack. Hard to tell."

In the midst of looking, Bellatara suddenly felt the sharpness of her vision fade to normal. She looked at Galethiel who winked.

"I can cast it again when we need it."

Quarion hitched rope to one of the twisting trunks that lined the side of the hill and they eased themselves to the bottom. Qerlak bent over nearly double when he stepped away, but pushed off help and murmured something in the Ancient tongue before straightening up and waving her to the front.

"I'll be fine," he assured with his confident smile, and Bellatara wanted to believe him. This immortal Pious Warrior was without question the most powerful fighter she had ever seen. Yet he didn't scare her the way he should, as Lord Beryllian did.

Galethiel stepped into line behind him, and the face she wore looking after Qerlak told Bellatara all she needed to know about who would be fine.

The going over rocks and dry channels was slow and surprisingly hard. Bellatara searched for paths that would require less jumping and landing, but the afternoon wore on and Qerlak exhorted her to hurry. During one brief rest stop, Quarion kept looking out to the left at the place where the body lay low and out of sight. Qerlak was sitting on a rock gently holding his side as he looked at the young Elf.

"You want to investigate."

Quarion nodded, as Galethiel clucked and muttered "Another carking Meandar," under her breath.

Qerlak quirked a grin and nodded for him to go. Ellesmera rose to join him and they made their way quickly to the side, looking and then leaping down from view for a few minutes. When they returned, Quarion was holding a sheathed sword.

"How did he die?" Qerlak asked.

"Not from bites or blows," Quarion replied, "I think maybe he got caught by a flood and drowned."

"The corpse is very old," Ellesmera commented, "that sheath cracked off the belt at the slightest touch."

"The sword is likely rusted through." Qerlak guessed, and Quarion shrugged as he worked the blade free.

"Mine's already chipped, and this might be too heavy, but I thought—"

The blade that flashed into the afternoon light was indeed dark, but not rusty or chipped. Its sheath crumbled to bits as Quarion brandished it aloft in one hand, a weapon longer than his cutlass but seemingly as light. For a moment Bellatara thought she heard a tone of music, but it fled her chasing ear and was gone.

Ellesmera leaned in to peer at the weapon. "There is writing on the blade."

Everyone gathered around and Quarion slowly read it to them all.

I am the Sword of No Master
Blood me, Wish me, Let me go

No one spoke for some time.

"Well," Galethiel said brightly, "what could possibly go wrong with that."

Qerlak grinned, "Don't spoil the celebration. Quarion, it's obviously a rather powerful artefact, I've heard nothing of it myself. I'm sure it will do no good to tell you it's dangerous, so…" He stood as if to continue, but caught Galethiel's judging eye and spread his arms. "What do you want? His sword is chipped."

"The sun is headed down," Ellesmera said, as the rest fell in line behind the Woodsman again.

Now Bellatara could not afford the luxury of an easy road. Straight toward the caves, which they only guessed would house the Bugs, the rocks became loose and harder to navigate as the river channel dominated the approach. Finally they all straggled to a small ledge, a place surely under the water when the river ran free, and looked up another two to three rods above them at two cave mouths, one slightly above and to the left of the other, almost directly under the dry fall. Just an arms' width trickle of water leaked down between them from the cliff top four rods further up.

"You really think this is the place?" Galethiel asked.

"You really can't hear the hum?" Bellatara shot back. Everyone looked at her, then cocked their heads.

First, Ellesmera nodded, then the rest chimed in. A low deep thrum as of dozens of large fans whipped the air echoing from the caves.

"How many do you think there are?" Quarion asked.

"The townsfolk reported hundreds, of each kind," Qerlak said, "but I think they may exaggerate."

"Still, there's no way we could beat them fighting as we have so far." This from Ellesmera, quiet and sure as usual.

"Then how?" Quarion shot back.

"Fire," Qerlak said. They looked at him.

"You mean, pile up wood at the entrances?"

"Or use my spell—"

"Perhaps these stones you gave us."

Qerlak nodded. "Any of that, all of it. I don't know but the key must be flame." He refused to elaborate, yet spoke with such certainty no one argued.

"Alright then," Galethiel said rising and smoothing her robe. "The wood is too far to get, and time is short. I will cast my fire spell into the higher cave, try to cook the flying things. Bellatara, you stand with me. The rest, use the Fire-Light stones in the lower cave and be ready for anything that gets out past the flames."

"Good!" Qerlak said, standing and pulling his gauntlets tight. "Tomorrow I'll return to the town and they will pull down that dam up there. If anything survives, hopefully they'll be trapped and drown, or at least stay quiet until after the raid." He looked around the group, as Bellatara realized it was suddenly time. "May Argens bless our attempt."

Bellatara reached a narrow ledge outside the higher cave and reached down to help Galethiel up. Every nerve on edge, she noted that the setting sun peeked through the ever-present Mon-Crulbagh clouds to poke a shaft of light almost directly down the tunnel they stood beside. The humming here was loud enough to destroy normal talk. The ceiling and sides of the tunnel was festooned with Bugs, clinging to rock and goopy strands of something they either wove, excreted or had chewed on.

Galethiel signaled with her palms that they needed to close the distance, so she tiptoed into the cave mouth with the mage and crept forward even as the stench and sound almost forced the urine from her before she clenched. Long after Bellatara stopped breathing through her nose Galethiel urged her forward. She could have stabbed a half-dozen of them when they finally stopped. Galethiel gestured and soundlessly shouted, as the width of the cave erupted into a bonfire of mystic flame.

They ran out and Bellatara turned with her throwing spear in hand, stabbing wildly at an avalanche of half-burning remnants of panicked Bugs. Galethiel too laid on with her staff sweeping to both sides; charred stinking bits piled the ledge around their ankles and still the creatures came. Many, many more simply roasted in place like a field sown with burning torches. The hum immediately grew dim, and the crackle of flames also died down. It was probably less than two minutes, and the fire continued to spread along the strands deeper and deeper into the cave.

"I'll watch here!" Galethiel assured her. "See how they're doing below."

Bellatara brushed herself off but still gagged from the smell of fried insect as she scrambled down the cliff to the second cave. Qerlak stood to one side, Quarion the other, while Ellesmera held the Fire-Light stone in her palm between them.

"Here, I'll throw mine too," Bellatara said.

Quarion pulled his new blade from where he'd stashed it in his belt. From nowhere there came a whispering hiss:

Blood me...

Qerlak called out "Luxar" and a ball of blue light sprang into being twenty paces into the cave, illuminating a wider single area in a chamber not as deep as the higher one. The floor looked like ocean chop, constantly wriggling or quaking. It was a few moments before Bellatara could make out it was simply a mass of the beetle-things, lying athwart each other and entangled in torpor, but now rousing in the presence of bright light. Unexpectedly they began to squeal on a pitch almost too high to hear, and Bellatara screamed even as she threw the stone.

It broke against a shell while Ellesmera's landed near the center of the chamber, and at once bright patches of flame sprang into being, catching on Bugs and burning fiercely. Bellatara began to feel useless again, as the fire combined with the light caused a mortal stampede, several tons of maddened insect cramming down the tunnel toward the flimsy bags of flesh in their way.

⊕ ⊕ ⊕

Foef of Mon-Crulbagh

"...nd thus, we the lords and laborers of Mon-Crulbagh affirm our ancient bond, established first by Aliatrake..."

Hitaelseran sat his horse and took in the light rain, listening to Squire Cecil read out the muster document to another cluster of peasants while the small wagon-line waited. The trained pike levy from the steads nearest the castle stood in column behind them, cutting a splendid figure for the two dozen or so peasants gathered around listening. Hitaelseran thought he saw perhaps eight adult males capable of bearing the pike among them.

"And in token of their intent they shall sign their names. May Argens bless all those who live in this foef, and make them first in courage, true forgers of Hope." Cecil finished reading and folded up the parchment again to put under his cloak away from the rain.

Hitaelseran had heard it read four times so far today, and it never felt less strange to his ear. A lord of the land, by voluntary compact, offered to his peasants—*offered*, not commanded—the chance to participate in the defence of the foef. He knew his father would not have known whether to laugh or cry at such a notion. Still, his heart tugged at him with each recitation: there was something to this, a knot he needed to untangle if he wished to understand his new home, and his new lord.

The peasants let the silence sit a moment before saying anything.

"That was well read, young fellow."

"Aye, it's been too long since we heard the words, never knew why."

"You never heard that before, have you Fren?"

"Me? Why, I've heard and signed to it three times, once before you did!"

"Such a lie, tell me the sun is shining next."

"Good people," Cecil called out from back by the wagon, "We have no intent here to discover anyone's age." Hitaelseran recognized the point, that Elves never liked to surrender their years to public knowledge. But until today, he had never dreamed that anyone would care how a commoner felt. Scanning their faces, he saw serious attention from them, and a few suspicious glances.

Cecil grinned, and added, "Why, I remember that day when Argens himself told me..." and let the chuckles finish the joke for him. Hitaelseran sensed the squire was probably about his own age, acting and looking less than thirty years old. Seldom Chased to the other side of him was perhaps five years older,

286

looking fit and in the prime of health; as a mortal Man, he could not hide his age if he had any.

"What say you, good villeins," Chased sang out in his booming ringing tones, "will you band together in defence of your homes? Step forward, and each man who votes to support his lord shall receive a pike and armor today."

"And in future," Cecil put in, "the shaft shall stay in your possession, together with the stone practice-head, so that you may train and stay ready in the event of another invasion."

"When, boy, not if." One man quipped to the general amusement, but he stepped forward to put his name to Cecil's list.

"Raculf, you're going then?"

"Sure and why not. The grump-tubers are in and my lad Fellis can handle the weeding for a few days. Will you come Hevassah?"

"Nay, I'll stay and watch the hutches. Too many foxes still, and my wife has her hands full with the baby."

"Your boy Hessan is old enough, nimble lad."

"He'll come along with his sling, but I'll stay this time."

Hitaelseran listened, hardly able to believe his ears as the people of this region, beyond all that he had ever known and respected, made up their own minds how many would go or not.

"You must all come!" he cried, his mouth sounding strange to himself with these words. "Your lord, Sir Qerlak, needs you."

The peasants stopped their chatter to look up at him. "And where is Lord Barleybane now?"

"Aye," said another, "this need is so great, he cannot read out the muster himself?"

"He is, he minds the serious business of the foef, no matter, but—"

"Bugs in Bultarr-r," Cecil put in.

Hitaelseran glared at first to the squire, bristling that one of inferior rank should interrupt. But the peasants who had been defensive with him now nodded their heads in understanding.

"Ah, the Bugs. Like in '47, recall that Raculf."

"I was here, it was '44. And it was Pritaelseran invaded that year too."

"Lord Barleybane promises to meet us at Sluicehill," Seldom Chased said, making it sound as if all the Barons of the realm would be there. "He shall read the muster once to all."

"And any man who takes the roll shall be relieved of a tenth of his tithing, upon his word that he shall spend that time in practice with the stone-headed pike."

"We must hurry," Hitaelseran added, "The Hawk is already stooping upon us."

"Flowery," one fellow in the back shot out. "Aye, but I'll come. The fence line can wait."

"It's a fence between us," another called, "you've nothing to fear, Aggles, my word on that."

Aggles spat, saying "You think I'm building it for show!" But then he grinned, gripped his neighbor's arm to seal the deal, and signed. In all, six full-grown males took up pikes and stood in the back of the levy, and the wagons rolled on.

And Hitaelseran still thought it strange. But the feeling he had, that something about this new idea was right, only grew.

Foef of Mon-Crulbagh

The remote cabin south of the Sodsluice burns very brightly, and the ever-present rain dampens the smoke to prevent its inhabitants, even in dying, from sending a warning. The knight's son in charge of the raiding patrol details four peasants to stand by with bows, and strict orders to shoot if either the villein or his wife manage to escape. He spurs his horse alongside his two retainers, advancing back to the main force now an hour's march ahead. The night will be well advanced before these four make the camp.

The peasant archers are none of them happy about the job, but clearly the most upset is a young bowman from Lann, who stands with arms hugging his bow beneath the cloak, no arrow on the string and hot tears disappearing in the drizzle that has soaked everyone's face. Never has he seen such wanton cruelty. That a freeman of any knighthood should be slain without offering resistance outrages the youth's untested sense of justice.

In Lann they have been ruled by Pritaelseran for more than two centuries. Even his father was not born the last time they tried to break away and regain the independence of their forefathers. But the Hawk Knight came with the levy of two foefdoms against their bows and staves, and the fight did not last long. Their lord controls three foefs of men, and tithing, and landed wealth; he has always coveted this fourth, and now he will not be denied.

But who will he rule here, the youth wonders, if he slays all he comes upon?

"Twas the fellow's smart mouth, as I hear it," one of the grown bowmen says, looking to the youth. "Shot an impertinence at the young lord, now gone. The Hawk, heard the tale from others, he'll have none of that lip from the common class, and him a Demonbender."

A large crackle and crash within makes the men jump and gives the youth hope, but it is only the center timber coming down in a geyser of sparks and hellish heat. Soon there is just a pile of cinders less than two feet high smoldering and sputtering as it loses the war with the water from above. Two of the archers poke among the ruins briefly and then they turn north to catch up to the levy.

The youth from Lann trudges after them with no spirit. Just yesterday, marching with the army he felt a thrill to be in such shining company on a grand adventure to right the wrongs Mon-Crulbagh had no doubt done to many in his home. The row of mounted men in metal armor and bearing lances was the most impressive parade he had ever seen, pennons dipping in time with each other and the spearmen practically marching in step to the drummer's cadence. And the wizard, surely four hundred years old in his long robes with his wagon tarped to cover forbidden materials. Such an army! What force ever assembled could resist it? Just yesterday, the youth from Lann was proud to be here.

Now he hears a faint and distant horn—one of the peasants nearby, giving a warning despite the rain's blanket over the smoke of that burning house. The youth from Lann knows his enemies will now gather; they will fight, and more will die. He fingers his handmade bow, scrutinizes one by one his arrows as he walks, making sure each is intact and will fly true. A feast of glory awaits, and still the youth cries a little, for he has lost his appetite.

When Quarion was just a lad, he had saved a little girl from a runaway wagon in the Wanlock mall. Anytime he wanted he could summon up the image of that day; people starting to shout and point, the toddling girl running after a stray cat, the wagon breaking loose when its unruly camel snapped the reins, and nobody else close enough. On that day Quarion learned what it felt like to have his body answer questions his mind was still framing. He dove across the stones, scooped up the girl, and managed to roll to his own back so the scars would be there rather than on his precious cargo.

He knew then he wanted to risk himself as often as he could. Every day if possible.

At the mouth of the lower cave, he saw Bellatara standing on the ledge over a fifteen foot drop of solid stone, directly in the path of the stampeding Bugs. These beetle-things were smaller than a wagon, but more numerous. The Stealthic knew there was no place to dive to, no chance to grab her back out of the way. He had no chance to repeat the path to glory that he had once as a lad.

But of course, back then, he wasn't holding a magical sword.

Blood Me, the weapon said in a chilling tone, and Quarion could raise no objection. Controlling his gorge at the nearness of the things he took one step in and slammed down with the long blade atop the first of them to emerge on his side.

The blazing flash of light only energized Quarion without blinding him, but it seemed to further confuse the Bugs, while the one he had hit fell in two as if he'd been chopping a cart-sized loaf of bread. Qerlak across from him brought his axe down on another with similar results. They both chopped again and again, not always lethally but often enough to foul even their six-legged balance. Squalls, spatters and a stench so thick Quarion wanted to use his blade to cut the air and hack a path to a wholesome scent. Down, he must chop down. Ellesmera and Bellatara poked and punched at anything falling or wedging through the press of Insectir, until one of the two edge-wielders could spare a strike their way. Yet they all slowly, steadily gave ground.

Now the ledge was less than two feet away and Ellesmera, without room to spin and weave, was starting to lose her composure. Still they came, dozens of these mastiff-sized Bugs, some without a mandible, some on four remaining legs, some on fire. Worse yet, Quarion as he hacked and slew could hear a hum returning from above, the sound he had heard from the flying Bugs Galethiel and Bellatara had attacked first. Were there more of them? Was Galethiel dead? He dared not spare an instant to look. Down, chop down.

The sword in his hand practically flew back and forth, it felt light as a rapier though the cutting surface was greater than a broadsword. When it struck the main carapace of the beetle-things, it sunk in easily doing dreadful lethal damage nearly every time. When Quarion missed a little and hit a mandible or leg, the blade cut so easily he barely felt the resistance. Qerlak on the other side swung more frequently, crying out with the pain of his rib every time, but his massive battle-axe in both hands hardly did better. Gore spackled the rocky ledge and all the combatants: the stench of their dead brethren seemed only to push the Bugs to greater efforts to escape.

It was a tide of shell and limbs, and four adventurers could not long stem the flow. As the hum behind him rose ever higher, beyond the pitch of the flying Insectirs, Quarion could feel his nape-hair begin to stand out, though how he could be more horrified he had no idea. Ellesmera had leaped atop one Bug and used the vantage to kick down at another climbing over it, following with a strong punch that cracked the shell and drove it half-back onto still more behind. Bellatara poked furiously with her short spear, doing little more than staving them back like mad dogs. One got Qerlak around his middle; the armor held but he bellowed in agony and could only bring the haft-end of his weapon down on the foe.

Quarion slipped in the gore, and next to him Bellatara ducked a foe while taking a step back that had no stone underneath it. Screaming for her, he reached and caught her arm. The front half of a dying Bug flopped into them, its mandibles clacking over his sword-arm as the added weight carried them all into air and down. Quarion desperately rolled back to put his body between his friend and the stone below. The impact jarred loose all the breath from his body, tearing off all but the two jaws of his foe, painting them both in ichor the color of rotted blood.

He could barely breathe, and saw stars well before sunset. The damn hum was a screech of fury now, and from this angle, he saw Ellesmera stumble off her unwilling mount and out of sight near Qerlak, who looked up and nodded fiercely while he fought to reach her.

Above at the second cave stood Galethiel, the golden ball atop of her staff spinning so fast it could no longer be seen as anything other than sparkling color of purest light. At Qerlak's signal, she raised the staff and pointed it dramatically at the mouth of the cave. A bolt of lightning struck the far side of the entrance and a cottage-width of solid rock blew into rubble. The entire cave-mouth filled with desperate, burning, fleeing Bugs disappeared in a raft of rocks, and Quarion saw Galethiel fall back one way as Qerlak, holding Ellesmera to his side, half-fell, half scrabbled back the other.

The sound of crumbling, avalanching rock continued as Quarion and Bellatara, directly in front and below the old cave, were pelted by a hail of smaller stones they had no chance to avoid from their backs. Quarion had time to wonder if he would be buried here with his blade and good friend. Certainly, he had no more strength to escape if Astor wished his career over today.

The hum disappeared at once. The rocks rolled to a stop, some of them fifty paces further behind the group and plonking into the dry river channel. Bug legs and jaws stopped moving long after they ceased bleeding. The rain let up a little and sunset was visible. Except for the pain he felt in two dozen places, Quarion thought the early evening had become rather peaceful. Might just lie here another hour, maybe nap, maybe die. For the first time in years, he felt he had taken enough risk.

He got upright looking for the sword which lay sticking between several fallen rocks to his left. Bellatara scrambled up near him, with blood trickling down the side of her face and looking a bit dazed. Galethiel clambered across the scree created by the collapse of the cave, looking unhurt but covered with rock dust from head to toe.

"Where is Qerlak?"

Quarion looked to the other side as Galethiel called out with urgency.

"We are well here," came the reply, "or at least well enough."

The Pious Warrior hove in view around the outcrop, limping with Ellesmera in his arms, her eyes drooping and blood beneath her chin.

"These rocks, almost sharp as blades, the fall caught us both."

The five gathered together and looked over Ellesmera, gave her water, tried to clean wounds.

"Can we make the forest before nightfall?" Qerlak asked Bellatara.

She looked at the group and shook her head. "How would we get you up the rope? But to the edge, maybe, and I could get wood from there."

"We need to rest, clearly," the knight heaved to his feet again with a wince, one hand on his rib, the other against his thigh.

"Lean on me," Galethiel said, stepping in and using her staff to crutch them both.

"I need my sword," Quarion announced, but Bellatara was closer.

"I'll get it—aagh!" As she grabbed the hilt there was a flash of power and the Woodsman dropped it to hold her hand against her chest.

Quarion came alongside and slowly reached down to tap, then touch, and finally grasp and lift the wondrous weapon again. A tone of music sounded quite clearly in the quiet dusk, and everyone heard a strong resonant voice of victory shout *Wish Me.*

Quarion was stunned, a voice inside telling him nothing could be more natural now than to panic. He looked to Qerlak.

"I have never encountered wish magic before. Most comes from sources foreign to Hope. But this blade seems so finely crafted… I cannot advise you Quarion. But choose your words carefully."

The tone of music grew stronger without getting louder, and Quarion felt his arm begin to vibrate with the vitality of the magic weapon. Riches? Great power? What questions could he ask, how could he use a wish to perhaps clear his companions' reputation? What should he do?

His hand and lower arm were numb and he dared not even switch the grip. With a prayer to Astor that nothing he did could be seen as cowardice, he raised the blade and shouted.

"Healing for all in my band!"

In a few seconds, he realized he had closed his eyes, and opened them again. Bellatara's cut was dried. Qerlak stepped apart from Galethiel, tested his leg and chuckled, then tapped his ribs and laughed. Ellesmera stood without wobbling, her eyes steady and clear as always.

"That was a selfless thought," she said to him with a touch of emotion. Quarion grinned and decided not to tell her that the scrapes on his shoulders were gone.

"My pouch!" Bellatara cried, pulling out a glass vial, "there are two bottles in here."

"I have them as well," Galethiel said, "these are healing salves."

"It fits," Qerlak nodded, "your wish was neither too large nor subject to any foul interpretation. Well done, sir."

The sword felt incredibly light in Quarion's hand now, and a soft, echoing tone returned. A hush fell over the group and heard a quiet voice say *Let Me Go*.

Quarion stared into space and in the time of two heartbeats saw a collage of fast-moving images. First, he saw a woman of heroic stature in full armor, forging and using the sword: she slew dozens of the dark race of Despair centuries ago. But eventually she was overwhelmed by the forces of evil and as her last act called out a powerful enchantment in the Ancient tongue before hurling the weapon from her to disappear. Following that, a flutter of images too fast to follow. Men, women, knights, commoners, merchants, base thieves and heroic beings, all wielding a dark long blade in combat and causing miracles afterwards. Some released the weapon, others held it and suffered a blast of eldritch force that slew them. The last fell into a small river in the middle of a rocky gorge, and the waters closed over him.

Quarion released his hand, and the blade floated free in the air for several seconds, its ashen metal glowing brighter and brighter, then fading into nothing. Quarion released a long, shuddering sigh, then jumped when Ellesmera put an affirming hand on his shoulder.

"You may feel remorse, someday," Ellesmera said quietly. "We all wonder 'what if' about our past."

Quarion grinned evilly at her. "You mean, I should have wished for more Bugs?"

"Never mind," Qerlak cried, "but notice this. You asked for healing to 'my band'. That means a great deal, in my view." He looked around at them. "We are indeed together in this, and I for one am pleased to have such a group again. I've missed it."

Smiling, they all set out from the wrack of the caves to the place where the rope let them back up onto the tableland and the edge of the forest.

"Just wait," Bellatara warned Galethiel before setting out to forage. The mage raised a ginger brow to that but held off as the Woodsman gathered down deadwood, struck tinder and got the fire going.

They sat up for two hours, eating and telling tales, everyone still energized by their quest and the miracle. With prodding, Ellesmera reluctantly told the tale of their meeting in Wanlock, and Qerlak was heartened to think how they had met some of his old comrades that day.

"It is so very strange, as if we who think like this, whom others call adventurers, it's as if we are drawn to each other somehow. And you say Engurra gave you some tutoring, lessons or whatever it is you Martial Wizards do?"

Ellesmera nodded and Qerlak sighed with satisfaction.

"If only you, Quarion, could have met Trekelny, or Treaman, Bellatara. They are truly magnificent heroic men."

"Where are they now?" Quarion asked, "And Spitz, Zoanstahr, the rest?"

"Oh around, somewhere, I'm sure still getting into trouble," the knight replied. "I've missed them, no denying. But there's so much to do I hadn't thought, until today." He shook his head as if to clear it and looked off east to the rising hillside in the distance. "And more ahead. We don't have much time, but I intend tomorrow to investigate those stones on my border. That song, there must be something there. And Bellatara, you've seen signs of some mounted beings in this forest. I cannot emphasize enough how important it is for us that we contact them, find out more about them."

"People living in this forest?" Ellesmera asked.

"I'm hoping it's our mysterious mounted allies, the ones mentioned in the journal of the foef. I don't know what deal my predecessors had, but right now Pritaelseran is coming and I need every advantage I can lay my hands on."

Bellatara volunteered for first watch again, and Quarion laid back completely sure that he'd be awake when his turn came. The miracle of the sword left him refreshed and as happy as he had been in months. Having Qerlak and Galethiel around was very reassuring—they had status, tremendous power, and confidence. He was proud to be serving such worthy… employers, he finally settled on the word in his mind. Comrades, that was still a bridge too far for him.

When Ellesmera awakened him, it was nearly dawn. Surprise, shame and fear combined as he shook his head. But seeing Ellesmera's face, shining with anxiety shifted his emotions toward only the fear.

"They're gone," she whispered, unusually upset.

"Who?" Quarion looked around and by the dying embers, he saw only Bellatara asleep under a blanket, lightly snoring in the growing light.

Qerlak and Galethiel were nowhere in evidence.

They roused Bellatara and as she rolled over groggily and demanded to know what was wrong, everyone heard the rustle of parchment beneath her blanket.

"It's a note!" She exclaimed and handed it to Ellesmera. Swallowing hard the martialist read it out.

Friends, my apologies but G and I must leave. She has dreamed of the enemy—it is a skill she has and trust me, not a random vision—and we cannot delay. She and I will trade our mounts for horses in town and head south. The Hawk Knight is burning and killing as he comes, and I must be at the Sodsluice in less than two days or else many more will die.

Nothing comes before the lives of my people. I hope you can understand that.

I left you here not because I lack faith in you, quite the opposite.

I need to you discover the riddle of the Border Stones. I know it's only a song, but I feel in my heart there's something there.

And if Bellatara can discover the ancient allies of Mon-Crulbagh, and bring them to Sluicehill right away, I would be most grateful to you!

Perhaps this seems impossible. Perhaps it is. I ask only that you do your best, for the people of Mon-Crulbagh, but also for the group, the band that we now are in.

I trust you.

Argens Bless your efforts. In Haste,
Q

⊕ ⊕ ⊕

Foef of Mon-Crulbagh

Spezh was definitely losing patience. The talking was interminable; he sat his horse and listened to Chased, and Cecil and Hitaelseran trying to cajole peasants into line that by rights should have no choice in the matter. Would they be any good at fighting? Argens Balls, of course not. But bang them together in the back row and let them hold a pike just to give a good look, that would be fine. Why ask them?

He looked in the eyes of men who in past months he'd collected tithing from, checked the labor projects of. Spezh saw their smug faces now as they hemmed and deliberated with each other, how they looked back at him with such deep satisfaction it made him want to use his axe right now. Peasants, defending the foef!

It was all upside down, and the dekentar felt his temper grow ever hotter. Lord Barleybane wasn't even here, but Spezh knew this was just the sort of lunacy he favored. Giving those who owed the taxes and work a voice in whether you go to war? Spezh shook his head as they rode the final furlongs into Sluicehill village, to beg for more volunteers. To the south smoke spiraled up from several points, and the horns continued to sound at intervals that the enemy was already within the borders, ravaging this time to conquer instead of raid.

In the lead wagon the breathless boy with the horn, the one who had come to warn the first time, sat next to the drover and chatted nervously about what was coming. His sling through his belt and a pouch of good river stones gathered from the lowered banks of the Sodsluice, he wagged about how he'd help in the coming battle as if he were without a care in the world. Pebbles flung against armor, Spezh had never believed it. Time and again he had argued to Sir Qerlak the need to hire more mounted bowmen and formal retainers, but Fennet, curse him, always whined about the cost. Now his mad lord thought he could beat his enemy on the cheap, and like as not they'd all be dead or prisoners within two days.

But the final straw, the sight he could not bear to look at long, was that of his nemesis in the back of the lead wagon. Ondaii, the strange little man who claimed to come from the fabled Southern Isles, sat with each arm protectively cradling two tarp-covered objects each a little larger than a laundry basket, and another thick-rolled package between his outstretched legs. Ever since the feast he had been the toast of the servants and guards, this odd-speaking foreigner who seemed immune to every jest and prank Spezh devised to put him in his place. And now the lord, still absent, had said that this useless fellow in his fancy robes could come along to war. It was all too much.

Plus the rain never stopped.

In the main village square, more than a hundred folk had gathered—certainly, what other entertainment could there be—to listen to Cecil read off the lunatic document again, probably the ravings of a lord high on lotus powder and now lobbed out as the foef's best defence. Seven men stepped up and signed without prompting, but Spezh marked at least two dozen more, standing there with arms akimbo and daring to ask questions. Spezh dismounted to stand ready in case things got ugly. He almost hoped they would, his mood now needed some relief.

"Good people," Seldom Chased was saying, "your lord needs you. You have heard the horns—"

"Aye," one fellow broke in, "and we've seen the smoke, sir. This time the Hawk is serious."

"I avow he is," Hitaelseran said, "I know well the temper of this knight. All the more reason to come."

"All the more reason to be careful, lad. When a man musters, he puts his name on yonder list, see. We lose and the enemy knows which of us defied him. The rest—", the fellow shrugged and crossed his arms.

"You think this bastard will hold back!" Spezh shouted. "Because your name's not on a piece of paper, he'll leave you alone?"

"That's the muster custom, we've always stood by it."

"You! Morons, do you see Pritaelseran's name on that list? This is no compact to fight fair. That scrap of parchment doesn't make you all nobles in his eyes, he'll burn this rathole to the ground."

"And start again, to plant crops and trade in craft, with who? Where will he grow new men from, smart mouth, tell me that. And anyway, if Sir Qerlak needs us so badly, where is he now?"

A murmur of assent rose, and before Spezh could put his mailed fist into the villager's mouth he felt a light tap on his shoulder. Ondaii was standing there, but as he bowed Spezh spat and turned away. No time for mind-games now.

"Lord Barleybane sallied out to Bultarr-r," Cecil shouted, gaining their attention. "Bugs have attacked the town again." Everyone seemed impressed with this excuse, and Cecil added with more hope than assurance, "He hastens here even now and will affirm your names and rights on the muster. But we must hasten."

"There it is," the stubborn villager said, "when—and if—the lord of Mon-Crulbagh arrives, I will put my name on the list and so will most every man here."

That tore it. Spezh was determined to crack that jaw now, but again came the tap on his shoulder from Ondaii. "What!" he hissed at the hated little man.

"The warrior's armor, requested by him, is ready."

"My what? I'm wearing my armor, leave me alone."

"The suit of black, which he requested, I have finished making."

Spezh stared at Ondaii and finally recalled, the day he was covered in ash and had to go to war looking like one of the jungle blacks.

"You... you made me a suit of armor?"

Ondaii bowed again and moved back to the wagon, pulling the rolled package closer and unraveling its wrapping cloth.

Inside was what looked at first like a widow's mourning dress.

It covered the arms and legs about halfway, lacing in the back and so perfectly ebon in color it was impossible to tell what texture his eyes were seeing. Reaching out instinctively to touch the material, Spezh felt something hard and shiny, yet

301

jointed in some bizarre fashion, as if his chain mail links were all rectangles instead of circular. Hundreds of small bars were hooked together in a fashion he could not devise.

"This is no armor suit, it's a lady's dress, what are you trying to pull here?" Spezh demanded suspiciously. Perhaps this was an attempt at payback for his innocent pranks.

"If remove the chain mail you will, this can cover you better and will arrows and blows deflect very well." Ondaii picked up the dress from within the skirt and held it out offering to equip Spezh personally. The fact that this little man could raise the garment without effort was more proof he could never survive combat with it on.

Hitaelseran walked back and stopped. "The peasants have determined to wait for Sir Qerlak. We'll have to decide—say, what it this?" He ran his hand under the small tiles of the armor. "This is a banded suit, I've heard of these but never seen. Extremely rare, cost a fortune. Is it yours?"

Spezh could say nothing, but Ondaii volunteered, "It now is."

Hitaelseran began to unlace Spezh's chain kirtle without asking, and Spezh felt trapped in the presence of the young noble. When the black armor went on Spezh could not trust something so light and flexible could possibly protect him. Ondaii produced black gauntlets and a solid metal helm with a full-face visor on a hinge, also the deepest black and shaped like the maw of a ferocious Reptile Man.

By now Cecil and Chased had drifted back to the wagon, and Spezh saw them both gaping in amazement at his new suit.

"Incredible! And this will deflect blows? What is this material?"

"Special kind of lacquer over bands steel made, many layers are needed, much drying."

"It's much lighter than plate. Fewer apertures than chain. Astounding."

Spezh looked about him and realized there would be no escape from this ebon prison.

"I am going to die."

"A knight! On the road," many voices called from the village's edge. Spezh moved with everyone else to see, hope rising in his heart. But the dark-armored shape coming on rode too easily to be Qerlak, and bore the sign of the jeweled boar on his pennon.

"Sir Coss," Hitaelseran called out, "how fare you this fine morning sir? I must say, your way back to Beryl would have needed the northern road."

"Milord Beryllian and retinue head that way now, Sir. I have been deputed by the Greatknight to observe the coming hostilities. And bear a witness should an adjudication of claims be needful."

"Well, and welcome, sir." Hitaelseran rallied nobly but his deflation was evident to Spezh. More so, the peasants of Sluicehill, who had not yet seen their lord ride, voiced glum mutters and began to disperse.

"More riders! More coming!" the children called out, running back into the square, and again Spezh allowed himself to wish for the best. But instead of Qerlak, in trotted the blasted bard Eversong, looking resplendent as usual and dismounting to the cheers of the crowd.

"Greetings all! Catching wind that some merry fracas might be afoot, I thought I'd take pains to come out on this miserable rainsome day and test whether any deeds here could be worth a ditty."

"Well met, Bleys Eversong," Chased replied, even his voice sounding for him rather subdued. "We merely await our lord, detained in the north and—"

"Riders, riders!" the children's shouts now brought nothing but groans from the cynical crowd, yet everyone remained just to sate their curiosity.

Two noble Elves in leathers cantered in, lance and shield quartered behind them.

"Are we too late? Where—"

"—is our brother? We didn't want to miss—"

"—father would never forgive us if we didn't have—"

"—all the news."

"Greetings milords Barleybane," Cecil said, stepping forward to handle the reins. "Sir Qerlak your brother has not yet arrived from his separate dispatch." The young squire looked glum as well. "It may be that we shall meet the foe without him"

"Riders coming!" and by now the grown-ups had had enough.

"Silence, you floor-crawlers, or I'll tan your backsides so well that Pritaelseran will hear your screams and turn around in fear!"

Everyone chuckled a bit at that, and the children kept screaming, and no one minded them. But Spezh looked out, because he was fast becoming a fool evidently. And distantly he saw two riders, trudging slowly down the road with heads hung low over their horse's necks. As if they had come far.

And one was a woman, wearing a robe and bearing a staff.

"Attend, you peasant twits! It is the lord of Mon-Crulbagh and his wizard, the sorceress Galethiel. He has ridden far to address you and by Argens you will hear him. The first man to try and leave this square, I will seize by the hair and rip his skin completely off!"

Spezh was well known for such violent bombast; he expected a few laughs. But everyone stared instead, and he realized, belatedly, that he cut a more fearsome figure now in his new mien.

The sound of hooves slowly plonking on the cobbles kept everyone quiet, and when Qerlak rode into the square every man doffed his cap. He looked about him a bit dazed, then slung his body off the mount with a groan that echoed from the buildings.

"Never again! I walk from this day forward, on my name. Well, for today at least."

Galethiel stayed aboard, saying "We took two horses each, and rode them in turns. The others are walking after us. Maybe."

"Have you read the document, Cecil?"

"Yes milord. Some have signed and the rest… ahm, await your pleasure."

"My friends," Qerlak raised his voice to the crowd, "there is no pleasure at all for me in what I must ask. You have the right to muster, by the ancient custom of this foef, and I affirm it. Without your help, I cannot hope to defeat Pritaelseran, though I would stand against his possession of this foef if I stood alone. My life is here in Mon-Crulbagh. And someday, perhaps today, my death will also be here."

He waited a bit while thinking of more to say. Finally, he shrugged.

"But I would prefer later." Everyone chuckled at that.

"You have seen the smoke," he went on. "We saw it too long before reaching here. That smoke means flame, of course. That is how Argens tests the faithful, with fire. I have passed his tests so far. By fire, the Bugs of Bultarr-r have been defeated." This brought a brief cheer. "And one more test of fire lies before us. Face it with me, for Argens and for freedom in Mon-Crulbagh."

The cheers then were immediate and strong, as men lined up to sign the charter once again. Spezh saluted as Qerlak turned to review his retinue, and the knight was stunned and delighted.

"My dear guard captain, look at your new armor! It suits your look very well I think."

Spezh swallowed hard to make an admission, "It was a gift milord. From Ondaii."

Hitaelseran said, "He looks once again the black giant we thought him last month."

"Sirs Hitaelseran and Chased, thanks for your loyal service so far. I fear we may not have nearly the knights of our foe, but every lance reduces our infirmity."

"More than you might have guessed, Sir Qerlak. Look you, your two brothers are here, and Sir Coss has also come."

"To observe," the knight of Beryl put in. After a moment, his lips twitched toward a grin and he added, "of course, I may find it needful to observe from a close distance. You know, to gain a better view of the situation."

"Of course!" Qerlak replied clasping his arm. "And Mo'lem, Larel, you have stayed as well."

"Bored all day—"

"—hanging around the castle, now no one there—"

"—except that stuffy castellan of yours!"

Qerlak took each of their arms together in a three-way embrace, and Spezh saw tears in his eyes. "I think I can promise you, today and tomorrow, boredom will not be a problem."

Spezh had to speak, "Still more than twice our number in lances, Sir Qerlak. I'll hold one for you, though I'm no good with it."

"Not to despair, Spezh. I've been hearing from my companion the sorceress here, about a little surprise Citizen Ondaii has put together. And we have the pikemen, the slingers. We shall see. And do our best."

$$\oplus \ \oplus \ \oplus$$

Foef of Mon-Crulbagh

"Yes, Ellesmera," Quarion said, "I get it, our best. But exactly what should we do? For example, what first?"

The Elves sat by the dawn fire Bellatara was tending and went over the same ground for the fourth time. They had two jobs, neither of which seemed feasible, and almost no time to get them done. Investigate the Border Stones, then find the forest's mysterious inhabitants. The Halfling chuckled at the absurdity in spite of how serious it was, and that drew both the others to look at her.

She chucked a small deadwood stick into the flames. "First, we have to split up."

"What?" "Absolutely not."

"There is no time," Bellatara replied, standing up. "You two will need several hours, at least, to get up to those stones from here."

"We two?" Ellesmera asked, "why aren't you coming?"

"You will save a little time without me," she said. "I'm shorter, though if either of you make one comment—"

"Bellatara, come with us," Quarion urged. "You can't stay in this forest alone, it's too dangerous."

"I won't be alone, not for long." On this point, Bellatara felt certain. "These beings, whatever they are, only hold off because we're in a group. They might kill me, or not, but they won't come near until I approach them by myself."

She stared them both down a moment. "Look, I know nothing about rocks. I've thought about what could be happening there and my brain is dry, I have no idea. But the woods I know something about." She took a breath. "Yes, it's a risk. But I can do this."

Quarion's face moved suddenly from resistance to a grin. "Well, but I'm the one who's supposed to take the risks!"

Ellesmera had been looking thoughtful. "Not this time, evidently." She looked back at Bellatara and smiled, that beautiful face so rarely seen. "I believe you are right, Bellatara, though I'm afraid of losing you. Suppose we are both successful, how will we find each other again?"

"Head back to Bultarr-r?" Quarion suggested.

Bellatara shook her head. "No, that would take too long. Meet on the southern side of the forest, let us say by sunset. Or if one of us doesn't make it, then head straight for Sluicehill across country."

"Straight across the foef!" Quarion cried, "There must be forty homesteads between us in that direction, each with a farmer who will stick a hay-fork in a strange intruder. If a swampy beast doesn't get us. Three days on foot if we don't stop to sleep."

He knelt in front of the Halfling. "Bellatara, don't leave us. We need to stay as a group."

She grabbed his hand and felt happy that this daring fellow cared so much. The part of her that feared monsters and undead creatures urged her to take him up on it. But Ellesmera answered for her and it was the right, the braver answer.

"We are a group, Quarion. And two of our number have broken from us already."

"That's different, they can take care—" Quarion choked off his words, then hung his head and laughed. "Well, Astor watch over you Bellatara. Holler to us if you can."

"You just take care of yourselves," the Woodsman shot back. "Not every foul creature lurks under the trees."

They nodded, broke up the little camp, kicked out the small fire, embraced, and took their separate paths. The Elves headed due east, through the forest fringe with occasional sight of the gorge on their left, toward the rising land. Bellatara could not see them after a hundred steps. Squaring her shoulders and testing again the point of a javelin, she scanned around for the paths she made out yesterday, and took one headed more southeast, directly for the center of the forest.

There was much to sense here. Bellatara could tell, from the thickness of moss, the depth of half-buried rock, roots near the surface as large as trunks, that this forest was very old. What had the townsfolk in Bultarr-r been on about? Mostly the Bugs, and Bellatara wasn't paying attention. But once or twice, wasn't it, complaints about wood cutting? Something about not being allowed, and some now taking matters into their own hands.

Bellatara realized, after an hour of cautious walking where the sun climbed higher yet the light grew less, that she had not been alone, truly all by herself, since before she could remember. As a foster child in the north, as a traveler seeking her fortune, as a victim taken slave, always there were others around. Everyone else seemed so noisy to her. The Woodsman was naturally quiet, small and light, but she had always been able to tell when someone or something else was nearby.

She was in a slight gully when she heard the lone hoofbeat. The Halfling stopped, lowered her javelin and listened hard. All the tales she'd heard as a child among the Men, of the undead and half-beasts and monsters, came crowding back upon her and the summer day seemed suddenly chill.

"*Ar Aralte!*" she called out, the only passphrase she could think of that might work with unknown beings. Of course, if they were savage, or Despairing, or mindless, she would only have given away her position for nothing. But Bellatara could sense, they already saw her.

Again a bearded face, perhaps the same one, leaned out from behind an ancient twisting bole. The man held a strong bow, and the strap of a quiver was the only adornment she could see on his body. He whistled low, and suddenly the surrounding trees released more than a dozen of his fellows. Bellatara had just moments to take in the view—rapid movement, bows and spears, women as well as men—before being seized from behind and parked on a broad back as the patrol raced off deeper into the glades.

She saw, but did not believe, and one thing for certain. Their horsemanship was beyond description.

⊕ ⊕ ⊕

The way to the hillside was much harder than Ellesmera had thought. Well past noon they broke from the eastern edge of the thick forest. She let Quarion set the pace and he was clearly pushing hard. He muttered beneath his breath about the urgency, the insane plan they'd chosen, how useless he felt in the wild lands. She let him. Ellesmera wasn't quite sure she could argue with anything he said.

From the open they could see a long way across this north-south rise, with few trees or places where anything could take cover. At least a half-dozen stone piles were visible left to right, and Quarion wasted little time angling for the one furthest south in view.

"Closer to Sluicehill", he remarked curtly.

"And we can see anything slower coming after us from a long way off."

"Certainly, and anything faster can see us."

That was a point, admittedly.

Through the afternoon hours they labored up the steady slanting slope getting incrementally closer to their chosen target. They spotted nothing larger than a roe deer in their vicinity, and as they came close enough to appreciate the massive piles, Ellesmera could no longer hear birds or even flies. From the hillside her view was spectacular, with the town walls smudging the distant horizon and scattered farms and steads sprinkled between small heath-hills and bogs, tiny creeks and copses, connected by slender paths. Many more were out of sight from here and Ellesmera reflected that this was so often the case.

They slowed on the last few furlongs, a reluctance they both felt akin to the nearness of a haunted place. As Ellesmera caught her breath, her habits took over and the trance state beckoned. Slowing the rate of breath even further, she strolled now through the thick grass as the Stealthic roamed ahead and put his hand to stone halfway up the pile. He touched all around, looking for loose rocks or portions, while Ellesmera filtered out whatever he was saying. He circled the mound, and Ellesmera looked at the scraped grass on the downhill side. Quarion stopped at no particular spot, looking closely at the rock but seeing nothing. Ellesmera calmly walked to the uphill side and recognized its front.

By now her focus was so strong that even standing was a distraction to be eliminated. She sat cross-legged with a straight back, sending her mind across all things looking for clues to this impossible mystery.

"So we're here," Quarion said. "What did the song say? *The border stones of Mon-Crulbagh have never justice seen.* Fine poetry but what does it mean?"

It was possible once more to incorporate Quarion's words in her stream of thought. Ellesmera recalled Qerlak, speaking to himself more than anyone, disappointed that an old journal record mentioned these stones but not much else of help. Long ago, in the age of heroes, miracles were more common. And tomes no longer read described how the elements were harnessed for a purpose unknown.

"They are moving," she quietly announced.

"Well sure, that's what this other lord claimed. But how could anyone have moved something this big all that way? And these aren't separate rocks, it's just one thing."

"Not a thing," Ellesmera replied. "Alive. Not moved. Moving."

"Are you mad? What bizarre tale ever—"

Ellesmera saw across her own time, about a forbidden tome and words on a random page, of Qerlak's speech and Galethiel's magic. A test of fire.

"Do you still have your Fire-Light stone?"

"What? Yes, here, are you thinking of lighting a campfire?"

"Of a sort." Taking the stone, Ellesmera rose and placed it directly against the base of the statue on the uphill side. She stood back and pointed to the top. "Can you see? The face, the eyes?"

"What do you—a face, hem, well I suppose." Quarion looked askance at his friend. "Not a very handsome one!"

"Wait. Just wait." Ellesmera sat again as Quarion sighed. They watched the stone in the absolute stillness of early evening.

"It hasn't moved."

"It is moving. Wait."

"I tell you it's a waste of—Astor's right hand!"

With the slightest of grinding noises and the tiniest bit of motion, the enormous pile came a little closer to the pair. The stone crushed beneath the edge of the pile, and flame broke forth. Unlike at the cave, the flames were small but steady, and seemed to slowly spread across all the surface of the stones quicker than they could realize.

The surety of the test, the power of ancient times, the utter lack of coincidence all came together in Ellesmera's mind and she spoke a set of words seen on a random page.

"*ignita dicta sud terror*"

The flames scattered across the giant pile flared a little higher, then seemed to sink into the stone, briefly illuminating it from within. Arms broke from its sides and the rocks in the eye-spots flared as if they reflected the light of the stars.

With a sound like ground gravel it spoke. "*Whyyy have youuu summmonnned meee, mortall?*"

"What are you?" Ellesmera called, "what do you here with all your brethren."

"*Wweee mark-th-k the borrder. Of Monn-Krulbagghkh.*"

"Then why do you move? What drives you?"

"*Jusstisss…*"

"Justice? It draws you to it?"

"*Nnayyy. It drivezz uzz awayyy. Wee never seeee jusstisss…*"

The giant stone strode forward perhaps a full inch this time showing the walking posture of a person thigh deep in water.

And Ellesmera saw it all clearly.

The flame-light faded and the stone before them was once more a shapeless pile. Ellesmera rose and grabbed Quarion by the hand, pelting downhill in the darkness with unaccustomed haste. Slight tears in the cloud cover above let just enough starlight through to help the Elves find their way, as she guided them south and west on another long angle toward distant Sluicehill.

"I don't suppose," Quarion panted, "you will tell me heads or tails about what just happened to us."

"We must reach Qerlak. Whatever happens, he must not be tempted, to try anything, I don't know, unchivalrous."

"But what if his restraint makes him lose?"

"He's already winning!" Ellesmera's voice was joyous and confident. "Don't you see? Here in Mon-Crulbagh, there is justice on this side. That's why the stones are moving uphill."

Quarion was so struck by the revelation that he stopped running while Ellesmera distanced him for nearly a furlong. He suddenly shouted at the top of his lungs.

"They never see justice!"

Then Ellesmera came up short, as ahead of them the Stealthic's cry was answered by a distant familiar voice above the clatter of dozens of hooves.

"Quarion! Ellesmera! Hurry," Bellatara shouted. "The centaurs say we can make it, but we'll need to ride all night."

And Ellesmera would have refused to believe her eyes, had she not already conversed with a Border Stone.

The night before the battle, Pritaelseran's camp was subjected to undue harassment. Voices in the night cried out "Now! Now!" followed by a hail of sling stones that gravely injured one of the peasant watchers and forced the retainers to re-arm to repel a raid. Nothing happened, and archers combing the nearby trees saw only a handful of children running off laughing. Guards were doubled, but when the cry of "Now!" came again an hour later, the camp was still disrupted. No stones hit and no figures showed. On the third cry, a sharp sentry identified it was but a single remaining youth, hiding in a tree. The boy's laughter turned gradually to begging and then to screams when the tree was set aflame: after the leaping fiery corpse hit the earth it was discovered that it was, in fact, a young girl.

Lacking rest and thus in even worse temper than before, the lord of Pritaelseran arrayed his forces the next morning for an expected encounter with the enemy. Moving directly toward the nearest village, Cran-Kalrith received his first disappointment of the day. The stream level was indeed somewhat lower than normal, but not enough to permit easy passage in the area near the hamlet. The rain never let up, and already men could see it rising again. From less than a bowshot away, a small crowd of women and children gathered on the opposite bank, not jeering nor much moving, but simply watching the invading force as it moved back and forth, like dogs hoping for food.

The Hawk knight set his force in order again and double-timed them west and around the river's curve, further away to an area where fords existed as the current slowed on its way to feed the swamp called Mon Morteissk. Cran-Kalrith put the bowmen loosely in front, the battle of his spearmen on the left side and the single line of cavalry to the right. In the last nearly-open field before the Sodsluice itself, he came upon the host of Mon-Crulbagh.

A first glance told him the battle would not last long.

Pitching a temporary camp—little more than circling his supply wagons and allowing the villeins to drop packs and bedrolls—Cran-Kalrith moved briefly to confer with his brother.

"How strangely the enemy is drawn up," Zantire observed, which the Hawk Knight found unnerving for a first remark.

"He believes a little elevation, one tiny hill in all his land, will be enough to douse the ardor of the finest knights in Argens. He will shortly learn otherwise. See to it, brother, that you trap and destroy the witch before Barleybane retreats. My men will not take long to put this rabble to rout."

"Rather more of the pike than you expected, though."

In truth, Pritaelseran had thought at least half of Mon-Crulbagh's forces would be dispatched to Bultarr-r. "Faugh! A peasant with a long spear is still a peasant. I doubt they will survive even the spearmen, but after my knights are victorious, we will roll them up like a carpet from the flank."

Zantire nodded, but did not smile. "I will search out their sorceress now as you request."

Why could he not bring himself to say 'command'?

314

"My hands itch to win retribution for her unspeakable crime."

"Good hunting. We shall celebrate with a goblet at lunch."

Then Sir Pritaelseran returned to the front line to review the enemy dispositions.

Mon-Crulbagh had drawn up its peasants with long spears six ranks deep on a slight rise to the left, with only a small space of room beyond it before the banks of the Sodsluice curved past. On the right the ground was more open between the rise and a small stand of thick trees, suitable for cavalry operations. And the enemy had properly placed what few he had there. Pritaelseran counted only nine mounted men, of which two were in leather like squires, and four bore bows rather than lances. One of them armored all in black must be the jungle giant the survivors of the raiding party had reported. The pennon of the jeweled boar concerned him a moment, as the involvement of a retainer from the Greatknight Beryl could mean further support from Barleybane's overlord. But scanning the field carefully Pritaelseran could see no evidence. Slingers, mainly young persons, stood loosely scattered in small groups to all sides.

Where was his foe? At last he made out a large armored figure striding behind the pikemen atop the rise. On foot? Was there no end to the ignobility of this usurper? Riding a few steps beyond the line of his sixteen lancers, Cran-Kalrith dipped his hawk pennon toward Barleybane, in proper challenge to duel. In response, the plated-mailed figure raised an arm in acknowledgement, but only strode down the slope between the ranks of his pikemen to stand a rod before them, bearing an enormous battle-axe. When Pritaelseran dipped his lance again, itself a mark of dishonor to the foe that he should need a second invitation, the churl only waved at him as if to come ahead, horse and lance and all, against him on the ground. Suicide to challenge a true knight thus. But Pritaelseran glanced back to the boar pennon, and thought about how it might look to others, before turning his horse back to the line as the peasants jeered and sang.

His mood was now so black that the skin's heat dried the sweat within his armor. Pritaelseran signaled his archers forward to harass the enemy, with the spearmen close behind to charge in as soon as the ranks were shaken. His knights, outnumbering the mounted foe more than three to one, would need little time to finish them and afterwards teach these peasants to raise hands against their betters.

As the archers moved in, their initial volley fell almost comically short. The rain, of course, not that it mattered but the villeins should have known and he would see to their discipline later. On the other side, Mon-Crulbagh's ragged gang of slingers suffered no such disability, focusing their fire on the spearmen behind the archers. Some even dared to hurl at the knights in line, causing several to shout with pain and injuring two of the horses, requiring replacement. Cran-Kalrith held them back, waiting a better moment. The hooves of his steeds would serve those children well when the time came.

But from the enemy lines the four mounted bowmen charged slantwise across the field, firing into the archers and putting them quite to rout despite the numbers. The advancing spearmen, now exposed, took even greater casualties from sling stones and their pace wavered without direct leadership. Even as Pritaelseran raised one arm to order his knights to advance, he sneered with satisfaction to see the remaining mounted men of Mon-Crulbagh fleeing at top speed, racing away and curving around the rise to escape.

And his foe, among the peasants he loved so well, had not even a mount to flee with them.

Bleys Eversong was more excited than he could say, to be observing his first real battle.

Curiously, no one else shared his enthusiasm. Lord Qerlak, his new patron, always spoke courteously when approached but was clearly very busy setting his lines right and going over aspects of some plan with his subalterns. Sir Hitaelseran did not even respond when hailed—seemingly distracted for some obscure reason. Seldom Chased grinned and promised drinking later, but no more. And that dekentar Spezh had become as furious as the expression on his new mien, growling when anyone but Sir Qerlak addressed him and annoyed that he had to help the strange little man in bright robes unpack his gear.

"No, no, Spezh, here," Qerlak said, pointing to a spot twoscore paces to one side. "You understand, they have limited range and we must hope the enemy will be where we want them."

Bleys studied the items even as the red-haired mage came up to oversee. Two very small engines, such as the catapults the bard had seen in other castles, sat atop wheel-less platforms cut from the shell of a gigantic turtle, each slightly larger than a table-top. Their firing arms were not quite as thick as a man's wrist, made of strong-looking metal which nevertheless could bend a little as the robed man cranked them down with a geared device attached to the back of each one.

"How ingenious," he remarked as Galethiel stooped down to be sure a small quartz stone was securely tucked in a pocket of the skin bag that would be the devices' only ammunition. "What, er, what will it do?"

"If we are lucky," the mage replied, "it will administer a test, of sorts." She grinned to signal her intention of keeping a secret and Bleys laughed. Yet the weapons were clearly pointed at nothing.

From the slight rise behind the rows of pike-bearing peasants he surveyed the field as the enemy came in view, and felt a wave of apprehension. The uniform colors, the precision of their lines, and especially the display of armor and horsemanship on the left side of the Hawk Knight's force was fearsome. Qerlak had declined to join his men, but was hardly hiding, standing instead in front of his infantry, evidently placing his highest hopes in their numbers to survive the day.

Bleys decided to catch him a moment before the combat, to hear his intentions and perhaps final wishes before such a clash. Walking between the pike-rows, he saw the boys and older men scattered in front and to the sides with their slings and strummed a few chords just to get his mind for rhymes moving. Whatever the outcome there should be a song to—

The fact suddenly hit him as he reached Qerlak's side. The Swamp Knight, having just turned back from a challenge across the way, was surprised to see the minstrel near him.

"Why Master Eversong, what brings you here? The business shall be hot enough in a moment, you should seek cover at once."

"I see, milord, I see now what you intend."

"Indeed, sir?" Qerlak was smiling but a bit uncertain of the jest.

Bleys pointed around the field even as the horns sounded. "You intend to break their bones. Using sticks. And stones."

Now the knight's grin became something complete and sure. "Well, that is certainly a part of the idea. Hie you now, to the top of the rise, and keep your horse handy should matters go awry. Argens with you, sir."

Bleys turned and trotted back uphill through the ranks, and gave them all a verse even as he laughed to hear his words come true.

The muster of the swamp stood fast.
THEY ALWAYS DO, THEY ALWAYS DO!
With pike in arm and sling they cast their vote and lo- their aim was true.

By the time he reached the top, the shouting and shooting was well underway. Bleys looked in all directions and the blur of images sank his heart. Slingers withdrawing to all flanks, and the few lancers of Mon-Crulbagh turning to ride away to

318

the rear, circling behind the small hill closer to the river fords. Oh base knaves! To the front, the enemy spearmen came on though several were down from missiles. Suddenly the right half of Qerlak's pike leveled their points and charged downhill toward their foes, now stripped of archer protection. Yet here came up the enemy horse on the bare left flank, slowly and with confidence. Only half the pike remained on the hilltop to face them, but could never hope to chase down a mounted foe at that range. The enemy was free to crush the other pike in flank, or to give chase to the fleeing horse for the ransoms.

Bleys spun to Galethiel, who clutched her staff and watched the enemy carefully as if seeking a single foe.

"Mistress mage, can you do nothing to help?"

She shook her head briefly. "He's coming. I have to be ready."

"Who is coming?"

With a soft puff of smoky air there appeared on the hilltop an aquiline figure bald and furious. Vaguely, Bleys recognized the man sitting in the left-hand chair when he had sung for Pritaelseran many years before. He looked angry all the time but now apoplectic with rage. As Galethiel whirled he shouted a single syllable in the tongue of sorcerers, causing a ripple of explosive force from where he stood out to ten feet in all directions. Two servants nearby were knocked down as was the man assigned to guard the Mon-Crulbagh mage. She reeled from the blast but held her footing.

"Mortal slut! This is for my Insis." Zantire drew himself to full height, gestured and called out "I command you to Sleep!"

Bleys stood to the side of the Mage Command but felt the power of its energy pulsing in a ray all before the Elven wizard. The shimmer of the spell moved too quickly to dodge or outrun. Why, then, Bleys had time to wonder, as the energy hit her body and made her fall to the ground helpless, did she laugh with fierce relief?

⊕ ⊕ ⊕

Pritaelseran ordered his knights forward at the walk, then into a half-turn to bring his line to bear on the flank of Barleybane's foolish pike-charge. In perfect position—and the slingers on this side of the field all fled, probably back across the river—he signaled again for a hold to let Mon-Crulbagh come forward further into the trap. Scanning the hill, he saw his brother appear and the red-haired mage's body fall. Well and good. Turning back to order the charge he froze in mid-call.

The enemy horse, having ridden behind the hill at breakneck speed, made a full circuit and now appeared across the field, working through that narrow space between rise and river and charging helter-skelter into the spearmen from their flank. Lances to one side and pikes before, the Pritaelseran spear company dropped to rout in an instant. Many fell, and some threw down their weapons. With no archery to cover their retreat, his levy had no chance to escape, though only the enemy pike pursued with vigor.

Pritaelseran was furious at his losses; this victory would cost him much more than he had expected, though of course it would come out of Mon-Crulbagh's plunder in the end. He threw his arm down to signal the charge. Barleybane was still on foot, caught in the open now and subject to death in the melee carrying none of the dishonor which would have clung to the absurd joust he had signaled for earlier. Now Qerlak Barleybane was subject to the fortunes of war.

His men shouted and spurred their horses forward, bringing lances to bear on the fast-closing foes ahead. Pritaelseran's eye caught a bright flare from the hilltop to his right, no doubt his brother exacting vengeance. Behind him by the copse of trees, he heard the screams of the Mon-Crulbagh slingers, perhaps rousted by some of his archers or a beast of these accursed swamps. All the better.

But he could not spare the time to look or listen, not even to the bizarre sounds of ratchet and spring from somewhere nearby. He could see Sir Qerlak ahead, turning to face the charge but not calling back his pikemen. Perhaps the churl would at least face his death as befit a noble.

⊕ ⊕ ⊕

Bleys Eversong knew what he would need to sing about now. He saw the female mage fall to the ground, dead asleep—certainly a useful phrase, that—and fell to his knees in horror at the murder he was about to witness. With crackling hands, Zantire Pritaelseran advanced to seize and shock the life from her helpless form.

Except she was not lying down.

Or rather she was, but Galethiel was also standing there.

Bleys had heard the tales of the Dreamseer before. The previous year, folks of all ranks and races had murmured of the tall, red-haired mortal wizard who sailed past during their dreams. Bad dreams, mainly, it was a time when everyone seemed to suffer nightmares constantly. Elves who did not require sleep left off it. Bleys was certain he had seen her himself; the resemblance when he met Galethiel a week ago was uncanny.

Zantire had mastered one of the fabled Mage Commands, and it just happened to be this powerful one. With Sleep, he could disable small armies within the sound of his voice. So absorbed in study, he probably had not slept in decades himself, and paid no heed to the maunderings of the common folk.

But Galethiel, a misty form of her standing next to her own body and chuckling soundlessly, was the Dreamseer. Evidently, the power of the Mage Command was not nearly so complete over her as all the others.

Sensing her good humor, Bleys was emboldened to take part. "Ah, sirrah, if I may?"

Zantire glanced in his direction and spat a curse. "Back, vagabond, or feel my wrath."

Rather than approach or reply, Bleys lifted a single finger to mean "just a moment" and then pointed it behind the Elf with a confident smile.

Zantire turned and beheld the ghostly form of his opponent floating as if in the air just a few inches off the ground. He cried out and plunged his hands into her space but made no contact as his eldritch energies faded. Before he could renew them, Galethiel reached to a place beyond sight and dragged into view a huge, monstrous form. Bleys descried multiple arms and eyes, jagged teeth in places where there should be no mouth, fur, horns, ridges, scales. Galethiel caught the creature up in one hand though it seemed larger than a wagon. As she brought it round closer to her foe the monster shrank to as small as her palm. Before he could retreat or duck she popped it into one ear.

Zantire screamed in terror and clapped both hands to the sides of his head, staggering back and nearly falling down. The ghostly Galethiel made a dusting gesture, then calmly lay back down within her body on the ground. A moment later she arose, winked at Bleys, and leveled her staff at the opponent still screaming.

"And this is for Garr, you arrogant Elvish carker."

A bolt of purest lightning flashed out catching Zantire full in the chest, and his screams choked to nothing before the bolt finally stopped, releasing his corpse to the mossy turf.

And Bleys knew he would sing of this, some day when he had enough words and the chords to match them.

But beyond the hilltop, he saw the knights of Pritaelseran, now angled oddly to their original line, charging pell-mell toward the host of Mon-Crulbagh. And the path of their charge was in line with a place that used to be nothing.

A pair of crank-chunk sounds preceded two blobby skins popping into the air and sailing forward perhaps a hundred paces. In mid-flight, something ignited on their sides and the skins themselves burst, their oil catching fire and scattering an irregular patch of flame directly athwart the path of the Pritaelseran knights.

Horses reared in panic, two riders were thrown, and only one in four came through with any speed, one of whom dropped his lance to put out his own arm. With a shout, Qerlak signaled the remaining pikemen on the hill, who swept down upon an enemy much closer and no longer galloping.

Bleys saw one retainer try to ride down Sir Qerlak, who ducked the lance and countered with a two-handed blow from his axe that cut from man into mount and brought them both down dead. Sir Hitaelseran charged into his brother's joust and both lances shattered to kindling: the latter was thrown and lay the field writhing from a shattered hip or leg. The Mon-Crulbagh pike charged into the near side of the Pritaelseran line, felling three armored knights yet losing several of their number after the initial shock.

Far off, Bleys could see some of the enemy archers and spearmen slowing and gathering by their wagons which offered good shelter. A ragged line of fleeing slingers headed behind the hill, shouting in horror and pointing back to the copse. From within it, Bleys heard a horn of pure ivory, sounding several notes in sequence.

Out of the stand of dense trees came horsemen. Of a certain kind.

⊕ ⊕ ⊕

None of this was possible. Pritaelseran was furious that Mon-Crulbagh had by various ignoble tricks managed to stave off defeat, but now it seemed the heroes themselves had arrayed against him. His rallying spearmen and archers fled in total rout at the sight of the legendary allies charging from the copse. Never mind there were less than twenty of them, none armored, only six with spears. No matter that the enemy's pike-levy also ran at the sight. None of that was important.

Creatures of tale, of near-myth, whose very existence his own father had curtly denied, were here to fulfill the whispered promise that peasants back home were whipped to repeat.

With a heavy heart, Cran-Kalrith shouted to turn his remaining knights against this new foe. Coughing from the smoke of the fire-bombs that broke their first charge, his retainers could not get much speed from their mounts, already exhausted and terrified. And the new enemy, nearly naked, yet had some powerful bows in their number which took down two or three before the first contact.

The lances of Pritaelseran all missed, for their foes could shift directions with a thought, like rabbits, like squirrels at play. Their spears were used only to stab, not joust, and if four blows in five hit armor, still the last found a weak point and drew blood. Worse, their appearance was so unnerving, abominations of half-man sprouting directly from their horse's necks. Above all, their deep voices mixed scream with song as they fought. The unearthly sound was too much and Pritaelseran could not control his mount as it joined the general rout.

Zantire had not reappeared to add his mystic might to the cause, but a glance showed the flame-tressed witch standing again atop the hill. The enemy mounted bowmen were already among the wagons, rousting those hiding to either flee or surrender. A scattered line of his men trailed back to the south and east, toward home, and everyone within his line of sight was still running.

Somewhat behind him, he saw Hitaelseran dismount and heft Zanrith's wounded body over Craltire's crupper, sending them back in retreat and shame without a word. Their eyes met, and the Hawk Knight saw only the cold regard of a victorious enemy before the young man remounted and rode to rally on his new overlord.

There would be judgment for this day. So many injuries that Crulbagh must atone for! Not least of these, he reflected in a moment of bitter honesty and true sadness, was how these events had exposed the mistake he had made, with the knight who was once his youngest son. Yet even as he raged and wept for what he had lost, Cran-Kalrith Pritaelseran took a savage comfort in knowing that though the victory had vanished, the foef was already his.

⊕ ⊕ ⊕

Qerlak stood in the spot on the field where there had been nothing at all. Now the tall grass smoldered with oil-based flames slowly losing the battle under the relentless warm rain of Mon-Crulbagh, and he felt an enormous weight slowly lifting from his back. As calls came in from every side, he remained where he was and became the center of everything for a time.

"Qerlak! I mean, Lord Barleybane," Bellatara cried as one of the centaurs cantered up to deposit her in the grass nearby. "You're alive, and we won!"

"Evidently, on both counts, and thanks to you."

"It was the centaurs, sir," she beamed as her compatriots also rode up and were let off the backs of two others. "They greeted me as, um, as your ambassador you see…" She gave him a desperate look and Qerlak played along.

"Of course, and well done for establishing contact with our ancient allies, so long ignored by my predecessors." Qerlak looked up at the trio of man-beasts, who nodded gravely even as their hooves kept shying away from each new arrival behind him.

"As I'm sure you are reluctant to leave your forest home for long…"

"Yes," Bellatara cut in, "they said they were happy to honor the old alliance, as long as you would affirm them in their right to the Tenser Deeping. And that you renew your forbiddance on wood-cutting by anyone within its borders."

"Ah. Yes, of course. I am delighted to affirm that condition."

"On pain of death."

"Hem! Well, yes, I shall impress this upon the people of the town, yes. And here is my hand on that."

The nearest centaur, after shying back at first as if against her own will, approached to take his hand briefly. After an awkward pause, she spoke, with that same unnerving song-speech they used in the charge.

"Wee thank thee also, for such braaave efforts as theee didst make upon the Bugs who plagued us certes as much as thine owwn."

"May the people of Hope always live in Hope, and in peace." Qerlak said, repeating a phrase his father often used though not with beings so different.

The three creatures nodded thoughtfully, then abruptly turned and cantered back to the rest, who joined them in a hasty withdrawal to cover, away from the sight of their fellow beings.

Qerlak walked a few paces after them, and behind him two score of his followers waited. He took a deep breath, the largest he had in days, and let it out slowly as he tried to convince himself this had truly happened.

His eye chanced to fall on the body of a Pritaelseran archer, a young lad who had taken a sling stone near the center of his forehead and probably died in an instant. Threescore paces away Qerlak's heart sank to see the body of the boy with the horn, who had brought warning to the foef twice. His chest sprouted an arrow with markings like the ones he saw in the quiver at his feet. Just two of the dead on this field, whose years between them did not add up to those of a true adult. Such a waste.

"You did it," came a quiet voice behind him and Qerlak spun to see Galethiel, whole and alive. Dropping his axe he embraced her with unaccustomed ferocity, which she returned.

"I didn't dare think about it," he whispered. "That mage, so powerful, and I had no way to help you."

"Silly man," she chuckled back, "I was here to help you, remember? Just another arrogant Elf." She broke away with a smile and tears on the same face. "You remember the type?"

"I believe I recall hearing something…" he replied, not pulling back from the slap she gave his arm.

"Can you believe it, he put me to sleep!"

Qerlak felt his face go slack, and then he seized her arms again as the import sank in. "He slept the Dreamseer? Oh, I could almost pity him."

A cough from one side pulled him back to regard Sir Tancrad Coss, sitting his horse in the front rank of his followers, visor and eyebrow both raised at the sight of such an ignoble display of emotion.

"Sir Coss! I am pleased that your observations did not bring you into any harm."

"Indeed," he replied with frosty seriousness and just a twitch from his lip, "I felt it best to, ah, make my observations from closer range."

"So I see. You appear to have broken your lance."

"Indeed, an unfortunate misinterpretation by one of Pritaelseran's retainers who took it ill that I showed him my pennon so clearly. I explained his error to him, and he lies there now, your prisoner sir."

"Yours rather, I'm sure Sir Coss. Based on what I can see, I shall suffer no shortage of prisoners here."

"Indeed. And that will form a part of my report to milord Beryllian, which I must make without delay." Coss set his visor down and saluted gravely. "You may expect a summons, of course, to adjudicate any issues arising from this dispute."

"Of course. I shall be prompt to answer."

"Hail and farewell, Sir Barleybane. I would wish the blessings of Argens upon you, but today's events convince me that would be redundant."

The men cheered as the Beryl knight trotted off with his prisoner tied to a second horse's saddle. Pikemen and slingers were gathering again, standing around in no order at all, chatting loudly and pointing to the copse where the centaurs had disappeared as if that were their ancestral lair.

"Inter the dead in flame as is proper. Then we march for home. Any man here is free to enter the keep with me where he shall sample food and ale enough to remember for a year. But if you must return to home and hearth, take with you your pike shaft, and keep the steel head upon it as you practice."

Qerlak heard the exclamations of surprise all around and smiled. "I shall not burden free Elves with the distrust of using stone heads, when they have proven their loyalty to me in combat. Practice hard against the day I call you again, that you may muster if you will and defend this land, the greatest foef in the Argensian Empire!"

As the field rang with cheers, the rain petered down and a break of sun appeared. Through it all he saw the three former prisoners standing together and clapping.

"I owe you all a debt. Without your aid against the Bugs, the centaurs might not have come, to say nothing of finding them! You have helped me keep my foef."

"And it's still growing!" Quarion said with a grin.

"Eh?"

"Wait until you hear," Ellesmera said with a rare smile of her own.

Foef of Beryl

All the way from Mon-Crulbagh to Beryl, members of the delegation grumbled and complained. It seemed everyone had a gripe, except their lord who stood to lose his foef upon their arrival.

"I am most loathe, milord, to see my father again." Hitaelseran said on the first day.

"I empathize, sir. But one of the items in Sir Pritaelseran's complaint against me is that I have kidnapped you."

"That is ridiculous! My letter made my volition plain. Surely Sir Chased would have been a more fit support to you."

"Seldom Chased guards the foef in our absence and could not be happier to do so." Qerlak looked back on the other riders and motioned his knight closer to whisper. "Evidently, the serving girl who held the feather on the night of our feast has never been seen without it in her hair. Sir Chased has become quite taken with her." He chuckled, and added, "I gather the blindfold from that night has also gone missing."

He clapped Hitaelseran on the back. "As for your letter, no doubt it would be evidence enough to clear you, if only we could lay hands upon it. But be of good cheer, mayhap your lady mother will be in attendance."

That first night by the road campfire, it was Galethiel's turn to carp at him.

"I have important researches, in my lab. And Garr is still recovering; I'm needed there, not in some stuffy Elf-noble fraternity celebration!"

Qerlak did not respond to his old companion but only gazed at her fondly.

"You'll be in no danger!" she cried, "All Beryl's guards around the castle, everyone will be oh-so decent. I don't know why you bothered to bring your battleaxe."

Qerlak still kept his peace, only glancing at Galethiel's marvelous staff.

She sighed and began to answer her own questions. "Of course, it's all about the look, making the right appearance. What carking nonsense. You're right, he's wrong. Answer him with a letter, I say, and if he doesn't like it let him come to you!"

Now Qerlak chuckled and put one hand on her shoulder in affection. Galethiel cursed and spat, then grinned back at him.

"Alright, you win. We shall make an appearance, and I shall defend myself against the charge—what did that moron say I did?"

"That would be 'assassination of a noble', I believe."

"Of course." Galethiel chuckled. "It will be all I can do not to roast him. And our handsome bard? He's a witness to what really happened."

"There is that," Qerlak agreed, glancing over at Bleys. "Plus, I think he's become taken with you, or at least with your legend. I doubt I could have gotten him to stay behind."

The following day, the three newcomers spurred up to speak with their comrade and lord as they approached the city.

"You see, Sir Barleybane," Quarion began, but the Swamp Knight lifted a finger.

"With you I am just Qerlak."

"You see, Qerlak, we have been forbidden to return to Beryl on pain of death."

"Quite correct. But I have been summoned to answer charges that I manipulated the border with my neighbor, that I accessed forbidden magics to defeat him by foul means, and, well a great many other things. Some I can answer on my own. But for the matter of the Border Stones, I need your witness, and perhaps it will require a demonstration."

He looked at them all fondly. "You three can tell the tale of the barricaded river, the Bugs and the Border Stones. You are under my protection for this trip and I have already been granted an exception to your sentence for the duration of this embassy."

He turned in the saddle as they came over a rise and saw the Greatknight's capital and fortress on a distant hill. "My friends, I need you all with me, to help defend that which is mine. It is a lengthy and weighty list, no question, and I cannot doubt but that my foe will have some other trick to play when they have all been answered. Let us see this through to the end. Unless there are further complaints I have not yet heard? No? Excellent, forward then to face our doom."

⊕ ⊕ ⊕

Greatknight Torquem'l Beryllian greeted each guest to enter with the gravity due their station. First his counterpart from the Barony of Dargor, Greatknight S'int gripped his arm and exchanged the ritual greetings before accepting one goblet of wine after another, sitting so far down and back in his chair as if to signal he were done speaking for the day.

Close behind him into the great chamber came Cran-Kalrith Pritaelseran, with his lady wife but none of his sons in attendance—and of course his brother was slain, one of the reasons for this adjudication. The Hawk Knight cut the perfect figure of a noble if ever there were one; Beryllian marked the sour face of S'int to his side and reckoned it would be no happy chore to be overlord for a knight who controlled perhaps as many retainers as oneself. Or, rumor had it, perhaps a few more.

No formal delegate came from Beryllian's own lord, the imprisoned Baron Colign of Dargor, as was to be expected. He would gain no guidance nor political cover as vassal to the traitor exposed by last year's rebellion. Beryl, along with all of Colign and S'int's lord Baron Dargor, had committed to the Loyalist cause which lost the Battle of Tor Perite; the rebels in victory had put a Dwarf upon the throne of Argens, who in short order ended slavery and banned the sect of Argens Demonbender. Every lord in the room walked under the shadow of that humiliating truth, that they had all unwittingly supported a demon in disguise as Emperor. They could afford no mistakes now; judgment must be as accurate as swift, and if that entailed the condemnation of a good knight to keep matters quiet, many would say so be it.

Last, and late, to the room came the delegation from Mon-Crulbagh, loud and without the discipline such proceedings called for. Qerlak Barleybane saluted each lord in the proper order with fair words, a relief; yet to one side stood the mortal sorceress bearing her tall staff, unspeaking but looking daggers across the room at Pritaelseran. He would have to bring the mage, just to show me up, Beryllian thought in a moment of pique.

The Swamp Knight had with him the young Hitaelseran, standing stiffly and also unspeaking; he let the lotus flower on his livery speak volumes. And the minstrel! Barleybane was pleased to inflict that gadfly on the court again, Beryllian thought with bitter humor. Eversong bowed gracefully enough and seemed too pleased with the entire proceedings. Another song to be sung about this day, no doubt. Now Beryllian thought his misery complete.

Until he laid eyes on the three prisoners, free and also liveried in the colors of Mon-Crulbagh. Was the man determined to be found guilty?

"Greetings Sir Qerlak. Will you have wine before we begin?"

"My thanks, Lord Beryllian, but is there any beer?"

Both his grin and his words signaled his intention not to go quietly.

"With regret, I did not prepare—"

"No matter, I took the liberty of bringing one of my own, as a gift for you. We can tap it now if you wish, milord."

"Please do. I well recall the marvelous brewing from your delightful feast."

"It was my pleasure to host you milord, and I hope again soon. May your visits always profit me so handsomely."

That was better, though a mystery. The servants hustled in to tap the uncouth drink and Beryllian watched as Pritaelseran waited with the patience of a statue. Too confident, that one.

When all had been served they toasted the Emperor's health, none more vigorously than Qerlak himself.

Pritaelseran could not forbear to remark at this. "Your enthusiasm, Sir Barleybane, reminds me that your father was one of the few from all our southern baronies to support the insurrection." His words so carefully formal belied his tone, an attempt to spit on a family who supported the cause of Hope over a blind loyalty to the knightly order.

Qerlak finished a sip before meeting his opponent's eyes and answering with disarming informality.

"Yula is a good man. I enjoyed meeting him."

The room stood still a moment at this casual claim. The mutual glare of the Hawk and Swamp Knights traced a line which seemed a tangible thing.

Beryllian coughed. "Be seated, Sir knights. Let us begin the adjudication."

Barleybane and Pritaelseran sat facing each other at opposite ends of a long table. The Hawk Knight's side was covered with notes, ribboned in packs with proper labels to arrange evidence, testimonials, letters of witness and more. Qerlak rested his tankard near to hand and placed both palms on the clear wood. Near the wall, the lady Pritaelseran sat and stared at her youngest son across the chamber. Four steps behind Qerlak stood the mage Galethiel, looking above his shoulder as if at animals in a menagerie, whom she might have to constrain any moment. That, Beryllian thought, that level of loyalty in a wizard he could welcome with relief. He turned to Tancrad Coss.

"Where is that mage we will have to hire as our court wizard?"

"You asked for her opinion on the miracle claimed by Barleybane, about the Border Stones. She is retrieving the tome she needs now and should be here in moments."

Beryllian nodded, sat back and signaled for the adjudication to begin as he and S'int bore witness. It would prove to be by far the most interesting disputation he had heard in his lifetime.

"We begin," Pritaelseran said holding an old map in one hand, "with the question of your invasion."

"Mine!"

"As clearly marked on this notated map of 1759 ADR, the boundary between our foefs is the Sodsluice River."

After a moment of silence in the hall, Qerlak burst into a peal of good-natured laughter.

"In the northeastern corner of my foef, milords, the Sodsluice indeed runs along our border, for perhaps half a league. Then it bears southwest. The border continues directly south until the jungle."

"The river is the only landmark mentioned in the documents."

"Aye, and a direction, good enough for anyone with common sense. Half my foef!"

"Every minim of land beyond the Sodsluice is Pritaelseran territory. Your invasion—".

"My defence, sir, on that point I must insist."

"Was your first violation." Pritaelseran sat with smug certainty.

"The Border Stones," Qerlak said evenly, "have always demarked the boundary between the Swamp and Hawk. You may ask any peasant, living either—"

"Nobles do not consult with peasants to settle their disputes."

"Aye, well have I seen how you treat with the peasants," Qerlak said rising with a smolder in his tone that made the room stiffen. "To be clear, you claim it was your own subjects, then, you encountered on the way to our battle? Those were villeins beholden to Pritaelseran that you sealed in their homes and set ablaze?"

"Traitors to their rightful lord!" Pritaelseran cried, also rising.

"Free men, sworn to follow me!" Qerlak replied, and now the guards had to step between the nobles.

"Sirs!" Beryllian shouted, "We do not tolerate displays of violence in this court. Be seated at once."

Qerlak sat and spoke low. "Those people died because I could not protect them. Because *your* men sabotaged the river you claim to respect, delaying my advance so that I could not reach the borders in time to make you mind your manners."

"Let their deaths trouble your conscience," the Hawk Knight sneered.

"Certainly I do, sir," Qerlak replied. "That proves beyond doubt that they were mine."

To Beryllian, it seemed Pritaelseran could find no good answer to this, so he reached into his stack of testimonials.

"As to the matter of the proper border, I offer here indisputable proof that Sir Barleybane is shifting them, continuously, not only to the line that he spuriously claims but even beyond! He swears I am stealing land from him; it is in fact the reverse."

Beryllian sat up in concern at this accusation, but saw that Qerlak seemed only to relax. Along with everyone he looked to Barleybane for answer, though expecting none.

"I do not dispute that the Border Stones have moved."

"Are you prepared, then, to confess guilt and make reparations?"

"By no means, sir. I maintain simply that they move of their own accord."

"What!" It was Lord S'int who roused himself to speak on this. "What can you mean by this, moving on their own?"

"I have not witnessed it personally, milord. But I brought two who have."

As Quarion and Ellesmera stood forward Pritaelseran rose again.

"I object! These are commoners and convicted criminals as I understand. Their word is worthless."

Beryllian felt his throat suddenly dry as he stared at the problem he thought he had sent from him. He glared to the Swamp Knight with an anger he didn't feel, but Qerlak was addressing his foe.

"I must ask you, Sir, to keep a more civil tongue as regards my comrades." Qerlak's firm declaration stilled the room completely. "If you prefer, you may summon one of your own men, or perhaps one of your sons, who surely led the detail blocking the river a fortnight ago."

"We have not come here to listen to your scandalous accusations!"

"Indeed. Yours, rather." Qerlak rose to signal for quiet after this jibe. "But hear them, milords, and rest assured that I can test them for truth in Argens' name should you doubt their story." He looked to Pritaelseran calmly, adding, "I would happily use the same test on any claim of yours, Sir, if you wish it."

Pritaelseran's face went splotchy red as he gasped in search of breath, for the first time his composure truly lost in a welter of rage and fear.

"You dare to suggest that a knight of the realm be subjected to a test of his honesty? This proves without doubt how little you deserve the title."

"Nay, sir, I am no wizard," Qerlak returned cheerfully, "but a Pious Warrior of Argens himself. Do you argue he was not a noble, then, who lends me the power of his miracle?"

With an expulsion of breath, Pritaelseran sat wordlessly, and Qerlak gestured to his companions.

"Milords," Ellesmera began, "these Border Stones are in fact spirits of the Earth, from ancient times called elementals."

"But there are scores of them!" S'int cried, carried away with interest despite himself. "For what reason would our ancestors have invested such staggering magical energy in a mere boundary?"

Quarion shrugged, then bowed to make up for it. "We understand, milord, that there have on occasions been ah, disputes between the knighthoods. Over their borders."

This brought a chuckle from everyone, including eventually Qerlak and even Pritaelseran.

"The method of adjudication here," Ellesmera continued, "is based on a powerful enchantment, acting to restrain either side that was in the wrong at a given time."

336

"What do you mean?" Pritaelseran demanded.

"The Border Stones are not fixed, milord. They move at all times, facing in the direction of that lord who has been, well, least fair in his dealings with the other."

"In other words," Bleys Eversong put in, "they never justice see!"

"Ridiculous," Pritaelseran cried, "nonsense at every point."

"Indeed?" Qerlak replied with interest. "Shall we cover those points then, Sir? These witnesses claim the stones move on their own. Shall I test them for truth on that point? No? Then where?"

"That a pile of rocks should have a sense of justice. What tripe, justice is not to be defined by some simple rule."

"Is it not?" This voice from behind Qerlak brought everyone's attention. Beryllian beheld the young knight Hitaelseran, his eyes blazing with comprehension. "Is justice so obtuse? Fair dealing to those over whom you hold authority, respect accorded to all until proven unworthy, and honesty from thine own self, to keep your given word."

Pritaelseran groped to answer, finally saying, "Well spoken. Sir. And evidence of noble training."

"Which I had not from you, milord, who was my father, but from this knight who took me prisoner with more courtesy and at greater exertion than seemed worth your while."

"Milords!" Pritaelseran cried, looking to Beryllian in preference to answering his estranged son. "This rogue Barleybane throws one crime in my face as answer to another. My list of complaints includes his refusal to ransom my imprisoned son."

"Did you write such calumny using my name!" Hitaelseran thundered, striding out into the room. "Did you utter such lies to my mother?"

From behind the Hawk Knight came a slight gasp, and Pritaelseran's eyes betrayed to Beryllian how quickly he sensed his edifice was crumbling. He had evidently failed to mention Hitaelseran's letters to Eli'se, and upon hearing such brave defiance from his youngest son, Pritaelseran's face revealed him a stranger to himself. Unable to look upon the son, he kept his gaze to the Greatknights as he listed his other complaints.

"Failure to ransom seventeen men taken in his lawless raid beyond the Sodsluice. Ignobly refusing a challenge to settle matters by joust thereby avoiding bloodshed." Pritaelseran paused to look at Galethiel with utter hatred. "Assassination of a noble, in the person of Zantire Pritaelseran my brother during that same illegitimate invasion when my other men were taken prisoner."

He paused long enough to pant for breath, while pulling his tunic straight. Holding out a sheaf of his evidence to the dais he made his voice ring to the chamber roof.

"I demand that he be made to answer for these crimes!"

Beryllian was trapped, without recourse to intervene, and signaled for Qerlak to speak. Though Pritaelseran's case was a bundle of twisted hate, the Greatknight saw no way to make an answer that could defuse all accusations.

Qerlak took a long drink, then laid his hands again on the table.

"A moment, milords, if you will indulge me. Truly, Sir Pritaelseran has shown me an entirely new way of looking at the world."

Beryllian indulged in an encouraging chuckle as Qerlak rose to pace a while.

"So then, let us review his history. Upon taking over a foef poor in rents and denuded of tenants, I immediately set about plotting an invasion of my neighbor. Well and good so far— one of us certainly invaded the other. But I took the course of rounding up the few peasants I had for my army. Because naturally there's nothing a farmer likes so well as being pulled from his land to risk life and limb, that his lord can acquire even more land which he cannot fill. Everyone knows the common folk cannot wait to fight in such a just cause!"

Qerlak's pace picked up as he warmed to the argument.

"Naturally my first move was to invade lands I already claim to hold. All this, mind you, in between finding a way to shift one hundred stone-piles taller than you can reach, each and every night, by a few inches more uphill along a line a league and more to the east of my levy. So that, after I conquered these lands, I could claim they belonged to Mon-Crulbagh." He smiled sweetly at Pritaelseran before finishing. "Since the fact they had been tithing me for a year means nothing."

He raised a commanding arm as the Hawk Knight opened his mouth to speak. "Nay milord, it boots nothing to banter this nonsense, I grant you that right readily. In fact, there is but one issue here and one alone. Where does the rightful border between our estates lie? If at the river as he claims, I accept that no misunderstanding on my part can excuse me from where I went and what I did. And, I trust milords, you will accept that the reverse is also true."

"He asks you to believe that I am senseless, vengeful, contrary and utterly disdainful of the lives entrusted to my care. This is a creed that declares some are permanently and enormously better than others, that the letter of the noble code outweighs the life and happiness of the many."

Qerlak looked from his foe to the Greatknights. "I have found, time and again, that to treat all with the respect due to equals, and to find nobility in deeds rather than descent; this is the way to face any obstacle with the hope needed to survive it. To place one's fortune, honor and life in the hands of one's companions—" here he stopped to gesture at his entourage, the mage and the three adventurers, "to share the risk is to summon justice."

He stood by his chair to conclude. "Pritaelseran asks you to believe in doom. I ask you to believe in a miracle."

In the silence that followed, Beryllian knew, in his heart, he would commit his word, his influence and if need be his sword to defend the best among his vassals. Battles he could lose, as he already had. But to stand against a noble fellow like this, whatever his eccentricities, that price Torquem'l Beryllian was unwilling to pay.

At that moment, the chamber door burst open and the blue-robed mage entered with a thick brown tome in her hands, reading in it even as she spoke.

"Milord! Milord Beryllian, it is just as you suggested. Our ancestors mastered these magics and I see the outlines of the lore in this tome. The spirits of the earth can be bound in fulfillment of instructions, and made to serve indefinitely—"

She had crossed the entire room in her excitement, referring to the words rather than notice the gathering. But before she could finish Beryllian heard interruptions from the former prisoners.

"That's the book! The one we were sent to retrieve."

"And she's the one who hired us!"

The blue-robed mage gasped in terror, spun to see the three, slightly adjusted her robe, and passed out on the spot. Beryllian felt a wave of relief drown him and had to steady himself against the arm of the chair before speaking.

"Coss, when she comes to, she is under arrest. Take her out from here."

"With great pleasure milord."

Beryllian turned to Qerlak's trio of recent companions. "You three, whatever else we decide here today, are hereby declared innocent of all charges in this most regrettable case. You were not the only persons taken in by this intrigue. And in light of your recent heroism, attested to by this letter I hold from my vassal Sir Barleybane, I consider the death of my guard to have been a regrettable accident."

Beryllian stood and looked at Ellesmera Altieri, the preacher's orphaned daughter, feeling a terrible weight lifting from him. "This puts the value of their testimony in a much different light, Sir Pritaelseran. Together with Sir Barleybane's disputation arguing that all depends on, in essence, the truth of their story, we must consider your entire slate of charges to be illegitimate."

Beryllian looked to S'int as he spoke his next words. "What say you, milord? We can credit the story of Sir Barleybane as to the power of our ancestors. Would you require him to submit to the test of truth?" He did not add that to vote against the Swamp Knight would expand the lands of his powerful vassal even further. Nor did he need to.

"I leave the judgment in your capable hands, Lord Beryllian." S'int settled back then into his chair with a gleam in the eyes that watched the Hawk Knight.

"Then I call upon you, Cran-Kalrith Pritaelseran, either to accept that the Border Stones represent the just judgment of Argens' day, or to accompany us to the border wherein the test shall be repeated."

The pent-up fury on the knight's face was truly marvelous to behold. Beryllian wondered if he might in fact burst his heart from rage. But Pritaelseran gradually mastered his breathing, calculated a moment, and then made a dismissive gesture to indicate that he accepted his foe's tale.

"But there is still the matter of compensation for the prisoners," he hissed with venom.

Qerlak furled his brow and pursed his lower lip. "Prisoners, milord? I can have no idea what you mean, my gaol is empty."

"Then you admit you had them slain!"

"Not one being was killed once you, ah, withdrew milord. On that I swear. None of your men died of their wounds either."

"You have not returned them! Name your price and be done, churl!"

Qerlak shook his head, clearly play-acting, then suddenly his face brightened.

"Ah, perhaps you mean my new settlers! Some men did come to me, in the days after we fought, indeed, and asked to stay. I would even say it was more than a dozen, and perhaps seventeen. I can write to my castellan and check."

"Villain! You stole them, as you have everything. My brother is dead, make you no restitution for that?"

Here, Beryllian thought, was a point difficult to defuse. Whatever the cause, the death of a noble had to be answered.

"You mean," Galethiel said, moving forward suddenly and putting a chill in Beryllian's spine though she looked only at the Hawk Knight. "You mean, the wizard who came with you into Mon-Crulbagh, on your invasion. Who after sending an assassin to kill me and my acolyte, came in person, shifted his body behind Qerlak's line of battle and aimed a Mage Command at me? You wish restitution for that?"

"The truth," Eversong added, "every word."

Pritaelseran was practically in a palsy now, sitting back in his chair with hands clearly visible and nearly foaming at the mouth with emotion. The mortal sorceress advanced beyond Qerlak's chair and approached the Hawk Knight with her staff in one hand and the other beneath her robe. Beryllian felt a shock to think she might assail a nobleman right here in open court. Qerlak's entire case would be lost in an instant: yet the Swamp Knight did not move.

She stopped a few feet away and withdrew a small wooden box inset with colored tiles in the shape of a lotus flower. She shoved it down the last foot to his hand and spoke calmly.

"I gathered his effects, all the items on his person to return to you. His body was burned in proper state, on a separate bier. But in here you can find his belt, some jewelry, a few papers and reagents, things of that sort." She tapped the upper end of her staff where the metal met the wood, drawing attention to a small pendant with the symbol of the stooping hawk. "This was his earring. I checked, it has no magical properties. This, I am keeping for myself."

She let Pritaelseran look upon the prize a moment, and then leaned slowly in as he angled away. "By the way," she said very quietly, "that is a lovely brooch you are wearing. It matches my eyes." Galethiel straightened up, cocked her head slightly, and then returned to her place behind Sir Qerlak.

The assembled lords were all suddenly thirsty and the silence was prolonged.

"Since you seem determined," Pritaelseran spat while rising, "to ignore my case and favor this upstart, I have no further business here."

"Pray be seated, Sir Pritaelseran," Beryllian replied. "For it is as Sir Barleybane has said: if we do not favor you, we must needs favor him."

"And so? No surprise there, milord Beryllian."

"Ah but then all your claims become his. Your invasion, sir, your murders, your reparations and apologies. We await your answer."

Beryllian wondered, as he held the Hawk Knight's glare, why the man was suddenly so calm and how his sneer had found its way back to his lips. Pritaelseran stepped to the table and seized a single small document, wielding it at him and toward Qerlak as if it were an edged weapon.

"Here, milords, is my answer. Deprive me of my rights to vengeance and deny the damages caused. Accept the words of commoners, of a witch, or a minstrel, of thieves over an Elven noble. Put the border wherever you please. It moots nothing," he said while his smile grew, "for I am Lord of Mon-Crulbagh whether you will it or no."

Unfurling the document, Pritaelseran read the words of a large loan now repaid in full, from the Wanlock Assurers. S'int sat forward again in concern, and Beryllian gripped his wine goblet so hard it left marks in the silver chasing.

Qerlak Barleybane sat still, his face looking as a man who has been struck by lightning.

"Your debt, sir, paid out by me and thus transferring full title to the property named herein. Scan the signatures and the official seal if you will. I lay claim to Mon-Crulbagh just as you attempted to."

Beryllian closed his eyes in prayer to the Stargazer, that Argens might show the way to a fair and proper future in the face of such calamity. No one spoke, and when he opened his eyes, he saw everyone in the room staring at Pritaelseran.

"Well then?" he cried, "No objections, thus I may as well take possession at once."

Beryllian noted the Hawk's Knight's triumphant voice somewhat at odds with the shake in his hands. And his gaze: he seemed unable to quite face his wife, his son, or his overlord and wound up delivering his speech of victory to his feet. What a strange thing, Beryllian thought, to win at the price of such regret. He never supposed he would see such emotion from the legendary knight of Pritaelseran.

"You do realize," Ellesmera said, "you will lose your own lands if you do this."

"Eh? Cease your babble, peasant foot-fighter!"

"She's right," the Stealthic cried eagerly, "those Border Stones have probably picked up their skirts and are running east by now. The maps will only show Mon-Crulbagh from next year on!"

"Nonsense! And why should I care where stones move?"

"Think it through," the Halfling said, "you know they're shifting, and you know it's because of what you have done. They will move east and on the way they will pass every person living in your foef."

"All of whom," Bleys added gaily, "could test the reason by use of fire and phrase. Such a fine lord they all will have, how glad they will be to serve him."

Pritaelseran looked to each speaker and his face began to crack.

"And you will rule it alone," came the slightest female whisper from Eli'se. Now the mien of the Hawk Knight showed a flash of terror.

Greatknight Beryllian knew this was his moment, and stood to aim a mortal blow atop these others.

"You forget yourself, Sir Pritaelseran. The lands of Mon-Crulbagh are subject to my rule, and I do not exchange vows based on the payment of a fee alone." He let those words sink in, and just as Pritaelseran opened his mouth to answer, found the counter-stroke to defeat them. "And before you avow your willingness to swear fealty to both Lord S'int and myself, think you this. By the power of the Border Stones, there shall no longer be a knighthood under which he can accept your vows. You would have only me, Cran-Kalrith Pritaelseran. Despite the unpleasantness, I am constrained to say, here in public court, that I would have grave questions about the character of Pritaelseran's current ruler as a suitable vassal to Beryl."

At last Lord S'int stirred himself to participate now that Beryllian had shown the way. "Aye, and with no lands to your name, Cran-Kalrith, you could lose your status as a knight altogether."

Under the weight of the room's eyes, Pritaelseran stood exposed as if wearing no clothing. He blinked and stayed in thought for a time, while the room waited. As Beryllian watched, the Hawk Knight read over the document again that gave him Mon-Crulbagh, as if every word meant something different to him now. He laid it gently down and turned first to his wife.

Bowing low to her he said, "Madam, in my anger I have misused you. I crave your pardon."

Lady Pritaelseran made no obvious response, and her husband nodded, unsurprised. "Time and deeds will show whether I deserve it. Mark you now, my first."

He turned to make his answer to the court.

"Every person must know his place. I have lived my life by this belief. Yet I wonder if it is time for me to take mine." He held his breath a moment before continuing, "My place, as my father's before me, was always found in gain. My foef has grown, through alliance as with my own marriage to Eli'se of Lann, and at times by force of arms. I sought always to grow it; and I came to see any obstacle to that growth as wrong by nature."

Pritaelseran tapped the document on the table, then laid his hand gently on the wooden box of his brother's effects.

"I never hesitated to pay the needful price. Yet I came to think all prices worth paying."

Qerlak stood to address his foe. "You, sir, inherited a feud, not I. As to loss, I may say I know something of that. The weight of death is dear when it comes by our own command."

Pritaelseran sneered again. "Make no mistake, Sir Barleybane. I have never liked you and doubt that will change."

Qerlak grinned in response, again ignoring the brunt of his foe's hatred. "I promise, on my word as a knight, not to reveal how much you paid for that document."

"I thought it nothing less than my place. But here again, I am outvoted," he snapped as if at a dirty word, and then raised one eyebrow at a new thought.

"Would you agree, sir," the Hawk Knight asked the Swamp Knight, "that one's own mistakes cannot excuse them from the demands of justice?"

"Certainly, the course of justice requires our best effort, and beyond that much is chance."

"Not the fairest answer I sought, but it will do. Justice requires of me to grow my lands, that my sons may each have their rightful place in the noble order. I have failed—for the moment—but the obligation remains."

Squaring his shoulders he faced Qerlak Barleybane. "Milords, listen to me. I own Mon-Crulbagh by right, this document attests to that and cannot be gainsaid in any court. My right," he said again emphasizing the word, "which I am willing to set aside."

To the intake of breath he added. "I say again, I will place this document in yonder fireplace and set it ablaze, if the knight before me will undertake to grant one demand."

Qerlak asked, "And what is that demand?"

Pritaelseran pointed dramatically at Hitaelseran and cried, "Adopt him."

The room rang with exclamation as Pritaelseran lowered his arm and waited, finally looking his fourth-born in the eye now that his gaze had changed to astonishment.

Beryllian could hardly believe this turn; at first, he suspected a clever trap to bring his vassal's lands under the Hawk banner by a back door. But he could tell from the look on the son's face, no such friendly relations would ever grow between these men. That gate was locked.

"He may claim," Pritaelseran sneered, "that I have made mistakes in his upbringing. One silver bit for his opinion, or for anyone's, especially those with no children. Hitaelseran is no longer my son, I accept that. But the code of the nobleman does not yield to such spins of fortune's wheel, and the obligation to secure my lands and place my offspring well is unchanged." He looked on the youth impassively while still speaking to Qerlak. "One day it may be that I shall wrest Mon-Crulbagh from him, instead of you."

He returned his gaze to his foe. "You sir, incur the same obligation, though your line is as poor as your foef. Make Hitaelseran your son, and agree to deed the foef to him upon your death unless you gain later issue from your marriage."

"But, sir," Qerlak choked, "I am a bachelor."

"Indeed? I had thought you and the mortal wench—but no matter, sir. Marry her! You are lord of a foef, however poor. It is not fitting that you throw your body around in wars and leave no plan in place for the future. I'm sure you would agree, it is in the best interest of your peasants." Here the Hawk Knight grinned ferally. "As I understand, that is important to you."

Greatknight S'int roused himself again, in puzzlement. "A lord marry a commoner? And an Elf with a mortal at that!"

Beryllian's eyes met Qerlak's a moment, and he knew this was again his time to speak.

"Be at peace, Lord S'int. I would not have my vassal's foef fall to ruin intestate. Would you be content to have the Hawk's lands and men exceed your own? Better we both resign our seats than to rule so intemperately." He drew a deep breath and spoke to the Swamp Knight. "Sir Qerlak Barleybane, if you and your, em, comrade are content with this arrangement, I shall lodge no objection to either the rank or race. In all my years I have never heard of issue in such a match. But with you, sir, I freely admit nothing would surprise me."

He sat back then, to watch as Qerlak turned to Galethiel in fear.

"I cannot ask this of you, my friend."

"I already said, Qerlak," the sorceress replied, "anything for you. That's how it's always been."

"But we haven't, I mean, we don't, I mean." He looked at her sheepishly. "Do we?"

Galethiel laughed. "Who carking knows! You and I will continue as we have, whatever paper these nobles need means nothing to me. It's a bucket of spit, as I said. Besides," She winked wickedly. "You told me once, I could keep the tower. This way, I get a shot at the whole castle."

Qerlak looked to Hitaelseran, then Galethiel and finally back to the Hawk Knight before giving a slight nod.

Pritaelseran immediately turned to place the document in the empty fire grate, here in the heat of summer needing no fuel.

"Milord, if you would summon a taper—"

With a hiss, a bolt of mystic flame hit the grate, passing Pritaelseran by less than a foot and incinerating the document.

The knight turned to face Galethiel and rallied with a grin. "Perhaps, Lady Mon-Crulbagh, you missed your target?"

The smile Galethiel returned to him had all her teeth in it. "Nice brooch."

To the general laughter Beryllian added his own, as Bleys Eversong broke into verse again and for once this time welcome.

Now from west to east at last there's peace… until next summer's been!
But the Border Stones of Mon-Crulbagh, have never justice seen.

The End

SIGN UP FOR WILL HAHN'S GENTLE REMINDERS

And get a free copy of "Two Tales" from the Lands of Hope.

Two short stories for your reading pleasure await you. Go to:

www.williamlhahn.com/reminders/

and grab them right away. Will will only contact you if there's something interesting to share, and you can unsubscribe at any time.

THE PLANE OF DREAMS

The greatest tales begin when the adventure ends.
Tales from the Tributarians II

In 2002 ADR, a band of upstarts, called the Tributarians, returns from the impassable desert bearing riches and winning momentary fame. But as the wizard Zoahnstar, preacher Cheriatte, new knight Qerlak, dream-seer Galethiel and the rest go their separate ways, the Tributarians discover that wealth beyond their dreams can bring on the nightmare.

Fortune, fame, and the fate of all who live are at risk from a threat to the waking world that lurks beyond the veil of sleep: a threat awakened, and resisted, by one of their own whom they thought dead.

Can the scattered group discover the clues they need to survive? Ambushed and bewildered by political and magical powers beyond their understanding, can they rally to defuse a conspiracy of robbers, defeat a primordial threat from the deepest swamps, and cross boundaries between the worlds to confront Nightmare himself?

How far beyond the adventurer lies the hero? To find out, each must enter... *The Plane of Dreams.*

soon available as eBook and in print
ISBN 978-3-95681-131-9

Shards of Light I: The Ring and the Flag

A Sword and Sorcery novel from the Lands of Hope.

In 2002 ADR, the jewel of the southern empire is the city of Cryssigens, where life is an unending carnival of display, while intrigue brews beneath the surface. Nobles, guilds and House Cups scheme with and against each other, even in the best of times. But civil war stripped the city of its Overlord, and now factions emerge daring all in a bid to succeed to the throne.

Newly-graduated imperial officer Justin is convinced he has no future, and hearing the details of the secret mission he's assigned for the Emperor won't change his mind. Civil War threatens the North Mark. Justin must race against time to form a company, and lead his men into the center of the web; but what happens when his loyalty to the Empire means the death of those who follow him?

available as eBook and in print
ISBN 978-3-95681-094-7

SHARDS OF LIGHT II: FENCING REPUTATION

A Sword and Sorcery novel from the Lands of Hope.

When the elven lords, preachers and merchants of Cryssigens need wrongs righted without clues, they look for the stealthic Feldspar to solve their problems. But the legend without a face is hard to find: and when Feldspar takes a commission from the most famous, and beautiful, priestess in the city, he finds problems of his own piling up, and is forced to choose between Hope and safety.

available as eBook and in print
ISBN 978-3-95681-095-4

SHARDS OF LIGHT III: PERILOUS EMBRACES

A Sword and Sorcery novel from the Lands of Hope.

One of the leading lights of Cryssigensian society is W'starrah Altieri, the Lavender Lady, high-ranking priestess of the sect of Argens Stargazer; while others see only her dazzling beauty her eyes are filled with foreknowledge of the future. She willingly risks life and reputation to save her city, but juggling visions, rivals, suitors and the occasional assassin pushes the real world further from her grasp. Who could expect that in the midst of this she would meet the promised love of her life, or foresee that he too is doomed?

available as eBook and in print
ISBN 978-3-95681-096-1

SHARDS OF LIGHT IV: SHARDS OF LIGHT

A standalone novel from the Lands of Hope

Captain Justin seeks to win political favor in Tralmachia and return in time to tip the balance. But will the brave officer instead find doom for himself and his loyal men in the haunted hills ruled by the Baron of Blood?

Feldspar the Stealthic threads through ancient streets and tunnels, past enemies villainous and monstrous, to locate a fabled artefact in the heart of abandoned Old Cryss. Peril only makes him smile: but how can he choose which of his many faces to honor when the danger bears down on those he loves?

Preacher W'starrah Altieri, who loved the Captain and hired the Stealthic, sees too late the shape of the conspiracy threatening her city, her family. Will her unknown allies ever meet, now that she is helpless to halt the release of the Shard Demon?

available as eBook and in print
ISBN 978-3-95681-097-8

Judgement's Tale: The Complete Omnibus
Two millenia of peace are coming to an end.

For twenty centuries the Lands of Hope prospered from their Heroes' peace, but suffer now from their absence. Chaos slowly grows in the central kingdom of the Lands of Hope known as the Percentalion. It no longer permits safe or reliable travel in or out. Even the bravest adventurers, who for centuries made a living foraying into its midst after lore and treasure, seem unable to do so anymore. The sundered populations of the Percentalion are trapped there, beyond communication and without hope.

Worse yet, the liche Wolga Vrule plots escape from his extra-worldly prison to unleash a tide of undeath, and enlists the Earth Demon Kog, who ruled the Percentalion millennia ago, as an uneasy ally.

On the western coast of the Lands of Hope, Solemn Judgement comes ashore, having journeyed with his father for two years across an ocean, Solemn steps onto these Lands both a stranger and and orphan, driven to complete the lore his father died to give him. Will he discover Wolga Vrule's plan in time to prevent the return of Despair?

The tale continues in "The Eye of Kog"

available as eBook and in print
ISBN 978-3-95681-026-8 (PB) & 978-3-95681-027-5 (HC)

THE EYE OF KOG: THE COMPLETE OMNIBUS
A Force of Ancient Despair Stirs Again...

...and twenty centuries of peace in the Lands of Hope are shattered. But in the chaotic Percentalion, evil's return goes unnoticed by all but a few. The grim young scholar Solemn Judgement, sails and walks a circuit of the northern kingdoms, in search of lore to fend off the plague of undeath. Meanwhile, the Woodsman Treaman struggles to guide his adventuring party to safety, but instead encounters deep loss and inherits a quest to pit all of their lives against desperate odds.

The demon Kog, formerly ruler of these lands, searches for his lost Eye which will render him again invincible. His uneasy ally, the liche Wolga Vrule, schemes to expand his undead army and overwhelm the unsuspecting kingdoms in his own bid for power. What part can a discovered scepter or a missing crown, a dwindling holy order of knights, a ghoul-guarded tomb, or an ancient prophecy play in the chance to ward off such threats?

The quest begun in "Judgement's Tale" reaches its climax

available as eBook and in print
ISBN 978-3-95681-082-4 (PB) & 978-3-95681-081-7 (HC)